'There are uncommon books and films that crack the "safe place," that have us forgetting it's only a story. Nobody knows exactly how this is done, but when it's done, we know it. FINAL GIRLS is operating on that plane; you will check your own arm for a wound a character suffers, you will look across the room when a character hears someone coming, and you will wonder if you yourself have the mettle to endure being a Final Girl'
—JOSH MALERMAN, author of *Bird Box*

'The tale builds to a fantastic conclusion that will have readers thinking of Gillian Flynn's *Gone Girl* and Paula Hawkins's *The Girl on the Train* … This brilliant horror/psychological thriller will fly off the shelves'
—*LIBRARY JOURNAL*

'You know the cold dread that washes over you while you're watching a slasher flick? That's how you'll feel reading this blood-spattered mystery'
—ENTERTAINMENT WEEKLY

'Inventive, well-crafted … A fresh voice in psychological suspense'
—KIRKUS

'Sager cleverly plays on horror movie themes from *Scream* to *Single White Female*, creating an homage without camp. Despite comparisons to *Gone Girl*, this debut's strong character development and themes of rebirth and redemption align more closely with Flynn's *Dark Places*'
—BOOKLIST

Final Girls is the first thriller from Riley Sager, a pseudonym for an author who has previously published under another name. Riley is a native of Pennsylvania, a writer, editor, and graphic designer who lives in Princeton, New Jersey.

'The first great thriller of 2017 is almost here: FINAL GIRLS, by Riley Sager. If you liked GONE GIRL, you'll like this'
—**STEPHEN KING**

'A terrific read!'
—**KARIN SLAUGHTER**, New York Times and international bestselling thriller writer

'The FINAL GIRLS need you. You must sit down with this book, you must read. You must start flipping pages, faster, faster, faster. The FINAL GIRLS are tough, everything survivors should be. But the new threat is clever, ominous, even closer than you suspect. You are about to gasp. You might drop the book. You may have to look over your shoulder. But you must keep reading.
This is the best book of 2017, the FINAL GIRLS need you'
—**LISA GARDNER**

'A great thriller that gave me goosebumps and kept me reading into the night. There were so many unexpected revelations that I had no idea where it was going. A must read.'
—**KATERINA DIAMOND,** bestselling author of *The Teacher* and *The Secret*

'An intriguing, original idea. We've all shuddered at bloodbath stories — but how **does** the survivor cope? It made me think outside the psychological box. Fresh voice, great characterisation and unexpected surprises. This stayed in my mind because it was different.'
—**JANE CORRY**, *Sunday Times* bestselling author of *My Husband's Wife*

526 795 24 2

'Phenomenally drawn characters and an intriguing premise make this one of my favorite books I've read this year. An outstanding debut'
—**HOLLIE OVERTON,** bestselling author of the Richard and Judy pick *Baby Doll*

'Original, fast-paced, and terrifying. FINAL GIRLS takes an unflinching look at the price to be paid for surviving. You will not be able to put this book down!'
—**AMY ENGEL,** author of *The Roanoke Girls*

'Captivating and compelling, with a refreshingly brilliant premise, Riley Sager is one to watch'
—**LISA HALL,** bestselling author of *Between You and Me* and *Tell Me No Lies*

'FINAL GIRLS is a compulsive read, with characters who are at once unreliable and sympathetic. Just when you think you've figured out the plot, the story pivots in a startling new direction. ... A taut and original mystery that will keep you up late trying to figure out a final twist that you won't see coming'
—**CARLA NORTON,** author of *The Edge of Normal* and *What Doesn't Kill Her*

'Part psychological thriller, part homage to slasher flicks and film noir, FINAL GIRLS has a little bit of everything: a suspicious death, a damaged heroine, an unwelcome guest who trades in secrets, and not a single character you can trust. Plenty of nail-biting fun!'
—**HESTER YOUNG,** author of *The Gates of Evangeline*

'Smart and provocative, with plenty of twists and turns, FINAL GIRLS will have the reader racing breathlessly toward its shocking conclusion'
—**SOPHIE LITTLEFIELD,** award-winning author of *The Guilty One* and *The Missing Place*

RILEY SAGER

FINAL
GIRLS

EBURY
PRESS

3 5 7 9 10 8 6 4 2

Ebury Press, an imprint of Ebury Publishing
20 Vauxhall Bridge Road,
London SW1V 2SA

Ebury Press is part of the Penguin Random House group of companies
whose addresses can be found at global.penguinrandomhouse.com

First published in the US in 2017 by Dutton, a division of Penguin Random House
First published in the UK in 2017 by Ebury Press

This edition published in 2018

www.penguin.co.uk

A CIP catalogue record for this book is available from the British Library

ISBN 9781785034046

Printed and bound in Great Britain by Clays Ltd, St Ives PLC

Penguin Random House is committed to a sustainable future for
our business, our readers and our planet. This book is made
from Forest Stewardship Council® certified paper.

To Mike

PINE COTTAGE
1 A.M.

The forest had claws and teeth.

All those rocks and thorns and branches bit at Quincy as she ran screaming through the woods. But she didn't stop. Not when rocks dug into the soles of her bare feet. Not when a whip-thin branch lashed her face and a line of blood streaked down her cheek.

Stopping wasn't an option. To stop was to die. So she kept running, even as a bramble wrapped around her ankle and gnawed at her flesh. The bramble stretched, quivering, before Quincy's momentum yanked her free. If it hurt, she couldn't tell. Her body already held more pain than it could handle.

It was instinct that made her run. An unconscious knowledge that she needed to keep going, no matter what. Already she had forgotten why. Memories of five, ten, fifteen minutes ago were gone. If her life depended on remembering what prompted her flight through the woods, she was certain she'd die right there on the forest floor.

So she ran. She screamed. She tried not to think about dying.

A white glow appeared in the distance, faint along the tree-choked horizon.

Headlights.

Was she near a road? Quincy hoped she was. Like her memories, all sense of direction was lost.

She ran faster, increased her screams, raced toward the light.

Another branch whacked her face. It was thicker than the first, like a rolling pin, and the impact both stunned and blinded her. Pain pulsed through her head as blue sparks throbbed across her blurred vision. When they cleared, she saw a silhouette standing out in the headlights' glow.

A man.

Him.

No. Not Him.

Someone else.

Safety.

Quincy quickened her pace. Her blood-drenched arms reached out, as if that could somehow pull the stranger closer. The movement caused the pain in her shoulder to flare. And with the pain came not a memory but an understanding. One so brutally awful that it had to be real.

Only Quincy remained.

All the others were dead.

She was the last one left alive.

1.

My hands are covered in frosting when Jeff calls. Despite my best efforts, the French buttercream has oozed onto my knuckles and into the hammocks between my fingers, sticking there like paste. Only one pinkie finger remains unscathed, and I use it to tap the speakerphone button.

"Carpenter and Richards, private investigators," I say, imitating the breathy voice of a film noir secretary. "How may I direct your call?"

Jeff plays along, his tough-guy tone pitched somewhere between Robert Mitchum and Dana Andrews. "Put Miss Carpenter on the horn. I need to talk to her pronto."

"Miss Carpenter is busy with an important case. May I take a message?"

"Yeah," Jeff says. "Tell her my flight from Chi-Town has been delayed."

My façade drops. "Oh, Jeff. Really?"

"Sorry, hon. The perils of flying out of the Windy City."

"How long is the delay?"

"Anywhere from two hours to maybe-I'll-be-home-by-next-week," Jeff says. "I'm at least hoping it's long enough for me to miss the start of Baking Season."

"No such luck, pal."

"How's it going, by the way?"

I look down at my hands. "Messy."

Baking Season is Jeff's name for the exhausting stretch between early October and late December, when all those dessert-heavy holidays arrive without reprieve. He likes to say it ominously, raising his hands and wiggling his fingers like spider legs.

Ironically, it's a spider that's caused my hands to be coated in buttercream. Made of double-dark chocolate frosting, its stomach teeters on the edge of a cupcake while black legs stretch across the top and down the sides. When I'm finished, the cupcakes will be posed, photographed, and displayed on my website's roster of Halloween baking ideas. This year's theme is "Revenge of the Yummy."

"How's the airport?" I ask.

"Crowded. But I think I'll survive by hitting the terminal bar."

"Call me if the delay gets any worse," I say. "I'll be here, covered in icing."

"Bake like the wind," Jeff replies.

Call over, it's back to the buttercream spider and the chocolate-cherry cupcake it partly covers. If I've done it right, the red center should ooze out at first bite. That test will come later. Right now, my chief concern is the outside.

Decorating cupcakes is harder than it seems. Especially when the results will be posted online for thousands to see. Smudges and smears aren't allowed. In a high-def world, flaws loom large.

Details matter.

That's one of the Ten Commandments on my website, squeezed between *Measuring Cups Are Your Friends* and *Don't Be Afraid to Fail.*

I finish the first cupcake and am working on the second when my phone rings again. This time there's not even a clean pinkie finger at my disposal, and I'm forced to ignore it. The phone continues to buzz while shimmying across the countertop. It then goes silent, pausing a moment before emitting a telltale beep.

A text.

Curious, I drop the icing bag, wipe my hands, and check the phone. It's from Coop.

We need to talk. Face 2 face.

My fingers pause above the screen. Although it takes Coop three hours to drive into Manhattan, it's a trip he's willingly made many times in the past. When it's important.

I text back. *When?*

His reply arrives in seconds. *Now. Usual place.*

A spot of worry presses the base of my spine. Coop is already here. Which means only one thing—something is wrong.

Before leaving, I rush through my usual preparations for a meeting with Coop. Teeth brushed. Lips glossed. Tiny Xanax popped. I wash the little blue pill down with some grape soda drunk straight from the bottle.

In the elevator, it occurs to me that I should have changed clothes. I'm still in my baking wear: black jeans, one of Jeff's old button-downs, and red flats. All bear flecks of flour and faded splotches of food coloring. I notice a scrape of dried frosting on the back of my hand, skin peeking through the blue-black smear. It resembles a bruise. I lick it off.

Outside on Eighty-Second Street, I make a right onto Columbus, already packed with pedestrians. My body tightens at the sight of so many strangers. I stop and shove stiff fingers into my purse, searching for the can of pepper spray always kept there. There's safety in numbers, yes, but also uncertainty. It's only after finding the pepper spray that I start walking again, my face puckered into a don't-bother-me scowl.

Although the sun is out, a tangible chill stings the air. Typical for early October in New York, when the weather seems to randomly veer between hot and cold. Yet fall is definitely making its swift approach. When Theodore Roosevelt Park comes into view, the leaves there are poised between green and gold.

Through the foliage, I can see the back of the American Museum of Natural History, which on this morning is swarmed with school kids. Their voices flit like birds among the trees. When one of them shrieks, the rest go silent. Just for a second. I freeze on the sidewalk, unnerved not by the shriek but by the silence that follows. But then the children's voices start up again and I calm down. I resume walking, heading to a café two blocks south of the museum.

Our usual place.

Coop is waiting for me at a table by the window, looking the same as always. That sharp, craggy face that appears pensive in times of repose, such as now. A body that's both long and thick. Large hands, one of which bears a ruby class ring instead of a wedding band. The only change is his hair, which he keeps trimmed close to the scalp. Each meeting always brings a few more flecks of gray.

His presence in the café is noticed by all the nannies and caffeinated hipsters who crowd the place. Nothing like a cop in full uniform to put people on edge. Even without it, Coop cuts an intimidating figure. He's a big man, consisting of rolling hills of muscle. The starched blue shirt and black trousers with the knife-edge creases only amplify his size. He lifts his head as I enter, and I notice the exhaustion in his eyes. He must have driven here directly from working the third shift.

Two mugs are already on the table. Earl Grey with milk and extra sugar for me. Coffee for Coop. Black. Unsweetened.

"Quincy," he says, nodding.

There's always a nod. It's Coop's version of a handshake. We never hug. Not since the desperate one I gave him the night we first met. No matter how many times I see him, that moment is always there, playing on a loop until I push it away.

They're dead, I had choked out while clutching him, the words gurgling thickly in the back of my throat. *They're all dead. And he's still out here.*

Ten seconds later, he saved my life.

"This is certainly a surprise," I say as I take a seat. There's a tremor in my voice that I try to tamp down. I don't know why Coop's called me, but if it's bad news, I want to be calm when I hear it.

"You're looking well," Coop says while giving me the quick, concerned once-over I'm now accustomed to. "But you've lost some weight."

There's worry in his voice too. He's thinking about six months after Pine Cottage, when my appetite had left me so completely that I ended up back in the hospital, force-fed through a tube. I remember waking to find Coop standing by my bed, staring at the plastic hose slithered up my nostril.

Don't disappoint me, Quincy, he said then. *You didn't survive that night just to die like this.*

"It's nothing," I say. "I've finally learned I don't have to eat everything I bake."

"And how's that going? The baking thing?"

"Great, actually. I gained five thousand followers last quarter and got another corporate advertiser."

"That's great," Coop says. "Glad everything is going well. One of these days, you should actually bake something for me."

Like the nod, this is another of Coop's constants. He always says it, never means it.

"How's Jefferson?" he asks.

"He's good. The Public Defender's Office just made him the lead attorney on a big, juicy case."

I leave out how the case involves a man accused of killing a narcotics detective in a bust gone wrong. Coop already looks down on Jeff's job. There's no need to toss more fuel onto that particular fire.

"Good for him," he says.

"He's been gone the past two days. Had to fly to Chicago to get statements from family members. Says it'll make a jury more sympathetic."

"Hmm," Coop replies, not quite listening. "I guess he hasn't proposed yet."

I shake my head. I told Coop I thought Jeff was going to propose on our August vacation to the Outer Banks, but no ring so far. That's the real reason I've recently lost weight. I've become the kind of girlfriend who takes up jogging just to fit into a hypothetical wedding dress.

"Still waiting," I say.

"It'll happen."

"And what about you?" I ask, only half teasing. "Have you finally found a girlfriend?"

"Nope."

I arch a brow. "A boyfriend?"

"This visit is about you, Quincy," Coop says, not even cracking a smile.

"Of course. You ask. I answer."

That's how things go between us when we meet once, twice, maybe three times a year.

More often than not, the visits resemble therapy sessions, with me never getting a chance to ask Coop questions of my own. I'm only privy to the basics of his life. He's forty-one, spent time in the Marines before becoming a cop, and had barely shed his rookie status before finding me screaming among the trees. And while I know he still patrols the same town where all those horrible things happened, I have no idea if he's happy. Or satisfied. Or lonely. I never hear from him on holidays. Never once got a Christmas card. Nine years earlier, at my father's funeral, he sat in the back row and slipped out of the church before I could even thank him for coming. The closest he gets to showing affection is on my birthday, when he sends the same text: *Another year you almost didn't get. Live it.*

"Jeff will come around," Coop says, again bending the conversation to his will. "It'll happen at Christmas, I bet. Guys like to propose then."

He takes a gulp of coffee. I sip my tea and blink, keeping my eyes shut an extra beat, hoping the darkness will allow me to feel the Xanax taking hold. Instead, I'm more anxious than when I walked in.

I open my eyes to see a well-dressed woman entering the café with a chubby, equally well-dressed toddler. An au pair, probably. Most women under thirty in this neighborhood are. On warm, sunny days they jam the sidewalks—a parade of interchangeable girls fresh out of college, armed with lit degrees and student loans. The only reason this one catches my attention is because we look alike. Fresh-faced and well scrubbed. Blond hair reined in by a ponytail. Neither too thin nor too plump. The product of hearty, milk-fed Midwestern stock.

That could have been me in a different life. One without Pine Cottage and blood and a dress that changed colors like in some horrible dream.

That's something else I think about every time Coop and I meet—he thought my dress was red. He'd whispered it to the dispatcher when he called for backup. It's on both the police transcript, which I've read multiple times, and the dispatch recording, which I managed to listen to only once.

Someone's running through the trees. Caucasian female. Young. She's wearing a red dress. And she's screaming.

I *was* running through the trees. Galloping, really. Kicking up leaves, numb to the pain coursing through my entire body. And although all I could hear was my heartbeat in my ears, I was indeed screaming. The only thing Coop got wrong was the color of my dress.

It had, until an hour earlier, been white.

Some of the blood was mine. The rest belonged to the others. Janelle, mostly, from when I held her moments before I got hurt.

I'll never forget the look on Coop's face when he realized his mistake. That slight widening of the eyes. The oblong shape of his mouth as he tried to keep it from dropping open. The startled huffing sound he made. Two parts shock, one part pity.

It's one of the few things I actually can remember.

My experience at Pine Cottage is broken into two distinct halves. There's the beginning, fraught with fear and confusion, in which Janelle lurched out of the woods, not yet dead but well on her way. Then there's the end, in which Coop found me in my red-not-red dress.

Everything between those two points remains a blank in my memory. An hour, more or less, entirely wiped clean.

"Dissociative amnesia" is the official diagnosis. More commonly known as repressed memory syndrome. Basically, what I witnessed was too horrific for my fragile mind to hold on to. So I mentally cut it out. A self-performed lobotomy.

That didn't stop people from begging me to remember what happened. Well-meaning family. Misguided friends. Psychiatrists with visions of published case studies dancing in their heads. *Think*, they all told me. *Really think about what happened*. As if that would make any difference. As if my being able to recall every blood-specked detail could somehow bring the rest of my friends back to life.

Still, I tried. Therapy. Hypnosis. Even a ridiculous sense-memory game in which a frizzy-haired specialist held scented paper strips to my blindfolded face, asking how each one made me feel. Nothing worked.

In my mind, that hour is a blackboard completely erased. There's nothing left but dust.

I understand that urge for more information, that longing for details. But in this case, I'm fine without them. I know what happened at Pine Cottage. I don't need to remember exactly *how* it happened. Because here's the thing about details—they can also be a distraction. Add too many and it obscures the brutal truth about a situation. They become the gaudy necklace that hides the tracheotomy scar.

I make no attempts to disguise my scars. I just pretend they don't exist.

The pretending continues in the café. As if my acting like Coop isn't about to lob a bad-news grenade into my lap will actually keep it from happening.

"Are you in the city on business?" I ask. "If you're staying long, Jeff and I would love to take you to dinner. All three of us seemed to like that Italian place we went to last year."

Coop looks at me across the table. His eyes are the lightest shade of blue I've ever seen. Lighter even than the pill currently dissolving into my central nervous system. But they are not a soothing blue. There's an intensity to his eyes that always makes me look away, even though I want to peer deeper, as if that alone can make clear the thoughts hiding just behind them. They are a ferocious blue—the kind of eyes that you want in the person protecting you.

"I think you know why I'm here," he says.

"I honestly don't."

"I have some bad news. It hasn't reached the press yet, but it will. Very soon."

Him.

That's my first thought. This has something to do with Him. Even though I watched Him die, my brain sprints to that inevitable, inconceivable realm where He survived Coop's bullets, escaped, hid for years, and is now emerging with the intent of finding me and finishing what He started.

He's alive.

A lump of anxiety fills my stomach, heavy and unwieldy. It feels like a basketball-size tumor has formed there. I'm struck by the sudden urge to pee.

"It's not that," Coop says, easily knowing exactly what I'm thinking. "He's gone, Quincy. We both know that."

While nice to hear, it does nothing to put me at ease. I've balled my hands into fists pressed knuckle-down atop the table.

"Please just tell me what's wrong."

"It's Lisa Milner," Coop says.

"What about her?"

"She's dead, Quincy."

The news sucks the air out of my chest. I think I gasp. I'm not sure, because I'm too distracted by the watery echo of her voice in my memory.

I want to help you, Quincy. I want to teach you how to be a Final Girl.

And I had let her. At least for a little while. I assumed she knew best. Now she's gone.

Now there are only two of us.

2.

Lisa Milner's version of Pine Cottage was a sorority house in Indiana. One long-ago February night, a man named Stephen Leibman knocked on the front door. He was a college dropout who lived with his dad. Portly. Had a face as jiggly and jaundiced as chicken fat.

The sorority sister who answered the door found him on the front steps holding a hunting knife. One minute later, she was dead. Leibman dragged the body inside, locked all the doors, and cut the lights and phone line. What followed was roughly an hour of carnage that brought an end to nine young women.

Lisa Milner had come close to making it an even ten.

During the slaughter, she took refuge in the bedroom of a sorority sister, cowering alone inside a closet, hugging clothes that weren't hers and praying the madman wouldn't find her.

Eventually, he did.

Lisa laid eyes on Stephen Leibman when he ripped open the closet door. She saw first the knife, then his face, both dripping blood. After a stab to the shoulder, she managed to knee him in the groin and flee the room. She had reached the first floor and was making her way to the front door when Leibman caught up to her, knife jabbing.

She took four stab wounds to her chest and stomach, plus a five-inch slice down the arm she had raised to defend herself. One more thrust of the blade would have finished her off. But Lisa, screaming in pain and dizzy from blood loss, somehow grabbed Leibman's ankle.

He fell. The knife skittered. Lisa grabbed it and shoved it hilt-deep into his gut. Stephen Leibman bled out lying next to her on the floor.

Details. They flow freely when they're not yours.

I was seven when it happened. It's my first memory of actually noticing something on the news. I couldn't help it. Not with my mother standing before the console television, a hand over her mouth, repeating the same two words: *Sweet Jesus. Sweet Jesus.*

What I saw on that TV scared and confused and upset me. The weeping bystanders. The convoy of tarp-covered stretchers slipping beneath yellow tape crisscrossing the door. The splash of blood, bright against the Indiana snow. It was the moment I realized that bad things could happen, that evil existed in the world.

When I began to cry, my father scooped me up and carried me into the kitchen. As my tears dried to salt, he placed a menagerie of bowls on the counter and filled them with flour, sugar, butter, and eggs. He gave me a spoon and let me mix them all together. My first baking lesson.

There's such a thing as too much sweetness, Quincy, he told me. *All the best bakers know this. There needs to be a counterpoint. Something dark. Or bitter. Or sour. Unsweetened chocolate. Cardamom and cinnamon. Lemon and lime. They cut through all the sugar, taming it just enough so that when you do taste the sweetness, you appreciate it all the more.*

Now the only taste in my mouth is a dry sourness. I dump more sugar into my tea and drain the cup. It doesn't help. The sugar rush only counteracts the Xanax, which is finally starting to work its magic. They clash deep inside me, making me antsy.

"When did it happen?" I ask Coop, once my initial shock reduces to a simmering sense of disbelief. "*How* did it happen?"

"Last night. Muncie PD discovered her body around midnight. She had killed herself."

"Sweet Jesus."

I say it loud enough to get the attention of my au pair look-alike seated a table away. She glances up from her iPhone, head tilted like a cocker spaniel's.

"Suicide?" I say, the word bitter on my tongue. "I thought she was happy. I mean, she *seemed* happy."

Lisa's voice is still in my head.

You can't change what's happened. The only thing you can control is how you deal with it.

"They're waiting on the tox report to see if she had been drinking or was on drugs," Coop says.

"So this could have been an accident?"

"It was no accident. Her wrists were slit."

My heart stops for a moment. I'm conscious of the empty pause where a pulse should be. Sadness pours into the void, filling me so quickly I start to feel dizzy.

"I want details," I say.

"You don't," Coop says. "It won't change anything."

"It's information. That's better than nothing."

Coop stares into his coffee, as if examining his bright eyes in the muddy reflection. Eventually, he says, "Here's what I know: Lisa called 911 at quarter to midnight, apparently with second thoughts."

"What did she say?"

"Nothing. She hung up immediately. Dispatch traced the call and sent a pair of blues to her house. The door was unlocked, so they let themselves in. That's when they found her. She was in the bathtub. Her phone was in the water with her. Probably slipped from her hands."

Coop looks out the window. He's tired, I can tell. And no doubt worried I might one day try something similar. But that thought never occurred to me, even when I was back in the hospital being fed through a tube. I reach across the table, aiming for his hands. He pulls them away before I can grasp them.

"When did you hear about it?" I ask.

"A couple hours ago. Got a call from an acquaintance with the Indiana State Police. We keep in touch."

I don't need to ask Coop how he knows a trooper in Indiana. Massacre survivors aren't the only ones who need support systems.

"She thought it'd be good to warn you," he says. "For when word gets out."

The press. Of course. I like to picture them as ravenous vultures, slick innards dripping from their beaks.

"I'm not going to talk to them."

This again gets the attention of the au pair, who looks up, eyes narrowed. I stare her down until she sets her iPhone on the table and pretends to fuss with the toddler in her care.

"You don't have to," Coop says. "But at the very least you should consider releasing a statement of condolence. Those tabloid guys are going to hunt you down like dogs. Might as well toss them a bone before they get the chance."

"Why do I need to say anything?"

"You know why," Coop says.

"Why can't Samantha do it?"

"Because she's still off the grid. I doubt she's going to pop out of hiding after all these years."

"Lucky girl."

"That just leaves you," Coop says. "That's why I wanted to come and tell you the news in person. Now, I know I can't make you do anything you don't want to do, but it's not a bad idea to start being friendly with the press. With Lisa dead and Samantha gone, you're all they've got."

I reach into my purse and grab my phone. It's been quiet. No new calls. No new texts. Nothing but a few dozen work-related emails I didn't have time to read this morning. I shut off the phone—a temporary fix. The press will sniff me out anyway. Coop is right about that. They won't be able to resist trying to get a quote from the only accessible Final Girl.

We are, after all, their creation.

Final Girl is film-geek speak for the last woman standing at the end of a horror movie. At least, that's what I've been told. Even before Pine Cottage, I never liked to watch scary movies because of the fake blood, the rubber knives, the characters who made decisions so stupid I guiltily thought they deserved to die.

Only, what happened to us wasn't a movie. It was real life. *Our* lives. The blood wasn't fake. The knives were steel and nightmare-sharp. And those who died definitely didn't deserve it.

But somehow we screamed louder, ran faster, fought harder. We *survived.*

I don't know where the nickname was first used to describe Lisa Milner. A newspaper in the Midwest, probably. Close to where she lived. Some reporter there tried to get creative about the sorority-house killings, and the nickname was the end result. It spread only because it was casually morbid enough for the Internet to pick up. All those nascent news sites starving for attention jumped all over it. Not wanting to miss a trend, print outlets followed. Tabloids first, then newspapers, and, finally, magazines.

Within days, the transformation was complete. Lisa Milner was no longer simply a massacre survivor. She was a straight-from-a-horror-flick Final Girl.

It happened again with Samantha Boyd four years later and then with me eight years after that. While there were other multiple homicides during those years, none quite got the nation's attention like ours. We were, for whatever reason, the lucky ones who survived when no one else had. Pretty girls covered in blood. As such, we were each in turn treated like something rare and exotic. A beautiful bird that spreads its bright wings only once a decade. Or that flower that stinks like rotting meat whenever it decides to bloom.

The attention showered upon me in the months after Pine Cottage veered from kind to bizarre. Sometimes it was a combination of both, such as the letter I received from a childless couple offering to pay my college tuition. I wrote them back, turning down their generous offer. I never heard from them again.

Other correspondence was more disturbing. I've lost count of how many times I've heard from lonely goth boys or prison inmates saying they want to date me, marry me, cradle me in their tattooed arms. An auto mechanic from Nevada once volunteered to chain me up in his basement to protect me from further harm. He was startling in his sincerity, as if he truly thought holding me captive was the most benevolent of good deeds.

Then there was the letter claiming I needed to be finished off, that it was my destiny to be butchered. It wasn't signed. There was no return address. I gave it to Coop. Just in case.

I start to feel jittery. It's the sugar and the Xanax, suddenly zipping through my body like the latest club drug. Coop senses my change in mood and says, "I know this is a lot to handle."

I nod.

"You want to get out of here?"

I nod again.

"Then let's go."

As I stand, the au pair again pretends to busy herself with the toddler, refusing to look my way. Maybe she recognizes me and it makes her uncomfortable. It wouldn't be the first time that's happened.

When I pass, two steps behind Coop, I snatch her iPhone off the table without her noticing.

It's slipped deep into my pocket before I'm out the door.

Coop walks me home, his body positioned slightly in front of mine, like a Secret Service agent. Both of us scan the sidewalk for members of the press. None appear.

When we reach my building, Coop stops just shy of the maroon awning that shields the front door. The building is prewar, elegant and spacious. My neighbors consist of blue-haired society ladies and fashionable gay gentlemen of a certain age. Every time Coop sees it, I'm sure he wonders how a baking blogger and a public defender can afford to rent an apartment on the Upper West Side.

The truth is, we can't. Not on Jeff's salary, which is laughably small, and certainly not on the money my website takes in.

The apartment is in my name. I own it. The funds came from a phalanx of lawsuits filed after Pine Cottage. Led by Janelle's stepfather, the victims' parents sued anyone and everyone possible. The mental hospital that allowed Him to escape. His doctors. The pharmaceutical companies responsible for the many antidepressants and antipsychotics that had clashed in His brain. Even the manufacturer of the hospital door with the malfunctioning lock through which He had escaped.

All of them settled out of court. They knew a few million dollars was worth avoiding the bad PR they'd get from going up against a bunch of grieving families. Even a settlement wasn't enough to spare some of them. One of the antipsychotics was eventually pulled from the market. The mental hospital, Blackthorn Psychiatric, closed its faulty doors within a year.

The only people who couldn't shell out were His parents, who had gone broke paying for His treatment. Fine by me. I had no desire to punish that dazed and moist-eyed couple for His sins. Besides, my share of the other settlements was more than enough. An accountant friend of my father helped me invest most of it while stocks were still cheap. I bought the apartment after college, just as the housing market was recovering from its colossal pop. Two bedrooms, two bathrooms, living room, dining room, kitchen with a breakfast nook that's become my makeshift studio. I got it for a song.

"Do you want to come up?" I ask Coop. "You've never seen the place."

"Maybe some other time."

Another thing he always says but never means.

"I suppose you need to go," I say.

"It's a long drive home. You going to be okay?"

"Yeah," I say. "Once the shock wears off."

"Call or text if you need anything."

That one he definitely means. Coop's been willing to drop everything to see me ever since the morning after Pine Cottage. The morning I, in the throes of pain and grief, had wailed, *I want the officer! Please let me see him!* He was there within half an hour.

Ten years later, he's still here, giving me a farewell nod. Once I return the gesture, Coop shields his baby blues with a pair of Ray-Bans and walks away, eventually disappearing among the other pedestrians.

Inside the apartment, I head straight for the kitchen and take a second Xanax. The grape soda that follows is a rush of sweetness that, coupled with the sugar from the tea, makes my teeth ache. Yet I keep on drinking, taking several gentle sips as I pull the stolen iPhone from my pocket. A brief examination of the phone tells me that its former owner's name is Kim and that she doesn't use any of its security features. I can see every call, web search, and text, including a recent one from a squarejaw named Zach.

Up for a little fun tonight?

For kicks, I text him back: *Sure.*

The phone beeps in my hand. Another text from Zach. He's sent a picture of his dick.

Charming.

I switch off the phone. A precaution. Kim and I may look similar, but our ringtones differ wildly. Then I turn the phone over, staring at the silvery back that's smudged with fingerprints. I wipe it clean until I can see my reflection, as distorted as if I were looking into a fun-house mirror.

This will do nicely.

I finger the gold chain that's always around my neck. Hanging from it is a small key, which opens the only kitchen drawer kept locked at all times. Jeff assumes it's for important website paperwork. I let him believe that.

Inside the drawer is a jangling menagerie of glinting metal. A shiny tube of lipstick and a chunky gold bracelet. Several spoons. A silver compact plucked from the nurses' station when I left the hospital following Pine Cottage. I used it to stare at my reflection during the long drive home, making sure I was actually still there. Now I study the warped reflections looking back at me and feel that same sense of reassurance.

Yes, I still exist.

I deposit the iPhone with the other objects, close and lock the drawer, then put the key back around my neck.

It's my secret, warm against my breastbone.

3.

I spend the afternoon avoiding the unfinished cupcakes. They seem to stare at me from the kitchen counter, seeking the same treatment as the two decorated ones sitting a few feet away, smug in their completeness. I know I should finish them, if only for the therapeutic value. After all, that's the First Commandment on my website—*Baking Is Better Than Therapy*.

Usually, I believe it. Baking makes sense. What Lisa Milner did does not.

Yet my mood is so dark I know that not even baking can help. Instead, I go to the living room, fingertips skipping over unread copies of *The New Yorker* and that morning's *Times*, trying to fool myself into thinking I don't know exactly where I'm heading. I end up there anyway. At the bookcase by the window, using a chair to reach the top shelf and the book that rests there.

Lisa's book.

She wrote it a year after her encounter with Stephen Leibman, giving it the sad-in-retrospect title of *The Will to Live: My Personal Journey of Pain and Healing*. It was a minor bestseller. Lifetime turned it into a TV movie.

Lisa sent me a copy immediately after Pine Cottage happened. Inside, she had written, *To Quincy, my glorious sister in survival. I'm here if you ever need to talk.* Beneath it was her phone number, the digits tidy and blocklike.

I never intended to call. I told myself I didn't need her help. Considering that I couldn't remember anything, why would I?

But I wasn't prepared for having every newspaper and cable news network in the country exhaustively cover the Pine Cottage Murders. That's what they all called it—the Pine Cottage Murders. It didn't matter that it was more of a cabin than a cottage. It made for a good headline. Besides, Pine Cottage was its official name, burned summer camp–style onto a cedar plank hung above the door.

Other than the funerals, I laid low. When I left the house, it was for doctors' appointments or therapy sessions. Because a refugee camp of reporters had occupied the lawn, my mother was forced to usher me out the back door and through the neighbor's yard to a car waiting on the next block. That still didn't keep my high school yearbook photo from being slapped on the cover of *People*, the words "sole survivor" brushing my acne-ringed chin.

Everyone wanted an exclusive interview. Reporters called, emailed, texted. One famous newswoman—repulsion forbids me from using her name—pounded on the front door as I sat on the other side, back pressed to the rattling wood. Before leaving, she shoved a handwritten note under the door offering me a hundred grand for a sit-down interview. The paper smelled of Chanel No. 5. I threw it into the trash.

Even with a broken heart and stab wounds still zippered with stitches, I knew the score. The press was intent on turning me into a Final Girl.

Maybe I could have handled it better had my home life been even the slightest bit stable. It wasn't.

By then my father's cancer had returned with a vengeance, leaving him too weak and nauseated from chemo to help soothe my ragged emotions. Still, he tried. Having almost lost me once, he made it clear my well-being was his first priority. Making sure I ate, slept, didn't wallow in my grief. He just wanted me to be okay, even when he obviously wasn't. Near the end, I began to think I had survived Pine Cottage only because my father had somehow made a pact with God, exchanging his life for mine.

I assumed my mother felt the same way, but I was too scared and guilt-ridden to ask. Not that I had much of a chance. By that point, she had descended into desperate housewife mode, determined to keep up appearances no matter the cost. She had convinced herself that the kitchen needed remodeling, as if new linoleum could somehow blunt the one-two punch of cancer and Pine Cottage. When she wasn't grimly shuttling my father and me to various appointments, she was comparing countertops and sorting through paint samples. Not to mention continuing her strict, suburban regimen of spin classes and book clubs. To my mother, bowing out of a single social obligation would have been an admission of defeat.

Because my patchouli-scented therapist said it was good to have a stable support system, I turned to Coop. He did what he could, God love him. He fielded more than a few desperate late-night phone calls. Yet I needed someone who had gone through an ordeal similar to Pine Cottage. Lisa seemed to be the best person for the job.

Rather than flee the scene of her trauma, Lisa stayed in Indiana. After six months of recuperating, she returned to that very same college and earned a degree in child psychology. When she accepted her diploma, the crowd at her graduation ceremony gave her a standing ovation. A wall of press in the back of the auditorium captured the moment in a strobe of flashbulbs.

So I read her book. I found her number. I called.

I want to help you, Quincy, she told me. *I want to teach you how to be a Final Girl.*

What if I don't want to be a Final Girl?

That's not your choice. It's already been decided for you. You can't change what's happened. The only thing you can control is how you deal with it.

For Lisa, that meant facing the situation head-on. She suggested I grant a few interviews to the press, but on my terms. She said talking about it publicly would help me deal with what had happened.

I followed her advice and granted three interviews—one to the *New York Times*, one to *Newsweek*, and one to Miss Chanel No. 5, who ended up paying me that hundred grand even though I didn't ask for it. It went a long way toward buying the apartment. And if you think I don't feel guilty about that, think again.

The interviews were awful. It felt wrong to be talking openly about dead friends who could no longer speak for themselves, especially when

I couldn't remember what had actually happened to them. I was as much of a bystander as the people eager to consume my interviews like candy.

Each one left me so empty and hollow that no amount of food could make me feel full again. So I stopped trying, eventually landing back in the hospital six months after I had left it. By then my father had already lost his battle with cancer and was simply waiting for it to make the knockout blow. Still, he was by my side every day. Wobbly in his wheelchair, he spooned ice cream into my mouth to wash down the bitter antidepressants I had been forced to take.

A spoonful of sugar, Quinn, he'd say. *The song doesn't lie.*

Once my appetite returned and I was released from the hospital, Oprah came calling. One of her producers phoned out of the blue saying she wanted us on her show. Lisa and me and even Samantha Boyd. The three Final Girls united at last. Lisa, of course, agreed. So did Samantha, which was a surprise, considering how she was already practicing her vanishing act. Unlike Lisa, she never tried to contact me after Pine Cottage. She was as elusive as my memories.

I too said yes, even though the thought of sitting before an audience of housewives clucking with sympathy almost made me plummet back down the rabbit hole of anorexia. But I wanted to meet my fellow Final Girls face-to-face. Especially Samantha. By that point, I was ready to see the alternative to Lisa's exhausting openness.

I never got the chance.

The morning my mother and I were scheduled to fly to Chicago, I awoke to find myself standing in her recently remodeled kitchen. The place had been completely trashed—broken plates covering the floor, orange juice dripping from the open refrigerator, countertops a wasteland of eggshells, flour clumps, and oil slicks of vanilla extract. Seated on the floor amid the debris was my mother, weeping for the daughter who was still with her yet irrevocably lost.

Why, Quincy? she moaned. *Why would you do this?*

Of course I had been the one to ransack the kitchen like a careless burglar. I knew it as soon as I saw the mess. There was a logic to the destruction. It was so utterly me. Yet I had no memory of ever doing it. Those unknown minutes spent trashing the place were as blank to me as that hour at Pine Cottage.

I didn't mean it, I said. *I don't know what happened, I swear.*

My mother pretended to believe me. She stood, wiped her cheeks, gingerly fixed her hair. Yet a dark twitchiness in her eyes betrayed her true emotions. She was, I realized, frightened of me.

While I cleaned the kitchen, my mother called Oprah's people and canceled. Since it was all of us or nothing, that decision scuttled the whole thing. There would be no televised meeting of the Final Girls.

Later that day, my mother took me to a doctor who basically gave me a lifetime prescription for Xanax. So eager was my mother to have me medicated that I was forced to swallow one in the pharmacy parking lot, washing it down with the only liquid in the car—a bottle of lukewarm grape soda.

We're done, she announced. *No more blackouts. No more rages. No more being a victim. You take these pills and be normal, Quincy. That's how it has to be.*

I agreed. I didn't want a troop of reporters at my graduation. I didn't want to write a book or do another interview or admit my scars still prickled whenever a thunderstorm rolled in. I didn't want to be one of those girls tethered to tragedy, forever associated with the absolute worst moment of my life.

Still buzzing from that inaugural Xanax, I called Lisa and told her I wasn't going to do any more interviews. I was done being a perpetual victim.

I'm not a Final Girl, I told her.

Lisa's tone was unfailingly patient, which infuriated me. *Then what are you, Quincy?*

Normal.

For girls like you and me and Samantha, there's no such thing as normal, she said. *But I understand why you want to try.*

Lisa wished me well. She told me she'd be there if I ever needed her. We never spoke again.

Now I stare at the face gazing from the cover of her book. It's a nice picture of Lisa. Clearly touched up, but not in a tacky way. Friendly eyes. Small nose. Chin maybe a bit too large and forehead a touch too high. Not a classic beauty, but pretty.

She's not smiling in the picture. This isn't the kind of book that warrants a smile. Her lips are pressed together in just the right way. Not too cheerful. Not too severe. The perfect balance of gravity and self-satisfaction. I imagine Lisa practicing the expression in a mirror. The thought makes me sad.

I then think of her huddled in her tub, knife in hand. An even worse thought.

The knife.

That's the thing I don't understand, more than the act of suicide itself. Shit happens. Life sucks. Sometimes people can't deal and choose to opt out. Sad as it may be, it happens all the time. Even to people like Lisa.

But she used a knife. Not a bottle of pills washed down with vodka. (My first preference, if it ever comes to that.) Not the soft, fatal embrace of carbon monoxide. (Choice Number Two.) Lisa chose to end her life with the very thing that almost stabbed it out of her decades earlier. She purposely slid that blade across her wrists, taking care to dig in deep, to finish the job Stephen Leibman had started.

I can't help but wonder what might have happened if Lisa and I had stayed in touch. Maybe we would have eventually met in person. Maybe we could have become friends.

Maybe I could have saved her.

I make my way back to the kitchen and open the laptop that's mostly used for blog business. After a quick Google search of Lisa Milner, I see that news of her death has yet to hit the Internet. That it will soon is inevitable. The big unknown is how much its impact will reverberate into my own life.

A few clicks later, I'm on Facebook, that insipid swamp of likes and links and atrocious grammar. Personally, I don't do social media. No Twitter. No Instagram. I had a personal Facebook page years ago but shut it down after too many pity follows and friend requests from strangers with Final Girl fetishes. Yet one still exists for my website. A necessary evil. Through that, I can easily access Lisa's own Facebook page. She was, after all, a follower of *Quincy's Sweets*.

Lisa's page has become a virtual memorial wall, filled with condolence messages she'll never read. I scroll past dozens of them, most of them generic but heartfelt.

We'll miss you, Lisa Pisa! XOXO

I'll never forget your beautiful smile and your amazing soul.

Rest in peace, Lisa.

The most touching comes from a doe-eyed, brown-haired girl named Jade.

Because you overcame the worst moment of your life, it inspired me to overcome the worst moment of mine. I'm forever inspired by you, Lisa. Now that you're among the angels in Heaven, keep watch over those of us still down below.

I find a picture of Jade in the many, many photos Lisa posted to her wall over the years. It's from three months ago, and it shows the two of them posing cheek to cheek at what appears to be an amusement park. Crisscrossed in the background are the support beams of a wooden roller coaster. An enormous teddy bear fills Lisa's arms.

There's no question that their smiles are genuine. You can't fake that kind of joy. God knows, I've tried. Yet there's an aura of loss around both of them. I see it in their eyes. That same subliminal sadness always creeps into pictures of me. Last Christmas, when Jeff and I went to Pennsylvania to visit my mother, we all posed for a picture in front of the tree, acting as if we were a real, functioning family. Later, while looking at the photos on her computer, my mother mistook my rigid grin for a grimace and said, *Would it have killed you to smile, Quincy?*

I spend a half hour poking around Lisa's photos, getting glimpses of an existence far different from mine. Although she had never married, settled down, and had kids, her life seemed to be a fulfilling one. Lisa had surrounded herself with people—family and friends and girls like Jade who just needed a kind presence. I could have been one of them, had I allowed it.

Instead, I did the opposite. Keeping people at a safe distance. Pushing them away if necessary. Closeness was a luxury I couldn't afford to lose again.

Scanning Lisa's photos, I mentally insert myself into each one. There I am, posing with her at the edge of the Grand Canyon. There we are, wiping mist from our faces in front of Niagara Falls. That's me tucked into a group of women kicking up our two-toned shoes at a bowling alley. *Bowling Buddies!!* reads the caption.

I pause at a picture Lisa had posted three weeks ago. It's a selfie, taken from a stretched, slightly overhead angle. In it, Lisa is raising a bottle of wine in what appears to be a wood-paneled dining room. For a caption, she had written, *Wine Time! LOL!*

There's a girl behind her, mostly cut out of the tilted frame. She reminds me of those alleged pictures of Bigfoot I sometimes see on cheesy paranormal shows. A blur of black hair turning away from the camera.

I feel a kinship with that unnamed girl, even if I can't see her face. I too turned away from Lisa, retreating into the background, alone.

I became a blur—a smudge of darkness stripped of all my details.

PINE COTTAGE
3:37 P.M.

At first, the idea of the cabin made Quincy think of a fairy tale, mostly because of its whimsical name.

Pine Cottage.

Hearing it conjured up images of dwarfs and princesses and woodland creatures eager to help with chores. But as Craig's SUV bucked along the gravel drive and the cabin finally came into view, Quincy knew that her imagination had let her down. The reality of the place was far less fanciful.

On the outside, Pine Cottage appeared squat, sturdy, and bluntly utilitarian. Only slightly more elaborate than something that could be built with Lincoln Logs. It sat among a cluster of tall pines that towered over the slate roof, making the place look smaller than it actually was. Huddled together with their branches intertwined, the trees surrounded the cabin in a thick wall, beyond which sat more trees, spreading outward in silent blackness.

A dark forest. That was the fairy tale Quincy had been looking for, only it was more Brothers Grimm than Disney. When she stepped out of the SUV and peered into the tangled thicket, an unwelcome tickle of apprehension flitted over her.

"So this is what the middle of nowhere looks like," she announced. "It's creepy."

"Scaredy-cat," Janelle said as she moved behind Quincy, lugging not one but two suitcases.

"Overpacker," Quincy shot back.

Janelle jutted out her tongue, holding the pose until Quincy realized she was supposed to grab her camera and capture it for posterity. Dutifully, she dug her new Nikon out of its bag and snapped a few shots. She kept on shooting once Janelle broke the pose and tried to lift both of her suitcases, thin arms straining.

"Quin-cee," she said in that singsongy voice Quincy knew all too well. "Help me carry these? Pretty please?"

Quincy looped the camera around her neck. "Nope. You're the one who brought all that stuff. I doubt you'll even use half of it."

"But I'm prepared for anything. Isn't that, like, what the Boy Scouts say?"

"Be prepared," Craig said, passing them both with a cooler perched on his sturdy shoulders. "And I hope one of the things you packed was the key to this place."

Janelle jumped at the excuse to ignore her suitcases and searched the pockets of her jeans until she found the key. She then bounded to the front door, giving a smack to the cedar sign that bore the cabin's name.

"Group portrait?" she suggested.

Quincy set the camera's timer and placed it on the hood of Craig's SUV. Then she rushed to join the others in front of the cabin. All six of them held their smiles, waiting for the shutter's telltale click. The East Hall Crew, as Janelle had dubbed them during freshman orientation. Still thick as thieves two months into their sophomore year.

Picture time over, Janelle ceremoniously unlocked the front door.

"What do you think?" she asked as soon as it creaked open, before the rest of them had more than a scant second to take in their surroundings. "It's cozy, right?"

Quincy agreed, although her idea of coziness wasn't bearskin on the walls and a well-trod rug tossed over the floor. She would have used the word "rustic," with an emphasis on the rust, which ringed the kitchen sink and tinted the water sputtering from the pipes in the only bathroom.

But it was big, as far as cabins went. Four bedrooms. A deck in the back that only shimmied slightly when they stepped onto it. A great room with a fieldstone fireplace roughly the size of the dorm room Janelle and Quincy shared, logs tidily stacked beside it.

The cabin—the whole weekend, actually—was a birthday present for Janelle from her mom and stepdad. They aspired to be the cool parents. The ones who thought of their children as friends. The ones who assumed their college-age daughter was drinking and getting high anyway, so they might as well rent her a cabin in the Poconos to do it all in relative safety. Forty-eight hours free of RAs, dorm food, and ID cards that had to be swiped at every door and elevator.

But before it could begin, Janelle ordered them all to place their cell phones inside a small wooden box.

"No calls, no texts, and definitely no pictures or video," she said before stuffing the box into the SUV's glove compartment.

"What about my camera?" Quincy asked.

"I'll allow it. But you can only take flattering pictures of me."

"Of course," Quincy said.

"I mean it," Janelle warned. "If I see anything that goes down this weekend on Facebook I *will* unfriend you. Online and in real life."

Then on her mark, all six of them sprinted to the bedrooms, each trying to claim the best one. Amy and Rodney grabbed the one with the waterbed, which sloshed wildly when they threw themselves on top of it. Betz, not having a boyfriend to bring along, dutifully took the room with bunk beds, flopping onto the bottom one with her dictionary-thick copy of *Harry Potter and the Deathly Hallows*. Quincy pulled Janelle into the one with twin beds pressed against opposite walls, just like their dorm room.

"Home sweet home," Quincy said. "Or at least a close enough approximation."

"Nice," Janelle said, the word sounding hollow to Quincy's ears. "I don't know, though."

"We can pick another room. It's your birthday. You've got first choice."

"You're right. And I choose"—Janelle grabbed Quincy by the shoulders, lifting her from the lumpy bed—"to sleep alone."

She steered Quincy into the hall, toward the room at the end of it. The cabin's largest, it boasted a bay window with a sweeping view of the woods. Several quilts adorned the walls in homespun kaleidoscopes of fabric. And there, seated on the edge of the king bed, was Craig. He looked at the floor, staring at the space between his Converse high-tops. His hands rested on his lap, fingers laced, thumbs rolling over each other. He looked up when Quincy entered. She noticed a hopeful lift in his shy smile.

"I'm sure this will be *much* more comfortable," Janelle said, a wink in her voice. "You two have fun."

She knocked a hip against Quincy, nudging her deeper into the room. Then she was gone, closing the door behind her and giggling back down the hall.

"It was her idea," Craig said.

"I assumed that."

"We don't have to—"

He stopped, forcing Quincy to fill in the blank. Room together? Sleep together like Janelle so blatantly planned for them to do?

"It's fine," she said.

"Quinn, really. If you're not ready."

Quincy sat beside him and put a hand on his trembling knee. Craig Anderson, the budding basketball star. Brown-haired, green-eyed, sexily lanky Craig. Out of all the girls on campus, he picked her.

"It's fine," she said again, meaning it as much as a nineteen-year-old contemplating the end of her virginity possibly could. "I'm glad."

4.

Jeff finds me on the sofa with Lisa's book in my lap and my eyes raw from an afternoon spent crying. When he drops his suitcase and sweeps me into his arms, I lay my head against his chest and weep some more. After two years of living together and two more of dating, he knows not to immediately ask what's wrong. He simply lets me cry.

It's only after I've soaked his shirt collar with tears that I say, "Lisa Milner killed herself."

Jeff's grip around me tightens. "*The* Lisa Milner?"

"The very one."

That's all he needs me to say. The rest he understands.

"Oh, Quinn. Hon, I'm so sorry. When? What happened?"

We settle back onto the sofa and I give Jeff the details. He listens with a heightened interest—a by-product of his job, which requires him to absorb all information before sifting through it.

"How do you feel?" he asks when I'm done talking.

"Fine," I say. "I'm just shocked. And in mourning. Which is silly, I guess."

"It's not," Jeff says. "You have every right to be upset."

"Do I? It's not like Lisa and I ever actually met."

"That doesn't matter. You two spoke a lot. She helped you. You were kindred spirits."

"We were victims," I say. "That's the only thing we had in common."

"You don't need to trivialize it, Quinn. Not with me."

That's Jefferson Richards the public defender talking. He lapses into lawyer-speak whenever he disagrees with me, which isn't often. Usually, he's simply Jeff, the boyfriend who doesn't mind cuddling. Who's a far better cook than I and whose ass looks amazing in the suits he wears to court.

"I can't begin to understand what you went through that night," he says. "No one can. No one but Lisa and that other girl."

"Samantha."

Jeff repeats the name absently, as if he knew it all along. "Samantha. I'm sure she feels the same way you do."

"It doesn't make any sense," I say. "I can't understand why Lisa would kill herself after everything she went through. It's such a waste. I thought Lisa was better than that."

Once again, I hear her voice in my head.

There's nobility in being a survivor, she had once told me. *Grace too. Because we've suffered and lived, we have the power to inspire others who are suffering.*

It was bullshit. All of it.

"Sorry for being such a mess," I tell Jeff. "Lisa's suicide. My reaction. All of it feels abnormal."

"Of course it does. What happened to you *was* abnormal. But one of the things I love about you is how you haven't let it define you. You've moved on."

Jeff's told me this before. Quite a few times, in fact. After so many repetitions, I've actually started to believe it.

"I know," I say. "I have."

"Which is the only healthy thing you can do. That's the past. This is the present. And I'd like to think that the present makes you happy."

Jeff smiles just then. He has the smile of a movie star. Cinema-Scope wide and Technicolor bright. It's what first drew me to him when we met at a work event so dull I felt the need to get tipsy and flirty.

Let me guess, I told him. *You're a toothpaste model.*

Guilty as charged.

What brand? Maybe I'll start using it.

Aquafresh. But I'm aiming for the big-time—Crest.

I laughed, even though it wasn't all that funny. There was something endearing about his eagerness to please. He reminded me of a golden retriever, soft and loyal and safe. Even though I didn't yet know his name, I clasped his hand. I haven't really let go of it since.

Between Pine Cottage and Jeff, my social life was quiet to the point of nonexistence. Once I was deemed well enough to return to school, I didn't go back to my old college, where I knew I'd be haunted by memories of Janelle and the others. Instead, I transferred to a school slightly closer to home, spending three years living alone in a dorm room designed for two.

My reputation preceded me, of course. People knew exactly who I was and what I had gone through. But I kept my head down, stayed quiet, took my daily Xanax and grape soda. I was friendly but friendless. Approachable yet purposefully aloof. I saw no point in getting too close with anyone.

Once a week, I attended a group therapy session in which a grab bag of afflictions was dealt with. Those of us who attended became sort of friends. Not close, exactly, but trusted enough to call when one of us was too anxious to go to the movies alone.

Even then, I had a hard time relating to these vulnerable girls who had endured rape, physical abuse, disfiguring car accidents. Their trauma was far different from my own. None of them knew what it felt like to have their closest friends snatched away in a single instant. They didn't understand how awful it was to not remember the worst night of your life. I got the sense my lack of memories made them jealous. That they too wanted only to forget. As if forgetting were somehow easier than remembering.

While at school, I attracted an interchangeable string of skinny, sensitive boys who wanted to unlock the mysteries of the shy, quiet girl who kept everyone at arm's length. I indulged them, to a degree. Awkward study dates. Coffeehouse chats where I amused myself by counting the ways they avoided bringing up Pine Cottage. Maybe a teasing kiss good night if I was feeling especially lonely.

Secretly, I preferred the jockish types found solely at frat parties and raucous keggers. You know the type. Big arms. Beefy pecs and slight beer gut. Guys who don't care about your scars. Who are incapable of being gentle. Who are all too happy to tirelessly fuck, piston-like, and definitely not upset when you slip out afterward without giving them your number.

After those encounters, I'd leave feeling sore and chafed and oddly invigorated. There's something energizing about getting what you want, even if that something is shame.

But Jeff is different. He's perfectly normal. Polo by Ralph Lauren normal. We dated an entire month before I dared bring up Pine Cottage. He still thought I was Quincy Carpenter, marketing grunt about to start a baking blog. He had no idea I was actually Quincy Carpenter, massacre survivor.

To his credit, he took it better than I expected. He said all the right things, ending with, *I firmly believe it's possible for people not to be harnessed to bad things from their past. People can recover. They can move on. You certainly have.*

That's when I knew he was a keeper.

"So how was Chicago?" I ask.

From the half shrug Jeff gives me, I can tell it didn't go well.

"I didn't get the information I was hoping for," he says. "Actually, I'd rather not talk about it."

"And I'd rather not talk about Lisa."

Jeff stands, struck with an idea. "Then we should go out. We should get dressed up, go someplace fancy, and drown our sorrows in too much food and booze. You game?"

I shake my head and stretch catlike across the sofa. "I just don't have it in me tonight. But you know what I'd really like?"

"Wine from a box," Jeff says.

"And?"

"Takeout pad thai."

I muster a smile. "You know me so well."

Later, Jeff and I make love. I am the initiator, tugging the case file out of his hands and climbing on top of him. Jeff protests. A little. It's more like feigned protest. Soon he's inside me, exceedingly gentle and attentive. Jeff is a talker. Having sex with him involves fielding a hundred questions. *Does that feel good? Too rough? Like that?*

Most of the time I appreciate his thoughtfulness, his vocal desire to meet my needs. Tonight is different. Lisa's death has put me in a mood. Instead of the ebb and flow of pleasure, dissatisfaction seeps into my body. I want the impersonal thrusting of those nameless frat boys who thought they were seducing me when it was the other way around. It's like an internal rash, irritated and itchy, and Jeff's earnest lovemaking doesn't come close to scratching it. Yet I pretend it does. I fake moan and squeal like a porn star. When Jeff asks for a progress report, I cover his mouth with mine, just so he'll stop talking.

Afterward, we cuddle while watching Turner Classic Movies. Our usual postcoital habit. Lately, that's become my favorite part of sex. The aftermath. Feeling his firm and furry body next to mine as rapid-fire '40s-speak lulls us to sleep.

But tonight sleep doesn't come easily. Part of it is the movie—*The Lady from Shanghai*. We've reached the ending. Rita Hayworth and Orson Welles in the hall of mirrors, their reflections shattering in a hail of bullets. The other part is Jeff, who shifts uneasily beside me, restless under the covers.

Eventually, he says, "Are you sure you don't want to talk about what happened with Lisa Milner?"

I close my eyes, wishing sleep would grab me by the throat and drag me under. "There's not really anything to talk about," I say. "Do you want to talk about your thing?"

"It's not a *thing*," Jeff says, bristling. "It's my job."

"Sorry." I pause, still not looking at him, trying to gauge his level of annoyance with me. "Do you want to talk about your job?"

"No," he says, before changing his mind. "Maybe a little."

I roll over and sit up, leaning on my left elbow. "I gather the defense isn't going well."

"Not really. Which is all I can legally say about it."

There's very little Jeff's allowed to tell me about his cases. Client confidentiality rules extend even to spouses. Or, in my case, eventual ones. It's another reason Jeff and I are a good fit. He can't talk about work. I don't want to talk about my past. We get to hopscotch over two of the conversational traps that usually ensnare couples. Yet for the first time in months, I feel like we're close to being caught in one and struggling mightily to avoid it.

"We should sleep," I say. "Don't you have to be in court early tomorrow?"

"I do," Jeff says, looking not at me but at the ceiling. "And did you even stop to consider that's why I can't sleep?"

"I didn't." I drop onto my back again. "I'm sorry."

"I don't think you understand how big this case is."

"It's been on the news, Jeff. I've got a pretty good idea."

Now it's Jeff's turn to sit up, lean on his elbow, look at me. "If this goes well, it could mean big things for me. For us. Do you think I want to be a public defender forever?"

"I don't know. Do you?"

"Of course not. Winning this case could be a huge stepping-stone. Hopefully to one of the big firms, where I can start making real money and not live in an apartment paid for by my girlfriend's victim fund."

I'm too hurt to respond, although I can tell Jeff instantly regrets saying it. His eyes go dead for a second and his mouth twists in distress.

"Quinn, I didn't mean that."

"I know." I slide out of bed, still naked, feeling exposed and vulnerable by that fact. I grab the first article of clothing I can get my hands on—Jeff's threadbare terry cloth robe—and slip it on. "It's fine."

"It's not fine," Jeff says. "I'm an asshole."

"Get some sleep," I tell him. "Tomorrow's important."

I pad into the living room, suddenly and irrevocably awake. My phone sits atop the coffee table, still turned off. I switch it on, the screen glowing ice-blue in the darkness. I have twenty-three missed calls, eighteen texts, and more than three dozen emails. Virtually all of them are from reporters.

Word of Lisa's death has gotten out. The press is officially on the hunt.

I scroll through my email inbox, which has gone neglected since the previous evening. Buried beneath the wall of reporter inquiries are earlier, more benign missives from fans of the website and various makers of baking tools eager for me to give their wares a test-drive.

One email address stands out from the flow of names and numbers, like a silver-scaled fish breaching the surface.

Lmilner75

My finger jumps off the screen. An involuntary recoil. I stare at the address until it sears itself onto my vision, the afterimage lingering when I blink.

I know of only one person who could have that address, and she's been dead for more than a day. The realization forms a nervous tickle in my throat. I swallow hard before opening the email.

Quincy, I need to talk to you. It's extremely important. Please, please don't ignore this.

Beneath it is Lisa's name and the same phone number written inside her book.

I read the email several times, the tickle in my throat transforming into a sensation that can only be described as fluttering. It feels like I've swallowed a hummingbird, its wings beating against my esophagus.

I check when the email was sent. Eleven p.m. Taking into account the several minutes it took for police to trace the 911 call and get to her house, it means that Lisa sent the email less than an hour before she killed herself.

I might have been the last person she ever tried to contact.

5.

Morning arrives gray and groggy. I awake to find Jeff already gone, off to meet his accused cop killer.

In the kitchen, a surprise awaits me: a vase filled not with flowers but baking tools. Wooden spoons and spatulas and a heavy-duty whisk with a handle as thick as my wrist. A red ribbon has been wrapped around the vase's neck. Attached to it is a card.

I'm an idiot. And I'm sorry. You will always be my favorite sweet. Love, Jeff.

Next to the vase, the unfinished cupcakes resume staring at me. I ignore them as I take my morning Xanax with two swallows of grape soda. I then switch to coffee, mainlining it in the breakfast nook, trying to wake up.

My sleep had been plagued with nightmares, a phase I thought had passed. In the first few years after Pine Cottage, I couldn't go a night without having one. They were the usual therapy fodder—running through the woods, Janelle stumbling from the trees, Him. Lately, though, I go weeks, even months, without having one.

Last night, my dreams were filled with reporters scratching at the windows and leaving bloody claw marks on the glass. Pale and thin, they moaned my name, waiting like vampires for me to invite them in. Instead of fangs, their teeth were pencils narrowed to ice-pick sharpness. Glistening chunks of sinew stuck to the tips.

Lisa made an appearance in one of the nightmares, looking exactly like the picture on her book jacket. The well-practiced form of her lips never wavered. Not even when she grabbed a pencil from one of the reporters and dragged its point across her wrists.

Her email was the first thing I thought of upon waking, of course. It spent the night sitting in my mind like a spring-loaded trap, waiting for the smallest bit of consciousness to set it off. It remains gripped to my brain as I down one cup of coffee, then another.

Foremost in my thoughts is the unshakable idea that, other than her aborted 911 call, I truly had been the last person Lisa tried to contact. If that's the case, why? Did she want me, of all people, to try to talk her off whatever mental ledge she had crawled onto? Did my failure to check my email make me in some way responsible for her death?

My first instinct is to call Coop and tell him about it. I have no doubt he'd drop everything and drive into Manhattan for the second day in a row just to assure me that nothing about this is my fault. But I'm not sure I want to see Coop on consecutive days. It would be the first time that happened since Pine Cottage and the morning after, and it's not an experience I long to repeat.

I text him instead, trying to keep it casual.

Call me when you get a chance. No rush. Nothing important.

But my gut tells me it *is* important. Or at least it has the potential to be. If it wasn't important, why did I wake up thinking about it? Why is my next thought to call Jeff just to hear his voice, even though I know he's in court, his cell phone switched off and shoved into the depths of his briefcase?

I try not to think about it, although that proves to be impossible. According to my phone, I've missed a dozen more calls. My voicemail is a swamp of messages. I listen to only one of them—a surprise message from my mother, who called at an hour when she knew I'd still be asleep. The latest of her constantly evolving attempts to avoid actual conversation.

"Quincy, it's your mother," her message begins, as if she doesn't trust me to recognize her nasal monotone. "I was just woken up by a reporter calling to see if I had a comment about what happened to that Lisa Milner girl you were friends with. I told him he should talk to you. Thought you'd like to know."

I see no point in calling her back. That's the last thing my mother wants. It's been that way ever since I returned to college after Pine Cottage. As a new widow, she wanted me to commute from home. When I didn't, she said I was abandoning her.

Ultimately, though, it was me who got abandoned. By the time I finally graduated, she had remarried a dentist named Fred who came with three adult children from a previous marriage. Three happy, bland, toothy children. Not a Final Girl in the bunch. They became her family. I became a barely tolerated remnant of her past. A blemish on her otherwise spotless new life.

I listen again to my mother's message, searching for the slightest hint of interest or concern in her voice. Finding none, I delete the voicemail and move on to that morning's copy of the *Times*.

To my surprise, an article about Lisa's death rests at the bottom of the front page. I read it in one distasteful gulp.

MUNCIE, Ind.—Lisa Milner, a prominent child psychologist who was the lone survivor of a sorority-house massacre that shocked campuses nationwide, died at her home here, authorities confirmed yesterday. She was 42.

Most of the article focuses on the horrors Lisa witnessed that long-ago night. As if no other moments of her life mattered. Reading it gives me a glimpse of what my own obituary will be like. It churns my stomach.

Yet one sentence gives me pause. It's near the bottom; almost like an afterthought.

Police are continuing their investigation.

Investigation of what? Lisa slit her wrists, which seems pretty straightforward to me. Then I remember what Coop said about the toxicology tests. To see if Lisa was on something at the time.

Tossing the newspaper aside, I reach for my laptop. Online, I skip the news sites and head straight for the true-crime blogs, an alarming number of which are solely devoted to Final Girls. The guys who run them—and they are all men, by the way; women have better things to do—still occasionally contact me through my website, trying to sweet-talk me into giving an interview. I never reply. The closest we've come to corresponding was after I received that threatening letter and Coop wrote them all asking if one of them had sent it. They all said no.

Normally I avoid these sites, fearful of what I might see written about me. Today, however, calls for an exception, and I find myself clicking through website after website. Nearly all of them have mentions of Lisa's suicide. Like the article in the *Times*, there's little to no new information. Most of them stress the irony of a world-famous survivor being responsible for her own death. One even has the gall to suggest other Final Girls could follow suit.

Disgusted, I close the browser window and slam the laptop shut. I then stand, trying to shake away some of the angry adrenaline scooting through my body. All that Xanax, caffeine, and misguided web surfing have left me antsy and aggravated. So much so that I change into workout clothes and lace up my running shoes. When I get like this, which is often, the only cure is to jog until it passes.

In the elevator, it dawns on me that there could be reporters outside. If they know my phone number and email address, there's every reason to think they also know where I live. I make a plan to start running as soon as I hit the street, instead of taking my customary stroll to Central Park. I begin while still inside the building, busting out of the elevator at a light jog.

Once outside, though, I see there's no need. Instead of a crush of reporters out front, I'm confronted by exactly one. He looks young, eager, and handsome in a nerdy way. Buddy Holly glasses. Great hair. More Clark Kent than Jimmy Olsen. He rushes toward me as I trot from the building, the pages of his notebook fluttering.

"Miss Carpenter."

He tells me his name—Jonah Thompson. I recognize it. He's one of the reporters who called, emailed, *and* texted. The nuisance trifecta. He then tells me the name of the paper he works for. One of the major daily tabloids. Judging by his age, it means he's either very good at his job or else incredibly unscrupulous. I suspect it's both.

"No comment," I say, breaking into a full run.

He makes an attempt to keep up, the flat soles of his Oxfords clapping against the sidewalk. "I just have a few questions about Lisa Milner."

"No comment," I say again. "If you're still here when I get back, I'm calling the police."

Jonah Thompson falls back while I keep moving. I feel him watch my retreat, his gaze a sunburn on the back of my neck. I increase my pace, quickly navigating the cross-blocks to Central Park. Before entering, I glance over my shoulder, just in case he somehow managed to follow me there.

Not likely.

Not in those shoes.

In the park, I head north toward the reservoir. My preferred jogging spot. It's flatter than other areas of the park, with better sight lines. No curving paths with God-knows-what waiting just around the bend. No pockets of trees thick with shadows. Just long stretches of gravel where I can clench my jaw, straighten my back, and *run.*

But on this crisp morning it's hard to focus on running. My thoughts are elsewhere. I think about fresh-faced Jonah Thompson and his annoying tenacity. I think about the article on Lisa's death and its refusal to acknowledge how what she went through messed her up so much she decided to sink a knife into both her wrists. Mostly, though, I dwell on Lisa herself and what possibly could have been going through her mind when she sent me that email. Was she sad? Desperate? Was the knife already gripped in her trembling hands?

It's suddenly all too much, and the adrenaline drains from my limbs as quickly as it filled them. Other joggers continually pass me, the gravelly crunch of their footsteps warning of their approach. Giving up, I slow to a stroll, move to the path's edge, and walk the rest of the way home.

Back at my building, I'm relieved to see that Jonah Thompson has departed. In his place, though, is another reporter, idling on the other side of the street. On second glance, I decide she's not a traditional reporter. She looks too edgy for mainstream media, reminding me of those aging Riot Grrrls who roamed Williamsburg before the hipsters took over. A woman who doesn't give a shit she's dressed like someone half her age. Leather jacket sitting over a hip-hugging black dress. Fishnet stockings rising out of scuffed combat boots. Her raven hair is a parted curtain that provides only a partial view of eyes ringed with liner. She wears red lipstick as bright as blood. A blogger, I surmise. One with a far different readership from me.

Yet there's something familiar about her. I've seen her before. Maybe. My stomach flips with the sensation of not recognizing someone even when I know I should.

She recognizes me, though. Her raccoon eyes assess me through the dark drapes of her hair. I watch her watch me. She doesn't even blink. She merely slouches against the building across the street, making no attempt to blend in with her surroundings. A cigarette juts from her ruby lips, smoke swirling. I'm about to head inside when she calls to me.

"Quincy." It's a statement, not a question. "Hey, Quincy Carpenter."

I stop, do a half turn, frown in her direction. "No comment."

She scowls—a storm cloud darkening the landscape of her face. "I don't want a comment."

"Then what *do* you want?" I say, facing her head-on, attempting to stare her down.

"I just want to talk."

"About Lisa Milner?"

"Yeah," she says. "And other stuff."

"Which makes you a reporter. And I have no comment."

She mutters "Jesus Christ" and tosses the cigarette into the street. She reaches for a large knapsack sitting at her feet. Heavy and full, whatever's inside presses against the frayed seams when she lifts it. Soon she's across the street, right in front of me, dropping the knapsack so close to me that it almost lands on my right foot.

"You don't need to be such a bitch," she says.

"Excuse me?"

"Listen, all I want to do is talk." Up close, her voice sounds husky and seductive. Cigarettes and whiskey ride her breath. "After what happened to Lisa, I thought it might be a good idea."

I suddenly realize who she is. She looks different from what I expected. A far cry from the yearbook photo that was printed everywhere one long-ago summer. Gone is the too-high hair, the ruddy cheeks, the double chin. She's thinned out since then, shed the cherubic glow of youth. Time has made her a taut and weary version of her former self.

"Samantha Boyd," I say.

She nods. "I prefer Sam."

6.

Samantha Boyd.

The second Final Girl.

Of the three of us, she probably had it the worst.

She was two weeks out of high school when it happened. Just a girl trying to scrape together enough money to pay for community college. She got a job cleaning rooms at a highway motel outside Tampa called the Nightlight Inn. Because she was new, Samantha had to work the red-eye shift, fetching towels for exhausted truckers and changing sheets that reeked of sweat and semen in rooms occupied only half the night.

Two hours into her fourth shift, a man with a potato sack over his head showed up and all hell broke loose.

He was an itinerant handyman with a boner for the parts of the Bible few like to talk about. Whores of Babylon. Smiting the sinners. Eyes for eyes and teeth for teeth. His name was Calvin Whitmer. But after that summer, he would be forever known as the Sack Man.

The name fit, for he carried lots of things in sacks. The back of his pickup was full of them. Sacks of empty tin cans. Sacks of animal skins. Sacks of sand, salt, pebbles. Then there was the sack of tools he carried to the Nightlight Inn, filled with saw blades and chisels and masonry nails. Police found twenty-one tools in all, most of them crusted with blood.

Samantha personally met two of them. One was a sharpened drill bit that found its way into her back. Twice. The other was a hacksaw that caught her upper thigh, severing an artery. Her brush with the drill bit came before the Sack Man lashed her to a tree behind the motel with a loop of barbed wire. The hacksaw was after she had somehow managed to break free.

Six people died that night—four motel guests, a nighttime desk clerk named Troy, and Calvin Whitmer. That last one was Sam's doing, once she freed herself and got her hands on the same drill bit that had entered her back. She leapt atop the Sack Man and plunged it into his chest again and again and again. The cops found her like that— trailing barbed wire, straddling a dead man, stabbing away.

I know all this because it was in *Time* magazine, which my parents assumed I never read. That issue I did, poring over the article under the covers, penlight clenched in my sweaty palm. I had nightmares for a week.

Sam's story, meanwhile, made the same rounds as Lisa's and, eventually, mine. Evening news. Front pages. Magazine covers. Oh, how the reporters came running. Probably the very ones who would later camp on my parents' front lawn. Sam granted a handful of print interviews, plus an exclusive one to that TV bitch with the Chanel-scented paper, likely for more or less the same price given to me.

Her only condition was that her face couldn't be shown on camera, nor could any new photographs be taken of her. All anyone saw was that single yearbook photo—the permanent face of her particular ordeal. That's why it was a big deal when she agreed to join Lisa and me in a chat with Oprah, on camera, for all the world to see. Which made it a bigger deal when I backed out. Because of me, no one got to glimpse another view of Samantha Boyd.

A year after that, she vanished.

It wasn't a sudden thing, her disappearance. Instead, it was a slow fading, like morning fog sapping away in the sun. Reporters writing about the tenth anniversary of the Nightlight Inn Murders suddenly had a hard time tracking her down. Her mother eventually came forward to admit she'd lost touch. Federal authorities, who like to keep tabs on victims of violent crimes, couldn't find her.

She was gone. Off the grid, as Coop puts it.

No one knows for sure what happened, but that didn't keep theories from sprouting and spreading like mold spores. One article I read surmised that she had changed her name and moved to South America. Another suggested that she was living in isolation somewhere out west. The murder-porn sites took a darker view, naturally, tossing out conspiracy theories involving suicide, kidnapping, government cover-ups.

But now she's here, right in front of me. Her appearance is so unexpected that I'm at a loss for words. All I can muster is, "What are you doing here?"

Sam rolls her eyes. "You really suck at this hello thing."

"Sorry," I say. "Hello."

"Good job."

"Thanks. But it still doesn't tell me why you're here."

"Isn't it obvious? I'm here to see you." Sam's voice brings to mind a speakeasy—smoky and booze-scented. It contains the dark lilt of something forbidden. "I thought we should finally meet."

We stare at each other a moment, each of us assessing the damage to the other. I get the feeling Sam has also read up on me, because she eyes my stomach first, then my shoulder. I, meanwhile, sneak a glance at her leg, trying to remember if there was a noticeable limp when she crossed the street.

Thoughts of Lisa slide into my head. *We're a rare breed*, she once told me. *We need to stick together.*

Now that she's gone, no one else can understand what we've been through. Sam and I are the only ones. And while I still don't fully comprehend why she's come out of hiding simply to see me, I find myself giving a reluctant nod.

"And so we have," I say, my voice still dulled by surprise. "Would you like to come up?"

We sit in the living room, not drinking the coffee I've set out in front of us. I've since changed out of my running clothes into blue jeans, red flats, and a turquoise blouse. A splash of color to counteract all of Sam's black.

I perch on a straight-backed chair upholstered in purple velvet.

Stiff and punishing, it's more for show than for sitting. Sam is on the antique sofa, looking equally as uncomfortable. She sits with her knees together, arms tight at her sides, trying to make small talk, which clearly isn't her forte. The words come out in short, intense bursts. Each one is like a cherry bomb that's been quickly tossed.

"Nice place."

"Thanks."

"Looks big."

"It's not bad. We only have the two bedrooms."

I cringe as I say it. *Only.* As if I'm somehow deprived. Judging from the bulging knapsack Sam brought with her, I'm not sure she has *a* room.

"Nice."

Sam shifts on the sofa. I get the sense she's trying hard to resist kicking off her boots and spreading herself across it. She looks as uncomfortable as I feel.

"Not that this place is small," I say, the words spilling out in a desperate attempt not to sound like I'm spoiled. "I understand how lucky I am. And the spare room is nice to have when Jeff's family comes to visit. Jeff. That's my boyfriend. His parents are in Delaware and his brother, sister-in-law, and two nephews live in Maryland. They like to visit a lot. It's fun having kids around sometimes."

I love Jeff's family, all of them as catalogue-perfect as Jeff himself. They all know about Pine Cottage. Jeff told them as soon as it was clear things between us were getting serious. Those solid, middle-class Protestants didn't bat an eye. His mother even sent me a fruit basket with a handwritten note saying she hoped it would brighten my day.

"What about your family?" Sam says.

"What about them?"

"Do they visit a lot?"

I think about my mother's one and only visit. She invited herself, using the excuse that she was going through a rough patch with Fred and just wanted to get away for a weekend. Jeff saw it as a good sign. Naïvely, I did too. I thought my mother would be impressed with the new life I had created. Instead, she spent the entire weekend criticizing everything from the clothes I wore to how much wine I drank at dinner. By the time she left, we were barely speaking.

"No," I tell Sam. "They don't. What about yours?"

"Same."

I once saw Mrs. Boyd in an interview on *20/20* shortly after the world realized Sam was missing. She was a scrubby thing, with red blotches on her skin and two inches of dark roots seeping into her bleached hair. During the interview, she came across as jarringly unsentimental about her daughter. The hard set of her jaw made her voice mealy and unkind. She looked tired and rubbed raw. Even though Sam has that same weary air about her, I can see why she wanted to escape such a woman. Mrs. Boyd resembled a house roughed up by too many storms.

My mother is the opposite. Sheila Carpenter refuses to let anyone see the wear and tear. When I was in the hospital after Pine Cottage, she showed up each morning in full makeup, not a hair out of place. Sure, her only child had barely escaped a madman who slaughtered all her friends, but that was no excuse to appear unkempt. If Sam's mother is a fixer-upper, mine is a suburban McMansion rotting on the inside.

"Last I heard, you sort of vanished," I say.

"Kind of," Sam says.

"Where were you all those years?"

"Here and there. You know, just laying low."

I find myself sitting with my arms locked across my chest, hands buried in my armpits. I pry them out and fold them primly on my lap. Within seconds, though, my arms have assumed their original position. My whole body thirsts for a Xanax.

Sam doesn't notice. She's too busy tucking her hair behind her ears to give the apartment another vaguely critical once-over. I've decorated the place with an emphasis on shabby chic. Everything is mismatched, from the blue walls to the flea-market lamps to the white shag carpeting I purchased ironically but ended up loving. It is, I realize, the apartment of someone trying to disguise how much money they really have, and I can't tell if Sam is impressed or annoyed by that.

"Do you work?" she asks.

"Yes. I'm, uh—"

I'm stalling, which I always do before telling someone my flighty, fanciful job. Especially someone like Sam, who carries an aura of life-long poverty. It's evident in the runs in her fishnets, her duct-taped boots, her hard eyes. Desperation hums off her like radio waves, shivery and intense.

"You don't have to tell me," she says. "I mean, you don't even know me."

"I'm a blogger?" It comes out sounding like a question. Like I have no clue what I am. "I have a website. It's called *Quincy's Sweets*."

Sam offers a polite half smile. "Cute name. Is it, like, kittens and shit?"

"Baked goods. Cakes, cookies, muffins. I post pictures and decorating tips. Recipes. Tons of recipes. It's been featured on the Food Network."

Jesus. Bragging about the Food Network? Even I want to smack myself. But Sam greets it all with a laid-back nod.

"Cool," she says.

"It can be fun," I say, finally wrangling my voice to a lower register.

"Why cakes? Why not world hunger or politics or—"

"Kittens and shit?"

This time, Sam's smile is full and genuine. "Yeah. That."

"I've always liked to bake. It's one of the few things I'm good at. It relaxes me. Makes me happy. After—" I hesitate again, for a very different reason. "After what happened to me—"

"You mean the Pine Cottage Murders?" Sam says.

At first, I'm surprised she knows the name. Then I realize it's natural that she would. Just like how I know about the Nightlight Inn.

"Yes," I say. "After that, when I was living at home, I spent a lot of time baking things for friends and neighbors. Thank-you presents, really. People were so generous. A new casserole every night, for weeks."

"All that food." Sam lifts her fingers to her teeth, gnawing at the cuticles. The sleeve of her leather jacket slips, revealing dark ink at her wrist. A tattoo, hidden just out of sight. "It must have been a nice neighborhood."

"It was."

Sam catches a hangnail in her teeth, tugs it off, spits it out. "Mine wasn't."

Silence follows as questions flicker in my mind. Personal ones Sam might not want to answer. How long did the barbed wire keep you against that tree? How did you get loose? What did it feel like plunging that drill bit into Calvin Whitmer's heart?

Instead, I say, "Should we talk about what happened to Lisa?"

"You make it sound like we've got a choice."

"We don't have to."

"She killed herself," Sam says. "Of course we do."

"Why do you think she did it?"

"Maybe she couldn't take it anymore."

I know what she means. *It* is the guilt, the nightmares, the lingering grief. Most of all, *it* is the gnawing, unshakable sense that maybe my survival wasn't meant to be. That I'm nothing more than a desperate, wriggling insect destiny forgot to squash.

"Is Lisa's suicide why you came out of hiding after all this time?"

Sam levels her gaze at me. "What do you think?"

"Yes. Because it rattled you as much as it did me."

Sam stays silent.

"I'm right, aren't I?"

"Maybe," she says.

"And you wanted to finally see me in person. Because you were curious about what I was like."

"Oh, I already know everything about you," Sam says.

She leans back onto the sofa, finally allowing herself to get more comfortable. She crosses her legs, the left boot thrown casually over her right knee. Her arms unlock from her sides, spreading like wings across the cushions. I perform a similar unfolding. My arms fall from around my chest as I lean forward in my chair.

"You'd be surprised."

Sam arches one of her brows. Both have been drawn on with black eyeliner, and the movement exposes a few downy hairs beneath the dark smudge.

"An unexpected challenge from Miss Quincy Carpenter."

"It's not a challenge," I say. "Just a fact. I've got secrets."

"We all have secrets," Sam replies. "But are you more than the young Martha Stewart you pretend to be on your blog? That's the real question."

"How do you know I'm pretending?"

"Because you're a Final Girl. It's different for us."

"I'm not a Final Girl," I say. "I really never have been. I'm just me. Now, I'm not going to lie and say I don't think about what happened. I do. But not a lot. I've moved past that."

Sam looks like she doesn't believe me. Both fake brows are now raised. "So you're telling me you've been cured by the therapeutic value of baking?"

"It helps," I say.

"Then prove it."

"Prove it?"

"Yeah," Sam says. "Bake something."

"Right now?"

"Sure." Sam stands, stretches, hauls me out of my chair. "Show me the real you."

7.

Baking is a science, as rigorous as chemistry or physics. There are rules that must be followed. Too much of one thing and not enough of another can lead to ruin. I find comfort in this. Outside, the world is an unruly place where men prowl with sharpened knives. In baking, there is only order.

That's why *Quincy's Sweets* exists. When I graduated college with a marketing degree and moved to New York, I still thought of myself as a victim. So did everyone else. Baking seemed the only way to change that. I wanted to pour my runny, sloshing existence into a human-shaped mold and crank up the heat, emerging soft, springy, and new.

So far, it's working.

In the kitchen, I spread twin lines of bowls across the counter, sized according to what they contain. The biggest ones hold the base—powdery mounds of flour and sugar heaped like snowdrifts. Medium bowls are for the glue. Water. Eggs. Butter. In the smallest bowls are the flavors, the tiniest amounts packing the largest punch. Pumpkin puree and orange zest, cinnamon and cranberry.

Sam stares at the array of ingredients, uncertain. "What are you going to bake?"

"*We* are going to bake orange pumpkin loaf."

I want Sam to witness firsthand the formula behind baking and to experience its safety; I want her to see how it's helped me become more than just a girl screaming through the woods away from Pine Cottage.

If she believes it, then maybe it's actually true.

Sam remains still, looking first at me and then at our surroundings. I think the kitchen is cozy, done up in soothing greens and blues. There's a vase of daisies on the windowsill and kitschy potholders hanging from the walls. The appliances are state-of-the-art but with a retro design. Sam eyes it all with barely concealed terror. She has the look of a feral child dragged suddenly into civilization.

"Do you know how to bake?" I ask.

"No," Sam says. "I microwave."

Then she laughs. A raucous, throaty one that fills the kitchen. I like the sound. When it's just me in the kitchen, all is silent.

"It's easy," I tell her. "Trust me."

I position Sam before one row of bowls and take my place before the other. I then show her, step-by-step, how to fold the butter and sugar together; combine them with the flour, water, and eggs; layer in the flavors one at a time. Sam forms the batter the same way she talks—in short, haphazard bursts. Tufts of flour and blots of pumpkin rise from her bowl.

"Um, am I doing this right?"

"Almost," I say. "You need to be more gentle."

"You sound like all my ex-boyfriends," Sam jokes, even though she's starting to follow my advice and mix the ingredients with slightly less force. The results are immediate. "Hey, it's working!"

"Slow and steady wins the race. That's the Tenth Commandment on my blog."

"You should write a cookbook," Sam says. *Baking for Idiots.*"

"I've thought about it. Just a regular cookbook, though."

"What about a book about Pine Cottage?"

I stiffen at the sound of those two words pushed together. Individually, they have no power over me. Pine. Cottage. Nothing but harmless words. But when combined they obtain the sharpness of the knife He shoved into my shoulder and stomach. If I blink, I know I'll see Janelle emerging from the trees, still technically alive but already dead. So I keep my eyes open, staring at the batter thickening in the bowl in front of me.

"It would be an awfully short book," I say.

"Oh, yeah." There's a false ring to Sam's voice, as if she's trying to make it sound like she's only just now considering my memory loss. "Right."

She's staring too, although at me and not at her bowl. I feel her gaze on my cheek, as warm as the afternoon sun coming through the kitchen window. I get the uneasy sense she's testing me somehow. That I'll fail if I turn to meet her stare. I continue to look at the bread batter, thick and glistening in the bottom of my bowl.

"Did you read Lisa's book?" I ask.

"Nah," Sam says. "You?"

"No."

I don't know why I lie. Which is itself a lie. I *do* know. It's to keep Sam slightly off balance. I bet she assumes I've read Lisa's book cover to cover, which I have. There's nothing as boring as being predictable.

"And the two of you never met?" I say.

"Lisa never got the pleasure," Sam says. "You?"

"We talked on the phone. About how to deal with trauma. What people expect of us. It wasn't quite like meeting in person."

"And sure as hell not like baking together."

Sam nudges my hip with hers and gives another laugh. Whatever test she was giving me, I think I've passed.

"It's time to put these in the oven," I announce.

I slide my batter into a loaf pan using a spatula. Sam simply tips her bowl over the pan, but her aim is off, and batter spills onto the counter.

"Shit," she says. "Where can I get one of those flat things?"

"You mean a spatula? In there."

I point to one of the counter drawers behind her. She tugs the handle of the one beneath it. The locked drawer. *My* drawer. Inside, something rattles.

"What's in here?"

"Don't touch that!"

I sound more panicked than I intend to, my voice lightly dusted with anger. My hand flutters to my neck, feeling for the key, as if it had somehow magically found its way into the drawer's lock. It's still there, of course, flat against my chest.

"It's recipes," I say, calming. "My top secret stash."

"Sorry," Sam says as she lets go of the drawer handle.

"No one can see them," I add.

"Sure. I get it."

Sam raises both hands. Her jacket sleeve rides down her wrist, fully revealing the tattoo there. It's a single word, etched in black.

SURVIVOR

The letters are capitalized. The font is bold. It's both declaration and dare. *Go on*, it says. *Just try to fuck with me.*

An hour later, all the cupcakes from yesterday are decorated and two orange pumpkin loaves sit cooling atop the oven. Sam surveys the results with weary pride, a smudge of flour across her cheek like war paint.

"So now what?" she says.

I begin to arrange the cupcakes on chunky Fiestaware, their black icing popping against the pale green of the plates.

"Now we design a table setting for both desserts and photograph it for the website."

"I meant about us," Sam says. "We met. We talked. We baked. It was magical. So now what?"

"That depends on why you came here," I say. "Is it really just because of what happened to Lisa?"

"Isn't that enough?"

"You could have called. Or emailed."

"I wanted to see you in person," Sam says. "After learning what Lisa had done, I wanted to see how you were doing."

"And how am I doing?"

"I can't tell. Care to give me a hint?"

I busy myself with the cupcakes, trying out different arrangements as Sam stands behind me.

"Quincy?"

"I'm sad, okay?" I say, whirling around to face her. "Lisa's suicide makes me sad."

"I'm not." Sam examines her hands as she says it, digging batter out from under her fingernails. "I'm pissed off. After all she survived, that's how she died? It makes me mad."

Although it's exactly the same thing I had said to Jeff last night, irritation ripples over me. I turn back to the display. "Don't be mad at Lisa."

"I'm not," Sam says. "I'm pissed off at myself. For never reaching out to her. Or to you. Maybe if I had, I—"

"Could have prevented it?" I say. "Join the club."

Although my back is still turned to Sam, I know she's staring again. This time a faint cold spot blunts the heat of her gaze. Curiosity, left unarticulated. I want nothing more than to tell her about the email Lisa sent me before she died. It would be a relief to talk about it, to let Sam shoulder some of the burden of my possibly misplaced guilt. But it's partly guilt that has brought her to my door. I'm not about to add to it, especially if this visit is some unspoken rite of atonement.

"What happened to Lisa sucks," she says. "I feel like shit knowing that I—we, actually—might have been able to help her. I don't want the same thing happening to you."

"I'm not suicidal," I say.

"But I wouldn't have known it if you were. If you ever need help or something, tell me. I'll do the same for you. We need to look out for each other. So you can talk to me about what happened. You know, if you ever need to."

"Don't worry," I say. "I'm happy."

"Good." The word rings hollow, as if she doesn't believe me. "That's good to hear."

"Really, I am. The website's going well. Jeff is fantastic."

"Will I be allowed to meet this Jeff?"

It's a nesting-doll question, concealing other, unspoken ones inside. If I crack open *Will I meet Jeff?* I'll find *Do you like me?* Out of which pops *Are we becoming friends?* Inside that is the most compact, most important question. The heart of the matter: *Are we the same?*

"Of course," I say, answering them all at once. "You have to stay for dinner."

I finish the table setting, the cupcakes angled so their frosted spiders will fill the frame. For the background, I've chosen a swath of fabric with a bold '50s pattern and vintage ceramic pumpkins picked up at a flea market.

"Cute," Sam says, the wrinkling of her nose indicating it's not a compliment.

"In the baking blog biz, cute sells."

We stand shoulder to shoulder, studying the display. Despite all those minute adjustments, it's still not right. There's something missing. Some intangible spark I've neglected to include.

"It's too perfect," Sam announces.

"It's not," I say, when, of course, it is. The whole display is flat, lifeless. Everything is so pristine the cupcakes might as well be fake. They certainly look that way. Plastic frosting atop a foam base. "What would you do differently?"

Sam approaches the display with an index finger on her chin, lost in thought. She then goes to work, tearing through it like Godzilla stomping Tokyo. Some of the plates are cleared of cupcakes and hastily stacked. A ceramic pumpkin is knocked on its side and a napkin is crumpled and casually tossed, bouncing into the middle of the scene. Wrappers are torn from three cupcakes and dropped into the mix.

The once-pristine display is now chaotic. It resembles a table after a wildly entertaining dinner party, messy and satisfying and real.

It's perfect.

I grab my camera and start taking pictures, zooming in on the disheveled cupcakes. Behind them sits an uneven stack of Fiestaware, some bearing globs of black icing dark against the green.

Sam grabs a cupcake and takes a gargantuan bite as crumbs drip and cherry filling oozes. "Take my picture."

I hesitate, for reasons she can't begin to understand.

"I don't put pictures of people on the blog," I say. "Only food."

Nor do I *take* pictures of people, even ones not intended for my website. No Lisa-esque selfies for me. Not since Pine Cottage.

"Just this once," Sam says, faking a pout. "For me?"

Hesitantly, I look into the camera's viewfinder and suck in a breath. It's like peering into a crystal ball and seeing not my future but my past. I see Janelle, standing in front of Pine Cottage, striking wacky poses with her too many suitcases. I didn't notice the similarity earlier, but now it's obvious. While Sam and Janelle don't physically resemble each other, they share the same spirit. Vivid and unapologetic and startlingly alive.

"Something wrong?" Sam says.

"No." I click the shutter, taking a single picture. "Nothing's wrong."

Sam hurries to my side, nudging me until I show her the photograph.

"I like it," she says. "You definitely need to put it up on your blog."

I tell her that I will, which pleases her, even though I plan to delete the picture the first chance I get.

Next, it's time to arrange and photograph the pumpkin bread. I let Sam saw away at one of the loaves, the uneven slices unfolding off it like pages torn from a book. The ceramic pumpkins are replaced with vintage teacups I found a week earlier in the West Village. I fill them with coffee, varying the amounts in each. When a splash of coffee hits the table, I leave it there, letting it pool around the base of a teacup. Sam finishes things by lifting the cup and taking a long, slurping sip. Her lipstick leaves a mark on the brim. A ruby kiss, mysterious and seductive. She stands back to let me photograph it. I click away, taking more pictures than necessary, drawn to the chaos.

8.

Dinnertime arrives in a panicked whirl of preparation and last-minute details. I whip up linguini with the homemade puttanesca sauce Jeff's mother taught me how to make. There's salad, freshly baked bread-sticks, wine from actual bottles, all perfectly laid out on the rough-hewn dining-room table we bought the previous summer in Red Hook.

Jeff comes home to find Rosemary Clooney standards drifting from the living-room stereo and me clad in the mid-'50s party dress I felt compelled to change into, my face pink and gleaming. God knows what's going through his mind. Definitely confusion. Perhaps worry that I've gone a little overboard, which I have. But I hope there's pride in the mix too. At what I've accomplished. At the fact that after so many crowded, informal meals with his family, I finally have a guest.

Then Sam emerges from the dining room with her face scrubbed of flour and a fresh coat of lipstick, and I know exactly what Jeff is thinking. Concern mixed with suspicion tinged with surprise.

"Jeff, this is Sam," I announce.

"Samantha Boyd?" Jeff says, more to me than to her.

Sam smiles and offers her hand. "I prefer Sam."

"Sure. Hi, Sam." The situation has jolted Jeff so much that he almost forgets to return Sam's handshake. When he does, it's weak. More hand than shake. "Quincy, can I talk to you for a sec?"

We go to the kitchen, where I quickly brief him on the afternoon's events, finishing with, "I hope you don't mind that I asked her to stay for dinner."

"It's certainly a surprise," he says.

"Yes, it happened very suddenly."

"You should have called me."

"You would have tried to talk me out of it," I say.

Jeff ignores the remark, mostly because he knows it's true.

"I just think it's very strange that she suddenly showed up like this. That's not normal, Quinn."

"You're sounding a bit too suspicious, Mr. Lawyer."

"I'd just feel better knowing more about why she's here."

"I'm still trying to figure that out," I say.

"Then why did you invite her to dinner?"

I want to tell him about that afternoon, how for a moment Sam was so much like Janelle that it took my breath away. But he wouldn't understand. No one would.

"I kind of feel sorry for her," I say. "After all that she's been through, I think she just might need a friend."

"Fine," Jeff says. "If you're cool with all this, then so am I."

Yet the shadow of a scowl crossing his face tells me that he's not entirely cool with it. Still, we go back to the dining room, where Sam politely pretends that we just weren't talking about her. "Everything good?" she says.

I smile so wide my cheeks hurt. "Perfect. Let's eat!"

During the meal, I play hostess, serving the food and pouring the wine, trying hard to ignore that Jeff is talking to Sam like she's one of his clients—genial but probing. Jeff's a conversational dentist that way. Extracting what needs to be removed.

"Quinn tells me you vanished for a few years," he says.

"I like to think of it as laying low."

"What was that like?"

"Peaceful. No one knowing who I was. No one knowing all the bad things that happened to me."

"Sounds more like being a fugitive," Jeff says.

"I guess," Sam replies. "Only I didn't do anything wrong, remember."

"So why hide?"

"Why not?"

When Jeff can't think of a good response, silence ensues, broken occasionally by the sound of cutlery scraping against plates. It makes me nervous, and before I know it, my wineglass is empty. I refill it before offering more to the others.

"Sam? Refill?"

She seems to intuit my nervousness and smiles to put me at ease. "Sure," she says, gulping down the rest of the wine in her glass just so I can pour more into it.

I turn to Jeff. "More wine?"

"I'm good," he tells me. To Sam, he says, "And where have you been living these days?"

"Here and there."

The same answer she had given me. One that doesn't satisfy Jeff. He lowers his fork to give Sam a cross-examination stare.

"Where, exactly?"

"No place you would have heard of," Sam says.

"I've heard of all fifty states." Jeff flashes a friendly smile. "I can even recite most of their capitals."

"I think Sam wants to keep it a secret," I say. "In case she wants to return there and live in anonymity."

Across the table, Sam gives me a grateful nod. I'm looking out for her. Just like she said we should do. Even if, in this case at least, I'm just as curious as Jeff.

"I'm sure she'll tell us eventually," I add. "Right, Sam?"

"Maybe." The hardness in Sam's voice makes it clear there'll be no maybe. Yet she tries to sandpaper her tone by adding a joke. "It depends on how good dessert is."

"It doesn't matter anyway," Jeff says. "What matters is that the two of you finally got the chance to connect. I know it means a lot to Quinn. She was really broken up about what happened with Lisa."

"Me too," Sam says. "As soon as I heard about it, I decided to come here and finally talk to her."

Jeff tilts his head. With his shaggy hair and big, brown eyes he looks like a spaniel faced with a bone. Hungry and alert. "So you knew Quinn was in New York?"

"Over the years, I kept tabs on both her and Lisa."

"Interesting. For what reason?"

"Curiosity, I suppose. I liked knowing they were doing okay. Or at least thinking they were."

Jeff nods, looks down at his plate, pushes the linguini from one side to the other with his fork. Eventually, he says, "Is this your first time in Manhattan?"

"No. I've been here a few times before."

"When was your last visit?"

"Decades ago," Sam says. "When I was a kid."

"So before all that stuff happened at that hotel?"

"Yeah." Sam gazes at him from across the table, eyes narrowed, on the razor's edge of a glare. "Before all that *stuff.*"

Jeff pretends not to notice the sarcastic spin placed on that last word. "So it's been a while, I guess."

"It has."

"And Quincy's well-being is the only reason you came here?"

I reach out to pat Jeff's hand. A silent signal that he's out of bounds, taking things too far. He does the same thing to me when we're visiting my mother and I get too argumentative about her views on, oh, everything.

"What other reason could there be?" Sam says.

"I suppose there could be plenty," Jeff replies, my hand still heavy over his. "Maybe you're seeking some publicity in the wake of Lisa's death. Maybe you need money."

"That's not why I'm here."

"I hope not. I hope you only came here to check in on Quinn."

"I suppose that was always Lisa's wish," Sam says. "To have the three of us meet, you know? And help one another."

The mood has irrevocably shifted. Suspicion hovers over the table, humid and sour. Impulsively, I raise my glass. It's almost empty again, a thin circle of red swirling around its bottom.

"I think we should make a toast," I announce. "To Lisa. Although the three of us never got the chance to meet, I think she's here in spirit. I also think she'd be pleased to see at least two of us together at last."

"To Lisa," Sam says, playing along.

I slosh more wine into my glass. Then more into Sam's, even though it's still half-full. When our glasses clink over the table, it's too hard, too loud, the crystal a hair's breadth from cracking. A wave of Pinot Noir breaches the edge of my glass, splashing onto the salad and breadsticks below. The wine seeps into the bread, leaving behind splotches of red.

I let out a nervous giggle. Sam pops out one of her shotgun-blast laughs.

Jeff, not amused, gives me a look he sometimes whips out during awkward work functions. The *Are-you-drunk?* look. I'm not. Well, not yet. But I can see why he thinks I am.

"So what do you do for a living, Sam?" he asks.

She shrugs. "A little of this, a little of that."

"I see," Jeff says.

"I'm between jobs at the moment."

"I see," Jeff says again.

I take another sip of wine.

"And you're a lawyer?" Coming from Sam, it sounds like an accusation.

"I am," Jeff says. "A public defender."

"Interesting. Bet all types of people come your way."

"They certainly do."

Sam leans back in her chair, one arm crossed over her stomach. The other grips her wineglass, holding it close to her lips. Smiling over the rim, she says, "And are all your clients criminals?"

Jeff mirrors Sam's stance. Reclined in his chair, clenching his wineglass. I watch the two of them face off, the half-eaten meal heavy and unsettled in the pit of my stomach.

"My clients are innocent until proven guilty," Jeff says.

"But most of them are, right? Proven guilty?"

"I suppose you could say that."

"How does that make you feel? Knowing the guy sitting next to you in court in a borrowed suit did all those things he's accused of?"

"Are you asking me if I feel guilty about it?"

"Do you?"

"No," Jeff says. "I feel noble knowing that I'm one of the few people giving that guy in the borrowed suit the benefit of the doubt."

"But what if he did something really bad?" Sam asks.

"How bad are we talking about?" Jeff says. "Murder?"

"Worse."

I know where Sam's going with this, and my stomach clenches even more. I put a hand over it, rubbing slightly.

"It doesn't get much worse than murder," Jeff says, also knowing what Sam's up to and not caring. He'll gladly follow her to the edge of an argument. I've seen it happen before.

"Have you represented a murderer?"

"I have," Jeff says. "In fact, I'm doing so right now."

"And do you like it?"

"It doesn't matter if I like it. It needs to be done."

"What if the guy killed several people?"

"He still needs defending," Jeff says.

"What if it's the guy who killed all those people at the Nightlight Inn? Or the guy who did all that shit at Pine Cottage?" Sam's anger is palpable now—a heat pulsing across the table. Her voice picks up speed, each subsequent word getting harder, rougher. "Knowing all of that, would you still happily sit next to that motherfucker and try to keep him out of jail?"

Jeff remains motionless, save for a slight working of his jaw. His eyes never leave Sam. He doesn't even blink.

"It must be convenient," he says, "to have something to blame for everything that went wrong in your life."

"Jeff." My throat is parched, my voice soft and easy to ignore. "Stop."

"Quinn could do that. God knows, she has every right to. But she doesn't. Because she's managed to put it behind her. She's strong like that. She's not some—"

"Jeff, *please.*"

"—helpless victim who skipped out on her family and friends instead of trying to move past something that happened more than a decade ago."

"Enough!"

I leap from my seat, tipping my wineglass, its contents gushing over the table. I sop it up with my napkin. White fabric turning red.

"Jeff. Bedroom. Now."

We stand by the closed door, facing each other, our bodies a study in contrasts. Jeff is calm and loose, arms at his sides. Mine are a straight-jacket across my chest, which lifts and falls in exasperation.

"You didn't need to be so harsh."

"After what she said to me? I think I did, Quinn."

"You have to admit, you kind of started it."

"By being curious?"

"By being suspicious," I say. "You were giving her the third degree out there. This isn't court. She's not one of your clients, Jeff!"

My voice is too loud, ringing off the walls. Jeff and I both look to the door, pausing to find out if Sam heard us. I'm sure she did. Even if she has managed to miss my increasingly shrill tone, it's obvious we're again talking about her.

"I was asking her pretty rational questions," Jeff says, lowering his voice to make up for my volume. "Don't you think she's being evasive?"

"She doesn't want to talk about this stuff. I can't blame her."

"That still gave her no right to talk to me like that. As if I'm the one who attacked her."

"She's sensitive."

"Bullshit. She was egging me on."

"She was defending herself," I say. "She's not an enemy, Jeff. She's a friend. Or at least she can be."

"Do you even *want* to be friends with her? Until yesterday, you seemed perfectly happy having nothing to do with this Final Girls stuff. So what's changed?"

"Other than Lisa Milner's suicide?"

A sigh from Jeff. "I understand how much it's upset you. I know you're sad and disappointed about what happened. But why this sudden interest in becoming friends with Sam? You don't even know her, Quinn."

"I know her. She went through the same thing I did, Jeff. I know exactly who she is."

"I'm just worried that if you two get close, you'll start dwelling on what happened to you. And you've moved past it."

Jeff means well. I know this. And living with me isn't always easy. I know this too. But that doesn't keep his comment from getting me riled up even more.

"My friends were *slaughtered*, Jeff. That's not something I'll ever move past."

"You know I didn't mean it like that."

I lift my chin, defiant in my anger. "Then what did you mean?"

"That you've become more than a victim," Jeff says. "That your life—our life—isn't defined by that night. I don't want that to change."

"My being nice to Sam isn't going to change anything. And it's not like I have a whole army of friends beating down the front door."

This isn't something I plan to admit. My loneliness is something I generally keep from Jeff. I smile sunnily when he comes home from work and asks me how my day was. Fine, I always say, when in fact my days are often a lonely blur. Long afternoons spent baking in isolation, sometimes talking to the oven just to hear the sound of my voice.

Instead of friends, I have acquaintances. Former classmates and coworkers. Ones with husbands and kids and office jobs that aren't conducive to regular contact. Ones I purposefully kept at a distance until they became nothing more substantial than occasional text messages or emails.

"I really need this, Jeff," I say.

Jeff grips my shoulders, kneading them. He looks into my eyes, seeing something out of place, something unspoken.

"What aren't you telling me?"

"I got an email," I say.

"From Sam?"

"Lisa. She sent it an hour before she—"

Offed herself, I want to say. Finished what Stephen Leibman didn't get the chance to do. "Passed away."

"What did it say?"

I recite the email word for word, the text etched into my memory.

"Why would she do that?" Jeff says, as if I somehow have an answer.

"I don't know. I'll never know. But for some reason she was thinking about me right before she died. And all *I* can think about is the fact that, if I had seen that email in time, I could have possibly saved her."

Tears form, hot in the corners of my eyes. I try to blink them back, to no avail. Jeff pulls me to him, my head against his chest, his arms tight across my back.

"Jesus, Quinn. I'm so sorry. I didn't know."

"You had no way of knowing."

"But you can't let yourself think you're responsible for Lisa's death."

"I don't," I say. "But I do think I missed my chance to help her. I don't want to do the same thing with Sam. I know she's rough around the edges. But I think she needs me."

Jeff sighs a long exhalation of defeat.

"I'll play nice," he says. "I promise."

We kiss and make up, tears salty on my lips. I wipe them away while Jeff lets go of me, jiggling his arms to release the tension. I give my shirt a tug and smooth out the tear-stained spot I left on his. Then we're out of the bedroom, moving down the hall with hands entwined. A unified front.

In the dining room, we find the table unoccupied, Sam's chair pushed away from it. She's not in the kitchen either. Or the living room. In the foyer, the spot by the door where her knapsack sat is now an empty patch of floor.

Once again, Samantha Boyd has vanished.

9.

My phone rings at three a.m., yanking me from a nightmare of running through a forest. Running from Him. Tripping and screaming, tree branches reaching out to circle my wrists. I'm still running even after I wake, my legs thrashing beneath the covers. The phone keeps ringing—an urgent beep slicing the silence of the room. Jeff, the heaviest of sleepers, trained only to wake to the Pavlovian bell of his alarm clock, doesn't stir. To keep it that way, I cover the screen when I grab the phone, blocking its glow. I peek through my fingers in search of the caller's identity.

Unknown.

"Hello?" I whisper as I slide out of bed and rush to the door.

"Quincy?"

It's Sam, her voice hard to hear over the din surrounding her. There's chatter and yelling and the harried clack of fingers on keyboards.

"Sam?" I'm in the hallway now, eyes bleary in the darkness, brain swimming in a soup of confusion. "Where did you disappear to? Why are you calling me so late?"

"I'm sorry. I really am. But something's happened."

I think she's going to say something about Him. Most likely because of the nightmare, which lingers sticky on my skin like drying perspiration. I brace myself to hear her tell me that He's resurfaced, as I always knew He would. It doesn't matter that He's dead. That I gladly watched Him die.

Instead, Sam says, "I need your help."

"What's wrong? What happened?"

"I was sort of arrested."

"What?"

The word echoes down the hallway, waking Jeff. From the bedroom, I hear the squeak of the mattress as he bolts upright and calls my name.

On the phone, Sam says, "Please come get me. Central Park Precinct. Bring Jeff."

She hangs up before I get the chance to ask her how she knew my phone number.

Jeff and I take a cab to the precinct, which is situated just south of the reservoir. I've jogged past it dozens of times, always slightly confused by its mix of old and new. It consists of low-slung brick buildings, around since the park's birth, bisected by a modern atrium that glows from within. Every time I see it, I think of a snow globe. A Dickensian village encased in glass.

Inside, I ask to see Samantha Boyd. The desk sergeant on duty is a ruddy-faced Irishman with love handles jiggling under his uniform. He checks the computer and says, "We haven't brought in anyone by that name, miss."

"But she told me she was here."

"How long ago was this?"

"Twenty minutes," I say as I adjust the half-tucked blouse bunched at my waist. Jeff and I had dressed in a hurry, with me throwing on the same clothes I had worn that afternoon. Jeff slipped into jeans and a long-sleeved T-shirt, his hair jutting off his head in wild thatches.

Officer Love Handles frowns at the computer. "I've got nothing."

"Maybe she's already been released," Jeff says, all but announcing his wishful thinking. "Is that a possibility?"

"She'd still be in the system. Maybe she gave you the wrong precinct. Or maybe you misheard her."

"It was this one," I tell him. "I'm sure of it."

I scan the open expanse of the precinct. High-ceilinged and bright, it looks more like a modern train depot than a police station. There's a sleek staircase, state-of-the-art lighting, the staccato click of foot-steps on the polished floors.

"Have any women been brought in recently?" Jeff asks.

"One," the desk sergeant says, still studying the computer. "Thirty-five minutes ago."

"What's her name?"

"I'm afraid that's confidential."

I look to Jeff, hopeful. "It could be her." I then look to the desk sergeant, pleading. "Can we see her?"

"That's not really allowed."

Jeff pulls out his wallet and flashes his work ID. He explains, in his unfailingly polite way, that he's a public defender, that we're not here to cause trouble, that a friend of ours claimed to be in police custody at this precinct.

"Please?" I say to the desk sergeant. "I'm worried about her."

He relents and passes us into the care of another officer, this one bigger, stronger, devoid of love handles. He guides us into the heart of the precinct. The room gives off a jittery, caffeinated vibe. All that institutional lighting brightening what's technically the dead of night. Sam is there after all, cuffed to a booking desk.

"That's her," I tell our escort. He grabs my arm when I try to surge forward, keeping me in place. I call her name. "Sam!"

The cop at the booking desk stands, asks her a question. I can read his lips. *Do you know that woman?* When Sam nods, the cop holding me back gently walks me to her, his hand like a vise on my arm. He lets go once I'm within arm's length of Sam's booking officer.

"Sam?" I say. "What happened?"

Her cop gives her another look, forehead creasing. "Are you sure you know this woman?"

"Yes," I say, answering for her. "Her name is Samantha Boyd and I'm sure whatever happened is simply a misunderstanding."

"That's not the name she gave the arresting officer."

"What do you mean?"

The cop coughs while shuffling through paperwork. "Says here that her name's Tina Stone."

I look to Sam. The late hour has made her cheeks puffy and red. Her eyeliner is smudged in spots—streaks of blackness that bleed into the circles beneath her eyes.

"Is this true?"

"Yeah," she says with a shrug. "I changed my name a while back."

"So your name is really Tina Stone?"

"Now it is. Legally. You know, just because."

I do know. I thought about doing the same thing a year after Pine Cottage, for the same reasons Sam has no need to articulate. Because I was tired of strangers vaguely recognizing it when I was introduced to them. Because I hated the way their features froze, if only for a second, when their memories clicked. Because it made me sick knowing my name and His will forever be associated.

Coop ultimately talked me out of it. He said I should hold on to my name as a stubborn point of pride. Changing it wouldn't separate the name Quincy Carpenter from the horrors of Pine Cottage. Keeping it could, if I moved on and made something of myself. Something beyond being the lucky one who lived when so many others had not.

"Now that we've got the name thing cleared up," Jeff says, "can someone tell me what she's been accused of?"

"Are you her attorney?" the cop asks.

Jeff sighs. "I guess."

"Miss Stone," the cop says, "faces charges of third-degree assault on a police officer and resisting arrest."

The details come in pieces, from both Sam and the booking officer. Jeff, calm and collected, asks the questions. I struggle to keep up, head pivoting between the three of them, my brain buzzing from lack of sleep. From what I'm able to gather, Sam, now also known as Tina Stone, went to a bar on the Upper West Side after leaving my apartment. After a few drinks, she went outside for a smoke, encountering a husband and wife in mid-argument. It was heated, according to Sam. Things got physical. When the man shoved the woman, she stepped in.

"I was breaking up a fight," she tells us.

"You attacked him," the cop counters.

Both agree on one thing—that Sam ultimately punched the man. He called the police while Sam asked the woman if she was okay, if fights like this were a regular thing, if the man had ever hit her. When a pair of cops arrived, Sam bolted across Central Park West, vanishing into the park itself.

The cops followed, caught up, brought out the cuffs. That's when Sam resisted.

"They were arresting me for no goddamn reason," she says.

"You hit a man," the cop says.

She sniffs. "I was trying to help. He looked like he was about to beat the shit out of that woman. He probably would have too, if I hadn't done something about it."

Frustrated by the injustice of it all—Sam's words, not mine—she took a swing at one of the cops, knocking off his hat and prompting her arrest.

"It was only his hat, for God's sake," she mutters in conclusion. "It's not like I hurt him or anything."

"It appeared to him like you wanted to," the booking officer says. "That harm certainly seemed to be your intent."

"Let's talk this through," Jeff says. "She's only being charged with what happened in the park, correct?"

The cop nods. "The man she punched declined to press charges."

"Then clearly we can work something out."

Jeff pulls the cop aside. They confer by the wall, their voices low but still loud enough for me to hear. I stand next to Sam, my hand on her shoulder, fingers digging into the soft leather of her jacket. She doesn't bother trying to listen in. She simply stares straight ahead, grinding her teeth.

"This all sounds to me like a big misunderstanding," Jeff tells the cop.

"Not to me," the cop replies.

"It's clear she shouldn't have done what she did. But she was trying to help that woman and emotions were high and she got a little wild."

"You're saying the charges should be dropped?"

The booking officer looks our way. I give him a smile, hoping it will somehow persuade him. As if seeing perky, harmless me at Sam's side will tip the scales in her favor.

"I'm saying she shouldn't have been charged in the first place," Jeff says. "If you knew what she's been through, you'd understand why she acted that way."

The cop's face is a blank. "Then tell me what happened to her."

Jeff whispers something to him that I can't fully make out. I catch only random words. One of them is "Nightlight." Another is "murders." The booking officer turns to look at Sam again. This time, his eyes contain a potent mix of curiosity and pity. I've seen that look a thousand times before. It's the look of someone realizing he's facing a Final Girl.

He whispers something to Jeff. Jeff whispers back. This continues a few more seconds until they shake hands and Jeff walks briskly toward us.

"Grab your things," he tells Sam. "You're free to go."

Outside, the three of us idle in the courtyard just beyond the precinct's glass front wall, the Irish desk sergeant watching us from his post. A chilly breeze courses through the park, nipping at my ears and nose. I was in too much of a hurry when we left to think of bringing a sweater and now hug myself for warmth.

Sam zips her leather jacket all the way to her chin, the collar popped. The knapsack is strapped to her back. Its weight makes her list sideways as she says, "Thank you for helping me in there. After the shit I said tonight, I wouldn't have blamed you for letting me rot in a holding cell."

"You're welcome," Jeff says. "I'm not such a bad guy now, am I?"

He gives us a pleased-with-himself grin. I turn away. Although I know I should be grateful, a rash of annoyance creeps across my skin. Sam, though, *is* grateful. She thrusts out her hand, her SURVIVOR tattoo peeking from her sleeve. Jeff looks to me as he shakes it, sensing something is wrong. I refuse to meet his eye.

Instead of a handshake, Sam gives me a quick hug. "Quincy, it was good to finally meet you."

"Wait—you're leaving?"

"I think I've caused enough trouble," she says. "I only wanted to see how you were doing. Now I have my answer. You're doing great. I'm happy for you, babe."

"But where will you go?"

"Here and there," Sam says. "Take care of yourself, okay?"

She starts to walk away. Or maybe she only pretends to, knowing I'll stop her. It's hard to tell, with the knapsack giving her a slow, uneven gait. Still, I know I can't let her slip away again. Not like this.

"Sam, wait," I say. "I know you don't have a place to stay."

Wind whips hair across her face as she turns around. "Don't sweat it. I'll be okay."

"You will," I tell her. "Because you're coming home with us."

10.

The minute we get home, Jeff and I confer in the bedroom, the door
closed, our voices emerging in exhausted half whispers so Sam can't
hear us from the living room.

"She can stay one night," Jeff says.

"The night's almost over," I say, still mad at him for reasons I can't
articulate. "Two nights. At least."

"This isn't a negotiation."

"Why are you so against this?"

"Why are you so gung-ho about it?" Jeff says. "She's a stranger,
Quinn. She didn't even bother to tell you her real name."

"I *know* her name. It's Samantha Boyd. And she's not a stranger.
She's a person who went through the same things I did, who now
needs a place to stay."

"We're in Manhattan," Jeff says. "There are thousands of places
she can go. Hotels."

"I'm pretty sure she can't afford a hotel."

Jeff sighs, sits on the bed, kicks off his shoes. "That alone should
give you pause. Who travels from God knows where to New York
without any money? Or any plan, for that matter?"

"Someone who's really upset about what happened to Lisa Milner
and now wants to do something about it."

"She's not our responsibility, Quinn."

"She came here to see me," I say. "That makes her our responsibility.
My responsibility."

"And I got those charges dropped. I think that's enough charity for someone we don't know."

Jeff shucks off his shirt, slides out of his pants, and crawls into bed, ready to put the whole night behind him. I remain by the door, arms crossed, sending out waves of unspoken anger.

"Yeah. You did a swell job."

Jeff sits up, blinking at me. "Wait. You're actually mad at me for that?"

"I'm mad that you were so quick to play the victim card. All it took was one mention of the Nightlight Inn."

"Sam didn't mind."

"Only because she didn't hear you. I'm sure things would be different if she had."

"I'm not going to apologize for keeping her out of jail."

"Nor should you," I say. "But you can at least acknowledge that there might have been a better way to do it. You should have seen the way that cop looked at Sam. Like she was a wounded dog or something. That's why she changed her name, Jeff. So people would stop pitying her."

But I'm angry at him for reasons that go beyond Sam. When he whispered to that cop, I caught a glimpse of Jefferson Richards at work. The lawyer. The guy willing to say anything to help his client, even if it meant reducing her to an object of pity. I didn't like what I saw.

"Listen," Jeff says, reaching out for me. "I'm sorry I did that. But at the time it seemed like the quickest way to resolve the whole thing."

I tighten my arms across my chest. "If the roles were reversed and it was me who had been arrested, would you have done the same thing?"

"Of course not."

I detect a streak of falsehood in his voice. There's a thinness to his words that brings the annoyed prickle back to my skin. I scratch my neck, trying to make it go away.

"But that's what I am, right?" I say. "A victim? Just like Sam?"

A frustrated sigh from Jeff. "You know you're more than that."

"So is Sam. And while she's staying with us, you need to treat her that way."

Jeff tries to utter another apology, but I cut him off by whirling around and throwing open the bedroom door. When I leave, I slam it shut so hard the walls shake.

The guest room is small, tidy, stuffy. The red shade of the nightstand lamp throws a rosy glow over the walls. Because of the hour, everything feels shimmering and dreamlike. I know I should try to sleep, but I don't want to. Not with Sam seemingly wide-awake, pulsing with heat and energy and life. So we huddle on the queen bed, shoes discarded on the floor, our feet shoved beneath the comforter for warmth.

Sam retreats to the knapsack she dropped in the corner and removes a bottle of Wild Turkey.

"A little pick-me-up," she says, climbing back into bed. "I think we need it."

The Wild Turkey is passed back and forth, both of us swigging directly from the bottle. Each swallow is a burning lump sliding down my throat. They ignite faint traces of memory. Me and Janelle on the first night in our dorm room. The two of us shoulder to shoulder, her drinking wine coolers she had flirted from a junior across the hall, me sipping a Diet Coke. We became best friends that night. I still think of her as that. My best friend. It doesn't matter that she's ten years in the grave and that I know our friendship wouldn't have survived even if she had.

"This is just for tonight, you know," Sam says. "I'll be gone in the morning."

"You can stay as long as you need."

"And I only need one night."

"You should have told me you were struggling," I say. "I'm happy to help. I can loan you money. Or whatever."

"I'm sure that'll go over real well with your boyfriend."

I take a swig of Wild Turkey and cough. "Don't worry about Jeff."

"He doesn't like me."

"He doesn't know you yet, Sam." I pause. "Or should I call you Tina?"

"Sam," she says. "The Tina thing is just a formality."

"How long has it been since you did that?"

Sam takes a drink, talking while swallowing. "Years."

"When you disappeared?"

"Yeah. I was sick of being Samantha Boyd, the Final Girl. I wanted to be someone else. At least on paper."

"Does your family know?"

Sam shakes her head and passes me the bottle before scooting off the bed. Her first destination is her knapsack, out of which is pulled a pack of cigarettes. Then it's on to the window, where she says, "Can I?"

I shrug my permission and Sam opens the window. Outside, thin clouds streak the bruise-black sky. The darkness hums with faint energy. Dawn is approaching.

"I need to quit," Sam says as she lights up. "Smoking's gotten too damn expensive."

"Not to mention deadly," I say.

She blows a stream of smoke through the window screen. "That part doesn't worry me. I've already cheated death once, right?"

"So you started after the Nightlight Inn?"

"I needed something to calm me down, you know?"

Oh, yes, I know. Besides the Xanax, my go-to relief valve is wine. Red, white, or in between, it doesn't matter. I'm certain Janelle would have found that ironic.

"I'm surprised you and Lisa never started," Sam says. "It seemed so natural to me."

"I tried it once. Didn't like it." A question pings into my head. "How do you know Lisa didn't smoke?"

"I assume she didn't," Sam says. "She didn't mention it in her book or anything."

The first half-inch of her cigarette has become a cylinder of ash, on the verge of dropping to the floor. She steps away from the window, the hand holding the cigarette remaining by the screen while her free arm reaches for the knapsack and pulls out a portable ashtray. Leather and baglike, it looks like a coin purse with a snap clasp. Displaying the dexterity of a longtime smoker, Sam flicks it open and, with a tap, deposits the ash dangling from the cigarette.

"So you *did* read her book?" I say.

Sam inhales, nods, exhales. "I thought it was okay. It sure as hell didn't help me deal with what happened to me."

"Do you think about it a lot?"

I take another swallow of Wild Turkey, getting used to its warmth in the back of my throat. Sam reaches out an arm, seeking the bottle. When I hand it to her, she takes two hard swallows, only a puff of her cigarette separating them.

"Constantly."

She passes the bottle back to me. I raise it to my lips, my quiet words reverberating against the glass. "Do you want to talk about it?"

Sam finishes her cigarette with a single, grand exhalation. It's then tapped out in the ashtray, which she promptly shuts. When the window is closed, smoke continues to sting the air of the room, lingering like a bad memory.

"You think it only happens in the movies," she says. "That it couldn't happen in real life. At least, not like that. And certainly not to you. But it happened. First at a sorority house in Indiana. Then at a motel in Florida."

She slides off her jacket, revealing more of the black dress underneath. Her arms and shoulders are exposed, the flesh tight and moon-pale. On her back, a tattoo of the Grim Reaper has been inked just below her right shoulder, its skeletal face momentarily bisected by the strap of her dress.

"Calvin Whitmer," she says, climbing back into bed. "The Sack Man."

The name prompts a deep, internal shiver. It feels like a chunk of ice is tangled among my organs.

"You said his name."

"Why wouldn't I?"

"I've never said His name." There's no need for me to clarify. She knows who I'm talking about. "Not once."

"It doesn't bother me," Sam says as she pulls the bottle from my grip. "I think about him all the time. I can still see him, you know? When I close my eyes. He had cut eyeholes into the sack. Plus a little slit right over his nose for air. I'll never forget the way it flapped when he breathed. He had tied string around his neck to keep the sack in place."

I sense another chunk of ice forming in my gut. I take the Wild Turkey from Sam even though she's not finished with it. I swallow two gulps, hoping it will melt the chill.

"Too many details?" Sam says.

I shake my head. "Details matter."

"What about you? You remember any details at all?"

"A few."

"But not much."

"No."

"I've heard it's not a real thing," she says. "All that repressed-memory stuff."

I help myself to another swallow, trying to ignore the vague needling from Sam. Despite all we have in common, she's incapable of peering into my brain and seeing the black hole where memories of Pine Cottage should be. She'll never know how comforting yet frustrating it is to remember the very beginning of something and then the tail end. It's like leaving a theater five minutes into the movie and returning right when the end credits start to roll.

"Trust me," I say. "It's real."

"And you don't mind not remembering?"

"I think it's probably better that I don't."

"But don't you want to know what really happened?"

"I know the end result," I say. "That's all I need to know."

"I heard it's still standing," Sam says. "Pine Cottage. I read it on one of those shitty true-crime sites."

I had read the same thing several years ago. Probably on the same website. Once the investigation was over, Pine Cottage's owner had tried to sell the land. No one wanted it, of course. Nothing sinks land values more than blood in the soil. When he went into bankruptcy, it passed into the hands of his creditors. They couldn't sell it either. So Pine Cottage remains, a cabin-size tombstone in the Pennsylvania woods.

"You ever think about going back there and taking a look?" Sam asks. "Maybe it would help you remember."

The very idea nauseates me. "Never."

"Do you ever think about him?"

It's obvious she wants me to say His name. Anticipation pulses like body heat off her skin.

"No," I lie.

"I figured you'd say that," Sam says.

"It's true."

I have another swallow of Wild Turkey and stare into the bottle, taken aback by how much we've had. Actually, by how much *I've* had. Sam, I realize, has barely touched it. I close my eyes, swaying a little. I can feel myself teetering on the edge of being drunk. One more drink will do the trick.

I tip the bottle back, take two gulps, relish their burn.

Sam's voice has become distant and tinny, even though she's right beside me. "You act like you're totally over what happened, but you're not."

"You're wrong," I say.

"Then prove it. Tell me his name."

"We should try to sleep," I say, looking to the window and the increasingly lightened sky. "It's late. Or early."

"There's no reason to be afraid," Sam says.

"I'm not."

"It's not like it'll bring him back to life."

"I know."

"Then why are you being such a pussy about it?"

She sounds exactly like Janelle. Nudging. Prodding. Goading me into something I don't want to do. Annoyance swells inside me, tinged with anger. When I try to tamp it down with more Wild Turkey I realize Sam's taken the bottle from my hands.

"You are, you know," she says. "Being a pussy."

"That's enough, Sam."

"If you're so over everything that happened, then a simple name shouldn't be that big of a deal."

"I'm going to bed."

Sam grabs my arm when I try to leave. I jerk free of her grip, slide off the bed, and hit the floor. Hard. Pain spreads up my hip.

Drunk on both Wild Turkey and lack of sleep, it takes some effort to stand. The whiskey sloshes sourly in my stomach. My vision swims. Sam makes things worse by saying, "I wish you'd say it."

"No."

"Just once. For me."

I turn on her, wildly unsteady. "Why are you making such a big deal out of this?"

"Why are you so against it?"

"Because He doesn't deserve to have His name spoken!" I yell, my voice loud in the predawn silence. "After what He did, no one should say His fucking name!"

Sam's eyes go wide. She knows she's pushed me too far.

"You don't need to freak out about it."

"Apparently I do," I say. "I'm doing you a favor by letting you crash here."

"You are. Don't think I don't know that."

"And if we're going to be friends, you need to also know that I don't talk about Pine Cottage. I've moved past it."

Sam looks down, both hands on the bottle, cradling it between her breasts. "I'm sorry," she says. "I didn't mean to be such a bitch."

A moment of sobriety arrives as I stand in the doorway, hand on my throbbing hip, trying my damnedest to not look as drunk as I truly am. "Maybe you're right. Maybe it is best if you leave in the morning."

Having spoken coherently, drunkenness again crashes over me. I sway out of the room, needing multiple attempts to close the door behind me. Then it's into my own room, where more wrangling with a door ensues.

Jeff is half-awake when I flop into bed, murmuring, "I heard shouting."

"It's nothing."

"You sure?"

"Yes," I reply, too exhausted to say more.

Before I free-fall completely into sleep, a thought cuts through the fuzz of my brain. It's a flash of memory—an unwelcome one. Him during the moment we first met. Before the killing started. Before he became Him.

A second thought arrives, one more troublesome than the first.

Sam wanted me to remember.

What I don't understand is why.

PINE COTTAGE
5:03 P.M.

Janelle decided she wanted to explore the woods, knowing full well the group agreed ahead of time to do the birthday girl's bidding. So off they went, tramping into the trees that practically nudged up against the cabin's back deck.

Craig, the former Boy Scout, led the way with a determination that was almost silly. He was the only one who brought along proper footwear—hiking boots with heavy-duty socks pulled over his taut calves to guard against ticks. He carried an absurdly long walking stick, which struck the ground in a rhythmic thud.

Quincy and Janelle were right behind him, less serious. Wearing jeans, striped sweaters, and impractical Keds, they kicked their way through the fallen leaves that coated the forest floor. More leaves continued to fall, the late-afternoon sunlight shining through their brittle thinness as they spun, tumbled, and whirled. Falling stars speckled red and orange and yellow.

Janelle grabbed a leaf in mid-fall and tucked it behind her ear, its fiery orange glowing against her auburn hair.

"I demand a picture," she said.

Quincy obliged, snapping off two shots before turning around and taking one of Betz, trudging heavily like she'd done all day. To her, this trip was more burden than gift. A weekend to be endured.

"Smile," Quincy ordered.

Betz frowned. "I'll smile when this hike is over."

Quincy took her picture anyway before moving on to Amy and Rodney, walking as one, their hips all but connected. Since they were never not together, everyone else had taken to calling them Ramdy.

Amy wore one of Rodney's flannel shirts, the too-long sleeves hanging past her fingertips. Beside her, Rodney resembled a grizzly bear, with his stoner scruff and thatch of chest hair peeking over the collar of his V-neck. Seeing Quincy, they squeezed tightly together, mugging.

"That's it," Quincy said. "Make love to the camera."

"You guys keeping up back there?" Craig called to them as they all began to scale a slight incline. Downed leaves made the ground slick, and Janelle and Quincy held hands, alternately hauling each other up the hill.

"Seriously, you don't want to fall behind," Janelle said with the authority of a tour guide. "These woods are haunted."

"Bullshit," Rodney replied.

"It's true. An Indian tribe used to live here hundreds of years ago. Then the white man came and wiped them out. Their blood is on our hands, guys."

"I don't see anything," Rodney said, turning his hands in mock examination.

"Be nice," Amy chided.

"Anyhow," Janelle said, "they say the spirits of these Indians haunt the woods, ready to kill any white man they see. So watch your back, Rodney."

"Why me?"

"Because Craig is too strong to be defeated by a ghost, Indian or otherwise," Quincy said.

"What about you?"

"I said the white *man* killed them," Janelle said. "We're women. They've got no beef with us."

"People really did die out here."

Betz is the one who said it. Quiet, observant Betz. She looked at them all with her too-large, slightly spooky eyes.

"A guy in my world lit class told me about it," she said. "A pair of campers were killed in the woods last year. A boyfriend and girl-friend. The police found them stabbed to death in their tent."

"Did they ever catch who did it?" Amy asked, sinking deeper against Rodney.

Betz shook her head. "Not that I know of."

No one spoke as they climbed the rest of the hill. Even the crunch of their feet on the leaf-strewn ground seemed to quiet down, letting them subconsciously listen for the sound of someone else in the woods. In that soft, new silence, Quincy sensed they weren't alone. She knew she was being foolish. That it was simply the by-product of what Betz had told them. Yet she couldn't shake the feeling that someone else was in the woods with them. Not very far at all. Watching.

A twig snapped nearby. Fewer than ten yards away. Hearing it made Quincy chirp out a half shriek. It set off a chain reaction of yelps, rising almost simultaneously from Janelle, Betz, and Amy.

Rodney, on the other hand, laughed. "God," he said. "Nervous much?"

He pointed to the source of the noise—a mere squirrel, its tail a white flag waving above the underbrush. The rest of them began to laugh too. Even Quincy, who instantly forgot how strangely jittery she had felt mere moments before.

At the crest of the hill, they found a large, flat-topped rock as wide as a king bed. Dozens of names had been carved into the surface— remnants of similar kids who'd made the same trek. Rodney picked up a sharp stone and began to add his name to the list. Beer cans and cigarette butts were scattered around the rock's perimeter, and an unrolled condom drooped from the spindly branch of a nearby sapling, prompting disgusted squeals from Janelle and Quincy.

"Maybe you and Craig can do it up here," Janelle whispered. "At least protection is provided."

"*If* we do it," Quincy said, "it certainly won't be on a rock that, from the looks of it, is an STD waiting to happen."

"Wait— You haven't decided yet?"

"I've decided not to decide," Quincy said, when in fact she already had. Agreeing to sleep in the same bed with Craig sealed that particular deal. "It'll happen when it happens."

"It better happen fast," Janelle said. "Craig is prime beef, Quinn. I'm sure lots of girls are dying for a taste."

"Interesting metaphor," Quincy replied dryly.

"All I'm saying is you don't want to wait so long that he loses interest."

Quincy looked to Craig, who had scrambled atop the rock and was studying the horizon. He was interested in more than just sex. Quincy was certain of that. They had been friends first—meeting on their official first day of college and spending all of freshman year engaged in a slow, budding flirtation. The dating part didn't happen until late August, when both returned to campus realizing how much they had missed each other over the summer. And if Quincy had started to sense some impatience about sex on Craig's part, she chalked it up to desire and not the kind of pent-up frustration Janelle was implying.

Now perched on the rock, Craig caught Quincy looking. She raised her camera and said, "Smile."

He did more than smile. He stood with his fists on his hips and his chest puffed out like Superman's. Quincy laughed. The camera's shutter clicked.

"How's the view?" she asked.

"Pretty swell."

Craig reached down and helped her climb onto the rock beside him. They were higher than Quincy expected, able to see how the rest of the forest sloped sharply downward for another mile before ending in a shadow-filled valley. The others joined them, with Janelle ordering another picture.

"Group shot," she said. "Everyone in. Even you, Quincy."

The six of them squeezed together and Quincy stretched out her arm until everyone had edged into the frame. Once the picture was taken, Quincy studied its frenzied composition. That's when she noticed something behind them in the far distance. A mammoth building, it sat in the middle of the valley, its gray walls barely visible among the trees.

"What's that?" Quincy asked, pointing it out.

Janelle shrugged. "Beats me."

Betz the wise owl knew. Of course.

"It's an insane asylum," she said.

"Jesus," Amy replied. "Are you purposely trying to freak us out?"

"I'm just telling you. It's a hospital for crazy people."

Quincy stared at the asylum. A low-lying breeze in the valley rustled the trees around it, giving the place a shifting, restless air. Almost as if the building itself were alive. There was a definite sadness to the asylum. Quincy felt it emanating from the valley all the way up to their lookout atop the rock. She imagined a storm cloud permanently hovering over the place, unseen but keenly felt.

She was about to take a picture of it but stopped herself. Something about keeping its image in her camera disturbed her.

Standing next to Quincy, Craig studied the sky. The sun had slipped below the tree line and become a fiery glow that warmed the woods. Trees sliced the brightness, their long shadows gridlike across the forest floor.

"We need to head back," he said. "We don't want to be out here when it gets dark."

"Because, you know, Indian ghosts," Janelle added.

Quincy joined in. "And crazy people."

Their departure was delayed by Rodney, who insisted on finishing his defacement of the rock. He added Amy's name beneath his own, connecting them with a plus sign and surrounding it all with a hastily scratched heart. Then they were off, heading back the way they had come. It took them no time at all to reach the flat expanse that led to the cabin, the incline having made their journey feel longer than it actually was. All told, the distance between the flat rock and Pine Cottage was less than half of a mile.

Still, the sun had fully set by the time they emerged from the woods, giving the cabin a pinkish, autumnal glow. Shadows crept from the tree line and brushed its fieldstone foundation. Craig, still in front, stopped suddenly. When Quincy bumped into him, he shoved her backward.

"What the—"

"Shush," he hissed, squinting at the half shadows gathering on the back deck.

At last, Quincy saw what he had. The others did too. Someone was on the deck. A stranger with hands cupped to the window in the back door, peering inside.

"Hey!" Craig called, stepping forward with his walking stick wielded like a weapon.

The stranger at the door—a man, Quincy now saw—spun around, startled.

He looked to be about their age. Maybe a couple of years older. It was hard to tell because of his glasses, which reflected the dying light, obscuring his eyes. He was thin, almost gangly, with his long arms pressed stiffly against the sides of his beige cable-knit sweater. A dime-size hole sat at the shoulder, the white T-shirt beneath it peeking through. His pants were green corduroy, scuffed at the knees and so loose around the waist that he had to crook an index finger through a belt loop to keep them from sagging.

"I'm sorry if I frightened you." Hesitation streaked each word, as if he didn't quite know how to talk. He spoke English the way a foreigner did, halting and formal. Quincy listened for a trace of an accent, not finding one. "I was looking to see if someone was here."

"That would be us," Craig said, taking another step forward, his bravery impressing Quincy, which just might have been his plan.

"Hello," the stranger said, waving with the hand not hooked to his waist.

"Are you lost?" Janelle said, more curious than afraid.

"Sort of. My car broke down a few miles away. I've been walking all afternoon. Then I finally saw the driveway to this place and hoped someone here would be able to help me."

Janelle broke away from the rest of them, emerging from the woods and crossing to the deck in three assured strides. The stranger flinched. For a moment, Quincy thought he was going to bolt, springing like a startled deer into the woods. But he stayed, keeping completely still as Janelle studied his shock of dark hair, his slightly crooked nose, the faintly sexy curve of his lips.

"All afternoon, huh?" she said.

"Most of it."

"You must be tired."

"A little."

"You should come in and party with us." Janelle shook his free hand as the index finger of his other one twisted around his belt loop. "I'm Janelle. These are my friends. It's my birthday."

"Happy birthday."

"What's your name?"

"I'm Joe." The stranger gave her a nod, followed by a cautious smile. "Joe Hannen."

11.

It's past ten when I wake up. Jeff's side of the bed has long been empty, the sheets there cool under my palm. In the hallway, I pause by the guest room. Although the door is open, I know Sam is still around. Her knapsack remains in the corner and the Wild Turkey still sits on the nightstand, only an inch of amber liquid remaining.

Noise bursts from the kitchen—drawers closing, pans banging. I find Sam there, a white apron tossed over a Sex Pistols T-shirt and a pair of black jeans.

My head hurts, less the product of Wild Turkey than the surreal circumstances in which it was consumed. Although the events of last night are hazy, I have no trouble recalling Sam's repeated attempts to get me to say His name. I'm annoyed at both her and the memory.

Sam knows this. I can tell from the apologetic way she smiles when she sees me. From the mug filled with coffee she all but shoves into my hands. From the blueberry-scented warmth that drifts from the oven.

"You're baking?"

Sam nods. "Lemon-blueberry muffins. I found the recipe on your blog."

"Should I be impressed?"

"Probably not," Sam says. "Although I was hoping you'd be."

Secretly, I am. No one has baked anything for me since my father died. Not even Jeff. Yet here's Sam, eyeing the oven timer as it counts down to zero. I'm reluctantly touched.

She removes the muffins from the oven, not giving them nearly enough time to cool before flipping the pan. Muffins drop onto the counter in a spray of crumbs and blueberry sludge.

"How'd I do, Coach?" Sam asks, giving me a hopeful look.

I take a judgmental nibble. They're slightly dry, which tells me she skimped on the butter. There's also a severe lack of sugar, which suppresses the fruit. Rather than either lemon or blueberry, the muffin is the flavor of paste. I take a sip of coffee. It's too strong. The bitter taste on my tongue bleeds into my words.

"We need to talk about last night—"

"I was a bitch," Sam says. "You're being all nice and I—"

"I don't talk about Pine Cottage, Sam. It's off limits, okay? I'm focused on the future. You should be too."

"Got it," Sam says. "And I'd like to make it up to you somehow. If you let me stay longer, of course."

She takes a deep breath, waiting for me to give her an answer. It might be an act. Part of me thinks she's certain I'll tell her she can stay. Just like she was certain I wouldn't let her trudge away with her knapsack last night. Only, I'm not certain about anything.

"It'll only be for another day or two," she says after I say nothing.

I take another sip of coffee, more for the caffeine than the taste. "Why are you really here?"

"Isn't wanting to meet you enough?"

"It should be," I say. "But it's not your only reason. All these questions. All this prodding."

Sam picks up a lumpy muffin, puts it down, checks her fingernails for crumbs. "You really want to know?"

"If you're going to continue to stay here, I need to know."

"Right. Truth-telling time. No bullshit." Sam takes a deep breath, sucking in air like a kid about to slip underwater. "I came because I wanted to see if you're as angry as I am."

"Angry about what Lisa did?"

"No," Sam says. "Angry about being a Final Girl."

"I'm not."

"Angry, or a Final Girl?"

"Both," I say.

"Maybe you should be."

"I've moved past it."

"That's not what you told Jeff last night."

So she *had* heard the two of us arguing in our bedroom. Maybe some of it. Probably all of it. Definitely enough to send her fleeing into the night.

"I know you're not past it," she says. "Just like I'm not. And we'll never get past it unless we pull a Lisa Milner. We got stuck with a raw deal, babe. Life swallowed us whole and shit us out and everyone else just wants us to get over it and act like it didn't happen."

"At least we survived."

Sam lifts her wrist, flashing the tattoo there. "Sure. And your life has been perfect ever since, right?"

"I'm fine," I say, cringing because I sound just like my mother. She uses the word like a dagger, fending off all emotion. *I'm fine*, she told everyone at my father's funeral. *Quincy and I are both fine*. As if our lives hadn't been completely shattered in the span of a year.

"Obviously," Sam says.

"What's that supposed to mean?"

She digs into the front pocket of her jeans, pulling out an iPhone that she slaps on the counter in front of me. The motion startles its screen to life, revealing the unmistakable image of a man's penis.

"I'm going to go out on a limb here and assume that's not Jeff," Sam says. "Just like this isn't your phone."

I look to the other side of the kitchen, the coffee and muffin suddenly sour in my stomach. The locked drawer—*my* drawer—is open. Dark scratches form a starburst pattern around the keyhole.

"You picked the lock?"

Sam lifts her chin in a pleased-with-herself nod. "One of my few skills."

I rush to the open drawer, making sure my secret stash is still there. I grab the silver compact and check my reflection in its mirror. I'm startled by how tired I look.

"I told you to leave it alone," I say, more embarrassed than angry.

"Relax. I'm not going to tell anyone," Sam says. "Honestly, it's a relief knowing there's something dark underneath all that happy-homemaker bullshit."

Shame heats my cheeks. I turn away and lean against the counter, my palms flat against it, sliding through muffin crumbs. "It's not what you think."

"I'm not judging you. You think I haven't stolen anything? You name it, I've probably taken it. Food. Clothes. Cigarettes. When you're as poor as I've been, you get over the guilt real fast." Sam dips a hand into the drawer, pulling out a stolen tube of lipstick. She gives it a twist and, mouth forming a perfect circle, swipes the cherry-red tip over her lips. "What do you think? Is this a good color on me?"

"That has nothing to do with what happened at Pine Cottage," I say.

"Right," Sam replies, lips smacking. "You're completely normal."

"Fuck you."

She smiles. A cherry-lipped grin that flashes like neon.

"Now, that's what I'm talking about! Show some emotion, Quinn. *That's* why I wanted you to say his name. *That's* why I broke into your secret goodie drawer. I want to see you get angry. You've earned that rage. Don't try to hide it behind your website with your cakes and muffins and breads. You're messed up. So am I. It's okay to admit it. We're damaged goods, babe."

I peer into the drawer again, looking at each item as if for the first time, and realize Sam is right. Only a seriously damaged woman would steal spoons and iPhones and silver-plated compacts. Humiliation grips my body, squeezing ever so slightly. I push past Sam and move woodenly to the cupboard where my Xanax is stored. I shake a pill into my palm.

"Do you have enough to share with the whole class?"

I stare at her dumbly, my mind elsewhere, neurons focused solely on getting that light-blue pill into my body.

"The Xanax," Sam says. "Give me one."

She plucks the pill from my hand. Instead of swallowing it, she crunches it between her teeth like a Flintstones vitamin. I take mine the usual way—chased down with grape soda.

"Interesting method," Sam says as she runs her tongue along her teeth, catching stray granules.

I take another gulp of soda. "A spoonful of sugar. The song doesn't lie."

"Whatever gets the job done, I guess." Sam holds out her hand. "Give me another."

I tap a second pill into her palm. It stays there, cradled like a tiny robin's egg, as she gives me a curious look.

"You're not having seconds?"

It's not a question.

It's a dare.

All of a sudden, I feel like we're replaying yesterday afternoon. Back in the kitchen, Sam watching, me inexplicably wanting to impress her.

"Sure," I say.

I take another Xanax, followed by more grape soda. Instead of chewing hers, Sam gestures for the soda bottle. She takes two hearty swallows, finishing up with a quick belch.

"You're right. That does make it go down easier." Again, she holds out her hand. "Third time's the charm."

This time, we take the pills simultaneously, passing the soda quickly between us. All that Xanax has left a bitter spot on my tongue, which is made even more obvious by the sticky fuzz of grape soda spreading over my teeth. I laugh at the ridiculousness of the situation. We're just two massacre survivors downing Xanax. Lisa would not have approved.

"Are we cool?" Sam says.

Soft morning light slants from the kitchen window onto her face. Although she's made sure to put on makeup, the sunlight exposes tiny webs of wrinkles starting to form around her eyes and the corners of her mouth. They draw my gaze the same way I'm drawn to a Van Gogh, always looking for the glimpses of canvas hidden between the dollops of paint. That's the real Sam I'm looking for. The woman behind the tough-girl mask.

The glimpse I get now is darkly alluring. I see someone who's still trying to comprehend what's become of her life. I see someone who's lonely and sad and uncertain about everything.

I see myself, and the recognition makes my body hum with relief that there's someone out there just like me.

"Yes," I say. "We're cool."

The Xanax kicks in fifteen minutes later while I'm in the shower. My body softens in increments, feeling as if the shower's steam is seeping into my pores, swirling inside of me, filling me up. I get dressed as if on a cloud—floating and lightweight, drifting down the hall, where Sam waits by the door, also floating, her eyes smiling.

"Let's go." Her voice is muffled, soft. A long-distance call.

"Where?" I ask, sounding like someone else. Someone happier and carefree. Someone who's never heard the name Pine Cottage.

"Let's go," Sam says again.

So I go, grabbing my purse before following her into the hallway, the elevator, the lobby, the street, where sunlight shimmers down on us, golden and warm and radiant. Sam is radiant too, with sun-orange highlights in her hair and face glowing pink. I try to pause at each door we pass, checking my reflection in the glass to see if I'm radiant too, but Sam pulls me away, into a cab that I never noticed her hail.

We float on. Into the steaming thickness of the city, then into Central Park, where a fall breeze trickles in through the cab window, cracked an inch or two. I close my eyes, feeling the air's caress until the cab stops and Sam is tugging at me again, me barely feeling it.

"We're here," she says.

Here is Fifth Avenue. *Here* is the concrete fortress of Saks. *Here* is us floating across the sidewalk, through the doors, into the gleaming pattern of perfume counters, passing scents so strong I can almost see them stretching in hues of pink and lavender. I trail Sam through the rainbowed air and up an escalator. Or maybe we're not going up at all. Maybe it's just me. Floating into the women's department, where another rainbow appears, made real in rows of cotton, silk, and satin.

Other women mill about. Bored salesgirls and haughty matrons and listless teenagers who should be in school but instead are here, sighing into their cell phones. They give us judging looks, if they bother to look at us at all.

Jealousy.

They know we're special.

"Hi," I say to one of them, giggling.

"Love that skirt," Sam says to another.

She leads me to a rack of blouses. White ones spattered with blooms of color. Grabbing one off the rack, she holds it up and says, "What do you think?"

"That would look *amazing* on you," I say.

"Really?"

"Yes, you have to try it on."

Sam grabs a blouse. "Give me your purse," she says.

My purse. I forgot I had brought it with me. Then a line of clarity cuts through the haze, its appearance so sudden that I grow dizzy.

"You're not going to steal it," I say.

Sam's expression is blank. The golden glow on her skin fades to gray. "It's not stealing if you've earned it. And after what we went through, babe, I'd say we earned this big-time. Purse, please."

With arms so numb I can barely feel them, I pass the purse to Sam. She tucks it under her arm and disappears into a dressing room.

While she's gone, a glint of gold catches my eye and lures me across the sales floor. It's a small display of accessories—thin belts and chunky bracelets and loops of beaded necklaces. But what holds my attention is a pair of earrings. The two dangling ovals remind me of twin mirrors, drawing the light until they glow.

Radiant.

Like me.

Like Sam.

I finger one of them, the light glinting. My reflection leaps off its surface, face oblong and pale.

"You want them, right?" It's Sam, out of the dressing room and suddenly behind me, whispering in my ear. "Go on. You know what to do."

She pushes the purse back into my arms. Without even looking, I know the blouse is in there. It radiates a heat that makes the whole purse pulse. I unzip it just a crack. Inside is a slip of white silk, a splash of color.

"It's not hurting anyone," Sam says. "You're the one who got hurt, Quinn. You and me and Lisa."

She drifts to a nearby rack of sweaters. She grabs two handfuls and drops them onto the floor, plastic hangers clattering. The noise draws a salesgirl, who zips to Sam's side.

"I'm so clumsy," Sam says.

That's my cue. As Sam and the salesgirl collect the downed sweaters, I snatch the earrings from their display and drop them into my purse. Then I speed-walk from the scene of my crime. I'm halfway out of the women's department when Sam catches up to me. She grabs my wrist, yanking me to a slow walk while whispering, "Easy, babe. No need to look suspicious."

But we *are* suspicious. And I'm certain all those bored salesgirls and haughty matrons and listless teenagers who should be in school know what we've done. I expect them to stare as we pass, but none of them do. We're so radiant we've become invisible.

Only one man notices us. A twentysomething in distressed jeans, Brooks Brothers polo, and shiny black sneakers with red stripes down the sides. He spies us over one of the fragrance counters, pausing midspritz to watch us float to the door. I watch him too, noticing something click just behind his eyes. It worries me.

"We've been spotted," I tell Sam. "Security."

My heart starts doing jumping jacks in my chest, thumping faster and faster. I'm scared and excited and breathless and exhausted. I want to run but Sam keeps gripping my arm, even as the man drops his cologne, picks up a newspaper sitting on the counter, and starts to follow.

He calls out to us. "Excuse me."

Sam curses under her breath. My heart beats even faster.

"Excuse me," the man says again, putting a more urgent spin on it, getting the attention of others, who look up, look at him, look at us. We're visible again.

Sam increases her pace, making me do the same. We reach the door and start to push through it, but the man is behind us, moving fast, reaching out to tap me on the shoulder.

Out on the street, Sam prepares to run. Her body tenses next to mine, readying for the sprint. I tense up too, mostly because the man is right at my back now. His hand drops onto my shoulder, making me spin around and hold the purse out to him, as if in offering.

The man looks not at the purse but at the two of us, a stupid grin on his face. "I *knew* it was you."

"We don't know you, man," Sam says.

"I know you," he says. "Quincy Carpenter and Samantha Boyd, right? The Final Girls."

The man fishes in the pocket of his jeans, pulling out a pen tangled in a ring of keys. He yanks it loose and hands it to me.

"It'd be awesome if I could get your autographs."

He then offers the newspaper. It's a tabloid, the cover stretched tight and facing us. When I look at it, I see my own face staring back at me.

"See?" the man says, proud of himself.

I teeter backward, dropping to Earth, the sidewalk under my feet suddenly hard and jarring. A second look at the newspaper confirms what I already know.

Somehow, Sam and I have become front-page news.

12.

Our picture takes up most of the front page, filling it all the way to the masthead. The image shows Sam and me during our first meeting, standing outside my building, sizing each other up. It captures me at my very worst—with my weight shifted to my right leg, hip jutting, arms crossed in suspicion. Sam's positioned slightly away from the camera, with just a slice of her pale profile visible. Her knapsack is still settling at my feet and her mouth yawns open as she speaks. I recall that moment with cutting exactitude. It was right before Sam started to say, *You don't need to be such a bitch.*

The headline sits below the photo in large, red letters: SOUL SUR-VIVORS.

Beneath it is a photo of Lisa Milner, similar to the one on her book cover. Next to it is a headline smaller in size but no less alarming: FINAL GIRLS MEET AFTER SUICIDE OF KILL-SPREE VICTIM LISA MILNER.

I look to the masthead again. It's the same tabloid that reporter idling outside my building yesterday said he worked for. His name lurches into my head. Jonah Thompson. That devious prick. He must have still been there, spying on us while scrunched in the front seat of a parked car, camera poised on the dashboard.

I snatch the newspaper from the autograph hound and start to walk away.

"Hey!" he says.

I keep walking, tripping down Fifth Avenue. Even though my legs are wobbly from Xanax, my muscles yearn for another. And then another.

As many as it takes to plunge me into oblivion for a few days. Which still wouldn't be enough to snuff out my anger.

I flip through the newspaper as I walk. Inside it is a bigger photograph of Lisa and a series of shots detailing the first conversation between Sam and me, all taken from the same angle. I look gradually less angry in those pictures, my stance and expression softening. As for the actual article, I can barely make it through the first two paragraphs.

"What does it say?" Sam asks as she hurries to keep up.

"That we're both in the city, united by Lisa's sudden suicide."

"Well, it's kind of the truth."

"And it's no one's goddamn business but ours. Which is exactly what I'm going to say to Jonah Thompson."

I toss through the newspaper until I find the address of its newsroom. West Forty-Seventh Street. Two blocks south and one block west. I surge forward, fueled only by rage. I go two steps before realizing that Sam hasn't moved. She stands on the corner, nibbling at her cuticles while watching my retreat.

"Let's go," I say.

Sam shakes her head.

"Why not?"

"Because it's not a good idea."

"Says the woman who just encouraged me to shoplift." This turns the heads of several people passing by. I don't care. "I'm still going."

"Whatever cranks your chain, babe."

"You're really not pissed off about this?"

"Sure, I'm pissed."

"Then we should do something about it."

"It won't make any difference," Sam says. "We'll still be on the front page."

More heads turn. I scowl at those who meet my gaze. Then I scowl at Sam, frustrated by her lack of anger. I want the Sam from an hour ago, urging me to embrace my rage, but she's been replaced by someone made mellow by the same Xanax that itches within me.

"I'm still going," I say.

"Don't," Sam says.

I start walking again, anger pushing me forward. I call to Sam over my shoulder, my words stretching into a taunt. "I'm *go-ing*."

"Quinn, wait."

But it's too late for that. I've reached the other end of the block and am crossing the street against the light. I think I hear Sam still calling after me, her voice blending into the din of the city. I keep going, newspaper in my fist, refusing to stop until I'm face-to-face with Jonah Thompson.

There's no getting past the security desk. It sits just inside the lobby, mere feet from the busy bank of elevators. I could make a run for the constantly opening and closing doors, but the guard on duty is a full foot taller than I. He'd be able to cross that lobby in a flash, blocking my path.

So I march right up to him, rolled newspaper in hand, and announce, "I'm here to see Jonah Thompson."

"Name?"

"Quincy Carpenter."

"Is he expecting you?"

"No," I say. "But I know he'll want to see me."

The guard checks a directory, makes a call, and tells me to wait by the mural positioned opposite the elevators. It's a massive Art Deco thing. A Manhattan skyline, painted in muted tones. I'm still looking at it when a voice sounds at my back.

"Quincy," Jonah Thompson says. "You change your mind about talking?"

I whirl around, the sight of him boiling my blood. He's wearing a checked shirt and skinny tie, trendy and smug. A bulging file folder is tucked under one arm. Probably dirt on his next victim.

"I'm here to get an apology, you son of a bitch."

"You've seen the paper."

"And now the whole goddamn city can see where I live," I say, waving said paper in his face.

He blinks behind his thick-framed glasses, more amused than

alarmed. "Neither the article nor the photo captions mention where you live. I made sure of that. I didn't even name the street."

"No, but you showed us. You identified who we are. Now the whole world can Google our names and see what Samantha Boyd and I look like. Which means any psycho can show up and stalk us."

This he hasn't thought of. The slight whitening of his face makes that abundantly clear.

"I didn't mean to—"

"Of course you didn't. You were just thinking about how many papers you'd sell. What kind of raise you'd get. How much the inevitable offer from *TMZ* would be."

"That's not the reason—"

"I could sue you," I say, interrupting again. "Sam and I both could. So you better pray that nothing happens to us."

Jonah gives a hard swallow. "So you came here to tell me you're going to sue the paper?"

"I'm here to warn you that there'll be hell to pay if I ever see another article about me or Samantha Boyd. What happened to us was years ago. Let it rest."

"There's something you need to know about that article," Jonah says.

"You can shove that article up your ass."

I move to leave but he grabs my arm, tugging me backward.

"Don't touch me!"

Jonah's stronger than he looks, his grip alarmingly tight. I try to get free, arm twisting, elbow aching.

"Just listen to me," he says. "It's about Samantha Boyd. She's lying to you."

"Let me go!"

I give him a shove. Harder than I intend. Hard enough to get the attention of the guard, who barks, "Miss, you need to leave."

As if I don't know that. As if I'm not aware that the longer I stay in Jonah's presence, the angrier I get. So angry that when Jonah moves toward me again, I give him another shove, this time intentionally harder than the first.

He rocks backward and the folder drops from his arm. It flaps open on the way down, spitting out its contents. Dozens of newspaper clippings fan out across the floor, their headlines shouting variations of the same story.

Pine Cottage. Massacre. Survivor. Killer.

Low-quality photos accompany most of the articles. To someone else, they'd mean nothing. Copies of copies, all pixels and smudges and Rorschach blots. Only I can see them for what they really are. Exterior shots of Pine Cottage, taken both before and after the murders. Yearbook photos of Janelle, Craig, the others. A picture of me. The same one that graced the cover of *People* against my wishes.

He's there too. His image is in a separate box right next to mine. I haven't seen that face in ten years. Not since that night. I shut my eyes, but it's too late. That single glimpse breaks something loose inside me, not far from where His knife went in. A croak belches from my throat, followed by a sick rattling as that broken chunk of myself pushes upward, black and bilious and thick.

"I'm going to throw up," I warn.

And so I do, spewing onto the floor until every single article there is covered.

PINE COTTAGE
6:18 P.M.

Quincy and Janelle stood in the cabin's kitchen area, separated from the great room by a waist-high counter. It was Janelle's suggestion that each of them prepare some aspect of dinner. A surprise, seeing as how the most elaborate thing Quincy had ever seen her cook was ramen noodles.

"Maybe we should just roast hot dogs," Quincy had said when they were planning the weekend. "We're camping, after all."

"Hot dogs?" Janelle replied, affronted. "Not on my birthday."

So there they were, colliding with Amy and Betz, who had been tasked with the main course of roast chicken and several side dishes. Quincy was on cake duty, and she had lugged along an entire bag of baking tools to use for the occasion. A cake pan. All the necessary ingredients. An icing bag with detachable tips. Yes, Janelle's mother and stepfather had paid for the cabin rental, but Quincy was determined to earn her keep in cake.

Janelle had an easy job—bartender. While Betz and Amy fussed with the chicken and Quincy decorated the cake, she set out several bottles of liquor. The large, cheap kind that came in plastic jugs and was meant to be poured into red Solo cups, of which Janelle had brought plenty.

"How long are you going to let Joe stay?" Quincy whispered to her.

"As long as he likes," Janelle whispered back.

"Like, all night? Seriously?"

"Sure," Janelle said. "It's getting late and there's plenty of room. It could be fun."

Quincy disagreed. So did everyone else, in their own muted way.

Even Joe, with his odd cadences and filthy glasses that clouded his eyes, seemed unenthused by the idea.

"Has it occurred to you that Joe might want to go home?" Quincy said. "Isn't that right, Joe?"

Their unexpected guest sat on the threadbare couch in the great room, watching Craig and Rodney kneel in front of the cavernous fireplace and bicker over the best way to start a fire. Realizing he was being addressed, he looked Quincy's way, startled.

"I don't want to be a bother," he said.

"It's no bother," Janelle assured him. "Unless you have somewhere you need to be."

"I don't."

"And you're hungry, right?"

Joe shrugged. "I guess."

"We've got plenty of food and drink. Plus we have a couch, not to mention an extra bed."

"We also have a car," Quincy said. "Full of cell phones. Craig could call a tow truck or drive him anywhere he needs to go. You know, like back to his own car. Or his house."

"Which will take hours. Besides, maybe Joe wants to join the party." Janelle looked his way, hoping he'd second that thought. "Now that we're all friends."

"Technically, he's still a stranger," Quincy said.

Janelle flashed the exasperated look she always got when she thought Quincy was being a goody-goody. Quincy had seen that same expression before her only sip of beer and her single hit of a joint. In both instances, Janelle had used sheer force of will to coax her into doing something she didn't want to do. Now, though, her frustration was amplified by the situation. Everything about the weekend—the cabin, her birthday, the absence of oversight of any kind—made her slightly manic.

"We're here to have fun, right?" she said. There was something accusing about the way she said it, as if she suspected she was the only one there intent on a good time. "So let's. Have. Fun."

That seemed to settle it. Joe would be staying as long as he liked. The birthday girl again got her wish.

"What's your poison?" Janelle asked Joe once the makeshift bar was complete.

He blinked at the bottles, alternately confused and dazzled by the choices. "I-I don't really drink."

"Seriously?" Janelle said. "Like, not at all?"

"Yes." He frowned. "I mean no."

"Well, which is it?"

"Maybe he doesn't want to drink," Quincy said, again the voice of reason, the angel perpetually perched on Janelle's shoulder. "Maybe, like me, Joe prefers to maintain control over his mental faculties."

"You don't drink because you're a wuss and Mommy and Daddy would get mad if they ever found out," Janelle told her. "Joe's not like that. Isn't that right?"

"It's just—I've never tried it," Joe said.

"Not even with your friends?"

Joe stammered, trying to push out a response. But it was too late. Janelle pounced.

"What? No friends either?"

"I have friends," Joe said, a prickle in his voice.

"A girlfriend?" Janelle asked, teasing.

"Maybe. I-I don't know what she is."

Behind Quincy, Betz whispered, "Imaginary is my guess."

Janelle glared at her before turning back to Joe, saying, "Then you'll have quite a story to tell the next time you see her."

She began to pour, splashing liquor from several bottles into a cup and filling it the rest of the way with orange juice. She took the cup to Joe, forcing his fingers around the red plastic.

"Drink up."

Joe tipped his face toward the cup instead of the other way around, his nose dipping birdlike beneath the rim. A cough rose from inside the cup. His first sip. When he came up for air, his eyes were wide and goofy.

"It's okay," he said.

"Okay? You totally love it," Janelle replied.

Joe smacked his lips. "It's too sweet."

"I can fix that." Janelle grabbed the cup from his hands as quickly as she had put it into them. Then she was back at the bar, snatching a lemon and searching her work area.

"Does anyone have a knife?"

She spotted one on the counter, a carving knife intended for the chicken Amy and Betz were preparing. Grabbing it, Janelle pushed it into the lemon, slicing through peel, pulp, and, ultimately, her finger.

"Dammit!"

At first, Quincy thought she was being dramatic for Joe's sake. Giving him what the rest of them had dubbed "The Janelle Show" behind her back. But then she saw the blood pumping from Janelle's finger, spilling over the paper napkin pressed against it, littering the counter in drops the size of rose petals.

"Ow," Janelle whimpered, tears forming. "Ouch, owie, ow."

Quincy swooped in behind her, cooing, performing her roommate-appointed duty to soothe. "It'll be okay. Lift your hand. Put pressure on it."

She flailed around the kitchen, searching for a first-aid kit while Janelle hopped from foot to foot, wincing at the sight of all that blood. "Hurry," she urged.

Quincy found a tin of Band-Aids beneath the sink. The old-fashioned kind with a hinged, flip-top lid. So old she couldn't remember the last time she had a similar pack in her own house. She grabbed the biggest Band-Aid she could find and wrapped it around Janelle's finger, begging her to hold still.

"All done," Quincy said, backing away, hands raised. "You're good as new."

The drama lured Joe off the couch. He hovered nearby, watching Janelle examine her bandaged finger. He lowered his gaze to the knife on the counter and its blood-splotched blade.

"That looks sharp," he said, picking up the knife and touching the pad of his index finger against its tip. "You need to be more careful."

He stared at Janelle and Quincy, as if seeking assurances that they would be. Beads of liquid clung to his bottom lip—remnants of his first cocktail. He wiped them away with the back of his hand and, knife still in his grip, licked his lips.

13.

Jeff retrieves me a half hour later, summoned by Jonah Thompson, who found his number on my cell phone, which I handed to him when he asked me the name of an emergency contact person shortly after I puked all over his shoes. I'm in the lobby ladies' room when he arrives, hunched over a toilet even though my stomach feels as squeezed dry as an empty water bottle. It's up to one of Jonah's coworkers to fetch me from the stall. A tiny bird of a reporter named Emily, who nervously calls to me from just inside the door like I'm someone contagious, someone to be feared.

Back at the apartment, Jeff puts me to bed in spite of protests that I'm feeling much better. Apparently, I'm not, for I'm asleep as soon as my head hits the pillow. I sleep fitfully for the rest of the afternoon, only vaguely aware of either Jeff or Sam popping into the bedroom to check on me. By evening, I'm wide-awake and famished. Jeff brings in a tray of food fit for an invalid—chicken noodle soup, toast, and ginger ale.

"It's not the flu, you know," I tell him.

"You don't know that for sure," Jeff says. "It sounds like you were pretty sick."

From a combination of lack of sleep and Wild Turkey and so many Xanax. And Him, of course. Seeing that picture of Him.

"It must have been something I ate," I say. "I'm much better now. Honest. I'm fine."

"Then I'm sure you'll be happy to know that your mother called."

I groan.

"She said the neighbors are asking why you're on the front page of the newspapers," Jeff continues.

"*One* newspaper," I say.

"She wants to know what to tell them."

"Of course she does."

Jeff snags a triangle of toast, takes a bite, puts it back on my tray. While chewing, he says, "It wouldn't hurt to call her back."

"And have her berate me for not being perfect?" I say. "I think I'll pass."

"She's concerned about you, hon. It's been an eventful few days. Lisa's suicide. Being in that newspaper. Sam and I are worried about how you're dealing with it all."

"Does this mean the two of you actually had a conversation?"

"We did," Jeff says.

"And it was civil?"

"Abundantly."

"Color me surprised. What did the two of you talk about?"

Jeff reaches again for the toast but I swat his hand away. He instead kicks off his shoes and pulls his legs onto the bed. On his side now, he scoots close, his body pressing against the entire length of my own.

"You. And how it might be a good idea to have Sam stick around for a week."

"Wow. Who are you and what have you done with the real Jefferson Richards?"

"I'm serious," Jeff says. "I spent all day thinking about what you said last night. And you're right. The way I got those charges against Sam dropped was wrong. She deserved a better defense. And I'm sorry."

I hand Jeff more toast. "Apology accepted."

"Plus," he says between bites, "this cop-killing case is going to start taking up more of my time, and I don't like the idea of you being home alone most of the day. Not after your picture's been plastered all over the city."

"So you're suggesting that Sam becomes my babysitter?"

"Companion," Jeff says. "And she's actually the one who suggested it. She mentioned the two of you did some baking together yesterday. It might be nice to have some help during Baking Season. You always said you wanted an assistant."

"Are you sure about this?" I ask. "It's a lot for you to handle."

Jeff tilts his head at me. "You sound like *you're* not sure."

"I think it's a great idea. I just don't want it to affect you. Or us."

"Listen, I'm going to be honest here and admit that Sam and I will probably never be friends. But the two of you have a connection. Or you could. I know we don't talk much about what happened to you—"

"Because there's no need to," I hastily add.

"I agree," Jeff says. "You say you'll never get past what happened, but you already have. You're not that girl anymore. You're Quincy Carpenter, baking goddess."

"Whatever," I say, although the description secretly pleases me.

"But maybe you *do* need some kind of support system to cope. Someone other than Coop. If Sam's that person you need, I don't want to stand in the way of it."

I realize, not for the first time, how lucky I am to have landed someone like Jeff. I can't help but think he's the one big difference between Sam and me. Without him, I'd be just like her—wild and angry and lonesome. A tempest never reaching shore, forever tossing about.

"You're awesome," I say, pushing the tray aside to throw myself on top of him.

I kiss him. He kisses back, pulling me tighter against him.

The stress of the day suddenly melts into desire and I find myself undressing him without even thinking about it. Loosening the tie still knotted around his neck. Popping open the buttons of his Oxford shirt. Kissing the rosy nipples surrounded by a thicket of hair before moving lower and feeling his arousal.

My phone buzzes on the nightstand. I try to ignore it, thinking it's a reporter. Or, worse, my mother. Yet the phone continues to rattle against the bedside lamp, insistent. I check the caller ID.

"It's Coop," I say.

Jeff sighs, his desire deflating. "Can't it wait?"

It can't. Coop had called me yesterday evening, responding to my pretending-not-to-be-worried text. At the time, I was too busy to answer, what with Sam hovering around me in the kitchen while I made dinner. If I don't pick up now, he'll definitely be concerned.

"Not while my picture is still on the front page," I tell Jeff.

Vibrating phone in hand, I spring out of bed and hurry into the master bathroom, closing the door behind me.

"Why didn't you tell me Samantha Boyd contacted you?" Coop says by way of greeting.

"How did you find out?"

"I got a Google alert," he says, the answer so unexpected he could have told me "aliens" and I wouldn't have been more surprised. "Although I would have preferred to hear it from you."

"I was going to call you," I say, which is the truth. I had planned to call him right after I got done confronting Jonah. "Sam showed up at my place yesterday. After Lisa's death, she thought it would be a good idea if we met."

I could have told Coop more than that, of course. How Sam had changed her name years ago. How she dared me into downing two Xanax too many. How I threw all three back up the moment I saw His picture.

"Is she still there?" Coop asks.

"Yes. She's going to be staying with us."

"How long?"

"I don't know. Until she figures out some stuff."

"Do you really think that's a good idea?"

"Why? You worried about me?"

"I always worry about you, Quincy."

I pause, unsure how to respond. Coop's never been this forthright before. I don't know if it's a good change or a bad one. Either way, it's nice to hear him admit out loud that he cares. It's definitely more heartwarming than a nod.

"Admit it," I finally say. "When you saw that Google alert, you almost drove out here to check on me."

"I got as far as the end of the driveway before stopping myself," Coop replies.

I don't doubt him. It's that kind of devotion that's made me feel safe all these years.

"What changed your mind?"

"Knowing that you can take care of yourself."

"So I've been told."

"But I'm still concerned that Samantha Boyd has come out of hiding," Coop says. "You have to admit, it's startling."

"You're starting to sound like Jeff."

"What's she like? Is she—"

The first words I think of are the same ones Sam used this morning. *Damaged goods.* Instead, I say, "Normal? Considering what happened to her, she's as normal as anyone can be."

"But not as normal as you."

I detect a smile in his voice. I imagine his blue eyes sparkling, which happens on the rare occasions he actually lets down his guard.

"Of course not," I say. "I'm the queen of normalcy."

"Well, Queen Quincy, what do you think about me coming into the city to meet Samantha? I'd like to get a read on her."

"Why?"

"Because I don't trust her." Coop softens his tone slightly, as if he knows he's starting to sound too intense. "Not until I meet her myself. I want to make sure she's not up to something."

"She's not," I say. "Jeff's already grilled her."

"Well, I haven't."

"I'd hate to put you out like that."

"You wouldn't be," Coop says. "I have the day off and the weather is nice. The leaves are starting to turn in the Poconos. Makes for a pretty drive."

"Then sure," I say. "How does noon sound?"

"Perfect." Even though we're on the phone, I know Coop is nodding. I can sense it. "The usual place."

"It's a date," I say.

Coop grows serious again, his voice husky and low. "Just please be careful until then. I know you think I'm being overly concerned, but I'm not. She's a stranger, Quincy. One who experienced a whole lot of bad stuff. We don't know if it messed her up. We don't know what she's capable of."

I sit on the edge of the bathtub, knees pressed together, suddenly cold. Jonah Thompson's voice flashes into my thoughts. *It's about Samantha Boyd. She's lying to you.* What a spineless asshole.

"Don't worry," I tell Coop. "I think you'll like her."

We say our good-byes, Coop finishing up with his usual invitation to call or text if I need anything.

At the sink, I splash water onto my face and gargle with a hearty dose of mouthwash. I pout at my reflection, trying to look sexy, mentally preparing myself to pick up where Jeff and I left off. Despite Coop's interruption, the desire I felt earlier is still very much intact. Perhaps even more so. I'm fully ready to jump back into bed and finish what I started with Jeff.

But when I exit the bathroom, I see that Jeff, tired of waiting and just plain tired, has fallen fast asleep.

Midnight finds my mind exhausted but my body wide-awake. All that napping earlier in the afternoon has left me thrumming with energy. I shift and roll beneath the covers, too warm with them, too cold without them. Jeff has no such problem. He snores lightly beside me, lost to the world. Rather than remain in bed, I get up and change into jeans, a T-shirt, and a cardigan. A little late-night baking feels in order. Old-fashioned apple dumplings. The next item on the *Quincy's Sweets* schedule, which has already been thrown off by a day.

I don't get past the guest room. Sam's room now, I suppose. A strip of light creeps from beneath the door, so I give it a single, tentative tap.

"It's open," Sam says.

I find her in the corner, rooting through the knapsack. She pulls out the earrings from Saks and tosses them onto the bed, their presence jarring my memory. I had forgotten all about them.

"I took the stuff out of your purse when you got home," she tells me. "In case Jeff decided to look in there."

"Thanks," I say, staring glumly at the earrings. "I'm not sure I want them anymore."

"I'll take them." Sam grabs the earrings off the bed and drops them back into the knapsack. "It's not like we can return them. How are you feeling?"

"Better," I say. "But now I can't sleep."

"Sleeping's not my strong suit either."

"Jeff told me about your talk earlier today," I say. "And I'm happy. *We're* happy. To have you here, I mean. Just yell if you need anything. Make yourself at home."

Which she's already done. A couple of books sit on the nightstand. Dog-eared science-fiction paperbacks and a hardcover copy of *The Art of War*. Although the window is open, it can't quite erase the cigarette smoke clinging to the air. Sam's leather purse/ashtray rests on the sill.

"I'm sorry I left you alone the rest of the day," I say. "I hope you weren't too bored."

"It's cool." Sam sits on one side of the bed, patting the mattress until I settle onto the other. "I took a walk around the neighborhood. Had that nice talk with Jeff."

"I'll make it up to you tomorrow," I tell her. "Which reminds me, we're meeting someone tomorrow. His name is Franklin Cooper."

"The cop who saved your life?"

I'm surprised she knows who he is. She really has been keeping tabs on me.

"Right," I say. "He wants to meet you. Say hi."

"And see if I'm a psycho," Sam says. "Don't worry. I get it. He needs to see if I can be trusted."

I clear my throat. "Which means you can't mention the Xanax."

"Sure," Sam says.

"Or the—"

"Five-fingered discount you sometimes take advantage of?"

"Yes," I reply, grateful I don't have to say it out loud. "That too."

"I'll be on my best behavior," Sam says. "I won't even swear."

"After that, we'll play tourist. The Empire State Building. Rockefeller Center. Wherever you want to go."

"Central Park?"

I can't tell if she's attempting a joke about what happened the night before. "If you'd like."

"Why wait? Why not go right now?"

Now I know she's joking.

"That's so not a good idea," I say.

"And was puking on that reporter a good idea?"

"That wasn't intentional."

"Did he say anything?"

Once more, Jonah Thompson's insistent voice tiptoes into my skull. Again, I ignore it. The only thing Sam lied about was her name change, and I know all about that now. Jonah's the one who was lying, trying to get me to spill my guts about being called a Final Girl. I spilled my guts, just not in the way he was expecting.

"Nothing important," I say. "I wasn't there to listen. I went there to yell."

"Good for you."

Another thought occurs to me, making my voice go soft. "Why didn't you go with me? Why didn't you even want me to go?"

"Because you need to pick your battles," Sam says. "I learned a long time ago that fighting with the press is useless. They'll win every time. And with guys like that Jonah Thompson punk, it only eggs him on. We'll probably be in the paper again tomorrow."

The thought makes my body go rigid with fear. "I'm sorry if that happens."

"It's no big deal. I'm just happy you finally got mad about something." A spark ignites just behind her eyes. "How did it feel to confront him?"

I think about it for a moment, parsing through my hazy memory, trying to sort how I really felt from what the Xanax made me feel. I think I liked it. Scratch that. I *know* I liked it. I felt righteous and energized and strong, right up until the nausea took over.

"It felt good," I say.

"Getting angry always does. And are you still mad?"

"No," I say.

Sam gives me a playful shove from across the bed. "Liar."

"Fine. Yes. I'm still mad."

"The question then becomes, what are you going to do about it?"

"Nothing," I say. "You just said it's useless to fight with the press."

"I'm not talking about the press now. I'm talking about life. The world. It's full of misfortune and unfairness and women like us getting hurt by men who should know better. And very few people actually give a shit. Even fewer of us actually get angry and take action."

"But you're one of them," I say.

"Damn right. You want to join me?"

I stare across the bed at Sam and the fiery glint crackling in her eyes. My heartbeat increases a tick or two as something stirs in my chest, as light as a butterfly's wings scraping the inside of its chrysalis. It's longing, I realize. A longing to feel the same way I felt with Sam that morning. A longing to be radiant.

"I don't know," I say. "Maybe."

Sam grabs her jacket, shoves it on, closes it with a forceful zip. "Then let's go."

14.

I can handle this.

That's what I tell myself.

We're only going to Central Park, for God's sake. Not a forest in the middle of nowhere. I have my pepper spray. I have Sam. We'll be fine.

But doubt takes over as soon as we step outside. The night air is shockingly cold. I rub my arms for warmth as Sam lights a cigarette beneath the building's awning. Then we're off, my heartbeat racing as we cross Columbus Avenue, Sam ahead of me, trailing smoke.

When we reach Central Park West, my anxiety only increases. The wrongness of the situation is obvious. I feel it in my gut, as if my conscience is an internal organ, crimson and fleshy, flaring with unexplained distress. We shouldn't be out here. Not at this hour.

I had wanted to feel radiant again. Instead, I feel dim and hollow and small.

"I think we've gone far enough."

My voice gets lost in the chilly breeze. Not that Sam would have turned back had she heard me. She's all determination as she crosses the street and makes a right, heading toward the park entrance one block south. I break into a run, following the route of my morning jogs, until I've caught up to her.

"What are we going to do out here?" I say.

"You'll see."

Sam ditches her cigarette and veers into the park. I pause at the threshold, the headlights cruising up Central Park West catching me in their glare and bending my shadow over the sidewalk. I want to turn back. I almost do. My body's prepared to sprint to the apartment and dive into bed, clinging to Jeff. But I can no longer see Sam. She's been swallowed by the park's dark mouth.

"Sam?" I say. "Come back."

There's no response.

I wait, hoping she'll reappear, grinning, saying this is just another one of her tests. One that I have failed. But when she doesn't come back, my nervousness ticks up another notch. Sam's alone in the park. In the dead of night. And even though I know she can take care of herself, I worry. So I curl my fingers around the slim canister of pepper spray in my pocket. I curse myself for not taking a Xanax. Then I inhale a deep, jittery breath and step into the park.

Sam stands just beyond the entrance. Not lost. Just blending with the shadows as she waits for me to catch up. She looks impatient. Or annoyed. I can't quite tell.

"Come on," she says, grabbing my arm and pulling me along.

I know this part of the park well. I've been here a thousand times. The Diana Ross Playground is to our left, its gates closed and locked. On our right sits the exit curve of the Seventy-Ninth Street Transverse. Yet night has transformed the park into something forbidden and unfamiliar. I barely recognize it. A mist has rolled in, shivery and thick. It whispers against my skin and haloes the lamps along the path, diffusing their glow. Muted circles of light creep across the grass and get tangled in the trees, making the park's woods seem thicker, more wild.

I try not to think about the woods surrounding Pine Cottage, even though it's all I can think about. That thick forest, filled with hidden dangers. It's like I'm back there again, ready to break out into my life-or-death race through the trees.

Sam heads deeper into the park. I follow, even as a chant of worry forms in my thoughts— *This is dangerous. Wrong.*

Through the mist, I see the hazy outline of the Delacorte Theater. Just beyond it is Belvedere Castle, a miniature fortress rising from a rock outcropping. Its fog-shrouded silhouette brings to mind fairy-tale forests.

One could get lost in a place like this, I think. One could stray from the path and never be seen again.

Just like Janelle.

Like all of them.

For now, Sam and I keep on the path as we head south, staying close to the park's western border. Despite the hour, we are not alone. I glimpse other people—moving shadows in the distance. A couple crossing the park swiftly, heads lowered against the mist. A late-night jogger behind us, breath heavy, tinny music drifting out of earbuds. Their appearances make my heart crash like cymbals.

Then there are the solitary men with fog-blurred faces who cruise the park's paths, looking for the erotic thrill of illicit, anonymous sex. Many of them wear similar clothes, as if there's a dress code involved. Track pants and expensive running shoes, hooded sweatshirts unzipped to expose tight T-shirts. They emerge from the mist in all directions. Roaming, circling, searching. They don't give Sam and me a second glance. We're not their type.

"We should go back," I say.

"Chill," Sam says.

She shares the same restlessness as those discreetly prowling men. There's something driving her. A hunger. A need. She plops onto a bench, her right leg fidgeting as she searches the horizon. A hardness has replaced the earlier fire in her eyes, her stare cold and coal-black.

I sit beside her, my heart beating so hard I'm surprised it doesn't shake the bench. Sam digs a cigarette out of her jacket pocket and lights up. The flare of her lighter in the fog gets the attention of one of the prowlers—a leather-clad moth drawn to the flame. I tense up as he gets closer. My hand tightens around the pepper spray in my pocket.

Once he reaches our bench, his features clear. He's handsome and lithe, with a peppery stubble tracing the line of his jaw. An air of dark sexiness radiates off him.

"Hey," he says, voice hushed and apologetic, as if talking isn't allowed. "Can I bum a smoke?"

Sam obliges, slipping a cigarette from her pocket and into his palm with the ease of a dime-bag dealer. She flicks her lighter and the man leans forward, cigarette tip catching, glowing hot a moment before darkening into a smolder. He nods at Sam, blowing out smoke that mingles with the mist.

"Thanks."

"No prob," Sam says. "Good luck tonight."

The man smiles, sly and sexy. He begins to walk away in a leather-clad strut, saying over his shoulder, "Luck has nothing to do with it, sweetie." Then he's gone, vanishing back into the fog from which he emerged.

I think about Him. In a different woods. In a different time. If only He had disappeared like that, slipping away, leaving us alone.

"Sam, I want to go home," I say.

"Fine," Sam replies. "Go."

"You're not coming with me?"

"Nope."

"What are we doing here?"

Sam shushes me, suddenly alert. She stands, looking in the direction we just came from, body taut, poised, ready to pounce. I follow her gaze, seeing what she sees. A woman has appeared in the mist, roughly a hundred yards away. Alone, she hurries through the park with an unwieldy canvas tote held tight against her chest. Young and hungry, probably. Crossing the park on foot to save on cab fare, not thinking about how spectacularly bad an idea that really is.

A man emerges from the fog right behind her, so close he could be her shadow. Shrouded in a black hoodie, he even looks like a shadow. He moves at a steady clip, faster than the girl, gaining on her. She realizes this and quickens her pace, on the cusp of a run.

"Sam?" I say as my heart begins to thud hollowly in my chest. "Do you think he's going to mug her? Or—"

Worse. That's what I'm about to say. *Or worse.*

I don't get the chance because the half-man, half-shadow is already upon the girl, a hand clamping down on her shoulder, the other reaching for either the tote bag or her breasts hidden behind it.

Sam takes off, sprinting up the path, the sound of her boots muffled in the haze. Instinct makes me run after her, even though I only vaguely know what's about to happen.

Up ahead, the girl sees Sam and recoils. As if Sam is aiming for her. She struggles under the man's grip, legs unsteady, the tote bag raised like a shield in front of her. Sam passes her in a wide arc, heading instead for the man, not slowing, smashing right into him.

The collision knocks him away from the girl and into the grass. Sam bounces off him, staggering backward. The girl hurtles away, wanting to look back but too scared to. I leap in front of her, hands raised, adrenaline frothing inside me.

"Friends," I say. "We're friends."

Behind her, the assailant slips over the grass as he tries to flee. Sam hurls herself at him, leaping onto his back. Quickly, I guide the almost-victim to the closest bench, set her down, order her to stay there. Then I'm off, rushing toward Sam.

Somehow, she's pushed the man onto his knees. He slumps more the longer she's on top of him, bending so far forward his face brushes the grass.

Something Coop said earlier fills my skull. *We don't know what she's capable of.*

"Sam, don't hurt him!"

My voice cuts across the park, distracting Sam. She looks up. Not long. Just a split second. But it's enough time for the man to kick at her. His foot hits her in the stomach and sends her rolling through the grass.

The man rises in a lunge, legs spaced apart and bent at the knees. A sprinter at the starting line. Soon he's off, shoes slipping a bit on the slick grass. Sam's still on her back, trying to flip onto her side, sucking in air to cool the pain in her stomach. Not down for the count, but close enough.

I break into a run, awkwardly, with one hand in my pocket fumbling for the pepper spray.

The man is completely up now, also running. But I'm faster, all those jogged miles paying off. I catch the man's sweatshirt, jerking the hood off his head. There's a baseball cap underneath, slightly askew. I see a shock of raven-black hair, cocoa skin on the back of his neck. One hard pull of the hood is all it takes to slow him down, sneakers sliding, arms flailing.

When he whirls around, I expect to see his face. Instead, all I see is the blur of his hand as it streaks toward me. Then the slap comes— a brutal backhand whipping my cheek so hard my entire head jerks to the right.

My vision clouds with a red pulse of pain that blocks out everything else. I haven't felt pain like that in years. Ten years, to be precise. Fleeing Pine Cottage. Screaming through the woods. That thick branch knocking me dizzy.

Suddenly it's like I'm right back there again, feeling the deep, throbbing hurt from that branch. Time contracts, becoming a dark tunnel that I'm about to fall through, not landing until I've returned to that cursed woods where all those bad things happened.

But I don't. I'm back in the present, shock numbing my body. I let go of the hood, my hand opening against my will. I can still see the man through the red haze clouding my vision. Now free, he's running south, getting farther away, soon gone.

His presence is replaced by two others, swooping in from different directions. One of them is Sam, hurrying up behind me, saying my name. The other is the girl we just saved. She's left her bench and comes toward me, hand deep in her tote bag.

"You're bleeding," she says.

I press a hand to my nose as something hot and wet trickles from my nostrils. Looking down, I see blood glistening on my fingers.

The girl hands me a tissue. While I dab at my nose, Sam presses against my back, encircling me with a hug.

"Goddamn, babe," she says. "We've got a fighter on our hands."

I breathe through my mouth, swallowing crisp air that smells faintly of grass. My entire body hums with a mixture of adrenaline and fear and pride that Sam might actually be right. I *am* a fighter, aglow with radiance.

The girl we saved—she never does give us her name—also seems astonished. She speaks in awed, hushed tones as we whisk through the fog on our way out of the park, asking us if we're vigilantes.

"No," I say.

"Yes," Sam says.

Once we're on Central Park West, I hail a cab and make sure the girl actually gets into it. Before closing the door, I shove a twenty into her palm, closing her fingers over the bill and saying, "Cab fare. Don't ever walk through the park alone this late again."

15.

My face still hurts when I wake up—a dull residual pain that trails along my cheekbone to my nose. In the shower, I make the water as hot as I can endure and spend a good five minutes sniffing steam into my nose, huffing it out, dislodging the dried blood caked to the insides of my nostrils. I then lift my face to the spray, the hot water stinging my skin.

When I think about last night, a tremor grips my legs so violently that I have to lean against the shower wall for support. It's hard to believe I was that foolish, that quick to leap into danger. The man in the park could have been armed. I could have been stabbed, shot, killed. All things considered, I'm lucky I got away with a mere backhand to the face.

Out of the shower, I swipe my hand over the bathroom mirror, making a clear streak across the fogged surface. The reflection staring back at me has the faintest of bruises on her cheek, barely noticeable. Yet it's tender to the touch. A little pressure from my fingertips is enough to make me wince.

The new pain along my cheek has awakened older wounds. Although the stab wounds I received at Pine Cottage didn't cause any lasting damage, they did leave scars. Today they're throbbing—the first time I've felt them in years. I arch my back slightly until the scar on my stomach is framed in the mirror. A milk-white line against my steam-reddened skin. I then lean forward, looking close at the two scars sitting an inch apart just below my shoulder. One is a vertical line. The other's slightly diagonal. Had the knife been bigger, the two would have intersected.

By the time I'm dried off and dressed, everything has subsided into a slight ache. Annoying, yes, but nothing I can't handle.

In the kitchen, I take my pre-Coop Xanax and grape soda, waiting for Sam to emerge from her room. She does a few minutes later, looking like a completely different person. Her hair is swept behind her ears, giving full view of a face that's been gently kissed with makeup. The eyeliner has been applied with a lighter hand, and instead of ruby red, her lips are touched with a peachy-pink gloss. Forgoing her usual black, she's dressed in dark jeans, blue flats, and the very same blouse she had taken from Saks yesterday. The gold earrings I stole dangle from her ears.

"Wow," I say.

"Not bad for a chick my age, right?"

"I'll say."

"I wanted to make a good impression."

While walking to the café, we catch a few looks from passersby, although it's impossible to know whether they're because of Jonah Thompson's article or Sam's new look. Probably the latter. Few eyes, I notice, glance my way, and when they do it feels like they're comparing me with Sam.

Even Coop does it when we arrive at the café and pass his usual spot by the window. Through the glass, I see a brief nod for me and an appraising look directed at Sam. A pinprick of irritation forms at the back of my neck.

Coop stands when we enter. Unlike our last meeting, he's dressed to blend in with the café's upper-class crowd. Today he wears khakis and a black polo shirt. It looks good on him, the short sleeves exposing his taut biceps, the veins popping just beneath his skin.

"You must be Samantha," he says.

He's slow with the handshake. Awkward. Uncertain. It's up to Sam to complete the gesture, reaching across the table to grasp his open palm.

"And you're Officer Cooper," she says.

"Coop," he says quickly. "Everyone calls me Coop."

"And everyone calls me Sam."

"Great," I say, forcing a smile as we take our seats. "We're all acquainted."

Two mugs sit on the table in front of Coop. His coffee and my tea. Looking at them, he says, "I wanted to order something for you, Sam, but I didn't know what you prefer."

"Coffee," Sam says. "And I can get it. You two catch up."

She edges around tables to the counter in the back of the café. One of them is occupied by a bearded guy wearing a backward baseball cap. A writer, judging from the laptop in front of him. Elsewhere on the table are a leather satchel, an iPhone, and a shiny Montblanc pen sitting atop a yellow legal pad. He looks at Sam as she passes, impressed. Sam smiles at him, wiggling her fingers in a flirtatious wave.

"So that's Samantha Boyd," Coop says.

"In the flesh." I gaze at him over the table, watching him watch Sam on the other side of the café. "Is something wrong?"

"I'm just shocked is all," he says. "I never expected her to show up like this. It's kind of like seeing a ghost."

"I was surprised too."

"She's not what I was expecting."

"What were you expecting?"

"Someone rougher, I guess. She looked different in that yearbook photo, don't you think?"

I could tell Coop that Sam is very different, that she's smoothed down her rough edges to impress him for my sake. I stay silent.

"I did some reading about the Nightlight Inn last night," Coop says. "I can't imagine what she's been through."

"She's had a hard life," I say.

"How are the two of you getting along?"

"Great. She and Jeff don't exactly see eye to eye."

Coop allows a half smile. "I can't say that surprises me."

"Jeff's the one you should be getting to know. This arrangement with Sam is only temporary. Like it or not, Jeff's permanent."

I don't know why I say it. It slips out, unplanned. And just like that, Coop's fraction of a smile vanishes.

"But thank you for coming," I say, guilt softening my tone. "It was nice of you to suggest it, even though I'm starting to feel like a burden."

"You're not a burden, Quincy. You've never been one and you'll never be one."

Coop stares at me with those eyes of his. I run a finger over my bruised face, wondering if he's somehow noticed that imperceptible line of pink along my cheekbone. Part of me hopes he'll ask about it, allowing me to use the lie I concocted to explain it away. *Oh, that? I bumped into a doorway.* I'm disappointed when he looks over my shoulder, watching Sam make her way back to us with a steaming mug in her hands. When she passes the writer again, she accidentally bumps the table, coffee mug tilting precariously.

"I'm so sorry!" she yelps.

The man looks up, smiling. "No problem."

"Nice laptop," she says.

Soon she's at our table again, sitting beside me, giving Coop the once-over before telling him, "I thought you'd look different."

"Good different or bad different?" Coop asks.

"Ugly different. And clearly you're not."

"So you knew who I was before today?"

"Of course," Sam says. "Just like you knew who I was. That's the power of the Internet. No one has secrets anymore."

"Is that why you went into hiding?"

"Mostly," Sam says. "But now I'm back among the living."

"You certainly are." There's an edge of disbelief in Coop's voice, as if he's not buying the good-girl act Sam's pushing so hard. He leans back, tilts his head, sizes her up the same way she did him. "Why'd you decide to return?"

"After I heard about what happened to Lisa, I thought I could possibly help Quincy," Sam says, adding, "*if* she needed help."

"Quincy doesn't need help." Coop says it like I'm not sitting directly across from him. Like I'm invisible. "She's strong like that."

"But I didn't know that," Sam says. "Which is why I'm here."

"Are you going to stay long?"

Sam gives a blithe shrug. "Maybe. It's too soon to tell."

I take a sip of tea. It's too hot, the liquid burning my tongue. But

I keep drinking in the hope the pain will erase the spot of annoyance that's once again found its way onto the back of my neck. This time it's the size of a thumbprint, pressing into my skin.

"Sam changed her name," I say. "That's why no one's been able to locate her."

"Really?" Coop's features rise in surprise. I'm expecting a lecture similar to the one he gave me when I suggested changing my name. Instead, he says, "I'm not going to ask you where you were or what name you were living under. I hope that, in time, you'll trust me enough to tell me that on your own. All I ask is that you contact your family and let them know."

"My family is one of the reasons I disappeared," Sam says, growing quiet. "It wasn't exactly the best environment, even before the Nightlight Inn. It just got worse after. I love them and all, but some families aren't meant to be around each other."

"I could contact them for you," Coop suggests. "Just to tell them you're safe."

"I couldn't ask you to do that."

Coop shrugs. "You didn't. I offered."

"Spoken like a true public servant," Sam says. "Were you always a cop?"

"Not always. Before that I was in the military. Marines."

"You see any action?"

"Some." Coop looks out the window, fixing those baby blues on the outside world to avoid eye contact. "Afghanistan."

"Shit," Sam says. "You must have seen some messed-up stuff."

"I did. But I don't like to talk about it."

"Well, you and Quincy certainly have that in common."

Coop turns away from the window, facing not Sam but me. Again, there's something unreadable in his expression. He looks suddenly, terribly sad.

"People deal with trauma in their own ways," he says.

"And how do you deal with yours?" Sam asks.

"I fish," Coop says. "And hunt. And hike. You know, typical Pennsylvania-boy stuff."

"Does it help?"

"Mostly."

"Maybe I should try it," Sam says.

"I'd be happy to take you and Quincy fishing sometime, if you'd like."

"Quincy's right. You really are the best."

Sam reaches across the table and squeezes Coop's hand. He doesn't pull away. My irritation grows. Tension fills my shoulders and pokes through the soft cushion of Xanax. I want to take a second pill. I worry that I've now become the kind of woman who *needs* to take a second pill.

"I have to go to the ladies' room," I say, grabbing my purse off the table. "Join me, Sam?"

"Sure." Sam gives Coop a wink. "Girls. We're so predictable, right?"

On our way to the back of the café, she gives another wave to the writer at the table. He waves back. Sam and I then cram ourselves into a bathroom built to accommodate only one person. We stand in front of the dust-mottled mirror, shoulders touching.

"How am I doing?" Sam says as she checks her makeup.

"The question is, *what* are you doing?"

"Being friendly. Isn't that what you wanted?"

"It is—"

"Then what's the problem?"

"Just tone it down a little," I say. "If you come on too strong, Coop will know it's an act."

"Would that be a problem if he does?"

"It could make things awkward."

"I don't mind awkward," Sam says.

I start to root through my purse, looking for any stray Xanax that might be resting inside. "Coop does."

"*Oh*," Sam says, the word a pool of innuendo. "So things have gotten awkward between you two."

"He's a friend," I say.

"Right. A *friend*."

"He is."

At the bottom of my purse I find a few loose sticks of gum and a lone, fuzz-covered Mentos. No Xanax. I zip it shut.

"I'm not arguing," Sam says.

"No, you're suggesting."

"Me?" Sam says, faux-offended. "I'm in no way suggesting that you want to get it on with that hot cop."

"I think you just did."

"All I'm saying is that he's hot."

"I never noticed."

Sam pulls out a tube of gloss and gives one quick swipe to both her bottom and top lips. "I call bullshit on that one, babe. It's kind of hard not to notice."

"Seriously, I never have. He saved my life. When someone does that, you tend not to think of them in that way."

"Guys do. They pretend they don't, but they totally do."

Sam's taken on a wiser, worldlier tone. The older sister giving sex advice. I wonder what kind of men she dates. Older guys, probably. Bikers with thick chests and thicker guts, their beards peppered with gray. Or maybe she likes them younger. Pale, wiry men so inexperienced they're grateful for even the most disinterested of hand jobs.

"If he did," I say, "Coop's too much of a gentleman to make a big deal out of it."

"Gentleman?" Sam says. "He's a cop. From my experience, they fuck like jackhammers."

I say nothing, knowing how she's only looking for my disapproval, seeking a chance to chide me for being such a prude. Janelle did it all the time.

"I'm joking," she says. "Lighten up."

That was another of Janelle's traits. To backtrack once she knew she'd gone too far, trying to shrug everything off as a joke. Today, Sam does her one better.

"I'm sorry, Quinn. I'll tone it down. Really." Her hand plunges into her pocket. "By the way, I thought you might like this. Something for your goodie drawer."

She pulls out a Montblanc pen as sleek and shiny as a silver bullet and presses it into my hand. It once belonged to the writer in the café. Now it belongs to us. Another one of our shared secrets.

PINE COTTAGE
6:58 P.M.

They were forced to dress for dinner. Another one of Janelle's rules. Before they left, she made sure to check that everyone brought the proper attire. "Slobs *will* be sent home," she warned.

Quincy had packed two dresses—the only two she brought with her to college. Both had been picked out by her mother, who had harbored dreams of Quincy going to mixers and pledging sororities just as she had done.

One dress was black, which Quincy had thought would be fine for the occasion. In the wan light of the cabin, though, it looked more widow-at-a-funeral than Audrey Hepburn in *Breakfast at Tiffany's*. That left the blue one, which appeared dowdier than she intended.

"I look dumpy," Quincy said.

She knew she was right because Janelle looked more horrified than when she'd sliced her finger half an hour earlier. She now pointed it at Quincy, Band-Aid crinkling.

"Worse," she said. "You look like a virgin."

"That's not a bad thing, you know."

"It is if you're trying to get some."

"Craig knows it will be my first time."

"Which that dress makes glaringly obvious," Janelle said, eyeing her from head to foot. "I have an idea."

She opened one of her two suitcases and tossed something at Quincy. It was a dress. White silk. As cool and shimmering as a swimming pool.

"Isn't white, like, the most virginal color?" Quincy asked.

"The color of the dress says virgin, but the cut says sex. It's the best of both worlds. Craig will love it."

Quincy rolled her eyes. Typical Janelle, who had been obsessed with the madonna-whore complex ever since they learned about it in Psych 101.

"What are you going to wear?"

Janelle turned back to her suitcase. "I brought extras, of course."

"Of course."

Quincy held the dress against her body, examining it in the room's grimy square of a mirror. The cut, with its plunging bodice and asymmetrical skirt, looked a little too sexy for her taste. Even with her back turned, Janelle could sense her hesitation. "Just try it on, Quinn."

Quincy slid out of the blue dress, which gave Janelle the opportunity to take a disapproving look at her bra and panties. Mismatched and worn, they were the antithesis of sexy.

"God, Quinn, really? Did you not plan any aspect of this weekend?"

"No," Quincy said, holding the recently removed blue dress to her chest, trying to hide behind it. "Because planning puts pressure on something. And I don't want any pressure. Whatever Craig and I do this weekend, I want it to happen naturally."

Janelle gave a sisterly smile and brushed a strand of blond hair from Quincy's face. "It's okay to be nervous."

"I'm not nervous." Quincy grimaced at the anxious quiver in her voice. "I'm just . . . inexperienced. What if I'm—"

"Lousy at sex?"

"Um, that's one way to put it."

"You won't know until you try it," Janelle said.

"What if Craig doesn't like it?"

Quincy thought back to what Janelle had said earlier, about Craig having plenty of options besides her. She knew all too well about the cheerleaders who fawned over him after games and the fangirls in school colors who yelled his name in the quad. They would be all too willing to take Quincy's place if Craig was disappointed in her.

"He'll like it," Janelle said. "He's a guy, after all."

"What if I don't like it?"

"You will. It just takes some getting used to."

Quincy felt a flutter in her stomach. More than a butterfly. A bird flapping. "How much getting used to?"

"It'll be fine," Janelle assured her. "Now, show me how that dress looks on you."

Quincy slid on the dress, the white silk tickling her bare legs. As she tugged and adjusted it over her shoulder, Janelle said, "What do you think of Joe? He's kind of hot, right?"

"More like creepy," Quincy said.

"He's mysterious."

"Which is practically the same as creepy."

"Well, *I* think he's mysterious. And hot."

"And taken," Quincy added. "You're forgetting the girlfriend."

Now it was Janelle's turn to roll her eyes. "Whatever."

"I just want to state for the record that the rest of us don't want him here. We're only letting him stay because it's your birthday."

"Duly noted," Janelle said. "And don't worry. I plan on keeping him very entertained."

Done with wrangling into the dress, Quincy backed up to Janelle, who zipped her up. Both of them examined her reflection in the mirror. Although the dress was tighter than Quincy normally liked, Janelle was right. She looked sexy.

"Wow," she said.

Janelle wolf-whistled. "You look so good, I might even try to fuck you."

"Thanks. I think."

Janelle made a few adjustments, giving a tight tug of the hem before smoothing some fabric bunched at Quincy's shoulders.

"Perfect."

"You think?" Quincy asked, despite already knowing that it was, indeed, perfect.

Yet something still bothered her.

"What's wrong?" Janelle asked.

"It's going to hurt, isn't it?"

"Yes," Janelle said, sighing out the word. "It does. But it also feels good."

"Which will I feel more of? The bad or the good?"

"That's the weird part. They're one and the same."

Quincy looked in the mirror, zeroing in on the eyes of her reflection, uneasy at the fear she saw in them. "You sure?"

"Trust me." Janelle wrapped her arms around Quincy, hugging her from behind. "Would I ever lead you astray?"

16.

Coop insists on walking us back to my place, even though Sam and I are perfectly capable of taking care of ourselves. Last night made that abundantly clear. Sam walks alongside him, matching his pace stride by careful stride.

I lag behind, my face lifted to the sun. It's a bright, hot afternoon—the last kiss of Indian summer before winter begins its slow takeover. The bruise on my face pulses a little, warmed by the sunlight. I picture it reddening into visibility along my skin. I want Coop to turn around, finally notice it, widen his eyes in concern. But he stays two steps ahead with Sam, their strides still matching as they round the corner onto Eighty-Second Street.

Both of them immediately stop.

I do too.

Something is going on outside my building. A horde of reporters has gathered there, so large and unruly we can see them from two blocks away.

"Coop." My voice is weak. An echo of its normal self. "Something's wrong."

"No shit," Sam says.

"Stay calm," Coop says. "We don't know for certain why they're here."

Yet I know. They're here for us.

I reach into my purse and grab my phone, which I turned off when Sam and I left the apartment. It springs to life with an explosion of alerts. Missed calls. Missed emails. Missed texts. Worry numbs my hands as I scroll through them. Many numbers I don't recognize, which means they're from reporters. Only Jonah Thompson's is familiar to me. He called three times.

"We should walk away," I say, knowing it will be only another minute or so before we're spotted. "Or get a cab."

"And go where?" Sam asks.

"I don't know. Jeff's office. Central Park. Anywhere but here."

"That's not a bad idea," Coop says. "It'll give us time to find out what's going on."

"And they can't stay out here forever." I squint at the crowd up the street, which seems to have grown in the past thirty seconds. "Can they?"

"I'm not waiting that long," Sam mutters.

She sets off up the street, marching straight for the reporters. I manage to grasp the back of her blouse and tug, trying to hold her in place. But it's no use. The silk slips from my fingers.

"Do something," I tell Coop.

He watches her advance, blue eyes narrowed. I can't tell if he's worried or impressed. Maybe it's a little of both. All I feel, however, is worry, which is why I rush after Sam, catching up just as she reaches my block.

The reporters see us, of course, their heads turning toward us more or less at the same time. A flock of buzzards spotting fresh roadkill. The TV people have cameramen with them, who jostle one another for prime position. The still photographers duck beneath them, shutters clacking.

Jonah Thompson is among them. No surprise there. He, like the other reporters, barks our first names as we approach. As if he knows us. As if he cares.

"Quincy! Samantha!"

We fall back a few steps, accosted on all sides by the surge of cameras and microphones. A hand lands on my shoulder, heavy and strong. I don't even need to look back to know it belongs to Coop, finally joining us.

"Come on, guys, step aside," he tells the reporters. "Let them get through."

Sam pushes forward, swinging her arms back and forth to clear a path, not caring who she hits.

"Get the fuck out of our fucking way," she says, knowing how all that swearing will prevent the footage from being used on newscasts. "We've fucking got nothing to fucking say to you."

"So that's no comment?" asks one reporter. He's a TV guy, the camera behind him swiveling toward Sam like the eye of an angry Cyclops.

"Sounds that fucking way to me."

She turns away from him, looking to me instead. All those flash-bulbs give her face a luminescent glow. The light flattens her features, making her expression as pale and blank as a full moon.

On the edge of my vision, I see Jonah nudge his way toward me.

"You're really not going to say anything about Lisa Milner?" he says.

Curiosity stirs in me, pushing me forward. Lisa's suicide happened days ago. In a twenty-four-hour news cycle, that's an eternity. This is something else. Something new.

"What about Lisa?" I say, sweeping in close. Cameras fill the spot I just vacated, surrounding me.

"She didn't kill herself," Jonah says. "Her death's been ruled a ho-micide. Lisa Milner was murdered."

These are the details:

On the night she died, Lisa Milner consumed two glasses of Mer-lot. She did not drink alone. Someone else was with her, also drinking wine. That same someone spiked Lisa's glass with a large quantity of anitrophylin, a mighty antidepressant sometimes used as a sleep aid for the seriously traumatized. Lisa had enough in her system to put an adult male gorilla into a coma.

The wine and anitrophylin were discovered during the toxicology tests performed in the wake of Lisa's death. Without them, everyone would have continued to think she killed herself. Even with them, it would have appeared that way. The responding officers found more anitrophylin on the kitchen counter. What they couldn't find was a bottle or a prescription from Lisa's doctor, but that means nothing in an age of online pharmacies that charge three times the going rate for pills shipped from Canada. Any drug your pharmaceutical-deprived heart desires is just a border hop away.

After the tox report lit up like a Vegas casino, a CSI unit was again dispatched to Lisa's house. They took the closer look they should have done days earlier but hadn't bothered to because everyone thought she had offed herself. They found Lisa's wineglass, its bottom crusted with granules of anitrophylin. They found two rings of dried Merlot on the dining-room table, created by the bottoms of two wineglasses. One wine ring contained anitrophylin. The other did not. What they couldn't find was that second glass. Or any signs of struggle. Or forced entry.

Lisa had trusted whoever killed her.

The medical examiner noticed something strange about the cuts on Lisa's wrists. They were deeper than most self-inflicted knife wounds. Especially if the person doing the cutting was drugged out of her mind. Even more telling was the direction of each cut—from right to left on Lisa's left wrist and left to right on her right one. In most cases, the opposite is the norm. And even though Lisa might have been able to slash herself in such an unusual manner, the angle of the wounds proved otherwise. There was no way she could have caused those cuts. Someone had done it to her. The same person who put pills in her wine and later took the glass with them.

The big question mark—other than who did it and why, of course—is when Lisa made the 911 call on her cell phone. Authorities in Muncie suspect it was after the drugging but before the cutting. Their theory is that Lisa realized she had been drugged and managed to call 911. Her assailant took the phone from her before she got the chance to speak and hung up. Knowing the police would be coming anyway, that person grabbed a knife, dragged a groggy Lisa to the bathtub, and sliced. It also explains why her wrists were slit when, in all likelihood, the anitrophylin would have killed her on its own.

What the police don't know, until they find it on Lisa's computer hard drive, is that she sent me an email roughly an hour before all this happened. It jumps into my thoughts as we gather around Coop's cell phone, set to speaker so all of us can hear the details.

Quincy, I need to talk to you. It's extremely important. Please, please don't ignore this.

We're in the dining room, me standing at the head of the table, too restless with anger and heartbreak to sit down. Lisa is still dead. This new revelation doesn't change that. But it does leave me grieving in a new, slightly raw way.

Murder is a stranger beast than suicide, although the end result of both is the same. Even the words themselves differ. "Suicide" hisses like a snake—a sickness of the mind and soul. "Murder," though, makes me think of sludge, dark and thick and filled with pain. Lisa's death was easier to deal with when I thought it was suicide. It meant that ending her life was her decision. That, right or not, it had been her choice.

There is no choice in murder.

Coop and Sam appear equally as stunned. They sit on opposite sides of the table, silent and still. Because he's never been in the apartment before, Coop's presence adds an extra layer of weirdness to what's already a surreal situation. It's jarring to see him in civilian clothes, uncomfortable in a dainty dining-room chair. Like he's not the real Coop but an impostor, lurking in a place he doesn't belong. The fake, cheery Sam, meanwhile, has been left behind at the café. Now it's the real one who gnaws her fingernails to the quick while staring at Coop's phone, as if she can see the person talking through it and not the featureless silhouette currently filling the screen.

The voice we hear belongs to Coop's acquaintance in the Indiana State Police. Her name is Nancy and she was a first responder to the sorority house after Stephen Leibman finished his bloody spree. She was also Lisa's version of Coop.

"I'm not going to lie to you all," she says in a voice made low by exhaustion and grief. "They've got very little to work with here."

I can only half hear her because the email plays on a loop in my mind, read aloud in Lisa's voice.

Quincy, I need to talk to you.

"Things might be different if those numbnuts had searched her place the minute they found her body, like I told 'em to do. But they didn't and God knows how many people tramped through there before they did. The whole scene is compromised, Frank. Fingerprints all over the place."

It's extremely important.

"So they might never know who did it?" Coop asks.

"I never say never," Nancy says. "But right now, it's not looking too good."

A brief silence follows in which all four of us think about the very real possibility of never getting more answers than what we already know. No killer brought to justice. No motive. No definitive reason why Lisa sent me an email not long before taking that first, unknowing sip of doom.

Please, please don't ignore this.

Another thought slithers into my head, sinuous and alarming.

"Should Sam and I be worried?" I ask.

Coop scrunches his brow, pretending the thought hadn't occurred to him, when, of course, it had.

"Well?" I say.

"I don't think there's cause for worry," he says. "Do you, Nancy?"

Nancy's wan voice emerges from the phone. "There's nothing to suggest this has anything to do with what happened to all of you."

"But what if it might?" I say.

"Quincy?" Coop gives me a look I've never seen before. There's a sternness to it, mingling with disappointment that I might be hiding something from him. "What aren't you telling me?"

Something I should have told him days earlier. I didn't because it seemed like Lisa's email was a desperate attempt to be talked out of killing herself. Now I know differently. Now I suspect that Lisa was really trying to warn me. About what, I have no idea.

"I got an email from Lisa," I announce.

Sam at last looks up from the phone, hand still at her mouth, the nail of her ring finger grasped between her teeth. *"What?"*

"When?" Coop says, concern burning bright in his eyes.

"The night she died. About an hour before, to be exact."

"Tell me what it said," he says. "Every word."

I tell them everything. The contents of the email. When I received it. When I actually read it. I even try to explain why I waited so long to tell anyone but Jeff about it, although Coop doesn't really care why. His only focus is the fact he didn't know about it sooner.

"You should have told me the second you got it, Quincy."

"I know," I say.

"This could have changed things."

"I *know* that, Coop."

It could have given the police a reason for doing a better search of Lisa's house, leading them to sooner conclude that she was murdered. It might have even yielded an important clue into who killed her. I know all of this, and the guilt it spawns makes me angry. At myself. At Lisa's killer. Even at Lisa, for thrusting me into this position. The anger fizzes through me, overtaking my heartbreak and surprise.

"It still doesn't mean you or Samantha are in danger," Nancy says.

"It might not mean anything at all," Coop adds.

"Or it could mean that she thought someone was targeting us," I say.

"Who would want to do that?" Coop asks.

"Lots of people," I say. "Crazy people. You've looked at those crime websites. You've seen how many freaks out there are obsessed with us."

"That's because they admire you," Coop says. "They're in awe of what you went through. What you managed to survive. Not many people could have done it, Quincy. But you did."

"Then explain that letter."

There's no need to clarify. Coop knows exactly which letter I'm talking about. The threatening one. The scary one. It unnerved him as much as it did me.

YØU SHØULDN'T BE ALIVE.
YØU SHØULD HAVE DIED IN THAT CABIN.
IT WAS YØUR DESTINY TØ BE SACRIFICED.

Whoever wrote it had used a typewriter. The keys had been struck so hard that, on the page, the letters looked like burn marks seared into leather. Every *o* was actually a zero, meaning that key was likely broken. Coop said this hint could possibly lead authorities to discover who wrote it. That was two years ago. I'm not holding my breath, especially since every other means of identifying its author have already been exhausted. There were no fingerprints on the paper or on the envelope, which had been sealed not with saliva but a sponge and water. The same goes for the stamp. As for the postmark, it was traced to a public mailbox in a town called Quincy, Illinois.

That wasn't a coincidence.

Jeff and I had been living together only a month when it arrived. It was his first real taste of what life with me would be like. I was, of course, hysterical to the point of insisting we had to move immediately. Preferably overseas. Jeff talked me out of it, saying the letter was a very sick but ultimately harmless prank.

Coop took it more seriously because, well, he's Coop and that's how he rolls. By that point, our relationship had dwindled to a text or two every few months. We hadn't actually seen each other in more than a year.

The letter changed all that. When I'd told him about it, he drove into the city to comfort me. Over coffee and tea at our usual place, he swore that he'd never let something bad happen to me, insisting on a face-to-face meeting at least every six months. The rest is history.

"That letter was sent by a deranged man," Coop says. "A sick man. But that was a long time ago, Quincy. Nothing came of it."

"Exactly," I say. "Nothing ever happened to the psycho creep who sent it. He's still out there, Coop. And maybe he wrote to Lisa or to Sam. Maybe he decided to finally take action."

I look to Sam, who's reverting by the minute back into her old self. Her hair has fallen from behind her ears and now covers most of her face like a protective veil.

"Have you received any death threats?"

Sam gives a tiny shake of her head. "I haven't gotten mail in a long time. One of the perks of no one knowing where you are."

"Well, they know now," I say. "It was on the front page."

A fresh wave of anger crashes over me as I think about Jonah

Thompson and what he's done. My hands ball into fists against my will, clenching and unclenching, aching for the sensation of smashing against his jaw.

"Did Lisa get any threats?" Coop says, leaning into the phone to address Nancy.

"A few," she answers. "Some more worrisome than others. We treated all of them seriously, even managing to track down some of the guys who wrote them. They were lonely cranks. Nothing more. Certainly not killers."

"So you don't think Sam and I could be targets?" I say.

"I don't know what to tell you, hon," Nancy says. "There's nothing to indicate that's the case here, but it's better to err on the side of caution."

Not what I want to hear, which keeps the anger rising. I long for an answer, good or bad. Something definitive and tangible I can use to guide me going forward. Without it, everything is as murky as the fog that shrouded Central Park last night.

"Isn't anyone else upset about this?" I say.

"Of course we're upset," Coop says. "And if we had answers, we'd give them to you."

I turn away, unable to see the earnest way his blue eyes try to offer comfort but reveal only uncertainty. Until today, Coop has always been something solid and strong that I could rely on, even when the rest of my world was tilting into oblivion. Now not even he can make sense of the situation.

"You're angry," he says.

"I am."

"That's understandable. But you shouldn't worry that what happened to Lisa is going to happen to you."

"Why not?"

"Because if that was a possibility, Nancy would have told us," Coop says. "And if I truly thought someone was trying to hurt you, we'd already be on our way out of the city by now. I'd take you so far away from here that not even Jeff would be able to find you."

He would too. Of that I have no doubt. It's finally the answer I've been looking for, and for a moment it's almost enough to snuff out the anger burning in my chest. But then Coop looks across the table and fixes Sam with a blue-eyed stare.

"You too, Sam," he says. "I want you to know that."

Sam nods. Then she starts to cry. Or maybe she's been crying for a while and Coop and I just haven't noticed it. But now she makes sure we notice. When she sweeps her hair off her face it's impossible to miss the tears slanting down her cheeks.

"I'm sorry," she says. "This—the whole situation—is really getting to me."

I stay where I am, trying to discern if Sam's tears are real, which makes me feel awful for even thinking they might not be. Coop, though, stands and rounds the table, edging toward her.

"It's okay to be upset," he says. "This is a bad situation all around."

Sam nods and wipes her eyes. She stands. She holds out her arms, seeking comfort in the form of an embrace.

Coop obliges. I watch him wrap his bulky arms around Sam and pull her against his chest, giving her the hug I've been denied for the past ten years.

I look away. I march into the kitchen. I take another Xanax and begin to bake.

17.

I'm preparing the dough for apple dumplings when Coop finally makes his way to the kitchen. Bowls of ingredients line the counter in front of me. Flour and salt, baking powder and shortening, a bit of milk to mix them with. Coop leans against the doorframe, silently watching me combine the dry ingredients, then the shortening, then the milk. Soon a large ball of dough sits on the countertop, malleable and glistening. I form a fist and give the dough several rough punches, mashing it into an uneven heap.

"Gets the air out," I say.

"I see," Coop says.

I continue to punch, the dough bulging under my knuckles. It's only after I feel the smack of countertop beneath it that I stop and wipe my hands.

"Where's Sam?"

"She went to lie down, I think," Coop says. "Are you okay?"

I offer a smile stretched as tight as a rubber band on the cusp of snapping apart. "I'm fine."

"You don't look fine."

"Really, I am."

"I'm sorry we don't know more about who killed Lisa yet. I know this is hard to deal with."

"It is," I say. "But I'll be fine."

The mounds of Coop's shoulders droop, deflating, as if I've also punched the extra air out of him. I grab a handful of flour and sprinkle it across the countertop. Then I slap the dough onto it, sending up tiny puffs of white. Rolling pin in hand, I flatten the dough in long, hard strokes. The muscles in my arms tighten with each push.

"Will you put that down and talk to me, Quincy?"

"There's nothing to talk about," I say. "Hopefully, they'll somehow catch whoever did this to Lisa and everything will go back to normal. Until then, I trust you'll do your best to keep me safe."

"That's my plan."

Coop chucks my chin, just like my father used to do. It was a common gesture when we baked together and I invariably messed something up. Spilling a tide of flour over the rim of a bowl or cracking an egg so poorly that fine bits of shell swam in the yolk. I'd get upset and he'd squeeze my chin between his thumb and forefinger, lifting it and thereby steadying me. Even though it's now Coop doing the steadying, the effect is the same.

"Thank you," I tell him. "Truly. I know I can be a handful. Especially on a day like today."

Coop starts to say something. I hear the pop of tongue on teeth as he opens his mouth, the word just starting to form. But then the front door opens and Jeff's voice fills the apartment.

"Quinn? You here?"

"In the kitchen."

Although Jeff is surprised by Coop's presence, he does a good job of hiding it. I notice only a slight double-take. It lasts barely a second before he comprehends the situation and realizes Coop is here for the same reason he's come home in the middle of the afternoon with a box of wine and two bags of takeout from my favorite Thai place.

"I left work as soon as I heard the news," he says as he deposits them in the fridge. "I tried to call but your phone went straight to voicemail."

That's because my phone has been turned off the whole time I've been home. By now the texts, emails, and missed calls are probably stacked so high I'll never be able to sort through them.

His hands now free, Jeff pulls me into a hug. "How are you doing?"

"She's fine," Coop says dryly.

Jeff nods at him—the first overt acknowledgment that he's even in the room. He turns to me. "Are you?"

"Of course not," I say. "I'm shocked and sad and angry."

"Poor Lisa. They know who did it, right?"

I shake my head. "They don't know who or why. All they know is how."

Jeff, refusing to let me go, turns to Coop again. My head remains against his chest, turning involuntarily with him. "I'm glad you were here with them, Franklin. I'm sure it was a big comfort to Quinn and Sam."

"I only wish I could do more," Coop says.

"You've already done so much," Jeff says. "Quinn is lucky to have you in her life."

"And you," I tell Jeff. "I'm so lucky to have you."

I press myself deeper into Jeff's chest, his tie slick on my cheek. He mistakes it for distress, which I suppose it is, and holds me tighter. I let myself be held, turning inward, Jeff's body edging across my field of vision, eclipsing the image of Coop staring at me from across the kitchen.

Later, Jeff and I watch another film noir in bed. *Leave Her to Heaven*, with Gene Tierney as an obsessive, murderous bride. So beautiful. So damaged. When the movie is over, we watch the eleven o'clock news until a story about Jeff's case comes on. The police union held a press conference with the dead cop's widow, urging stiffer penalties for those convicted of crimes against officers. Before Jeff can grab the remote and switch off the TV, I get a split-second glance of the widow's face. It's pale, deeply creased, smudged with sorrow.

"I wanted to see that," I say.

"I thought you'd want a break from bad news."

"I'm fine," I say.

"Just like Sam's fine. And Coop's fine."

Coop had left minutes after Jeff arrived, mumbling excuses about the long drive back to Pennsylvania. A clearly subdued Sam spent most of dinner trying to avoid the need to speak. And I remained mad, despite the Xanax and the baking and probably half the box of wine. I still am, hours later. It's an irrational, all-encompassing anger. I'm mad at everything and nothing. I'm mad at life.

"I know this is hard on you."

"You have no idea," I say.

That's more than anger talking. It's the stone-cold truth. Jeff doesn't know what it's like to have one of only two people just like you snatched from this earth. He doesn't know how sad and scary and confusing that feels.

"I'm sorry," he says. "You're right. I don't. I never will. But I do understand that you're angry."

"I'm not," I lie.

"You are." Jeff pauses. I tense up, knowing he's about to say something I don't want to hear. "And since you're already mad, I might as well tell you that I have to go back to Chicago again."

"When?"

"Saturday."

"But you were just there."

"The timing sucks, I know," Jeff says. "But a new character witness has come forward."

I look at the television's blank screen, still picturing the face of that cop's widow.

"Oh," I say.

"The guy's cousin," Jeff continues, even though I have no desire to hear about his client's character. "He's a pastor. The two of them grew up together. Got baptized together. It could really help his defense."

I flip onto my side and face the wall. "He killed a cop."

"Allegedly," Jeff says.

I think about Coop. What if he had been gunned down by this guy? Or what if Jeff's client had murdered Lisa? Would I still have to pretend to be happy that some niceties from a preacher cousin could reduce his sentence? No, I wouldn't. Yet Jeff seems to expect exactly that.

"You do know that, in all likelihood, he's guilty, right?" I say. "That he shot that detective just like everyone says he did."

"That's not for me to decide."

"Isn't it?"

"Of course not," Jeff says, matching me in testiness. "It doesn't matter what he's been accused of. He deserves as good a defense as anyone else."

"But do you think he did it?"

I sit up slightly, peering over my shoulder at Jeff. He's still on his back, hands behind his head, staring at the ceiling. He blinks once, and I can see the truth in that swift flutter of his eyelids. He knows his client is guilty.

"It's not like I'm some expensive criminal defense attorney," he says, as if that makes it slightly better. "I'm not getting rich from defending obvious murderers. I'm upholding a cornerstone of the American justice system. Everyone has the right to a fair trial."

"What if you were assigned to defend someone really bad?" I say as I flop back onto my side, unable to look at him.

"I'd have no choice."

But he would. If his client were Stephen Leibman, he of the swinging knife, or Sack Man Calvin Whitmer, he'd have that choice to say no, that men like them don't deserve defending.

Yet I know deep down Jeff wouldn't make that choice. He'd choose to be on their side. To defend them. To help them.

Even Him.

"There's always a choice," I say.

Jeff says nothing. He simply stares at the ceiling until his eyes grow heavy and eventually close. Minutes later, he's asleep.

For me, sleep is an impossibility. I'm still too angry. So I thrash under the covers in search of a comfortable position. If I'm being completely honest, there's a part of me that's doing it just to wake up Jeff. To make him as sleepless as I am. But he doesn't wake as the clock moves from eleven to midnight, then midnight to one.

At quarter past the hour, I crawl out of bed, slip on some dirty clothes, and tiptoe into the hallway. Light still peeks from under Sam's door, so I knock.

"Come on in, Quinn," she says.

I find her sitting cross-legged on the bed, reading an Asimov paperback bent at the spine. She's changed her clothes, returning to the black jeans and Sex Pistols T-shirt of yesterday. Her leather jacket has been added to the ensemble. When she looks up at me, I assume she can sense my anger. She certainly knows why I'm there.

Sam wordlessly leaves the bed and roots through her knapsack, removing a purse, of all things. It's a pleather monstrosity with short handles that can only be slipped to the elbows. Next out of the knapsack is a pile of paperback books, which Sam stuffs into the purse.

"Here," she says, snapping it at me like a football.

I catch it, surprised by its heft. "What's it for?"

"Bait."

I say nothing. I simply follow Sam out of the room, the purse's handles gripped in my sweaty palm as we slip out into the night.

18.

Outside, unseasonable warmth clings to the clear air, raw and oppressive. The heat of the day seeping into night. By the time we reach the park, I've broken into a sweat, my face slick and shining.

Inside the park, it's so hot that most of the men we see have discarded their hoodies, content to prowl the park in sticky-tight T-shirts. We nod to some of them when we pass, as if we're one of them, cruising the night for supple flesh.

In a way, we are.

There's no mist in the park this time. The night is almost brittle in its clarity. Blades of grass catch the moonlight, glowing white, looking like sharpened teeth. In the trees, leaves droop from their branches like recently hanged men.

We choose a bench not far from the one we sat on last night. I can see it just across the way, a triangle of streetlight thrown over its seat. I picture me sitting there twenty-four hours earlier, nervously wanting nothing more than to go home. Now I scan the night-shrouded corners of the park. Every shadow seems to tremble with untold danger. I'm ready for it. Eager.

"See anything?" I say.

"Nope," Sam says.

She pulls the pack of cigarettes from her pocket and taps one out. I hold out my hand.

"Give me one."

"Seriously?"

"I used to smoke," I say, when in truth it was only once and only after being goaded into it by Janelle. One puff made me cough so violently that she had to take it from me, fearful of inflicting more damage. Tonight, I do better, taking two tiny half puffs before the first cough erupts.

"Amateur," Sam says, inhaling deep and blowing smoke rings.

"Show-off," I say.

I merely hold my cigarette while she smokes the remainder of hers, always on the lookout, our eyes never leaving the dark horizon of the park.

"How are you feeling?" Sam asks. "About Lisa."

"Mad."

"Good."

"What happened to her is so wrong. I think it was easier—"

I can't say the rest of what I'm thinking. That it was easier to deal with when we thought Lisa had killed herself. It's not something you want to articulate, even if it's true.

"Do you really think someone's out to get us?" Sam says.

"It's a possibility," I say. "We're famous, in our way."

Rather, we're infamous. Notable for going through unthinkable situations with our lives intact. And some people—like the sicko who drove to Quincy, Illinois, to send me that letter—might see it as a challenge. To finish off what others couldn't complete.

Sam sucks in the last dregs of smoke from her cigarette. She then puffs it out, talking as she does it. "Were you ever going to tell me about that email from Lisa?"

"I don't know," I say. "I wanted to."

"Why didn't you?"

"Because I didn't know what it meant."

"Now it means we might be in danger," Sam says.

Yet here we are, sitting in Central Park at an ungodly hour, just asking for trouble. Hoping for it, in fact. But I see nothing in the clear night. Only our streetlamp-enabled shadows stretching across the path in front of us, dotted with the smoldering butts of our two cigarettes.

"What happens if we don't see anyone?" I say.

Sam jerks her head toward the purse still looped over my forearm. "That's why we brought that."

"When can we use it?"

She lifts one drawn-on brow and smiles in spite of herself. "Now, if you want."

Quickly, we form a plan. Because I'm smaller and therefore an easier target, I'll stroll through the park alone, the purse a tease dangling from my arm. Sam will follow at a discreet distance, staying off the path, where it's less likely she'll be noticed. If and when someone strikes, we'll be ready to strike back.

It's a solid plan. Only mildly reckless.

"I'm ready," I say.

Sam points the way down the tree-shrouded path. "Go get 'em, tiger."

At first, I walk too fast, the purse swinging as I tear down the path in a hurried gait that would give even the most experienced muggers second thoughts. I move so quickly that Sam has trouble keeping up. Looking over my shoulder, I glimpse her far in the distance, skirting around trees and hurrying over the grass.

After that, I slow down, reminding myself the aim is to look vulnerable and easy to catch. Also, I don't want Sam to fall so far behind that she can't rescue me if the need arises. Eventually I settle into a nice, even pace and head south along the path that hugs the shore of Central Park Lake. I see no one. I hear nothing but the occasional car on Central Park West and the scuffing of my soles against the ground. To my right is a sliver of empty park, bordered by high stone walls. On my left sits the lake, its placid surface reflecting a smattering of lights from buildings along the Upper West Side.

I've lost track of Sam, who's still somewhere behind me, creeping through the darkness. I am alone, which doesn't unnerve me as much as it should. I've been alone in the woods before. In situations more dangerous than this.

It takes me fifteen minutes to make a loop back to my starting point. I stand right where I began, my skin slimy with perspiration and two damp patches under my arms. Now is a rational time to find Sam and head back to the apartment, to bed, to Jeff.

But I'm not feeling rational. Not after the day I've had. A hollow ache has formed like hunger in my gut. My single pass through the park isn't enough to make it go away. So I set off on a second one, again walking beside the lake. This time, fewer lights reflect off the water's surface. The city around me is winking to sleep one window at a time. When I reach Bow Bridge at the lake's southern end, everything is darker. The night has swept me into its arms, wrapping me in shadows.

With that dark embrace comes something else. A man. Drifting through the park on a separate path fifty yards to my right. Immediately, I can tell he's not one of the prowling men looking for sex. His walk is different, less confident. Head down and hands thrust into the pockets of his black jacket, his progress is more amble than walk. He's trying hard to look inconspicuous and nonthreatening.

Yet he's watching me. I notice how his Yankees cap keeps turning my way.

I slow down, taking half-steps, making sure he'll be in front of me when our paths connect roughly twenty yards ahead. I long to check behind me and see if Sam has caught up, but I can't. That might tip him off. A risk I need to avoid.

The man whistles as he walks. The nondescript trill cuts through the silence of the park, high-pitched and airy. I get the feeling he's trying to put me at ease. An attempt, innocent or not, to get me to let down my guard.

Up ahead is the spot where our paths meet. I stop and mime rooting through the purse, making sure he notices. He has to. The purse is too big to miss. Yet he pretends not to see it, continuing his exaggerated stroll until he's on the same path, just ahead of me. He keeps up the whistling, trying not to scare me, trying to get me moving again. The Pied Piper.

I start walking. One, two, three steps.

The whistling stops.

He does too.

Suddenly he's whirling around to face me. His pupils ping-pong around his sockets, crazed and dark. The eyes of an addict in need of a fix. On the surface, though, he's hardly threatening. Gaunt cheeks. Body as thin as a broom handle. He's practically the same height as me, maybe even shorter. The jacket gives him some girth, but it's all show. He's a featherweight.

The hardness of his face is amplified by the sweat slicking his high forehead and razor-blade cheeks. His skin is as taut as a drum. He practically vibrates with hunger and desperation.

When he speaks, his voice is a sluggish mumble. "I don't wanna bother you, okay? But I need some money. For food, you know?"

I say nothing. Stalling. Giving Sam enough time to get closer. If she's even there.

"You hear what I'm sayin', mama?"

The silence continues on my end. I leave everything up to him. He can leave. He can stay. If he does and causes trouble, Sam will certainly strike.

Maybe.

"I'm real hungry," the man says, gaze flicking to my purse. "You got food in there? Some cash you can give?"

I look behind me at last, seeking out Sam's approaching shadow.

She's not there.

No one is.

It's just me and the man and a purse that'll make him really pissed if he looks inside and sees it's stuffed with nothing but paperbacks. I should be scared. I should have been scared this entire time. But I'm not. Instead, I feel the opposite of fear.

I feel radiant.

"No," I say. "I don't."

I stare at him, monitoring his movements, waiting to see the flex of an arm or the curl of a fist. Anything to suggest he's thinking of doing harm.

"You sure you got nothin' at all in there?" he says.

"Are you threatening me?"

The man raises his hands, takes a step back. "Whoa, mama. I ain't doin' nothin'."

"You're bothering me," I say. "That's something."

I turn, start to walk away, the purse dangling limply from my hands. The man lets me go. He's too strung out to put up a fight. All he can muster is a parting insult.

"You're one cold bitch."

"What did you just say?"

I spin around and stride toward him, pushing close enough to smell his breath. It stinks of cheap wine, stale smoke, and rotting gums.

"You think you're tough shit, don't you?" I say. "Bet you thought I'd quake at the sight of you and hand over whatever you wanted."

I give him a shove that sends him rocking back on his heels. His arms pinwheel as he tries to maintain balance. One of his hands knocks against my face, so light I hardly feel it.

"You just fucking hit me."

The man's face goes slack with shock. "I didn't mean—"

I interrupt him with another shove. Then another. When the man crosses his arms, blocking a fourth push, I drop the purse and start to swat at his arms and shoulders.

"Hey, stop it!"

He ducks away from my blows, dropping to his knees. Something tumbles from his jacket and plops onto the path. It's a pocketknife, folded shut. My heart seizes at the sight of it.

The man reaches for the knife. I slam into him, hip against his shoulder, nudging him away from it. When he stands, I start slapping at him again, swinging wildly, hitting his chest, his shoulders, his chin.

The man lunges forward, pushing back now. I fight him off, still swatting, kicking at his shins.

"Stop!" he yelps. "I didn't do nothin'!"

He grabs a fistful of my hair and yanks. The pain tugs me into stillness. My eyes close against their will, lids dropping. Something flickers in the sudden darkness. Not a pain, exactly. A memory of it. Similar yet foreign to the one I feel now as the man pulls me backward.

The memory pain explodes like fireworks across the backs of my eyelids. Bright and burning hot. I'm outside. Near the trees. Pine Cottage vague in my muffled vision. Someone else has grabbed my hair and is pulling me back while people are screaming.

My fingers wrap around the man's jacket collar, dragging him to the ground with me. We hit the ground hard, me on my back, him on my chest, both of us puffing out shocked breaths. When he goes for my hair again, I'm ready. I roll my head along the ground, evading his tug. Then I tilt forward, slamming my head against his own. My forehead connects with his nose, the cartilage bending.

The man cries out and rolls off me, a hand to his blood-gushing nose. He rises to his knees. His fingers are stained red.

Real pain and the memory pain spark through me like live wires on a car battery, jump-starting my muscles. It cracks the brittle shell around my memory. Tiny flecks of it fall away, beneath which are shimmering glimpses of the past.

Him.

In a similar crouch on the floor of Pine Cottage.

A bloody knife within His grasp.

Although I'm vaguely aware this is a different place in a different time, I see only Him. So I dive on top of Him, curled fists smashing against His face. I punch Him a second time. A third.

Rage takes over. Like a black ooze that's filling me up, spilling out of my pores, covering my eyes. I can no longer see. Or hear. Or smell. The only remaining sense is touch, and all I feel is pain in my fists as they smash into His face. When it becomes too much to bear, I rise to my feet, directing a kick at His skull.

Then another.

And another.

Each blow comes with a name, bubbling forth against my will. I spit them out as if they're poison, spewing them onto Him, covering Him.

"Janelle. Craig. Amy. Rodney. Betz."

"Quincy!"

That's not my voice. It's Sam's. Suddenly, she's right behind me, crushing me under her arms, dragging me away.

"Stop," she says. "For God's sake, stop."

I spend a few seconds fighting Sam's grip, thrashing and snarling. A feral dog trapped by a leash. I only ease up once I see the blood. It's a smear on Sam's hand, slick and dark. Seeing it makes me think I've hurt her. The very thought saps the rage out of me.

"Sam," I gasp. "You're bleeding."

I'm wrong. I realize that when I glimpse my own hands, seeing them soaked with blood. The same blood that got on Sam. The same blood that trickles down my arms, stains my clothes, splatters my face and neck in hot dollops.

Some of it is mine.

Most of it is not.

"Sam? What happened? Where were you?"

Instead of answering, she releases me, knowing I'm not going anywhere. In a flash, she's beside the man in the grass. He lies on his side, an arm flung out behind him and the other curled inward.

I can't look at his face but can't help but look at his face. What's left of it. His eyes are swollen shut. His broken nose seeps blood darker than the rest of his blood. He doesn't move. Sam pushes two fingers into the slick of blood at his neck, seeking a pulse. Worry creases her face.

"Sam?" I say as dizziness and fear and shock somersault through me. "He's still alive, right?"

My vision blurs, Sam and the maybe-dead man veering in and out of focus.

"Right?"

Sam says nothing. Not when she runs her jacket sleeve across the spot she touched on the man's neck, erasing the indentation left by her fingers. Not when she snaps up the knife lying in the grass and drops it into her pocket. Not even when she drags me from the scene, unable to look at me as I wail, "What did I do, Sam? *What did I do?*"

19.

We move quickly, a pair of fugitives hurtling through the darkness. Sam's thrown her jacket over my shoulders, her hand pressing the small of my back, pushing me forward. I keep going because I have to. Because Sam won't let me stop, even though all I want to do is collapse onto the ground and stay there.

Breathing has become a chore. Each inhalation is hampered by an anxious shudder. Each exhalation is accompanied by a sob. My chest expands from the lack of oxygen, my desperate lungs pushing themselves against my ribs.

"Stop," I gasp. "Please. Let me stop."

Sam increases the pressure at my back, forcing me onward. Past trees. Past statues. Past bums stretched across benches. When we come upon others—a man on a bike, three friends drunkenly walking arm in arm—she turns inward, shielding my blood-soaked body from view.

We stop only when we reach the Conservatory Water, that elaborate pool where in the daytime kids watch their toy sailboats traverse the shallow water. I'm guided to the pool's edge, lowered to my knees, hands plunged into the water. Sam cleans me off as much as possible, splashing water onto my arms, my neck, my face. On the other side of the pool, a homeless man is doing the same thing to himself. When he stares at us, Sam yells, her voice skipping over the water.

"What the fuck are you looking at?"

The man backs away, grabbing his fistfuls of trash bags and disappearing in the darkness.

Sam dips a hand in the water, scooping liquid onto my forehead.

"Listen," she says. "I think he's still alive."

I want to believe her, but I can't let myself.

"No," I murmur. "I killed him."

"I felt a pulse."

"Are you sure?"

"Yeah," Sam says. "I'm sure."

Relief pours over me, more cleansing than the water she continues to splash onto my bloodstained skin. I can breathe easier. My throat opens up, releasing another sob, this one grateful.

"We need to call for help," I say.

Sam lowers my hands into the water again, rubbing them beneath her own, erasing the evidence of my sin. "We can't do that, Quinn."

"But he needs to get to a hospital."

I try to pull my hands from the water but Sam holds them under.

"Calling 911 will get the police involved."

"So?" I say. "I'll tell them I was acting in self-defense."

"And were you?"

"He had a knife."

"Was he going to use it?"

I can't answer that. Maybe he would have, eventually. Or maybe he would have walked away. I'll never know.

"He still had it," I say, unsure of who I'm trying to convince, Sam or myself. "The police wouldn't charge me if they knew that."

Sam finally lifts my hands from the water, turning them over to see if any blood remains. It's all gone. My palms are pale and glistening.

"They would if they knew our reason for being out here," she says. "If they knew we were trying to lure someone. Especially if they found out you could have gotten away."

The only way she could know this is if she had been there. Hiding. Watching me the whole time. Watching even as the man's knife dropped from his pocket. For a moment, that particular truth eclipses everything else.

"You saw me?"

"Yeah."

"You were *there*?"

I start to hyperventilate again, my body wracked by a series of lung-scraping gasps. The sudden lack of air makes me woozy. Or maybe that's just from shock. Either way, I have to steady myself against the pool's edge to keep from tilting over. When I speak, it's in sharp, ragged bursts. "Why—didn't you—help?"

"You didn't need help."

"He had a *knife*," I say, a warm slick of anger rising in my throat. It feels like a swallow of Wild Turkey moving in reverse, inching its way higher. "You just sat back and fucking watched?"

"I wanted to see what you would do."

"And I almost killed a man. Happy? Was that the reaction you were looking for? Why didn't you try to stop me?"

"The question you should be asking is why you didn't try to stop yourself."

I manage to stand, shaking water from my hands before striding off. Away from the pool. Away from Sam.

"Quinn," she yells to my back. "Don't go."

"I'm going!"

"Where?"

"To the police."

"They're going to arrest you."

It's the way she says it that stops me. Her voice is flat, the words alarmingly matter-of-fact. She's right, and I know it. Panic boils in the depths of my stomach. I'm the moth that got careless with the flame. Now I'm engulfed.

"Knife or not, the cops aren't going to understand," Sam says. "They'll only see you as a vindictive bitch who came here looking for trouble. You'll be arrested for aggravated assault. Maybe worse. The kind of charges your boy, Jeff, won't be able to talk the cops into dropping."

I think of Jeff, mere blocks away, oblivious in his slumber. This could ruin him. He has nothing to do with it, but no one would care. My guilt is enough to destroy us both.

The dizziness returns, bringing with it a harsh tremble that paralyzes my legs. I sway, unsure how much longer I can remain upright. Sam keeps talking, only making it worse.

"You'll be in the papers again, Quinn. Not just one, but all of them."

Oh, I'm sure of that. I picture the headlines: FINAL GIRL SNAPS, GOES INTO VIOLENT RAGE. Jonah Thompson will have an orgasm over it.

"There's no recovering from that," Sam says. "If you go to the cops, life as you know it will be over."

The words are ugly in her mouth, even though she's only telling the truth. Yet I hate her all the same. Hate her for showing up, barging into my life, bringing me into this park. Mixed with that hate is another, more unwieldy emotion.

Despair.

It bubbles inside me, making me sweat and cry and feel so helpless that I long to plunge into the pool's water and never resurface.

"What are we going to do?" I say, hopelessness splitting my voice.

"Nothing," Sam says.

"So we just leave the park and pretend it never happened?"

"Pretty much."

She picks up her jacket, which I had shrugged off at the water's edge. She puts it around my shoulders again, nudging me forward. Our pace is slower this time, both of us keeping watch for signs of police. We take a different route out of the park.

Few people see us on our way from Central Park West to my building. Those who do probably write us off as two drunk girls stumbling home. My dizzy swaying helps sell the charade.

Once home, I fill the tub in the guest bathroom and peel off my clothes. The amount of blood on them is gut-churning. It's not as bad as the white-dress-turned-red at Pine Cottage, but close. Bad enough that I start sobbing again as I lower myself into the tub. Tendrils of pink form in the water, swirling slightly before vanishing into nothingness. I close my eyes and tell myself everything about tonight will disappear in the same manner. A flash of color quickly gone. The man in the park will live. Because he was carrying a knife, he won't mention what I did to him. Everything will be forgotten in a few days, weeks, months.

I examine my knuckles and see that they've turned a ghastly bright pink. Pain pulses through them. A similar ache throbs in the foot I had used to kick the man into unconsciousness.

More sensations from earlier in the night come back to me. The pulling of my hair. Seeing Him crouched on the floor, bloody knife within his grasp.

Memories.

Not of tonight but of ten years ago.

Of Pine Cottage.

Of things I thought I had forgotten.

I tell myself that they can't be. That almost everything bad about that night has been sliced from my mind. But I know I'm wrong.

I had remembered something.

Rather than sit up, I hunch down farther in the tub, hoping the hot water will wash it all away. I don't want to remember what happened at Pine Cottage. That's the reason I've mentally cut it out of my brain, right? Because it was all too horrible to keep in my head.

Yet like it or not, there's no denying something has come back to me tonight. Nothing major. Just a brief flash of memory. Like a faded photograph. But it's enough to make me shiver even while neck-deep in the steaming tub.

There's a quick knock at the door. A warning from Sam that she's about to enter. She manages one step before being stopped cold by my bloody clothes on the tiled floor. Wordlessly, she scoops them up.

"What are you going to do with them?" I ask.

"Don't worry about it. I know what to do," she says before carrying them out of the bathroom.

Yet I am worried. About the memories that have suddenly scurried back into my consciousness. About the man in the park. About why Sam stayed back and watched as I beat him senseless, as if it were simply another one of her unspoken tests.

Suddenly, I'm struck with a thought. A question, really, made hazy and distant by the steam rising off the water and my own exhaustion.

How does Sam know what to do with my bloody clothes?

And another: Why was she so calm as we fled the scene of my crime?

Now that I think about it, she was more than calm. She was utterly thorough in the way she whisked me from the scene, making sure to shield me and the blood from onlookers, finding a water source in which I could be cleansed.

No one could be that efficient in such a situation. Not unless they had done it before.

Those thoughts are quickly followed by another one. Not a question this time. A certainty, screaming into my brain so fast and loud that I bolt upright in the tub, water sloshing over the sides.

The purse.

We left it behind in the park.

20.

"Don't worry about it, babe."

That's what Sam tells me after I inform her about the missing purse.

"I already know that. If it was important, I would have taken it with us."

We're in her room, she smoking by the window, me nervously perched on the edge of the bed.

"And you're positive there's nothing incriminating in it?" I ask.

"Positive," Sam says. "Now, get some sleep."

There's so much more I should be asking. What did she do with my bloody clothes? Why did she let me snap like that in the park? Was I so violent and unhinged that it summoned that brief glimpse of Him at Pine Cottage? All remains unsaid. Even if I asked, I know Sam wouldn't answer me.

So I leave, heading to the kitchen for a Xanax and grape-soda chaser before lying down on the sofa, ready for another sleepless night. To my surprise, I do manage to drift off. I'm too exhausted to fight it.

Yet my slumber is brief, interrupted by a nightmare of Lisa, of all people. She's standing in the middle of Pine Cottage, blood gushing from her slit wrists. In her hands is Sam's purse, getting splashed with gore. She holds it out to me, smiling, saying, *You forgot this, Quincy.*

I awake with a start, sitting up on the sofa, limbs flailing. Although the entire apartment is silent, I sense the reverberations of an echo in the living room. A scream, probably, bursting from my mouth.

A minute passes in which I wait for someone to inevitably wake up. Surely Jeff and Sam heard it. Or maybe I didn't scream after all. Maybe it was just in the dream.

Outside the window, the night sky is quickly thinning. Dawn's on its way. I know I should try to get more sleep, that I'll collapse soon without it. But my nerves are a sparking jumble. The only way to calm them is to go back to the park and see if the purse is still there.

So I tiptoe into the bedroom, relieved to find Jeff fully asleep, snoring lightly. Quickly, I wrap myself in running clothes. I then slip fingerless gloves onto my hands to hide the abrasions that roll over my knuckles, already beginning to scab.

Once outside, I cross the blocks to the park at a dead sprint. I blast over Central Park West, crossing against the light, making an approaching cab slam on its brakes to avoid hitting me. The driver honks. I ignore him. In fact, I ignore everything as I fly to the spot where the purse had been knocked from my hands. The same spot where I had beaten a man so much his face resembled a rotting apple.

But now that man is gone. So is the purse. They've been replaced by police—a dozen officers milling around a wide square of yellow police tape. It looks like a murder scene. The kind you see on cop shows. Officers search the taped-off area, conferring with one another, sipping coffee from steaming paper cups.

I hang back, jogging in place. Despite the hour, several other onlookers are also there, standing in the blue-gray dawn.

"What happened?" I ask one of them, an older woman with an equally geriatric-looking dog.

"Guy got attacked. Beat real bad."

"That's awful," I say, hoping I sound appropriately sincere. "Will he be okay?"

"One of those cops says he's in a *coma*." She practically whispers the word, putting a scandalous spin on it. "City's full of sickos."

Inside, I feel a thorn bush of emotions, tangled and jagged. There's joy that the man is still alive, that I haven't killed him after all. Relief that his coma means he can't talk to the police just yet. Guilt for being so relieved.

And worry. That, above all else. Worry about the purse, which could have been found by the police. Or stolen. Or dragged into the thicket by the coyotes that sometimes, inexplicably, find their way to the park. It doesn't matter what happened to it. As long as it remains out of our possession, that purse has the potential to tie me to the beating. My fingerprints are all over it.

Which is why I come home with my mouth set in a grim scowl. Jeff is awake when I slip through the front door, standing in the kitchen in a T-shirt and boxers.

"Quincy? Where have you been?"

"I went for a jog," I say.

"At this hour? The sun's not even up."

"I couldn't sleep."

Jeff peers at me through puffy eyes, the lingering fog of sleep hovering around him. He scratches his head. He scratches his crotch. He says, "Is everything okay? This isn't like you, Quinn."

"I'm fine," I say, clearly not. My body feels hollow, as if my insides have been scraped out by the ice-cream scoop I use to drop batter into muffin tins. "Just fine."

"Is this about last night?"

I freeze in front of him, wondering what, if anything, he heard last night. That I'm keeping a secret from him at all makes me quiver with guilt. That he could possibly know about it only makes it worse.

"Me having to go to Chicago," he says.

I exhale. Slowly, so as not to arouse suspicion.

"Of course not."

"You seemed pretty annoyed about it. Believe me, I am. I don't love the idea of leaving you alone with Sam."

"We'll be fine," I say.

Jeff squints slightly, frowning just-so. The perfect picture of concern. "Are you sure everything is okay?"

"Yes," I say. "Why do you keep asking me that?"

"Because you were out jogging before six," Jeff says. "And because you just found out that Lisa Milner was murdered and that there are no suspects."

"Which is why I couldn't sleep. Which led to the jogging."

"But you'd tell me if something was wrong, right?"

I force a smile, trembling from the effort. "Of course."

Jeff pulls me into a hug. He's warm and soft and smells faintly of sweat and fabric softener from the sheets. I try to hug him back but can't. I'm undeserving of such affection.

Later, I make him breakfast while he gets ready for work. We eat in silence, me hiding my injured hand under a dish towel or on my lap while Jeff leafs through the *New York Times*. I take furtive peeks at each turning page, positive I'll see an article about the man in the park even though I know it's too early. My crime was past their deadline. That particular hell will have to wait until tomorrow's edition.

As soon as Jeff leaves, I pull the key from around my neck and open my secret kitchen drawer. The pen Sam stole in the café is there. I pick it up and scrawl a single word across my wrist.

SURVIVOR

Then I hop into the shower, forcing myself not to blink as I watch the water smear the ink away.

Sam and I don't talk.

We bake.

Our tasks are well defined. Apple tarte tatin with caramel sauce for me. Sugar cookies for Sam. Our workstations are laid out on separate ends of the kitchen, like opposing sides in a war sharing a common front. While I make the dough for the tarte, I keep checking my hands for signs of blood, certain I'll find lingering crimson stains across my palms. All I see is flesh turned puffy and pink from being washed too many times.

"I know you're having second thoughts," Sam says.

"I'm fine," I say.

"We did the right thing."

"Did we?"

"Yes."

I've started on the Honeycrisp apples, my hands trembling slightly. I stare at the red-yellow apple skins, which fall in long, drooping spirals. My hope is that if I concentrate on them hard enough Sam will stop talking. It doesn't work.

"Going to the police now won't make things right again," she says. "No matter how much you want it to."

It's not that I want to go to the police. I think I *have* to. I know from Jeff's work that it's always better for a criminal to come forward rather than get caught. Cops have at least a grudging respect for those who confess. So do judges.

"We should tell Coop," I say.

"Are you out of your goddamn mind?"

"He might be able to help us."

"He's still a cop," Sam says.

"He's my friend. He would understand."

At least I hope he would. He's said many times that he'd do anything to protect me. Is that the truth, or is there a limit to Coop's loyalty? After all, he made that promise to the Quincy he thinks he knows, not the one who actually exists. I'm not sure it would still apply to the Quincy who's already taken two Xanax since returning from the park this morning. Or the Quincy who steals shiny objects just so she can see her reflection in them. Or the Quincy who pummels a man until he's comatose.

"Let it drop, babe," Sam says. "We're good. We got away. It's over."

"And you're absolutely certain there was nothing in that purse that could lead to us?" I ask for what's probably the fiftieth time.

"I'm positive," Sam says. "Chill out."

Yet an hour later, my phone rings as I'm pulling the tarte tatin from the oven. I place the tarte on the counter, tear off an oven mitt, and grab the phone. Answering it brings a woman's voice to my ear.

"May I speak to Miss Quincy Carpenter?"

"This is Quincy."

"Miss Carpenter, I'm Detective Carmen Hernandez with the NYPD."

Fear freezes me—a sudden, numbing chill. How I manage to keep hold of the phone is a mystery. The fact I can still speak is a minor miracle.

"How can I help you, Detective?"

Hearing this, Sam whirls away from the counter, a large mixing bowl hugged to her stomach.

"I was wondering if you had time to come to the station today," Detective Hernandez says.

I only half listen to the rest of what she has to say. The deep freeze of fear has made its way to my ears, blocking out a good deal of it. Yet the key words are clear. Like blows of a pickax against the ice.

Central Park. Purse. Questions. Lots of questions.

"Of course," I say. "I'll be there as soon as I can."

Once I end the call, the frigid grip of fear subsides. Taking its place is the hot burn of despair. Trapped between cold and heat, I act accordingly, melting into a puddle on the kitchen floor.

TWO DAYS AFTER PINE COTTAGE

Their names are Detective Cole and Detective Freemont, although they might as well have been called Good Cop and Bad Cop. Each had a role to play, and they performed them well. Cole was the nice one. He was young—probably not yet thirty. Quincy liked his friendly eyes and the warm smile that sat beneath a wispy mustache grown in an attempt to make him look older. When he crossed his legs, Quincy saw that his socks matched the green of his tie. A nice touch.

Freemont was the gruff one. Short, stout, and balding, he had the jowls of a bulldog. They flopped slightly when he said, "We're confused by something."

"More curious than confused," Cole added.

Freemont shot him an annoyed look. "Things just don't add up, Miss Carpenter."

They were in Quincy's hospital room, she too sore to leave the bed. Instead, she was propped into a sitting position by several pillows. There was an IV needle in her arm, its low, perpetual sting distracting her from the detective's words.

"Things?" she said.

"We have questions," Cole said.

"A bunch of them," Freemont said.

"I've already told you everything I know."

That was the previous day, when Quincy had been so groggy with painkillers and grief that she wasn't sure what she had said. But she covered the basics. She was certain of that.

Yet Freemont glared at her, his eyes bloodshot and weary. His suit had seen better days, the cuffs frayed. A yellow splotch of dried mustard marred one of the lapels. A ghost of lunches past.

"That wasn't a whole lot," he said.

"I don't remember a lot."

"We're hoping that you might be able to remember more," Cole said. "Could you try? Just for me? I'd really appreciate it."

Leaning back into the pillows, Quincy closed her eyes, searching for something else she could remember from that night. But it was all a black stew, turbulent and dark.

She saw before: Janelle emerging from the woods. The flash of blade.

She saw after: Running through the forest, the branch whacking her face as rescue appeared on the horizon.

The in-between, however, was gone.

Still, she tried. Eyes and fists clenched, she swam through that mental stew, diving under, searching for the tiniest memory. She came up with only fragments. Glimpses of blood. Of the knife. Of His face. They didn't add up to anything substantial. They were lost puzzle pieces, giving no hint of the complete picture.

"I can't," Quincy finally said as she opened her eyes, shamed by the tears threatening to slide from them. "I'm sorry, but I really can't."

Detective Cole patted her arm, his palm surprisingly smooth. He was even more handsome than the cop who had saved her. The one with the blue eyes who immediately rushed to her side yesterday after she cried out that she wanted to see him.

"I understand," Cole said.

"I don't," said Freemont, the folding chair beneath him creaking as he shifted his weight. "Did you really forget everything that happened the other night? Or do you just want to forget it?"

"It's completely understandable that you do," Cole quickly added. "You suffered a great deal."

"But we need to know what happened," Freemont continued. "It doesn't make sense."

Confusion clouded Quincy's thoughts. A headache was coming on. A light, pulsing pain that exceeded the angry pinch of the IV needle in her arm.

"It doesn't?" she said.

"So many people died," Freemont said. "Everyone but you."

"Because that cop shot Him." Already she had decided to never speak His name. "I'm sure He would have killed me too if that cop—"

"Officer Cooper," Cole said.

"Yes." Quincy wasn't sure if she already knew that. Nothing about the name was familiar. "Officer Cooper. Did you ask him about what happened?"

"We did," Freemont said.

"And what did he say?"

"That he was instructed to search the woods for a patient reported missing from Blackthorn Psychiatric Hospital."

Quincy held her breath, waiting for him to speak that patient's name, dreading it. When he didn't, a warm rush of relief coursed through her.

"During the search, Officer Cooper heard a scream coming from the direction of the cabin. On his way to investigate, he spotted you in the woods."

Quincy pictured it, the moment superimposed over the image of the two detectives beside her bed. Officer Cooper's surprise when he noticed a flash of white fabric at her knees, realizing how her dress had been dyed red with blood. Her stumbling toward him, gurgling those words that continually echoed through her pill-stuffed brain.

They're dead. They're all dead. And he's still out here.

Then her latching onto him, pressing herself hard against him, smearing the blood—her blood, Janelle's blood, everyone's blood—all over the front of his uniform. They both heard a noise. A rustling in the brush several yards to their left.

Him.

Breaking through the branches, arms flapping, skinny legs churning. Coop drew his Glock. Aimed. Fired.

It took three shots to take Him down. Two in the chest, their impact making His arms flail even more, like a marionette in the act of being abandoned by his puppeteer. Yet He kept coming. His glasses had slipped off one ear, the frames slanted across His face, magnifying only one surprised eye as Coop fired the third shot into His forehead.

"And before that?" Freemont said. "What happened then?"

Quincy's headache expanded, filling her skull like a balloon about to pop. "I truly, honestly can't remember."

"But you have to," Freemont said, pissed off at her for something she had no control over.

"Why?"

"Because certain things about that night don't add up."

The headache kept growing. Quincy shut her eyes and winced. "What things?"

"To be blunt," Freemont said, "we can't understand why you lived when all the others died."

That's when Quincy finally heard it—the accusation hiding in his voice, peeking out suspiciously between his words.

"Can you tell us why?" he asked.

Just then, something inside of Quincy snapped. An angry shudder vibrated in her chest, followed by a surge of agitation. The balloon in her skull burst, tossing out words she never intended to say. Ones she regretted as soon as they took flight off her tongue.

"Maybe," she said, her voice like steel, "I'm just tougher than they were."

21.

Detective Hernandez is one of those women you can't help but admire even as you envy them. Everything about her is precisely put together, from the maroon blouse beneath a black blazer to the impeccably tailored slacks and boots with just a hint of a heel. Her hair is the color of dark chocolate, pulled back to display the perfect bone structure of her face. When she shakes my hand, it's both firm and friendly. She makes a point of pretending not to notice my battered knuckles.

"Thank you for coming on such short notice," she says. "I promise this will only take a few minutes."

I breathe. I try to keep calm. Just the way Sam instructed after she picked me up off the kitchen floor.

"I'm happy to help," I say.

Hernandez smiles. It doesn't appear strained. "Fantastic."

We're in the Central Park Precinct. The same place from which Jeff and I fetched Sam days earlier, although now it feels like years. The detective leads me up the same set of steps I climbed that long-ago, not-long-ago-at-all night. I'm then guided to her desk, which is free of clutter, save for a framed photograph of her, two kids, and a barrel-chested man I can only assume is her husband.

There's also a purse.

Placed on the center of the desk, it's the same purse Sam and I left in the park. Its presence isn't a surprise. We suspected it was the reason for the call and spent the walk to the precinct constructing an excuse as to why it—and we—were in the park last night. Yet my body freezes at the sight of it.

Hernandez notices.

"Do you recognize it?" she asks.

I have to clear my throat before answering, dislodging the words stuck there like an accidentally swallowed chicken bone.

"Yes. We lost it in the park last night."

I want to retract the words as soon as I say them, pulling them back into my mouth like a serpent's tongue.

"*We?*" Hernandez says. "You and Tina Stone?"

I take a deep breath. Of course she knows about Sam and her new name. The detective is as smart as she looks. That realization makes me feel weak. Exhausted, really. When she sits behind her desk, I drop into a chair next to it.

"Her real name is Samantha Boyd," I say meekly, nervous about correcting the detective. "She changed it to Tina Stone."

"After what happened to her at the Nightlight Inn?"

I take another deep breath. Detective Hernandez has certainly done her homework.

"Yes," I reply. "She went through a lot. We both have, but I'm sure you know all about that."

"It's a terrible thing that happened. To both of you. Crazy world, right?"

"It is."

Hernandez smiles again—this time in sympathy—before opening the purse and pulling out several battered paperbacks.

"We found the purse early this morning," she says, stacking books on the desk between us. "We traced it to Miss Stone after finding her name in one of these books. It came up in a quick scan of our records. Seems she was taken into custody a few nights ago. Assault on an officer and resisting arrest, I think it was."

"That was a misunderstanding." I clear my throat again. "I believe the charges were dropped."

"And so they were," Hernandez says as she inspects one of the books. Its cover bears a robot in the shape of a woman roaming a purple starscape. "You picked her up that night, correct?"

"I did. Me and my boyfriend, Jefferson Richards. He's with the Public Defender's Office."

His name clangs a bell in the detective's memory. She gives me another smile, this one painfully strained. "He's got quite a case on his hands, doesn't he?"

I swallow, relieved I didn't call Jeff and ask him to come to the station with me. I wanted to, of course, but Sam talked me out of it. She said bringing a lawyer, even one who was my boyfriend, would instantly arouse suspicion. Turns out it also would have brought him into contact with a detective none too pleased about him defending a man accused of killing a fellow cop.

"I don't know much about it," I say.

Hernandez nods before skipping back to the original subject. "Since we don't have a contact number for Miss Stone, I thought it wise to have a chat with you and see if you know of her whereabouts. Is she staying with you, perhaps?"

I could lie, but there'd be no point to it. I get the sense the detective already knows the answer.

"She is," I say.

"And where is she now?"

"Waiting outside, actually."

At least, I hope she is. Although Sam was calm when we left the apartment, I suspect it was purely for my sake. Now that she's alone, I picture her pacing outside, finishing up her third cigarette in a row while sneaking glances through the precinct's glass-walled entrance. It occurs to me that while I'm in here, Sam could easily just leave town, again leaping off the grid. Honestly, I'm not sure that would be a bad thing.

"I guess it's my lucky day," Detective Hernandez says. "Do you think she'd want to come in and answer some questions?"

"Sure." The word is high-pitched, akin to a squeak. "I suppose so."

The detective reaches for the phone, taps a few numbers, and informs the desk sergeant on duty that Sam can be found outside.

"Bring her in and have her wait outside my office," she says.

"Is Sam in some kind of trouble?" I ask.

"Not at all. An incident occurred in the park overnight. A man was severely beaten."

I keep my hands on my lap, the ugly, scabby right one covered by the less-ugly left. "That's terrible."

"A jogger found him this morning," Hernandez continues. "He was unconscious. A complete, bloody mess. God knows what would have happened if he hadn't been discovered in time."

"That's terrible," I say again.

"Since Miss Stone's purse was found near the scene, I was wondering if she saw anything last night. Or you, for that matter, since you were apparently with her."

"I was," I say.

"And what time was this?"

"About one. Maybe a little after."

Hernandez leans back in her chair, steepling her well-manicured fingers. "A bit late to be roaming the park, no?"

"It was," I say. "But we had been drinking. You know, girls' night out. And since I live near the park, we thought it would be quicker to cross it on foot instead of taking a cab."

It's the alibi Sam and I had concocted on the way here. I worried that I might not be able to tell it, yet the lie comes without hesitation, slipping from my mouth with such ease it surprises even me.

"And that's when Miss Stone—"

"Boyd," I say. "Her real name is Samantha Boyd."

"That's when Miss Boyd lost the purse?"

"It was taken, actually."

Hernandez arches a perfectly sculpted brow. "Taken?"

"We stopped at a park bench so Sam could have a smoke." A pebble of truth, tossed into the churning river of falsehood. "While we were there, a guy ran by, grabbed the purse, and took off. We didn't report it stolen because, as you can see, there's nothing valuable in it."

"Why was she carrying it in the first place?"

"Sam's a little paranoid about things," I say, furthering the lie. "I can't blame her, considering what happened to her. To us, really. She told me she carries the purse for protection."

A nod from Detective Hernandez. "Like a decoy?"

A nod from me. "Exactly. A mugger aims for the big stuff, like that purse, while neglecting the items of true value, such as her wallet."

Hernandez studies me from across the desk, parsing the information, taking time to respond. It looks as if she's counting the seconds, waiting until a suitably intimidating length of time has passed. Finally, she says, "Did you get a good look at the man who stole the purse?"

"Not really."

"Nothing at all?"

"It was dark," I say. "And he was wearing dark clothes. A puffy jacket, I think. I don't really know. It all happened so fast."

I lean back in my chair, relieved and, I'll admit, exceedingly proud of myself. I had given our false alibi without a hitch. It was so convincing that even *I* almost believe it. But then Hernandez reaches into a drawer, removes a photograph, slides it across the desk.

"Could this be the man you saw?"

It's a mug shot of a young punk of a man. Wild eyes. Neck tattoo. The papery skin of a junkie. The very same junkie whose nose collapsed beneath my forehead. Seeing his face makes my heart momentarily stop.

"Yes," I say with a gulp. "That's him."

"This is the same guy who was found almost beaten to death this morning," Hernandez says, although I already know this. "His name is Ricardo Ruiz. Rocky, for short. He's homeless. An addict. The usual sad story. Cops patrolling the park know him pretty well. They say he didn't seem like the type of guy to get into much trouble. Only wanted a place to sleep and his next fix."

I continue to stare at the photo. Knowing the man's name and what he's like makes my heart crack with guilt and remorse. I don't think about the fear I felt in the park. I don't think about the knife he carried and that Sam scooped up. All I can focus on is the fact that I hurt him. Badly. So bad that he might never recover.

"That's awful," I manage to mutter. "Will he be okay?"

"Doctors say it's too soon to tell. But someone sure did a number on him. You two didn't happen to see anything suspicious last night? Someone running away from something, maybe? Or anyone acting shady?"

"After the purse was taken, Sam and I left the park as fast as we could. We didn't see anything like that." I shrug, frowning for emphasis, showing her how much I long to help. "I'm sorry I can't tell you anything else."

"When I talk to Miss Stone—I mean, Miss Boyd—she'll tell me the same thing?"

"Of course," I say.

At least, I hope she will. After last night, I'm not sure Sam and I are on the same side.

"You two are close, I imagine," Hernandez says. "Going through similar ordeals. What's that name the papers call you?"

"Final Girls."

I say it angrily, with all the scorn I can muster. I want Detective Hernandez to know that I don't consider myself one of them. That I'm beyond that now, even if I no longer quite believe it myself.

"That's it." The detective senses my tone and wrinkles her nose in distaste. "I guess you don't like that label."

"Not at all," I say. "But I suppose it's better than being referred to as victims."

"What would you like to be called?"

"Survivors."

Hernandez leans back in her chair again, impressed. "And *are* you and Miss Boyd close?"

"We are," I say. "It's nice to be around someone who understands me."

"Of course it is." She sounds like she means it. There's sincerity there, I think. Yet her face is pinched just a fraction. "And you said she's staying with you?"

"For a few days, yes."

"So the fact that she's had prior brushes with the law doesn't bother you?"

I swallow. "Prior? As in, more than what happened the other night?"

"I guess Miss Boyd neglected to tell you about those," Hernandez says, consulting her notes. "I did a little digging into her recent history. Nothing big. Just the past five years or so. In addition to being picked up for assault two nights before Rocky's unfortunate accident, she had a drunk and disorderly arrest in New Hampshire four years ago, another one in Maine two years after that, and an unpaid speeding ticket following a traffic stop just last month in Indiana."

The world stops just then. A sudden, screeching halt that sends everything tilting. My hands slide off my lap and grip the underside of my chair, as if I might fall right out of it.

Sam was in Indiana.

Just last month.

I try to smile at Detective Hernandez, to show her I'm unflappable, that I know everything there is to know about Sam. In reality, my mind fills with memories, flipping like pages of a photo album. Each memory is a snapshot. Bright. Vivid. Full of detail.

I see Lisa's email on my phone, glowing ice-blue in the darkness.

Quincy, I need to talk to you. It's extremely important. Please, please don't ignore this.

I see Jonah Thompson gripping my arm, his features tight.

It's about Samantha Boyd. She's lying to you.

I hear Coop's low, concerned voice.

We don't know what she's capable of.

I see Sam in the park, covering my stained clothes with her jacket, steering me toward water, washing the blood from my hands. So swift and decisive. I see those same clothes being scooped into her arms, as if it were a normal occurrence.

Don't worry about it. I know what to do.

I see her swearing a path through the crush of reporters outside, unafraid of the cameras, completely unfazed when Jonah tells us that Lisa's been murdered. Her face is painted white by the flashbulbs, turned the same shade as a corpse on the slab. There's no expression there. No sadness or surprise.

Nothing.

"Miss Carpenter?" The detective's voice sounds faint among the shuffling memories. "You okay?"

"I'm fine," I say. "I know all about those. Sam has never lied to me."

She hasn't. At least there's nothing I can definitively pinpoint as a lie. But she hasn't exactly told me the truth either. Since her arrival, Sam hasn't told me much of anything.

I don't know where she's been.

I don't know who she was with.

Most of all, I have no idea what horrible things she might have done.

22.

The chill has returned to the park in full force, shocking in the same way water feels when you take that first plunge into a swimming pool. Change hangs in the air—a sense of time running out. Fall has officially arrived.

Because of the weather, everyone moves with manic energy. Joggers and cyclists and nannies pushing ridiculous double-wide strollers. It makes them look like they're fleeing something, even though they travel in all directions. Willy-nilly ants evading the foot about to crush their hill.

I, however, am stillness personified as I stand outside the precinct's tall glass window. Sam is inside, talking to Detective Hernandez, hopefully telling her the same things I did. And although I appear content to remain motionless, all I really want to do is run. Not toward home, but away from it. I long to run until I reach the George Washington Bridge, where I'll keep running. Through New Jersey. Through Pennsylvania and Ohio. Vanishing into the heartland.

Only then will I be away from the reality of what I'd done in the park. Away from the brief, confounding flashes of Pine Cottage that still cling to me like a sweat-soaked shirt. Most of all, I'd be away from Sam. I don't want to be here when she emerges from the police station. I'm afraid of what I'll see, as if one look will reveal the guilt on her face, as bright and glaring as her red lipstick.

But I stay, even though my legs tremble with pent-up energy. I want a Xanax so badly I can already taste the grape soda on my tongue.

I stay because I could be wrong about Sam.

I *want* to be wrong.

So she was in Indiana while Lisa was still alive. In all likelihood, their paths never came close to crossing. Indiana is a big state, after all, with more to it than just Muncie. Sam's presence there certainly doesn't mean she went to see Lisa. And it's definitely no reason to suggest Sam killed her. That I immediately jumped to that conclusion says more about me than it does her.

At least, that's what I try to tell myself as I huddle against the chill, my legs twitching, wondering what exactly Sam is saying deep inside the building behind me. She's been in there twenty minutes now—far longer than I. Worry nudges my sides, riling me up, making me want to run even more.

I yank my phone from my pocket and run the pad of my thumb across its screen. I think about calling Coop and confessing all my sins, even if it means he'll hate me. Short of running, it's the only logical course of action. Face my misdeeds. Let the chips fall.

But then Sam emerges through the precinct's glass doors, smiling like a kid who's just gotten away with something. The grin sets off a lightning bolt of fear in my heart. I'm afraid that Sam has told the truth about last night. Worse, I'm afraid she's now on to my suspicions. That she instinctively knows what's going through my mind. Already, she sees something off about my expression. Her grin flattens. She tilts her head, assessing me.

"Relax, babe," she says. "I stuck to the script."

She has the purse with her. It dangles from her forearm, giving her a disconcertingly dainty appearance. She tries to pass it to me, but I take a step back. I want nothing to do with it. Nor do I want anything to do with Sam. I keep an arm's length between us as we walk away from the police station. Even walking is a chore. My body still longs to sprint.

"Hey," she says, noticing the distance. "You don't have to be so tense now. I told Detective McBitch exactly what we discussed. Girls' night out. Drunk in the park. That dude stole the purse."

"He has a name," I say. "Ricardo Ruiz."

Sam hits me with a sidelong glance. "Oh, you're into saying names now?"

"I think I have to."

I feel compelled to start repeating it every day, like a Hail Mary, atoning for my sins. I would do it too, if I knew it would help.

"Just so we're clear," Sam says, "it's okay to say his name, but I'm not allowed to say—"

"*Don't.*"

The word emerges like the crack of a whip, sharp and stinging. Sam shakes her head. "Damn. You *are* tense."

I have every right to be. A man is in a coma because of me. Lisa was murdered. And Sam—Maybe? Possibly?—was there.

"Where were you before you came to New York?" I ask. "And don't tell me 'Here and there.' I need someplace specific."

Sam stays silent a moment. Just long enough for me to wonder if she's picking through several possible lies stored in her brain, deciding on the best one to use. Finally, she says, "Maine."

"Where in Maine?"

"Bangor. Happy now?"

I'm not. It tells me nothing.

We keep walking, heading south, deeper into the park. Red oaks line both sides of the path, their leaves barely clinging to the branches. Acorns have already started to drop, scattered in wide, unruly circles around the tree trunks. A few fall as we pass. Each one makes a tiny plunking noise when it hits the ground.

"How long were you there?" I ask Sam.

"I don't know. Years?"

"And did you go anywhere else during that time?"

Sam lifts her arms, the purse swinging, and assumes a haughty voice. "Oh, nowhere special. You know, just the Hamptons in the summer and the Riviera in winter. Monaco is simply gorgeous this time of year."

"I'm serious, Sam."

"And I'm seriously getting annoyed by all these questions."

I want to shake Sam so hard that the truth finally dislodges and plunks to the ground like the acorns dropping all around us. I want

her to tell me everything. Instead, I calm the emotional storm swirling inside me long enough to say, "I'm just making sure there are no
secrets between us."

"I've never lied to you, Quincy. Not once."

"But you haven't told me your full story," I say. "I just need to
know the truth."

"You really want the truth?"

Sam nods at the path just ahead of us. It's only then that I realize
how far we've walked, that Sam has used the distance I put between us
to her advantage, subtly steering us to the spot we had fled last night.

The cops have gone, taking their fluttering partition of police
tape with them. The only sign of their former presence is a wide swath
of grass that's been flattened against the ground. Tamped down, no
doubt, by officers searching for evidence. I study the grass, looking
for heel prints left by Detective Hernandez's boots.

A cluster of candles blocks the path where Rocky Ruiz was found.
They're tall, skinny glass ones with pictures of the Virgin Mary on
the sides, sold for a dollar in nearly every bodega in the city. There's
also a cheap teddy bear holding a heart, a hastily scrawled poster
board sign reading JUSTICE 4 ROCKY, and a helium balloon held in place
by a plastic weight tied to its string.

"Right there is the truth," Sam says. "You did that, babe, and I'm
covering for you. I could have told that detective everything, but I
didn't. That's all the truth you need to know."

She says nothing else. Nor does she need to. I understand loud and
clear.

Sam resumes walking, still pointed south, heading God knows
where. I stay where I am, guilt, fear, and exhaustion holding me in
place. I can't remember the last time I had a full night's sleep. It was
before Sam showed up, I know that much. Her arrival has whittled my
rest down to nothing. I don't see that changing anytime soon. I envi-
sion weeks of sleeplessness, my nights disrupted by dreams of Sam, of
Rocky Ruiz, of Lisa being held down while her wrists are slit.

"You coming?" Sam asks.

I shake my head.

"Suit yourself."

"Where are you going?"

"Here and there," Sam says, dripping sarcasm. "Don't wait up."

She heads off, glancing back at me only once. Although she hasn't gotten very far, I can't make out her expression. The same clouds that brought the chill have muted the afternoon sun, breaking its glow, splitting her face between light and shadow.

PINE COTTAGE
9:54 P.M.

Instead of sophisticated, as Janelle intended, the meal was muted and awkward—a pantomime of adult dining. Wine was poured. Food was passed. Everyone was too focused on not spilling something on their clothes, wishing to be free of their silly party dresses and stuffy neckties. Joe was the only one who looked remotely comfortable, snug in his worn sweater, oblivious to how much he stood out from the rest of them.

Things loosened up only after dinner, when Quincy brought out the cake, its twenty candles aflame. After blowing them out, Janelle used the same knife that had sliced her finger to cut the cake into haphazard pieces.

Then the real party began. The one they had delayed all day. Drinks were poured. Entire bottles of liquor were emptied into their dwindling supply of Solo cups. Music blasted from the iPod and portable speakers Craig brought along. Beyoncé. Rihanna. Timberlake. T.I. It was the same music they listened to in their dorm rooms, only now it was louder, wilder, finally unleashed.

They danced in the great room, Solo cups aloft, booze sloshing. Quincy didn't have any alcohol. She had picked her poison and it was Diet Coke. Yet it didn't inhibit her in the least. She danced right along with the others, twirling in the middle of the great room, surrounded by Craig and Betz and Rodney. Amy was beside her, bumping her hip, laughing.

Janelle joined the fray, lugging Quincy's camera, taking her picture. Quincy smiled, struck a pose, did a little disco move that threw

Janelle into a laughing fit. Quincy laughed too. As the music pulsed and she danced and the room swirled, she couldn't recall another time when she had felt this good, this free, this happy. Here she was, dancing with her catch of a boyfriend, reaching out to her best friend, the college life she had always imagined right here in front of her.

After a few more songs, they tired. Janelle refilled their cups. Amy and Betz sprawled across the great-room floor. Rodney produced a bong and waved it over his head like a flag. When he took it onto the deck, Janelle, Craig, and Amy surrounded him, lining up for hits.

Quincy didn't like pot. The one time she had tried it, it made her cough, laugh, then cough again. Afterward she felt wobbly and unmoored, which took away from whatever high she had experienced. While the others smoked, she stayed in the great room, sipping her Diet Coke, which she was pretty sure Janelle had splashed with rum when she wasn't looking. Betz, the perennial lightweight, was there too, drunk on the floor after three vodka-and-cranberries.

"Quincy," she said, cheap vodka stinging her breath, "you don't have to do it."

"Do what?"

"Fuck Craig." Betz giggled, as if it were the first time she'd ever sworn.

"Maybe I want to."

"*Janelle* wants you to," Betz said. "Mostly because she'd rather be the one doing it."

"You're drunk, Betz. And talking nonsense."

Betz was insistent. "I'm right. You know I'm right."

She let out another giggle, one that Quincy tried hard to ignore. Yet Betz's drunken laughter stuck with her as she went to the kitchen. There was knowledge in that laugh, hinting at something everyone but Quincy seemed to comprehend.

In the kitchen, she found Joe leaning against the counter, nursing one of the awful concoctions Janelle had made for him. His presence startled Quincy. Ever since dinner, he had been so quiet that she forgot he was even there. The others seemed to have done the same thing. Even Janelle, who discarded him like a toy on Christmas afternoon.

But he was there. Watching them all through his dirt-smeared glasses, observing their drinking, their dancing. Quincy wondered what he thought of their frivolity. Had it made him happy? Jealous?

"You're a good dancer," he said, staring into his cup.

"Thanks?" It emerged like a question, as if Quincy didn't quite believe him. "If you're bored, I could take you back to your car."

"It's okay. It's probably not a good idea to drive."

"I haven't been drinking," Quincy said, although more and more she suspected that was a lie, thanks to Janelle. She was starting to feel the faintest trace of a buzz. "I'm sorry that Janelle roped you into staying. She can be very, um, persuasive."

"I'm having fun," Joe said, although he sounded like the complete opposite was true. "You're very nice."

Quincy thanked him again, once more adding that uncertain inflection at the end of it. An invisible question mark.

"And pretty," Joe said, this time daring to look up from his cup. "I think you're very pretty."

Quincy looked at him. Really looked at him. And in doing so, she finally saw what Janelle seemed to see. He *was* cute, in a dorky way. Like one of those nerds in movies who blossomed once they removed their glasses. An aura of intensity swirled around his shy demeanor, making it seem like he meant every word he said.

"Thank you," she replied, sincerely this time. Minus the question mark.

The others burst back inside just then, the pot having made them hyper and slaphappy. Rodney lifted Amy over his shoulder and carried her shrieking into the great room. Janelle and Craig leaned on each other, stoned smiles on their faces. Janelle had a thin arm wrapped around Craig's waist, refusing to remove it even as he ambled toward Quincy. She trailed after him, arm stretching.

"Quincy!" she said. "You're missing all the fun."

Janelle's face was flushed and glistening. A strand of sweat-darkened hair stuck to her temple. Her features dimmed when she noticed Joe was also in the kitchen, and she looked from him to Quincy and back again.

"There you are!" she said to Joe, greeting him like a long-lost friend. "I've been looking for you!"

She guided him to one of the worn easy chairs in the great room, squeezing into it with him, legs pulled up so that her knees were on his lap.

"Having a good time?" she asked him.

Quincy looked away, focusing on Craig walking toward her. He too was drunk and high. But he wasn't a giggly drunk, like Betz, or a hyper one, like Janelle. There was a mellowness about him, an ease with his toned body that Quincy found seductive. He pressed against her, heat leaping off his skin, and whispered, "Up for a little fun tonight?"

"Sure," Quincy whispered back.

She felt herself being whisked toward the hall, unable to ignore the judgmental way Betz stared at her as they passed. When she turned to the great room, she noticed Janelle still squeezed into the chair and stroking Joe's hair, only pretending to pay attention to him. In reality, her eyes were locked on Quincy's departing form, glinting darkly with either satisfaction or jealousy.

Quincy couldn't tell.

23.

Exhaustion catches up to me as soon as I return home. I get as far as the living room before collapsing face-first onto the sofa and plummeting into sleep. I awaken hours later, with Jeff kneeling beside me, nudging my shoulder.

"Hey," he says, concern writ large on his face. "You okay?"

I sit up, eyes bleary, squinting at the late-afternoon sun pouring through the window. "I'm fine. Just tired."

"Where's Sam?"

"Out," I say.

"Out?"

"Exploring the city. I think she's getting tired of being cooped up here."

Jeff gives me a peck on the lips. "A sentiment I know well. Which means we should go out too."

He tries hard to act like he came up with the idea on the spot, although I can easily detect his rehearsed eagerness. He's been waiting for a Sam-free moment for days.

I agree, even though I don't really want to go. Exhaustion and anxiety have caused my back, shoulders, and neck to ache. Then there's the matter of my website, which is perilously close to careening off schedule. Responsible me would take an Advil and spend the evening doing some catch-up baking. But irresponsible me needs a diversion from the fact that I actually know nothing about Sam. Why she's here. What she's up to. Even who she really is.

I've invited a complete stranger into our home.

In the process, I've become a stranger myself. One who can beat someone to a pulp in Central Park and then lie to the police about it. One who used to be so content with Jeff but now itches to be alone.

Outside, the setting sun is at our backs. My shadow stretches before me on the sidewalk, slender and dark. It occurs to me that I have more in common with that shadow than the woman creating it. I feel just as insubstantial. As if, once darkness arrives, I'll dissolve until I vanish completely.

We end up walking a few blocks to a French bistro we claim to love but seldom patronize. And even though it's chilly, we huddle at an outside table, Jeff in a secondhand Members Only jacket he bought during a brief '80s phase and me wrapped in a shawl-collared cardigan.

We refuse to talk about Sam. We refuse to talk about his case. That leaves little else to discuss as we pick at our ratatouille and cassoulet. I have no appetite to speak of. What little I eat has to be forced down. Each minuscule bite seems to lodge in my throat until I wash it down with wine. My glass is emptied at record speed.

When I reach for the carafe of house red, Jeff finally notices my hand.

"Whoa," he says. "What happened there?"

Now would be the perfect time to tell Jeff everything. How I almost killed a man. How scared I am of getting caught. How I'm even more afraid of having another memory of Pine Cottage. How I know Sam was in Indiana around the time of Lisa's death.

Instead, I plaster a smile on my face and do my best imitation of my mother. Nothing is wrong. I'm completely normal. If I believe it enough, it'll come true.

"Oh, it's just a silly burn," I say, giving the words an airy spin. "I was so stupid this morning and accidentally touched a baking sheet that was still hot."

I try to jerk my hand away but Jeff catches it, studying the topography of the scabs across my knuckles.

"That looks pretty bad, Quinn. Does it hurt?"

"Not really. It's just ugly."

I again try to pull away, but Jeff keeps my hand trapped in his. "Your hand is shaking."

"Is it?"

I look to the street, pretending to be absorbed by the passing of a silver Cadillac Escalade. There's no way I can look Jeff in the eyes. Not when he's being so sweetly concerned about me.

"Promise me you'll see a doctor if it gets any worse."

"I will," I say brightly. "I promise."

I drink more wine after that, emptying the carafe and ordering another before Jeff can protest. Frankly, wine is exactly what I need. The alcohol combined with the Xanax I took as soon as I got home from the park makes me feel deliciously relaxed. Gone is the pain in my back and shoulders. I barely even think about Sam or Lisa or Rocky Ruiz. When I do, I simply reach for more wine until the thought passes.

On the way back from the bistro, Jeff holds my good hand. He leans down to kiss me when we stop at a crosswalk, slipping his tongue into my mouth just enough to send a heady shiver of desire running through me. Once home, we make out in the elevator, not caring about the camera installed in the corner or the sweaty, potbellied security guard probably watching us on a monitor in the basement.

Inside the apartment, we get as far as the foyer before I'm on my knees, taking Jeff into my mouth, liking the way he moans so loud I'm sure the neighbors can hear through the walls. When one of his hands holds my head in place, I reach back and curl his fingers around a length of hair, hoping he'll tug on it.

I need it to hurt. Just a little.

I deserve the pain.

Later, in bed, Jeff lets me pick the movie. I choose *Vertigo*. When the opening credits start to swirl across the screen in all their trippy, Technicolor glory, I lie down tight against Jeff and spread my arm across his chest. We watch the movie in silence, Jeff dozing off and on through most of it. But he's awake during the climax, when Jimmy Stewart drags poor Kim Novak up those bell-tower steps, begging for the truth.

"I don't have to go," he says once the movie's over. "To Chicago. I can stay here if you want."

"It's important that you go. Plus, you won't be gone long, right?"

"Three days."

"They'll fly by."

"You can come with me," Jeff says. "I mean, if you want."

"Won't you be busy?"

"Swamped, actually. But that doesn't mean you can't enjoy yourself. You love Chicago. Think of it—a nice hotel, deep-dish pizza, some museums."

Lying with my head on Jeff's shoulder, I can hear the quickening of his heart. It's clear he really wants me to go. I do too. I'd love to replace this city with another, just for a few days. Long enough to forget about what I've done.

But I can't. Not with Sam still around. By leading me to the spot where I attacked Rocky Ruiz, Sam made it abundantly clear that she's doing me a favor by keeping quiet. One wrong move on my part could upset the careful balance of our lives. Sam now has the power to destroy us.

"What about Sam?" I say. "We can't just leave her here alone."

"She's not a dog, Quinn. She can take care of herself for a couple of days."

"I'd feel bad. Besides, it's not as if she's going to be staying here much longer."

"It's not about that," Jeff says. "I'm worried about you, Quinn. Something's not right. You've been acting strange ever since she got here."

I start to slide away from him. It had been such a good night until he started talking.

"I've had a lot to deal with."

"And I know that. It's a crazy, stressful time for you. But I just feel like there's something else going on. Something you're not telling me."

I lie on my back and close my eyes. "I'm fine."

"And you swear you'd tell me if you weren't?"

"Yes. Now, please stop asking me that."

"I just want to make sure you'll be okay when I'm gone," Jeff says.

"Of course I will. I have Sam."

Jeff rolls away from me. "That's what worries me."

I wait an hour for sleep to arrive, flat on my back, breathing evenly, telling myself that at any moment I'll sink into slumber. But my thoughts are an unruly bunch, always on the move, in no hurry to settle down. I picture them as part of the dream sequence from *Vertigo*—bright spirals that are forever spinning. Each one has its own color. Red for thoughts about Lisa's murder. Green for Jeff and his concern. Blue for Jonah Thompson's assurance that Sam is lying to me.

Sam's spiral is black, barely visible as it rotates through the sleepless gloom of my brain.

When one a.m. comes and goes, I get out of bed and pad down the hallway. The door to the guest room is closed. No light peeks out from under it. Maybe Sam has returned. Maybe she hasn't. Even her presence has become uncertain.

In the kitchen, I fire up my laptop. Since I'm awake, I might as well do some much-needed work on the website. Yet instead of *Quincy's Sweets*, my fingers lead me to my email. Dozens of new messages from reporters have poured into my inbox, some from as far away as France, England, even Greece. I scroll past them, their addresses a monotonous blur, stopping only when I spot an address not from a reporter.

Lmilner75

I open the email, even though I've committed its contents to memory. Neon pink, if I were to use the *Vertigo* thought-color scale.

Quincy, I need to talk to you. It's extremely important. Please, please don't ignore this.

"What happened to you, Lisa?" I whisper. "What was so important?"

I open a new browser window, heading straight to Google. I type in Sam's name and am greeted with the predictable jumble of items about the Nightlight Inn, Lisa's death, and the Final Girls. Despite a smattering of articles about Sam's disappearance, I see nothing that hints at where she might have been.

Next, I search for Tina Stone, which yields an avalanche of information

about the many, many women who bear that name. There are Facebook profiles and obituaries and LinkedIn updates. Finding anything
about a specific Tina Stone seems impossible. It makes me wonder if
Sam understood this when she chose the name. That she, like I'm doing now, saw the pool of Tina Stones in the world and decided to dive
in, knowing she wouldn't resurface.

I click away from Google, going back to Lisa's email.

*Quincy, I need to talk to you. It's extremely important. Please, please
don't ignore this.*

As I read it, Jonah Thompson's words seem to sneak into the text,
transforming it into something else.

It's about Samantha Boyd. She's lying to you.

I'm about to do another Google search when I hear something
behind me. It's a muted cough. Or maybe the slightest creak of the
floor. Then suddenly someone is there, right at my back. I slam the
laptop shut and spin around to see Sam, silent and still in the dark
kitchen. Her arms are at her sides. Her face is an inscrutable blank.

"You startled me," I say. "When did you get home?"

Sam shrugs.

"How long have you been there?"

Another shrug. She could have been there the entire time or
merely for a second. I'll never know.

"Can't sleep?"

"No," Sam says. "You?"

I shrug. Two can play this game.

The corners of Sam's lips twitch slightly, resisting a smile. "I've
got something that might help."

Five minutes later, I'm sitting on Sam's bed, Wild Turkey in my lap,
trying to keep my hands from shaking as Sam paints my fingernails.
The polish is black and shiny—a miniature oil slick atop each finger. It
pairs well with the scabs on my knuckles, now the same shade as rust.

"This color looks good on you," Sam says. "Mysterious."

"What's it called?"

"Black Death. I picked it up at Bloomingdale's."

I nod in understanding. She used the five-finger discount.

Several minutes pass in which we say nothing. Then Sam, out of nowhere, says, "We're friends, right?"

It's another of her nesting-doll questions. To answer one is to answer them all.

"Of course," I say.

"Good," she says. "That's good, Quinn. I mean, imagine what it would be like if we weren't."

I try to read the expression on her face. It's a blank. A void.

"What do you mean?"

"Well, I know so much about you now," she says quietly. "The things you're capable of. The things you've actually done. If we weren't friends, there's so much I could use against you."

My hands tense within hers. I fight the urge to pull them away and run from the room, fingernails half-painted and streaked with black. Instead, I gaze at her sweetly, hoping she'll think it's sincere.

"That'll never happen," I say. "We're friends for life."

"Good," Sam replies. "I'm glad."

Once again, the room plunges into silence. It stays that way for another five minutes. That's when Sam stuffs her black-polished brush back into its bottle, smiles tightly, and says, "You're finished."

I leave the room before my nails are completely dry, forced to turn the doorknob awkwardly with my palms. I blow on my hands in the hallway, waiting for the polish to become a glistening shell. Then I head to the master bedroom and take a quick look at Jeff, making sure he's sound asleep before I slip inside the bathroom.

I don't bother turning on the light. It's better without it. I lie on the floor, my spine flat, shoulder blades cold against the tile. Then I dial the phone, Coop's number permanently fixed in my memory.

It takes several rings for him to answer. When he does, his voice is husky with sleep.

"Quincy?"

Just hearing him makes me feel better.

"Coop," I say. "I think I'm in trouble."

"What kind of trouble?"

"I think I've gotten myself into something I can't get out of."

I hear the faint rustle of sheets as Coop sits up in bed. It crosses my mind that he might not be alone. It's likely he has someone sleeping next to him most nights and I just don't know it.

"You're worrying me," he says. "Tell me what's going on."

But I can't. That's the most twisted part about all this. I can't tell Coop my suspicions about Sam without also mentioning the terrible thing I've done. They're intertwined, one inseparable from the other.

"That's not a good idea," I say.

"Do you need me to drive out there?"

"No. I just wanted to hear your voice. And to see if you had any advice for me."

Coop clears his throat. "It's hard to give advice when I don't know what's going on."

"Please," I say.

There's a moment of silence on Coop's end. I picture him sliding out of bed and slipping into his uniform, getting ready to come here and help whether I want him to or not. Eventually, he says, "All I can tell you is that if you're in a bad situation, the best thing to do is try to deal with it head-on."

"What if I can't?"

"Quincy, you're stronger than you think."

"I'm not," I say.

"You're a miracle and you don't even know it," Coop says. "Most girls in your situation would have died that night at Pine Cottage. But not you."

My mind flashes back to that scary and tantalizing memory I had in the park. Him. Crouched on the floor of Pine Cottage. Why did that image, of all things, return to me?

"Only because you saved me," I say.

"No," Coop tells me. "You were already in the process of saving yourself. So no matter what you've gotten yourself into, I know you have the power to get yourself out of it."

I nod, even though I know he can't see it. I do it because I think it would make him happy if he could.

"Thank you," I say. "I'm sorry I woke you."

"Never feel sorry for reaching out to me," Coop says. "It's what I'm here for."

I know that. And I'm grateful beyond words.

I stay where I am once Coop hangs up, the phone still in my grip. I stare at it, squinting at the glow, watching the clock at the top of the screen tick off one minute, then another. After eleven more minutes come and go, I know what I need to do, even though the very idea makes me sick to my stomach.

So I search my phone for one of the texts Jonah Thompson sent me. I text back, my fingers fighting every tap.

ready to talk. bryant park. 11:30 sharp

24.

Late morning.

Bryant Park.

A lull before the impending lunchtime crowds. A few office workers have already started to trickle in from adjacent buildings, sneaking away from their cubicles early. I watch them from my seat in the shadow of the New York Public Library, jealous of their camaraderie, their carefree lives.

It's a clear morning, although still on the chilly side. The leaves that canopy the walkways have turned a dusty gold. Surrounding the trees are patches of ivy already girding for winter.

I spot Jonah on the other side of the park—a head of shining hair bouncing through the crowd. He's dressed as if arriving for a first date. Checked shirt. Sport coat with pocket square. Burgundy chinos with rolled cuffs. No socks despite the fact that October's shivery side has settled in. What a preppy douche bag.

I'm wearing the same clothes I wore yesterday, having been too tired to pick out something fresh. The call to Coop had calmed me enough to get some sleep, but even five or six hours wasn't enough to erase the deprivation from earlier in the week.

When Jonah reaches me, he smiles and says, "A coworker and I bet ten dollars over whether you'd come or not."

"Congrats," I say. "You just won ten dollars."

Jonah shakes his head. "My money was on a no-show."

"Well, I'm here."

I don't even try to hide my weariness. I sound like someone with either a serious sleeping problem or a massive headache. In reality, I have both. The headache sits just behind my eyes, making me squint Jonah's way as he says, "So now what?"

"Now you have one minute to convince me to stay."

"Fine," he says, looking at his watch. "But before the clock starts, I have a question."

"Of course you do."

Jonah scratches his head, his hair immobile. He must spend hours grooming. Like a cat, I think. Or those monkeys forever plucking things from their fur.

"Do you even remotely remember me?" he asks.

I remember him staking out the sidewalk outside my building. I remember barfing at his feet. I certainly remember him telling me the true, horrible nature of Lisa Milner's death. But other than that, I have no recollection of Jonah Thompson, which he deduces from my lack of a speedy answer.

"You don't," he says.

"Should I?"

"We went to college together, Quincy. I was in your psych class."

Now, that's a surprise, mostly because it means Jonah is a good five years older than I first thought. Or else he's sorely mistaken.

"Are you sure?" I say.

"Positive," he says. "Tamburro Hall. I sat one row behind you. Not that there was assigned seating or anything."

I do remember the classroom in Tamburro Hall. It was a drafty half-circle that sloped sharply to ground level. The rows of seats were arranged stadium-style, with the knees of the person behind you mere inches from the back of your head. After the first week, everyone more or less sat in the same spot every class. Mine was near the back, slightly to the left.

"I'm sorry," I say. "I don't remember you at all."

"I definitely remember you," Jonah says. "A lot of times you'd say hi to me when taking your seat before class started."

"Really?"

"Yeah. You were very friendly. I remember how happy you always seemed."

Happy. I honestly can't remember the last time someone used that word to describe me.

"You sat with another girl," Jonah continues. "She came in late a lot."

He's talking about Janelle, who would sneak into class after it started, often hungover. On several occasions she fell asleep, head on my shoulder. After class, I'd let her copy my notes.

"You were friends," he says. "I think. Maybe I'm wrong. I remember a lot of bickering going on."

"We didn't bicker," I say.

"You totally did. There was some passive-aggressive thing going on between you two. Like you pretended to be best friends but actually couldn't stand each other."

I don't remember any of this, which doesn't mean it's not the truth. Apparently it happened with enough frequency to make Jonah remember.

"We were best friends," I say quietly.

"Oh God," Jonah says, doing a shitty job of pretending to piece it together just now. Surely he already knew. Two girls who sat in class in front of him, neither of them coming back after one October weekend. "I shouldn't have brought it up."

No, he shouldn't have, and I would lecture him about it if my head wasn't hurting and I wasn't so eager to change the subject.

"Now that we've established how I have a poor memory, it's time for you to tell me why I'm here," I say. "Your minute starts now."

Jonah dives right in, a salesman making his elevator pitch. I suspect he's practiced this routine. It has the smoothness of multiple rehearsals.

"You've made it very clear you don't want to talk about what happened to you. I understand that and I accept it. This isn't about your situation, Quincy, although you know I'm here if you ever do want to discuss it. This is about Samantha Boyd and *her* situation."

"You said she was lying to me. About what?"

"I'll get to that," he says. "What I want to know is how much *you* know about her."

"Why are you so interested in Sam?"

"It's not just me, Quincy. You should have seen the interest that article about the two of you generated. The Internet traffic was insane."

"If you mention that article again, I'm leaving."

"I'm sorry," Jonah says, the base of his neck slightly reddening. It makes me happy to see that he's at least a little embarrassed by his actions. "Back to Sam."

"You want me to spill some dirt on her," I say.

"No," he says, the too-high pitch of his protest telling me I'm right. "I simply want you to share what you know. Think of it as a profile of her."

"Would this be off the record or on?"

"I'd prefer it to be on," Jonah says.

"Too bad." I'm getting irritated. It makes my headache pulse just a little more and sends restlessness coursing through my legs. "Let's walk."

We start to stroll away from the library, toward Sixth Avenue. More people have crowded into the park, filling the slate walkways and angling for the coveted chairs that line them. Jonah and I find ourselves pushed tightly together, moving shoulder to shoulder.

"People really want to know about Sam," Jonah says. "What she's like. Where she's been hiding all this time."

"She hasn't been hiding." For some reason, I still feel the need to defend her. As if she'll know if I don't. "She was just laying low."

"Where?"

I wait a split second before telling him, wondering if I should. But that's why I'm here, isn't it? Even though I keep telling myself it's not.

"Bangor, Maine."

"Why did she suddenly stop laying low?"

"She wanted to meet me after Lisa Milner's suicide," I say, quickly realizing my mistake. "Murder, I mean."

"And you've gotten to know her?"

I think of Sam painting my nails. *We're friends, right?*

"Yes," I say.

It's such a simple word. Three little letters. But there's so much more to it than that. Yes, I've gotten to know Sam, just as she's gotten to know me. I also know I don't trust her. And I'm pretty sure she feels the same way about me.

"And you're positive you're not going to share what you know about her?" Jonah asks.

We've come to Bryant Park's Ping-Pong tables—one of those "only in New York" things. Both tables are occupied, one of them by an elderly Asian couple and the other by two office drones, their ties loosened as they smack the ball back and forth. I spend a moment watching them as I try to form a suitable answer to Jonah's question.

"It's not that simple," I say.

"I know something that might change your mind," Jonah tells me.

"What do you mean?"

It's a stupid question. I already know what he means. The big lie that Sam's been telling me. That Jonah has information I don't annoys me to no end.

"Just tell me what you know, Jonah."

"I'd like to, Quincy," he says, again scratching his head. "I really would. But good journalists don't readily share what they know with sources who aren't cooperative. I mean, if you really want me to give you some top secret intel, I'd need a little something in return."

More than ever, I want to leave. I know it's what I should do. Tell Jonah to leave me alone and then head home for a much-needed nap. Yet I also need to know just how much Sam's been lying to me. One overrules the other.

"Tina Stone," I say.

"Who's that?"

"Samantha Boyd's name. She had it legally changed years ago, to avoid people like you. That's how she was able to keep a low profile all those years. Samantha Boyd technically no longer exists."

"Thank you, Quincy," Jonah says. "I think I'll do some digging into the life of Tina Stone."

"You'll tell me what you find out."

It's not a question. Jonah acknowledges that with a terse nod.

"Of course."

"Now it's your turn," I say. "Tell me what you know."

"It concerns that article I swore I'd never mention again. Specifically the photos that ran with it."

"What about them?"

Jonah takes a deep breath and raises his hands, proclaiming his innocence before saying a word.

"Remember, I'm just the messenger," he finally says. "Please don't kill me."

25.

Sam's in the kitchen, apron on, pretending to be Betty Fucking Crocker. Pretending to be anything other than a devious bitch. When I enter, she's hovering over a mixing bowl, whisking eggs into a snowy pile of sugar and flour.

"We need to talk," I say.

Her eyes never leave the bowl. "Just give me a minute."

I rush to her. In a flash, the bowl is off the counter and slamming against the floor. A line of cake batter traces its descent, trailing from the countertop, down the cupboard beneath it, and across the floor to the bowl itself.

"What the fuck, Quinn?" Sam says.

"That's exactly what I'm thinking, Sam. What the fuck?"

She leans against the counter and looks at me warily. And then she understands. She knows exactly what I'm talking about.

"How much did he tell you?"

"Everything."

I know it all. How she went to Jonah's newsroom the day after news of Lisa's death broke. How she told him who she was and that she was in New York to see me. How she asked if he wanted the photo op of a lifetime.

"You knew he was still there when you introduced yourself," I say. "You planned it that way. You *wanted* us to be on the front page."

Sam doesn't move, her boots planted on the kitchen floor, a slow sludge of cake batter pooling around one of them.

"Yeah," she says. "So?"

I grab a nearby spatula and fling it across the room. It hits the wall next to the window, a blotch of cake batter sticking to the paint after it falls. It doesn't make me feel better.

"Do you realize how stupid that was? People saw those pictures, Sam. Lots of them. Strangers now know who we are. They know where I *live*."

"I did it for you," Sam says.

I slam my hand against the counter. I don't want to hear any of it. "Shut up."

"Honest. I thought it would help you."

"Shut up!"

Sam flinches, her drawn-on brows rising into startled arches. "I need you to know why I did it."

There's a carton of eggs sitting just to my right, a half dozen remaining. I pick one up.

"Shut—"

The egg goes flying toward Sam's head. She ducks out of its path, the egg exploding against the cupboard behind her.

"—the—"

I toss another. Like a grenade. A quick flick of the wrist. When it joins the bowl on the floor, I grab two more, flinging them in quick succession.

"—fuck—up!"

Both eggs hit Sam's apron. Chaotic detonations of yellow slime that push her against the counter, more from surprise than velocity. I reach for the others, but Sam rushes forward, unsteady across the slick tile. She yanks the carton away, sending the remaining eggs smashing to the floor.

"Will you just let me explain?" she shouts.

"I already know why you did it!" I shout back. "You wanted me to get angry! And I almost killed a man! Is that angry enough for you? What else do you want me to do?"

Sam grabs me by the shoulders, shaking me. "I want you to wake up! You've been hiding all these years."

"You should talk. I'm not the one who vanished. I'm not the one who hasn't even told her mother she's still alive."

"I don't mean it like that."

"Then what do you mean, Sam? I wish that for once you'd make some sense. I've tried to understand you, but I can't."

"Stop pretending to be someone you're not!" Sam also decides to throw things. There's another bowl on the counter, which she slaps onto the floor. It rolls into a corner, spinning on its rim. "You act like this perfect girl with this perfect life making perfect cakes. But that's not you, Quinn, and you know it."

She pushes me against the dishwasher, its handle poking into the base of my spine. I shove back and send her sliding through the muck of eggs and flour.

"You don't know anything about me," I say.

Sam comes at me again, this time slamming me against the counter.

"I'm the *only* one who knows you. You're a fighter. One who'll do anything to survive. Just like me."

I squirm against her, trapped. "I'm nothing like you."

"You're a fucking Final Girl," Sam says. "*That's* why I went to Jonah Thompson. So you couldn't hide anymore. So you could finally live up to the name you've earned."

Her face is so close to mine that I stop breathing. Her presence is like a fire sucking all the oxygen from the room. I shove her away, clearing enough space to turn around in. Sam latches onto my hand, trying to drag me toward her. My other hand fumbles along the countertop, reaching for anything I can find. Measuring cups bump against my knuckles. A spoon slips from my grip and hits the floor. My fingers finally close around something and I whirl toward her, brandishing it, thrusting it outward.

Sam cries out, scrambling backward. She drops to the floor and presses herself against a cupboard door.

I stalk across the kitchen, vaguely aware that she's saying my name on repeat. The sound watery and distant, as if shouted from the depths of a well.

"Quinn!"

That one is loud enough to rattle the cupboards. Loud enough to pierce the furious haze surrounding me.

"Quincy," Sam says, now merely whispering. *"Please."*

I look down.

There's a knife in my hand.

It's tilted, the flat of the blade facing the ceiling, reflecting the overhead kitchen light in a starburst glint.

I drop it, hand tingling. "I didn't mean to do that."

Sam stays on the floor, curled into a ball, knees touching apron straps. She can't stop shaking. It's like a seizure.

"I wasn't going to hurt you," I say, tears at the back of my throat. "I swear."

Sam's hair hangs across her face. I see her ruby lips, a pebble of a nose, one eye peeking from between the strands, bright and terrified.

"Quincy," she says. "Who *are* you?"

I shake my head. I honestly don't know.

26.

A buzz at the front door breaks the silence that's fallen over the kitchen. The building's intercom system. Someone's outside. When I press the intercom button by the door, a woman's voice crackles at me from the street.

"Miss Carpenter?"

"Yes?"

"Hi, Quincy," the voice says. "It's Carmen Hernandez. Sorry to just show up like this, but I'm going to need a moment of your time."

Soon Detective Hernandez is in the dining room, smartly dressed in a gray blazer and red blouse. The bracelet wrapped around her right wrist clicks as she takes a seat. A dozen circular charms dangle from the sterling silver. An anniversary present from her husband, maybe. Or perhaps a treat she purchased herself after getting tired of waiting for him to do it. Either way, it's lovely. A bolder version of me would try to steal it. I imagine looking into the charms and seeing a dozen different versions of myself.

"Is this a good time?" she says, knowing it's not. The kitchen is visible to anyone passing through the foyer on the way to the dining room. It's a gloppy mess of batter and egg yolks. Even if she somehow missed it, there's Sam and me, two flour-coated, egg-smeared shambles sitting across from her.

"No," I say. "It's fine."

"Are you sure? You look flustered."

"It's been one of those days." I flash a peppy smile. All teeth and gums. My mother would be proud. "You know how crazy it can get in a kitchen."

"My husband does the cooking," Hernandez says.

"Lucky you."

"Why are you here, Detective?" asks Sam, speaking for the first time since the intercom buzzer sounded. She's tucked her hair behind her ears, giving the detective a full view of her hard stare.

"I've got just a few follow-up questions about the Rocky Ruiz assault. Nothing serious. Just doing my due diligence."

"We've already told you everything." I try not to sound worried. I really do. Yet an anxious squeak hides inside every word. "There's really nothing else to add."

"You sure about that?"

"Positive."

The charms of the detective's bracelet clatter again as she plucks a notebook from inside her blazer and flips through it. "Well, I've got two witnesses who say otherwise."

"Oh?" I say.

Sam says nothing at all.

Hernandez jots something down in her notebook.

"One of them is a hustler who works the Ramble," she says. "His name's Mario. A plainclothes officer brought him in last night. Not a big surprise to anyone. He's got a list of solicitation charges a mile long. When the cop asked Mario if he saw anything the night of Rocky's assault, he said no. But he did mention seeing something unusual the night before. Two women sitting in the park. Around one in the morning. One of them was smoking. He said she gave him a cigarette."

I remember him. The handsome guy in leather. The mention of him makes me anxious, with good reason. Sam spoke to him. He saw our faces.

"He identified those two women for me," Hernandez says. "The two of you."

"How would he know that?" Sam says.

"He recognized you from the newspaper. I'm assuming the two of you know you were front-page news the other day."

I keep my hands on my knees, where Hernandez can't see them. Both are balled into nervous fists. The more she talks, the tighter I squeeze.

"I remember him," I say. "He came up to us while we were sitting in the park."

"At one a.m.?"

"Is that illegal?" Sam asks.

"No. Just unusual." Detective Hernandez cocks her head at us. "Especially considering that you were there two nights in a row."

My forearms ache as my fists stay clenched in my lap. I try to relax them one finger at a time.

"We told you why we were there," I say.

"Out drinking, right?" Hernandez says. "That's what you were doing the night Mario the Gigolo saw you too?"

"Yes," I say, chirping out the word.

Sam and I look at each other. Hernandez jots something down in her notebook, makes a show of crossing it out, writes something else.

"Fair enough," she says. "Now, let's talk about this second witness."

"Another man-whore?" Sam asks.

Detective Hernandez is not amused. She frowns at Sam, saying, "A homeless man. He spoke to one of the cops canvassing the park about Rocky Ruiz. He says he saw two women at that fancy pool where kids sail their boats. That place was in a book, I think. I read it to my kids. Something about a mouse?"

"*Stuart Little*," I say, unsure why.

"That's it. Nice place. That homeless man sure thinks so. He sometimes sleeps on a bench near there. But on the night Rocky was assaulted, he said he was chased away by those two women. They caught him watching as one of them washed her hands in the water. He said it looked like one of them was bleeding."

I don't dare ask if he described these women. Clearly, he has.

"The two of you match the description he gave us," Hernandez says. "So I'm just going to take a wild guess and assume it really was you. Would either of you like to explain what was going on there?"

She folds her hands atop the table, bracelet hand on top. Under the table, my fists have become rocks. Nuggets of coal being squeezed into diamonds. The pressure splits one of the scabs on my knuckles. A trickle of blood slips between my fingers.

"It was exactly what it looked like," I say, spinning the lie with no thought. It just comes out of my mouth. "I tripped when we were crossing the park. Scraped my hand up in the process. It was bleeding pretty hard, so we went to the pool so I could rinse it off."

"Was this before or after the purse was stolen?"

"Before," I say.

Hernandez stares me down, her gaze hard. Beneath the neat hair and tailored blazer is one tough cookie. She probably had to work hard to get where she is. More than the men, that's for damn sure. I bet they all underestimated her.

Yet so have I, and now here we are.

"That's interesting," she says. "Our homeless friend didn't mention seeing a purse."

"We—"

For some reason, I stop myself. The lie disappears like a pinch of salt melting on my tongue.

Hernandez leans forward, almost friendly, preparing to begin a just-us-girls chat. "Listen, ladies, I don't know what went down in the park that night. Maybe Rocky was high out of his mind. Maybe he tried to hurt you and you fought back a little too hard. If that's the case, it would be in both of your best interests to come forward."

She pulls back, friend time over. The bracelet scrapes across the table as she grabs her notebook again.

"I even get why you might not want to do that. The man's in a coma. That's a serious situation. But I swear I won't judge you. Not until I have the full story." Hernandez consults her notes, looks to Sam. "Miss Stone, I'll even overlook your past brushes with the law."

To her credit, Sam doesn't react. Her face is a mask of calm. But I can tell she's seeking out my reaction. My lack of one tells her everything she needs to know.

"I just want to be clear that none of those things will in any way affect your treatment," Hernandez says. "Should one of you decide to turn yourself in, of course."

"We won't," Sam says.

"Take some time to think about it." Across the table, Hernandez stands and tucks the notebook under her arm, bracelet singing. "Talk it over. But don't take too long. The more you wait, the worse it will get. Oh, and if one of you did, you know, happen to do it, you better pray Rocky Ruiz comes out of that coma. Because if I find myself with an involuntary manslaughter in my lap, all bets are off."

"We're not saying anything," Sam announces once Hernandez leaves.

"We have to," I say.

The two of us remain in the dining room, trapped in a heady, unbearable stillness. Sunlight slants through the window, illuminating the dust motes swirling just off the table's surface. Not daring to look at each other, we watch them like people awaiting a storm. All raw nerves and unspoken dread.

"Actually, we don't," Sam says. "She's grasping. She's got nothing on us. It's not illegal to sit in Central Park at night."

"Sam, there were witnesses."

"A homeless man and a gigolo who saw nothing."

"If we tell the truth now, she'll take it easy on us. She understands."

Even I don't believe this. Detective Hernandez has no intention of helping us. She's just a very smart woman doing her job.

"Jesus," Sam says. "She was lying, Quinn."

The silence resumes. We watch the dust motes dance.

"Why didn't you tell me you were in Indiana?" I say.

Sam finally looks my way. Her face is foreign, unreadable. "You don't want to go there, babe. Trust me."

"I need answers," I say. "I need the truth."

"The only truth you need to know is that what happened in the park is all on you. I'm just trying to save your ass."

"By lying?"

"By keeping your secrets," Sam says. "I know too much about you now. More than you think."

She pushes away from the table. The movement prompts a rush of questions from me, each one more pleading than the last.

"Did you meet Lisa? Were you at her house? What else aren't you telling me?"

Sam turns away, dark hair whipping outward, her face a blur. It unlocks a memory of a similar sight. So faint it's more like a memory of a memory.

"Sam, please—"

She leaves the dining room in silence. A moment later, the front door closes behind her.

I remain seated, too tired to move, too worried that if I try to stand, I'll simply drop to the floor. The way Sam looked when she left replays in my head, gnawing at my memory. I've seen it before. I know I have.

Suddenly I remember, which sends me hurrying to my laptop. I log on to Facebook, seeking out Lisa's profile. More condolences fill her page. Hundreds of them. I ignore them and head to the pictures Lisa had posted, quickly finding the one I'm looking for—Lisa lifting a bottle of wine with a happy glow.

Wine time! LOL!

I study the woman in the background of the photo. The dark blur that had so fascinated me the first time I saw it. I stare at the picture, as if I can will the image into focus. The best I can do is squint, trying to make my vision as blurry as the object in the photo and hope they balance each other into clarity. It works to an extent. A white smudge emerges in the far edge of the dark blur. Within that smudge is a drop of red.

Lipstick.

Sam's lipstick.

As bright as blood.

Seeing it makes my body hum with an internal acceleration. I feel as if I've been strapped to a bottle rocket, hurtling through the ozone, streaking sparks until we both explode.

27.

The kitchen is cleaned and my bags are packed by the time Jeff gets home from work. One suitcase. One carry-on. He stands in the doorway to our bedroom, blinking, as if I'm a mirage.

"What are you doing?"

"I'm going with you," I say.

"To Chicago?"

"I bought my ticket online. Same flight, although we can't sit together."

"You sure?" Jeff asks.

"It was your idea."

"True. It's just very sudden. And what about Sam?"

"You said yourself that we can leave her alone for a few days," I say. "She's not a dog, remember?"

In truth, I hope she'll be gone when we return. Quietly. Without fuss. A scorpion in such a hurry to get away that it forgets to sting.

Jeff, meanwhile, looks around the bedroom as if for the last time and says, "Let's hope there's something left when we get back."

"I'll take care of that," I say.

Sam doesn't return until late in the night, long after Jeff and I have gone to bed. Before we leave for the airport in the morning, I knock on the door to her room. After several knocks and no answer, I crack open the door and peer inside. Sam's in bed, comforter pulled to her chin. The blanket ripples as she thrashes beneath it.

"No," she moans. "Please don't."

I rush to the bed and shake her by the shoulders, barely getting out of the way before she bolts upright, wide-awake.

"What's going on?" she says.

"A nightmare," I say. "You were having a nightmare."

Sam stares at me, making sure I'm not part of the bad dream. She looks like a woman just rescued from drowning—red-faced and damp. Hair sticks to her sweat-soaked cheeks in long, dark strands that resemble seaweed. She even does a little shake, as if trying to flick away excess water.

"Whoa," she says. "That was a bad one."

I sit on the edge of the bed, tempted to ask her what she was dreaming about. Was it Calvin Whitmer and his sack-covered face? Or was it something else? Maybe Lisa, bleeding out in the bathtub. But Sam keeps looking at me, knowing something is about to happen.

"Jeff and I are going away for a few days," I say.

"Where?"

"Chicago."

"Are you kicking me out? I can't afford a hotel."

"I know," I say, keeping my tone calm and even. Nothing I say can upset her. That's vital. "You can stay here while we're gone. Kind of like a house sitter. Maybe do some baking, if you feel like it."

"I'm down with that," Sam says.

"Can Jeff and I trust you?"

A pointless question. Of course I don't trust her. It's why I'm going to Chicago with Jeff in the first place. Leaving her behind is my only option.

"Sure."

I remove the cash I had stuffed into my pocket right before coming into the room. Two rumpled hundred-dollar bills. I hand them to Sam.

"Here's some walking-around money," I say. "Use it for food, maybe go to the movies. Whatever."

It's a bribe and Sam knows it. Rubbing the bills together, she says, "Don't house sitters also get some sort of fee? You know, for looking after the place. Making sure everything's fine."

While she frames it as a perfectly reasonable question, it doesn't keep the betrayal I feel from stinging like a slap. I remember Sam's first night here, how Jeff flat-out asked if she had come seeking money. She denied it, and I had believed her. Now I get the feeling that's the only reason she's here. The late-night talks, the baking, the entire friendship was just a means to that end.

"How does five hundred sound?" I say.

Sam appraises the room. I can see her doing the math in her head, weighing the potential value of each object.

"A thousand sounds better," she says.

I grit my teeth. "Of course."

I leave to fetch my purse, returning with a check made payable to Tina Stone and postdated for the day after Jeff and I are scheduled to return. Sam says nothing when she sees the date. She simply folds the check in half and places it with the cash on the nightstand.

"Do you still want me here when you get back?" she says.

"That's up to you."

Sam smiles. "It really is, isn't it?"

On the plane, the solo traveler next to me kindly agrees to switch places with Jeff, allowing us to sit together. During takeoff, Jeff grabs my hand and gives it a gentle squeeze.

After landing and checking into our hotel, we have an entire afternoon and evening alone together. Gone is the awkwardness of two nights ago, when Sam's absence was as noticeable as a missing pinkie finger. We stroll the downtown blocks around our hotel, the tension from the past week thawing in the breeze blowing off Lake Michigan.

"I'm glad you came along, Quinn," Jeff says. "I know it didn't seem that way last night, but I mean it."

When he reaches for my hand, I gladly take it. It helps having him in my corner. Especially considering what I intend to do.

On the walk back to the hotel, we're both taken with a dress in a boutique window. It's black and white, with a cinched waist and a skirt that flares outward like a 1950s-era Dior.

"Right off the Paris plane," I say, quoting Grace Kelly in *Rear Window.* "Think it will sell?"

Jeff stammers, Jimmy Stewart–style. "Well, see, that depends on the quote."

"A steal at eleven hundred dollars," I say, still Grace.

"That dress should be listed on the stock exchange." Jeff drops the charade, becoming himself again. "And I think you should buy it."

"Really?" I say, also turning into myself again.

Jeff flashes that widescreen smile. "It's been a rough week. You deserve something nice."

Inside the shop, I'm relieved to learn the dress's price tag is slightly less than my Grace Kelly estimate. Discovering that it fits brings more relief. I buy it on the spot.

"A dress like that deserves an occasion to match," Jeff tells me. "I think I know just the place."

We dress for dinner, me in my new frock and Jeff in his sharpest suit. Thanks to the hotel concierge, we're able to get a late reservation at the city's hippest, most crazy-expensive restaurant. At Jeff's encouragement, we splurge on the nine-course tasting menu, washing it down with a bottle of Cabernet Sauvignon. Dessert is a chocolate soufflé so divine that I beg the pastry chef for the recipe.

Back at the hotel, buzzed on wine and our foreign surroundings, we're flirtatious and sensual. I kiss him slowly while unknotting his tie, the stubbled silk winding around my fingers. Jeff takes his time with my dress. I shiver as he inches the zipper lower, my back arching.

His breath grows heavier when the dress drops to the floor. He grips my arms, hurting them just a little. There's lust in his eyes. A wildness I haven't seen for ages. It makes him look like a stranger, dangerous and unknowable. I'm reminded of all those rough-and-tumble frat boys and football players I had slept with after Pine Cottage. The ones not afraid to yank off my panties and flip me over the bed. The ones who didn't care who I was or what I wanted.

My body trembles. This is promising. This is what I need.

But then it's gone, the mood falling away with the same ease as Jeff's tie slipping from my hands. I'm not even aware of its passing until we're on the bed and Jeff is inside me, suddenly his usual maddeningly conscientious self. Asking me how I feel. Asking me what I want.

I want him to stop caring about my needs.

I want him to shut up and take what *he* wants.

None of that happens. The sex ends the way it normally does—with Jeff spent and me stretched on my back, a tight lump of dissatisfaction in my gut.

Jeff showers afterward, returning to bed pink and tender.

"What's on your agenda for tomorrow?" he asks, voice distant, already sailing on the boat to dreamland.

"The usual sights. The Art Institute. The Bean. Maybe some more shopping."

"Nice," Jeff sleepily murmurs. "You'll have fun."

"That's why I came along," I say, when, in fact, it's not.

Fun has nothing to do with my reason for coming here. Jeff has nothing to do with it either. While he was in the shower, washing off the sweat and smell of humdrum sex, I was on my phone, reserving a rental car.

In the morning, I'm going to drive to Indiana and finally get some answers.

28.

Roughly 230 miles lie between Chicago and Muncie, and I drive them as fast as my rented Camry will allow. My goal is to get to Lisa's house and see if I can learn something—anything—before returning to the city by evening. The trip is long, about seven hours total, but if I keep a quick pace, I can be back before Jeff knows I'm gone.

On the way there, I make good time, stopping just once at a convenience store off I-65. It's one of those sad, generic places that wants you to think it's part of a chain. But the seams show. All those sticky soda cans, scuffed floor tiles, and racks of nudie mags wrapped in condoms of clear plastic. I buy a bottle of water, a granola bar, and a pack of cheese crackers. The breakfast of champions.

A rack of silvery lighters sits on the counter. When the stoner clerk cracks open a fresh roll of pennies for the register, I grab one and stuff it into my pocket. He catches me, smiles, sends me off with a wink.

Then I'm back in the car, marking my time by the way the sunlight slants across the flat ribbon of asphalt. The scenery streaking past the window is rural and stark. The houses have stripped siding and leaning porches. Miles of fields fly by, their cornstalks reduced to stubs. Exit signs point to small towns with misleadingly exotic names. Paris. Brazil. Peru.

By the time the sun has become an unblinking yellow eye directly overhead, I'm steering through Muncie, searching for the address Lisa gave me in case I ever wanted to write.

I find her house on a quiet side street full of ranch homes and sycamore trees. Lisa's is noticeably nicer than the others, with fresh paint on the shutters and pristine patio furniture on the front porch. A circular flower bed sits in the middle of the well-trimmed lawn, a fiberglass birdbath rising from its center like a giant mushroom.

A station wagon with a PBA sticker slapped to its back bumper sits in the driveway. Definitely not Lisa's car.

After parking on the street, I check myself in the rearview mirror, making sure I look somber and curious, not deranged and stalkerish. At the hotel, I had taken great care in picking an outfit that walked the fine line between casual and mourning. Dark jeans, deep-purple blouse, black flats.

I head to the front door using the flagstone walkway that cuts through the yard. When I ring the doorbell, I hear it echo back at me from deep inside the house.

The woman who answers the door is dressed in a monochrome outfit of tan slacks and beige polo shirt. Tall and angular, she might have resembled Katharine Hepburn in her younger years. Now, though, webs of wrinkles surround her hazel eyes. She brings to mind an Okie in a Walker Evans photo—thin, hard, and bone-tired.

I know exactly who she is.

Nancy.

"Can I help you?" she says in a voice as blunt as a Plains wind.

I have no plan about what to do or say. All that mattered was getting here. Now that I've arrived, I don't know what my next step will be.

"Hi," I say. "I'm—"

Nancy nods. "Quincy. I know."

She looks at my fingernails, messily painted black. My right hand, with its mottled scabs smarting like a sunburn across my knuckles, catches her attention. I shove it deep into my pocket.

"You here for the funeral?" she says.

"I thought that already happened."

"Tomorrow."

I should have known there'd be a delay. There had been an autopsy to contend with, plus that all-important tox report.

"Lisa thought a lot about the two of you," Nancy says. "I know she would want you there."

As would members of the press, who I assume will be arriving in droves, the clicking of their cameras punctuating the Twenty-Third Psalm.

"It's probably not a good idea," I say. "I'm afraid I'd be a distraction."

"Then it'd be real nice if you told me why you're here. I'm no genius, but I sure as hell know that Muncie's not exactly a stone's throw from New York."

"I'm here to learn about Lisa," I say. "I'm here for details."

Inside, Lisa's house is a tidy, depressing affair. The bulk of it is taken up by the living room, dining area, and kitchen, which merge together to form one giant room. The walls are covered in wood paneling, making the place feel musty and old-fashioned. It's the home of a widowed grandmother, not a forty-two-year-old woman.

I see no signs that a murder took place here. There are no cops dusting for prints, no grim-faced CSI grunts picking through the carpet with tweezers. Those tasks are complete, results hopefully pending.

Stacks of cardboard boxes—some folded, others not—clutter the living room, which has already been stripped of a few knickknacks. End tables bear dust-free circles where vases and bowls once sat.

"Lisa's family asked if I could start packing up her things," Nancy says. "They don't want to set foot in the place anymore. Can't say I blame them."

We sit at the oval dining-room table. In front of her is a laminated place mat. I assume it's where Lisa usually ate her meals. A table setting for one. We talk while sipping tea from mugs with pink roses around the rims.

Her full name is Nancy Scott. She's been an Indiana State Trooper for twenty-five years, although she'll probably be retired by this time next year. She's single, never married, owns two German shepherds that are decommissioned police dogs.

"I was one of the first people to enter that sorority house," she says. "And I was the first person to realize Lisa wasn't dead like the rest. All the other guys—and they were all guys except me—took one look at those bodies and assumed the worst. I did too, I guess. Oh, it was bad. The blood. It was just everywhere."

She stops, remembering who she's talking to. I nod for her to continue.

"When I took one look at Lisa, I knew she was still alive. I didn't know if she'd stay that way, but somehow she pulled through. After that, I took a shine to her. She was a fighter, that girl."

"And that's how the two of you became close?"

"Lisa and I were close in the way that you and Frank are close."

Frank. It's disconcerting to hear him called that. To me, he's simply Coop.

"She knew she could call me whenever she needed to," Nancy says. "That I was there to listen and help in whatever way I could. That kind of thing is delicate, you see. You need to let them know you're there for them, but not get too involved. You have to keep a distance. It's better that way."

I think of Coop and all the invisible barriers he's built between us. Always nodding, never hugging. Not coming up to the apartment until he absolutely had to. It's likely Nancy gave him this same spiel about keeping a distance. She doesn't strike me as the kind of woman who keeps her opinions to herself.

"It was only in the past five years or so that we became what you'd call friends," she says. "I became close with her family as well. They'd have me over for Thanksgiving dinner, family birthdays."

"They sound like good people," I say.

"They are. They're having a hard time with this, of course. That grief will be with them for the rest of their lives."

"And you?" I say.

"Oh, I'm furious." Nancy takes a sip of tea. Her lips pucker from the heat before flattening into a harsh line. "I know I should feel sad, and I do. But more than that, I'm mad as hell. Someone took Lisa away from us. After all she went through."

I know exactly what she means. Lisa's murder feels like a defeat. A Final Girl finally vanquished.

"Did you always suspect foul play was involved?"

"I sure as hell did," Nancy says. "I knew Lisa couldn't have killed herself. Not when she'd fought so hard to survive and had done so much with the hand she'd been dealt. I'm the one who ordered that tox report, conflict of interest be damned. I was right, of course. They found all those pills in her system but no prescription bottle in the house to keep them in. *Then* they looked at the knife wounds, which is something that should have been done in the first place."

"When we all spoke on the phone, you said there weren't any suspects. Has that changed?"

"Nope," Nancy says.

"What about a motive?"

"Still nothing."

"You sound like you don't think they'll ever catch who did it."

"Because I don't," Nancy says with a sigh. "By the time those idiots realized what really happened, it was too late. The scene was already compromised. Me with those boxes. Some of Lisa's friends and cousins. All of us clomping in here and dragging in God knows what."

She leans forward, looks to the table.

"The whole time, that circle of wine sat right here. From the glass no one knew was missing. Whoever killed Lisa took it with them. It's probably smashed on the side of the road somewhere. Tossed out a car window."

My hands are resting on the table's surface, palms flat. I quickly pull them away.

"They already dusted for prints," Nancy says. "Couldn't find any. Same with the bathroom, the knife, and Lisa's phone. All wiped clean."

"And none of her friends know anything?" I ask.

"They're asking around. But it's been hard. Lisa liked to be around people. She was very *social*."

Nancy's disapproval is obvious. She spits the word out as if it might leave a bad taste in her mouth.

"You don't think she should have been," I say.

"I thought she was too trusting. Because of what she went through, she was always willing to help people in need. Girls, mostly. Troubled ones."

"Troubled how?"

"Girls who were at risk. Having trouble with their parents. Or maybe running away from a boyfriend who liked smacking them around. Lisa took them in, looked out for them, helped them get back on their feet. I saw it as her trying to fill the void in her life caused by that night at the sorority house."

"Void?" I say.

"Lisa didn't date very much," Nancy says. "She didn't trust too many men, with good reason. Like most girls, she probably once had dreams of getting married, having kids, being a mom. That day at the sorority house took all that away from her."

"So she never dated?"

"A little," Nancy replies. "Nothing that ever got very serious. Most guys split once they found out what happened to her."

"Did she mention any of them to you? Maybe about one of them harassing her? Or did she ever talk about having problems with one of the girls she befriended?"

Sam. That's who I really mean. Did Lisa ever mention Samantha Boyd?

"Not to me." Nancy drains her teacup. She looks at mine, clearly hoping I'll do the same and take my leave. "How long are you in town for, Quincy?"

I check my watch. It's a quarter past one. I need to be on the road by two thirty if I want to make it back to Chicago without arousing Jeff's suspicions.

"Another hour." I look around the half-packed room, then the empty boxes leaning flat against the wall. "Need some help?"

29.

I offer to work in Lisa's bedroom while Nancy continues in the living room. She agrees, although she bites the inside of her mouth before consenting, as if she's unsure I can be trusted. But then she hands me two boxes.

"Don't worry about trying to sort stuff," she says, pointing me down the hallway. "Her family will do that. We just need to empty the place."

Finally out of her sight, I linger in the hall, looking into each of the three rooms located there.

The first one is a guest room, sparsely furnished and immaculately clean. I step inside and roam its perimeter, my index finger running along the dresser, the bed, the nightstand. There's no trace of Sam, even though I can picture her smoking by the open window, just like she's probably doing in my apartment at this very moment.

I move back to the hall, pausing at the bathroom. This room I refuse to enter. Doing so would feel like invading a crypt. Besides, I have a good enough view from the hall. From sink to tub to toilet, the bathroom is a sea of light blue, still smudged in spots by traces of the aluminum powder used to dust for prints. I stare at the tub, unnerved.

Lisa died right there.

I think of her lying in that tub, surrounded by cloudy pink water. I then think of Sam standing in the doorway just like I'm doing. Watching. Making sure the job is complete.

When I can't look at that tub a second longer, I head to Lisa's bedroom, trying hard to shake off the chill that's suddenly come over me. The bedroom is all cream and pink. Cream carpet, pink curtains, rose-colored comforter over the bed. A treadmill stands in the corner, covered with dust and draped with clothes.

I wonder if Lisa ever spent one of our phone conversations in here, doling out advice while walking on the treadmill, or maybe sprawled across the bed. The memory of her phone voice returns.

You can't change what's happened. The only thing you can control is how you deal with it.

I go to Lisa's dresser, the top of which is littered with hair accessories, plastic bins overflowing with makeup, and an old-school jewelry box. When I lift its lid, a porcelain ballerina in a tiny tulle skirt pops up and begins to spin.

On the other side of the dresser are several snapshots stuck into plastic frames meant to resemble wood. There's Lisa at the beach with Nancy, both of them squinting into the sun. Lisa with whom I can only assume are her parents, standing before a Christmas tree. Lisa at the Grand Canyon, at a bar with neon behind her and a hand on her shoulder bearing a red ring, at a birthday party with cake smeared on her face.

I empty the dresser one drawer at a time, grabbing bunches of Lisa's bras, socks, and granny panties. I remove the clothes quickly, trying to ignore the guilt-inducing fact that I'm snooping. It feels like a violation of sorts. As if I've broken into her home and started to ransack the place.

It's the same thing when I go to the closet and begin clearing it of dresses, pantsuits, and sad floral skirts that went out of style years ago. But then I find what I was hoping for. There's a gray lockbox in a back corner of the closet, partially obscured by a hamper. It's small, boasting a single drawer. I notice a tiny keyhole in that lone drawer, similar to the one located in my secret drawer at home. And just like on my drawer, the keyhole is circled by a pattern of scratch marks made when the lock was picked.

Now I know for certain that Sam was here. Those scratch marks were her handiwork. They had to be.

My hand drifts to the necklace that holds the key to my drawer. I still wear it, despite being so far from home. It gives me a sense of normalcy when, in truth, everything about my life has been upended by Sam.

I give the drawer a tug and it slides open. Three neatly stacked file folders sit inside it.

The top one is blue and unlabeled. Opening it, I see a scrapbook of sorts. Page after photocopied page of newspaper clippings, magazine articles, stories printed off the Internet. All of them are about the sorority-house massacre. Some of the articles have sentences underlined in blue pen. Question marks and sad faces crowd the margins.

The other two folders are red and white. One is about Sam. The other concerns me. I know that even without opening them. The math is simple: Three Final Girls, three folders.

Sam's folder is the red one. Inside are articles about the Nightlight Inn, including the one from *Time* magazine that traumatized me as a child. Lisa made notes in those too. Words, phrases, and whole sentences have been scribbled in the margins.

In the back of the folder are two newspaper clippings, both of them missing dates.

HEMLOCK CREEK, Pa.—Authorities are continuing to investigate the deaths of two campers found stabbed to death last month. Police discovered the bodies of Tommy Curran, 24, and Suzy Pavkovic, 23, inside a tent in a heavily wooded area two miles outside of town. Both victims had been stabbed multiple times. Although there were signs of a struggle at their campsite, authorities say nothing appeared to be taken from the scene, leading them to conclude robbery was not a factor in their deaths.

The grisly crime has left many in this quiet town on edge. It comes barely a year after the body of a 20-year-old woman was found along Valley Road, a little-traveled access road used by employees of Blackthorn Psychiatric Hospital. The woman, whom authorities could never identify, was strangled to death. Police think she was killed elsewhere and later dumped in the woods.

Police say the two crimes are unrelated.

HAZLETON, Pa.—A man was found stabbed to death yesterday inside the home he shared with his wife and stepdaughter. Responding to emergency calls, Hazleton police found Earl Potash, 46, dead in the kitchen of his Maple Street duplex, the victim of multiple stab wounds to the chest and stomach. Authorities have ruled the incident a homicide. The investigation is continuing.

I press a hand to my forehead. My skin is hot to the touch. That's because of the reference to Blackthorn in the first article. The name always makes me break into a nervous sweat. Although I can't remember how, I know I've heard about those murders in the woods. They took place a year or so before Pine Cottage, in the very same forest. Why Lisa kept this news clipping in a folder devoted to Sam is beyond my comprehension.

A second read doesn't make things any clearer, so I tuck the clippings back into the folder and put it away. Now it's time for the white folder.

My folder.

The first thing I see upon opening it is a single sheet of paper. My name is on it. So is my phone number. Now it starts to make more sense. Now I know how Sam got my phone number to call me the night she was arrested.

Next are articles about Pine Cottage, fastened together with a pink paper clip. I flip the stack over without looking at it, fearing I'll see another picture of Him. Beneath the articles is a letter.

The letter.

The bad one that made even Coop nervous.

YØU SHØULDN'T BE ALIVE.
YØU SHØULD HAVE DIED IN THAT CABIN.
IT WAS YØUR DESTINY TØ BE SACRIFICED.

Shock blasts through me. I start to gasp but stop myself, afraid Nancy will be able to hear it. Instead, I stare at the letter, not blinking, those out-of-place zeroes like several sets of eyes staring back.

A single question stabs into my thoughts. The obvious one.

How the fuck did Lisa get a copy?

Another, more pressing question follows.

Why did she have it?

Behind the letter, also paper-clipped, is the transcript of a police interview. At the top is my name and a date. One week after Pine Cottage. Neatly typed below that are the names of two people I haven't thought of in years—Detective Cole and Detective Freemont.

Nancy's voice rings out from the end of the hall, on the move, getting closer.

"Quincy?"

I shut the folder with a snap. I lift the back of my shirt, press the folder flat against my spine, and shove it down the seat of my pants far enough so that it won't flop out when I walk. I then tuck in my blouse, hoping Nancy won't notice how it was untucked when I arrived.

The other two folders are dropped back into the filing cabinet. The drawer is shoved shut just as Nancy sweeps into the room. She eyes the boxes first, then me, rising from my crouch in front of Lisa's closet.

"Your time's about up," she says.

She's back to looking at the boxes. Both are only partially filled. One of them has a pair of Lisa's jeans flopped over the side.

"I'm sorry I didn't get more done," I say. "Packing up Lisa's stuff is harder than I thought it would be. It means she's really gone."

We each carry a box to the living room, me letting Nancy lead the way. When we say our good-byes at the door, I worry she'll attempt a hug. I stiffen at the prospect of her bony arms sliding over the folder jutting at my back. But apparently she's like Coop when it comes to hugs. She doesn't even shake my hand. She simply purses her lips, the wrinkles around them bunching.

"Take care of yourself, hon," she says.

ONE WEEK AFTER PINE COTTAGE

Good Cop and Bad Cop stared at Quincy, expecting something she couldn't provide. Detective Freemont, that old bulldog, looked rough around the edges, as if he hadn't slept in days. Quincy noticed he wore the same jacket from their first interview, its glaring mustard stain still intact. Detective Cole, on the other hand, remained a handsome devil, in spite of the bristle on his upper lip that wanted to be a mustache. Its edges flared when he smiled at her.

"You're probably nervous," he said. "Don't be."

Yet Quincy was very nervous. Only two days out of the hospital and she was in a police station, pushed there in a wheelchair by her exasperated mother because it still hurt to walk.

What a hassle, her mother said on the drive there. *Don't they see how much of an inconvenience this is?*

Her mother had been cleaning the upstairs bathroom when the call came, answering the phone with hands encased in flopping rubber gloves. Hassle or not, she nonetheless changed into a floral print dress before leaving for the station. Quincy remained in pajamas and a bathrobe, much to her mother's abject horror.

"Is something wrong?" Quincy asked as she stared at the two detectives from her wheelchair, wondering why she had been summoned there.

"We just have a few more questions," Cole said.

"I've already told you everything I know," Quincy said.

Freemont gave a sorry shake of his head. "Which is a whole lot of nothing."

"Listen, we don't want you to think we're harassing you," Cole said. "We just need to make sure we know everything that happened out at that cabin. For the families. Surely you can understand that."

Quincy didn't want to think about all those grieving parents and siblings and friends. Janelle's mother had visited her in the hospital. Red-eyed and trembling, she begged Quincy to tell her that Janelle hadn't suffered, that her daughter had felt no pain when she died. *She didn't feel a thing*, Quincy lied. *I'm sure of it.*

"I understand," she told Cole. "I want to help. I really do."

The detective reached into a briefcase at his feet and pulled out a file folder, which he placed on the table. Next came a metallic rectangle—a tape recorder, now set atop the folder.

"We're going to ask you a few questions," he said. "If you don't mind, we'd like to record the conversation."

Anxiety flickered through Quincy as she stared at the tape recorder. "Sure," she said, the word emerging in an uneasy wobble.

Cole pressed the Record button before saying, "Now, tell us, Quincy, to the best of your ability, what you remember about that night."

"The whole night? Or when Janelle started screaming? Because I don't remember much after that."

"The whole night."

"Well—" Quincy paused, shifting slightly to peer out the window set into the upper half of the door. The door itself had been closed once her mother was asked to wait outside. The window's square pane revealed only a bit of ivory-colored wall and the corner of a poster warning about the dangers of drunk driving. Quincy couldn't see her mother. She couldn't see anyone.

"We know there was drinking," Freemont said. "And marijuana use."

"There was," Quincy admitted. "I didn't do either."

"A good girl, eh?" Freemont said.

"Yes."

"But it *was* a party," Cole said.

"Yes."

"And Joe Hannen was there?"

Quincy flinched at the sound of His name. Her three stab wounds, still stitched tight, began to throb.

"Yes."

"Did something happen during the party?" Freemont asked. "Something that made him angry? Did anyone tease him? Abuse him? Maybe hurt him in a way that would make him want to lash out?"

"No," Quincy said.

"Did anything happen that made *you* angry?"

"No," Quincy said again, stressing the word, hoping it would make the lie somehow ring true.

"We looked at the results of your sexual-assault forensic exam," Freemont said.

He was referring to the rape kit Quincy endured once her wounds had been stitched up. She didn't remember much. Only staring at the ceiling and trying to hold back sobs as the nurse calmly talked her through each step.

"It says you had engaged in sexual intercourse that night. Is that true?"

Shame scorched Quincy's cheeks as she gave a single nod.

"Was it consensual?" Freemont said.

Quincy nodded again, the hot flush spreading to her forehead, her neck.

"Are you sure? It's okay to tell us if it wasn't."

"It was," Quincy replied. "Consensual, I mean. I wasn't raped."

Detective Cole cleared his throat, as eager as Quincy to change the subject. "Let's move on. Let's talk about what happened after your friend Janelle came out of the woods and you were stabbed in the shoulder. Are you certain you can't remember anything that happened after that?"

"Yes."

"Try," Cole suggested. "Just for a few minutes."

Quincy closed her eyes, trying for what felt like the hundredth time that week to conjure even the faintest memory of that missing hour. She took deep breaths, each one straining her stitches. Her head began to hurt. Another headache ballooning in her skull. All she saw was blackness.

"I'm sorry," she whimpered. "I can't."

"Nothing at all?" Freemont said.

"No." Quincy was trembling now, on the verge of tears. "There's nothing."

Freemont crossed his arms and gave her an annoyed huff. Cole simply stared at her, squinting slightly, as if he could see her better that way.

"I'm a little thirsty," he announced, turning to Freemont. "Hank, could you be a sport and get me a coffee from the vending machine?"

The request seemed to surprise Freemont. "Really?"

"Yes. Please." Cole looked to Quincy. "Are you allowed to have coffee?"

"I don't know."

"We better not risk it," Cole decided. "Caffeine and those pain meds you're on might not mix too well, am I right? That wouldn't be good for you. Sheesh."

It was the last word that tipped Quincy off. Spoken with such forced cheer, it all but announced that it was nothing more than an act. Cole's handsome face. Those warm, vaguely sexy smiles. All of it was just a charade.

Cole confirmed this once Freemont was out of the room.

"I'll give you credit," he told her. "You're good."

"You don't believe me," Quincy said.

"Not one bit. But we're going to find out the truth eventually. Think about that, Quincy. Imagine how your friends' parents will feel when they find out you've been lying all this time. *Sheesh.*"

That time, he winked as he said it. His way of telling Quincy he knew that she knew.

"Now, you can talk all you want about how you don't remember anything," he said. "But you and I both know you do."

Again, a strange shift began to take place inside Quincy. An internal hardening. Everything galvanized. She pictured her skin turning to metal, polished and gleaming. A shield protecting her from Cole's accusations. It made her feel strong.

"I'm sorry my lack of memory makes you angry," she said. "You can spend years asking me stuff, but until my memory comes back, my answers will always be the same."

"I might just do that," Cole replied. "I'll go to your house. Every month. Hell, once a week. I suspect your parents will soon start to wonder why that handsome detective keeps coming over asking questions."

Quincy flashed a smart-assed smile. "Only mildly handsome."

"I wouldn't be smiling if I were you," Cole said. "Six kids are dead, Quincy. Their parents want answers. And the only survivor is you, a wispy little girl who claims she can't remember a thing."

"You actually think I did it?"

"I think you're certainly hiding something. Possibly protecting someone. Maybe I'll change my mind if you finally tell me everything you saw that night, including the stuff you've conveniently forgotten."

"I've told you everything I know," she said. "What makes you think I'm lying?"

"Because it doesn't add up," Cole replied. "Your prints are on the knife that killed all your friends."

"And so are everyone else's." Anger swelled in Quincy's chest as she thought about how many times that knife switched hands. Janelle, Amy, and Betz all definitely touched it. *He* did too. "And I shouldn't have to remind you of this, but I was also stabbed. Three times."

"Two stab wounds to the shoulder and one in the abdomen," Cole said. "None of them life-threatening."

"Not for lack of trying."

"You want to hear what the others experienced?"

Cole reached for the folder atop the table. When he opened it, Quincy saw photographs. *Her* photographs. Taken with her camera. Of course the police had found it at Pine Cottage and downloaded the pictures stored within it.

The detective slid a photograph across the table. It showed Janelle sticking out her tongue in front of Pine Cottage, mugging for the camera.

"Janelle Bennett," he said. "Four stab wounds. One each to the heart, lung, shoulder, and stomach. Plus a slit throat."

The comforting mental shell Quincy had felt earlier suddenly faded into nothingness. Now she was all exposed underbelly.

"Stop," she murmured.

Cole ignored her, whipping out another photograph. Craig this time. Standing heroically atop the rock they had hiked to.

"Craig Anderson. Six stab wounds, ranging in depth from two to six inches."

"Please."

Next came the photo of Rodney and Amy squeezing each other on the hike. Quincy remembered what she'd said while taking it: *Make love to the camera.*

"Rodney Spelling," Cole said. "Four stab wounds. Two to the abdomen. One on his arm. One in the heart."

"Stop!" Quincy screamed, loud enough to bring in Freemont and a uniformed cop who hovered in the doorway. She recognized him immediately. Officer Cooper, fixing her with a protective blue-eyed stare. The mere sight of him filled her with relief.

"What's going on in here?" he asked. "Quincy, are you okay?"

Quincy looked at him, still on the verge of tears but refusing to let them see her cry.

"Tell him," she begged. "Tell him I didn't do anything. Tell him I'm a good person."

Officer Cooper moved to her side, making Quincy think he was about to hug her. She welcomed it. She wanted to feel safe in someone's arms. Instead, he put a large, steady hand on her shoulder.

"You're a wonderful person," he said, addressing her but looking squarely at Detective Cole. "You're a survivor."

30.

A big rig thunders by, horn streaking as it rocks the Camry parked on the highway's shoulder. I sit in the front passenger seat, legs bent out the open door. The interior light throws a dim halo over my hands and the folder gripped between them.

It's opened to the transcript of my interview with Freemont and that asshole Cole. Seeing the first few lines is all it takes to remember.

COLE: *Now, tell us, Quincy, to the best of your ability, what you remember about that night.*

CARPENTER: *The whole night? Or when Janelle started screaming? Because I don't remember much after that.*

COLE: *The whole night.*

I toss the transcript aside, unwilling to read further. I don't need to relive that conversation. Once was enough.

Beneath the transcript are several pages of emails, printed out and stapled together. All were sent during the same time period—three weeks ago.

Miss Milner,

Yes, I do know who you are and what happened all those years ago. I humbly offer my belated condolences and wish to say I admire the courage and fortitude you've displayed all these years. That is why I've attached the transcript of our recorded interview with Miss Carpenter that you so kindly requested. Although others may not, I understand your curiosity about Miss Carpenter. You two went through very similar ordeals. It's been a long time since my dealings with Miss Carpenter, but I remember them well. My partner and I interviewed her several times after the events at Pine Cottage. We both felt she wasn't telling the truth. It was my gut feeling that something preceded the horrible events that occurred at the cabin that night. Something that Miss Carpenter wanted to keep secret. This led my partner to believe she might have had something to do with the deaths of her friends. I didn't share his opinion then nor do I share it now, especially in light of the compelling testimony given by Officer Cooper at a hearing on the matter. Still, even to this day, I do think Miss Carpenter is hiding something about what happened at Pine Cottage. What that might be is something only Miss Carpenter knows.

Sincerely,
Det. Henry Freemont

I've said all there is to be said regarding the matter of Pine Cottage. My opinion of Quincy Carpenter has not changed.

Cole

Other than Detective Freemont's eloquence, nothing about the content of the emails surprises me. Cole thinks I'm guilty. Freemont is in the middle. Yet their existence gives me pause, even more than seeing those folders hidden in Lisa's closet. This is proof that she was looking into my past. Mere weeks before she was killed, no less.

I try to tell myself that one isn't related to the other, but that's not possible. They are. I know it.

Two more printed emails sit beneath the ones from Cole and Freemont. Unlike those, this pair rattles me.

It's good to hear from you again, Lisa. As always, I hope you're well. Quincy is also doing well, so your questions regarding what happened at Pine Cottage surprise me. However, I am thankful you didn't pose them to Quincy herself and I hope you continue to display such discretion. I can only tell you what I've been saying all along: Quincy Carpenter endured a terrible experience, as you well know and can certainly relate to. She's a survivor. Just like you. It's my firm belief that Quincy is telling the truth when she says she can't remember much about that night. As a child psychiatrist, you of all people know that repressed memory syndrome is a real condition. Considering what happened to Quincy, I can't blame her mind for wanting to forget.

Franklin Cooper

P.S. I won't tell Nancy what you're doing. I'm sure she'll frown upon it.

At first, disappointment nudges my ribs as I wonder why Coop never bothered to tell me that Lisa had recently contacted him. It seems like something I should have known about, especially in the wake of her murder. But I soften once I reread his earnest defense of me. It's just so Coop. Firm, polite, revealing nothing personal. That's when I realize why he didn't tell me about it: He didn't want to upset me.

As surprised as I am by Coop's email, nothing prepares me for the one beneath it.

Hello Lisa! Thank you for contacting me instead of writing to Quincy directly. You're right. It's best that we keep this under wraps. There's no point in upsetting her. Unfortunately, I can't say I'll be of

much help. Quincy and I aren't in touch as much as we used to be,
but that's how things go! Always so busy! If you'd like to talk, I'll
give you my phone number and you can call me when you're able.

Sheila

The email's such a shock that at first I'm not quite sure it's real. I
blink, expecting it to be gone when I reopen my eyes. But it's still
there, the words bold on the snow-white page.

That bitch.

Furious, I hop out of the car and stand on the road's edge. Next to
my feet is a spray of broken glass. A bottle, probably, yet I can't help
but think it's the wineglass missing from Lisa's house. Tossed out the
window of a speeding car, its driver still high on a post-killing adrenaline rush.

I dig the lighter out of my pocket and hold it to the bottom corner
of the folder. It's a cheap thing that requires several flicks to spark a
flame. No wonder the clerk let me steal it. The store probably gives
them out for free.

Once lit, the fire smolders a moment, taking time to sink its teeth
into the folder. Soon a flame is running up its side. When the flame
threatens to burn my hand, I drop the folder, fingers of fire shimmering in midair. The driver of a passing rig sees it, blares his horn, keeps
on trucking. On the ground, the folder burns until it's just ash caught
in the breeze of vehicles barreling down the road.

Once I'm convinced that every page has been destroyed, I snag
the water bottle sitting in the car's cup holder and pour it onto the
folder, the flames vanishing into hisses of smoke.

Destroying evidence. That's the easy part.

What I have to do next is going to be a whole lot harder.

Back in the car, I swerve back onto I-65, heading north. I steer
with one hand and dial my phone with my other. Then I lay the phone
flat on the passenger seat, set to speaker mode. Each ring sounds out
loud and clear inside the car. The noise reminds me of my phone calls

on Mother's Day, when I count each ring, guiltily hoping no one will pick up. Today, someone does.

"Quincy?" my mother says, clearly shocked to be hearing from me. "Is something wrong?"

"Yes," I say. "Why didn't you tell me Lisa Milner contacted you?"

31.

There's a pause on my mother's end. Long enough to make me think she's hung up. Seconds pass in which I hear nothing but the whoosh of air sliding across the car's exterior. But then my mother speaks. Her voice is lukewarm and without inflection—the aural equivalent of melted vanilla ice cream.

"What a strange question, Quincy."

I huff out an angry sigh.

"I saw the email, Mom. I know you gave her your phone number. Did she call you back?"

Another pause. A bit of static crackles from my phone before my mother says, "I knew you'd be angry if you found out."

"When did you talk?" I say.

"Oh, I don't know."

"You do, Mom. Now, tell me."

More pausing. More static.

"About two weeks ago," my mother says.

"Did Lisa say why she was so suddenly interested in me again?"

"She told me she was worried."

This sends a chill scudding through me.

Quincy, I need to talk to you. It's extremely important. Please, please don't ignore this.

"Worried *for* me? Or *about* me?"

"She didn't really say, Quincy."

"Then what did you talk about?"

"Lisa asked me how you were doing. I told her you were doing great. I mentioned your website, your nice apartment, Jeff."

"Anything else?"

"She asked—" My mother stops herself, thinks, carries on. "She asked if you've recovered any memories. Of what happened that night."

Another chill goes through me. I switch on the car heater, hoping that will make it go away.

"Why would she do that?"

"I don't know," my mother says.

"And what did you tell her?"

"The truth. That you can't remember a thing."

Only, it's not the truth. Not anymore. I remember something. A keyhole-size peek into that night.

I take a deep breath, inhaling the dusty hot air rushing from the heating vents. It does nothing to warm me. All it manages to do is make my throat itchy and dry. My voice is a rasp when I say, "Did Lisa mention why she wanted to know this?"

"She said she'd been thinking about you lately. She said she wanted to check in on you."

"Then why didn't she call me?"

Instead, Lisa had reached out to Cole, Freemont, Coop, and my mother. Everyone but me. By the time she did reach out, it was too late.

"I don't know, Quincy," my mother says. "I guess she didn't want to bother you. Or maybe—"

Another pause. A lengthy one. So long that I can feel the distance stretching between my mother and me. All those fields and cities and small towns that sit between this Indiana highway and her too-white house in Bucks County.

"Mom?" I say. "Maybe what?"

"I was going to say that maybe Lisa thought you wouldn't be honest with her."

"She didn't actually say that, did she?"

"No," my mother says. "Nothing like that. But I got a feeling—and I could be wrong—I got the feeling that she knew something. Or suspected something."

"About?"

My mother goes quiet. "About what happened that night."

I squirm in the driver's seat, suddenly unbearably hot. Beads of sweat have popped along my brow line. I wipe them away and click off the heater.

"What gave you this feeling?"

"More than once, she stressed how lucky you were. How you re- covered so quickly. How your wounds weren't that bad. Especially compared with what happened to the others."

In ten years, this is the most my mother has ever talked about Pine Cottage with me. Four lousy sentences. I'd consider it some sort of warped breakthrough if the situation weren't so dire.

"Mom," I say, "did Lisa suggest that I had something to do with what happened at Pine Cottage?"

"She didn't suggest anything—"

"Then why do you think she suspected something?"

"I don't know, Quincy."

But I do. It's because my mother also suspects something. She doesn't think I killed the others. But I'm certain that, just like Cole and Freemont, she wonders why I lived when no one else did. Deep down, she thinks there's something I'm not saying.

I think about the way she had looked at me after I trashed the kitchen all those years ago. The hurt darkening her eyes. The utter fear quivering in her pupils. I wish to God I could forget that look as thoroughly as I've forgotten that hour at Pine Cottage. I want it erased from my memory. Painted so black I can never see it again.

"Why didn't you tell me about this?"

"I *tried*," my mother says, going heavy on the faux indignation. "I called you two days in a row. You didn't call back."

"You talked to Lisa two weeks ago, Mom," I say. "You should have called me as soon as it happened."

"I wanted to protect you. As your mother, that's my job."

"Not from something like this."

"All I want is for you to be happy," my mother says. "That's all I ever wanted, Quincy. Happy and content and normal."

Within that last word lies all my mother's hopes and all my

failings. It's as powerful and potent as a grenade dropped into the conversation. Only I'm the one who explodes.

"I'm not normal, Mom!" I scream, my words bouncing off the windshield. "After what happened, there's no possible way for me to be normal!"

"But you are!" my mother says. "You had a problem, but we took care of it and now everything is fine."

Tears burn the corners of my eyes. I try to mentally force them not to fall. Yet they leak out anyway, slipping down my cheek as I say, "I'm as far from fine as you can possibly get."

My mother's tone softens. In her voice is something I haven't heard in years—concern.

"Why didn't you ever tell me this, Quincy?"

"I shouldn't have had to," I say. "You should have seen that something was wrong."

"But you looked fine."

"Because you forced it on me, Mom. The pills and the refusing to talk about it. That was all because of you. Now, I'm—"

I don't know what I am.

Screwed up, obviously.

So screwed up that I could tally for my mother the many ways in which I've failed as a human being. I'm likely in trouble with the police. I'm possibly harboring Lisa's murderer in an apartment I could only afford because my friends were butchered. I'm addicted to Xanax. And wine. I pretend I'm not depressed. And angry. And alone. Even when I'm with Jeff, I sometimes feel so unbearably alone.

What's worse is that I never would have realized this without Sam crashing into my life. It took some prodding on her part, of course. All those tests and dares and nudges to reveal something about myself, to remember tiny details of something I'm all too happy to have forgotten.

Then it hits me. Hard. I'm like a nail just struck by a hammer—brittle, quivering, sinking deeper into something from which there is no escape.

"Mom, what did Lisa sound like on the phone?"

"What do you mean? She sounded like I imagined her to sound."

"I need specifics," I say. "How did her voice sound? Hoarse? Raspy?"

"I really didn't notice." My mother's confusion is evident. I picture her staring at the phone, befuddled. "You're the one who talked to Lisa all those years ago. I don't know what she's supposed to sound like."

"Please, Mom. If you can think of anything."

For the last time, my mother lapses into a deep silence. I clutch the steering wheel, hoping she'll come up with something. And while she's failed me many, many times in the past, in this instance, Sheila Carpenter comes through.

"There were a lot of pauses," she says, ignoring the irony coiled in that statement. "Lisa would talk, then pause. And with each pause, I heard a little exhale."

"Like a sigh?"

"Quieter than that."

It's all I need to know. In fact, it tells me everything.

"Mom, I need to go."

"Will you be all right?" my mother asks. "Tell me that you'll take care of yourself."

"I will. I promise."

"I hope that whatever's going on, I was able to help."

"Yes, Mom," I say. "Thank you. You helped more than you'll ever realize."

Because now I know that those pauses my mother had heard definitely wasn't sighing. It was the sound of someone smoking.

Which means she hadn't spoken to Lisa.

My mother had talked to Sam.

Curious, inquisitive Sam. She knows more than she let on. She's known it all along. That's why she showed up out of the blue. It wasn't to connect with me. It wasn't for money.

She's trying to find out everything she can about Pine Cottage.

About what I did there.

I end the call and roll down the window, letting myself be hit with bursts of crisp, Midwestern air. My grip tightens around the steering wheel as my foot presses on the accelerator. I watch the speedometer creep higher, passing seventy, seventy-five, flirting with eighty.

It doesn't help, no matter how fast I drive. I still feel like a fly, wriggling in a web of Sam's making. I realize there are only two ways to get free—fight or flight.

I know which one it needs to be.

Back at the hotel, I change my airline reservation. There's an eight p.m. flight from Chicago to New York. I'm going to be on it.

Jeff, of course, doesn't understand why I need to fly back to New York so suddenly. He peppers me with questions as I stuff clothes into my suitcase. I answer each one twice—the lie out loud, the truth in my head.

"Does this have something to do with Sam?"

"No."

Of course it does.

"Quincy, did she do something wrong?"

"Not yet."

Yes, she's done something terrible. We both have.

"I just don't understand why you need to leave this second. Why now?"

"Because I need to get back as soon as possible."

Because Sam knows things about me. Horrible things. Just as I know horrible things about her. Now I need to get her out of my life for good.

"Would it help if I went with you?"

"That's sweet, but no. You still have work to take care of."

You can't go with me, Jeff. I've been lying to you. About many things. And if you find them out, you won't want to be anywhere near me.

Once I'm packed and heading for the door, Jeff grabs me and pulls me tight against him. I long to remain in that exact spot, held in place, comforted. But that's not possible. Not with Sam still in my life.

"Will you be okay?" he asks.

"Yes," I tell him.

No. Despite what you might think, I'll never be okay.

The plane is small, barely booked. A money-losing trip that exists solely to get the aircraft to JFK for a more profitable flight in the morning. I have an entire row to myself. After takeoff, I stretch across the empty seats.

Lying there, I do everything possible not to think about Sam. Nothing works. There's no way to ignore the suspicion that skitters into my thoughts as if on spider legs. I imagine her dropping pills into Lisa's wineglass, seeing her sip them into her system, waiting until they take effect. I picture Sam with the knife, slicing Lisa's wrists, watching the results as she bites her fingernails.

Is she capable of doing such a thing?

Maybe.

Why would she do such a thing?

Because she was on the hunt for information about me. Perhaps she roped Lisa into helping her. But Lisa had second thoughts, pushed her away, threatened to kick her out. Now it's my turn to do the same thing. I pray the results are different.

Somehow, I manage to sleep for most of the flight, although even that offers little relief. I dream of Sam sitting stiff-backed on my living-room sofa. I'm in a chair across from her.

Did you kill Lisa Milner? I ask.

Did you kill those kids at Pine Cottage? she says.

You're avoiding the question.

So are you.

Do you think *I killed people at Pine Cottage?*

Sam smiles, her lipstick so red it looks like her mouth has been smeared with blood. *You're a fighter. One who'll do anything to survive. Just like me.*

A flight attendant snaps me awake as we make our descent into New York. I get into the upright position, shaking the dream away. I look out the window, the night sky and plane's interior lights turning it into an oval mirror. I barely recognize the reflection staring back at me.

I can't remember the last time I did.

PINE COTTAGE
10:14 P.M.

In the bedroom, Craig wasted no time in shedding his pants. Quincy didn't even realize they were off until he was on top of her, drunkenly kissing her, pushing the dress up to her stomach while grinding hard against her inner thigh. When he reached for Quincy's breasts, she put her hands over his, nodding her consent.

She was ready for this. Janelle had prepared her. She knew what to expect. She was a vestal virgin, tossed upon the altar, waiting for eternity.

But then Craig's breathing grew ragged and rough. So did his movements, which had been made brutish by too much alcohol and pot. When he slid his knees between her legs and pried them open, Quincy's whole body tensed.

"Wait," she murmured.

"Just relax," Craig said. His face was buried against her neck, sucking it, skin sticking to his hungry mouth.

"I'm trying."

"Try harder."

Craig made another attempt at parting her legs with his knees. Quincy kept them shut, thigh muscles straining.

"Stop."

Craig thrust his mouth upon hers, his flopping tongue silencing her. He was heavy on top of her, pinning her down, breathing like a bull while bucking against her closed thighs. Quincy felt like she was being smothered, suffocated. Craig's hands fell from her breasts to her knees, prying at them.

"*Stop*," Quincy said, putting more force into it this time. "I mean it."

She gave Craig a shove, slid out from under him, and sat up, back against the headboard. Craig's smile lasted a few more seconds before fading as realization set in.

"I thought we agreed to do this," he said.

"We did."

"Then what's the problem?"

Quincy didn't know if there even was a problem. Her body pulsed with desire, aching for Craig to be on top of her, against her, inside her. Yet a small part of her knew it didn't have to be like this. If they continued, it would be rushed and blunt, almost like they were following another one of Janelle's stupid rules.

"I want my first time to be special."

She thought it would make sense to him. That he would see how much this really meant to her. Instead, he said, "This isn't special enough for you? It's better than what I had."

The words confirmed something Quincy had always suspected but never wanted to ask. This wasn't Craig's first time. He had been through this before. The revelation felt to Quincy like a betrayal, small yet painful.

"I thought you knew," Craig said, easily reading her thoughts.

"I just assumed you were too."

"I never told you I was a virgin. I'm sorry if that's what you thought, but it wasn't my doing."

"I know," Quincy said.

She wondered how many other girls had been in the same position with him and if all of them had simply given in to the pressure. She hoped someone else had resisted. She hoped she wasn't the only one.

"I didn't lie to you, Quincy. So you're going to have to come up with a better excuse than that for saying no."

"But I'm not saying no," Quincy said, suddenly backtracking, mad at herself for doing so. "I just thought—"

"That it would be candles and flowers and romance?"

"That it would mean something," Quincy said. "Don't I mean anything to you?"

Craig rolled off the bed, suddenly shy. He searched for his pants while stretching the bottom of his shirt over his crotch. It was all the answer Quincy needed. Still, she reached for him, trying to lure him back to bed before he could get fully dressed.

"This doesn't have to be a problem," she said. "I still want to spend the night together. Who knows what will happen."

Despite her efforts, Craig found his pants on the floor next to the bed and started to stuff his legs into them. "Nothing is going to happen. I think you've made that very clear."

"Please come back to bed. I just need to give it some more thought."

"Think all you want." Craig zipped his fly and headed for the door. "But I'm done thinking."

Then he was gone, rejoining the party, leaving Quincy curled up in bed and crying. Large tears dripped onto the borrowed white dress, each one spreading, darkening the silk.

32.

It's past midnight when I reach home. Rather than well rested from my nap on the plane, I am drowsy and weak. My hands tremble as I unlock the door, partly from exhaustion, partly from uncertainty. I don't know what's awaiting me inside the apartment. I imagine opening the door to see the place stripped of every item we own, my post-dated check tossed onto the bare floor. And even that's better than finding Sam waiting for me in the shadows of the foyer, knife raised.

I drop my bags just inside the door, freeing my hands in case I need to defend myself. But there's no Sam gripping a knife. No Sam offering a glass of wine swimming with pills. A quick look around seems to confirm everything that was here before I left remains here still. The apartment is dark and, from the feel of it, empty. The place has an air of abandonment, as if someone has only recently departed, leaving bits of their essence swirling like dust.

"Sam? It's me."

My heart begins to pound as I wait for a response that doesn't arrive.

"I decided to come back early," I call out as my chest fills with hope. "I caught a late flight."

I roam the apartment, flicking on lights. Kitchen, dining room, living room. No trace of theft. No trace of Sam.

She's gone. I'm certain of it. She's skipped town, just as I had hoped. Taking her secrets with her and leaving mine.

I dig through my purse in search of my phone. I texted Jeff when

I landed, telling him I'd arrived safely and that I'll call him when everything is over. Now it *is* over, and I'm in the hallway, phone in hand, about to hit Dial.

That's when I notice the door to the guest room is still closed. Light seeps from beneath the door, crossing my shoes as I stand in front of it. Music plays on the other side, muffled behind the wood.

My heart hits the floor.

Sam is still here.

"Sam?"

I reach for the doorknob. It's loose in my hand, the door unlocked. Without hesitation, I swing it open and look inside.

The room is bathed in red-and-gold light. The red is from the nightstand·lamp. The gold comes from several candles that sit beside it. Music plays from an old CD player that's been pulled from the storage closet. Peggy Lee, purring out "Fever."

In the soft half-light, I can make out Sam on the edge of the bed. At least I think it's her. She looks so unlike her normal self that recognition is slow to arrive. She wears a dress far different from the grungy black one she first showed up in. This one is red, with capped sleeves, an A-line skirt, a scooped neck that gives a tantalizing peek of cleavage. Matching heels are on her feet. Her hair is pulled up, exposing her pale neck.

She's not alone.

A man sits beside her in a crisp black polo shirt and khakis. I have no trouble recognizing him.

Coop.

His hand is on Sam's neck, caressing the pale skin just beneath her chin. Sam is touching him too, her index finger riding the swell of his left biceps. They lean into each other, faces turned, on the verge of a kiss.

"What—"

What the fuck is going on?

That's what I mean to say, but only the first word comes out. Sam drops her hand from his arm. Coop's hand remains at her neck, his whole body stilled by surprise. I haven't seen him so shocked since our first meeting outside Pine Cottage. He wears the same expression he did that night. It's not as extreme, not as horrified. But it's there. A slightly smudged copy of the original.

"Quincy," he says. "I'm so—"

"Get out."

He manages to stand and steps toward me. "I can explain."

"Get out," I say again, growling the words.

"But—"

"Get out!"

Suddenly I'm upon him, scratching at him with one hand while unleashing a series of slaps with the other. My hands soon turn to fists, flying at him, not caring what part of him I hit as long as I hit something. And I do, landing blow after blow as Coop merely stands there and takes it. But then Sam swoops in, a flash of red, all but tackling me against the wall.

"Go!" she hisses to Coop.

He pauses at the door, watching me wail and thrash and pound my head against the wall, each thump harder than the last.

"Get the fuck out!" Sam yells.

This time, Coop obeys and slips out of the room. I slide down the wall, weeping. Pain makes me double over, arms folded across my stomach. It feels like a sharpened blade is pushing into my gut, stabbing me again and again and again.

PINE COTTAGE
10:56 P.M.

Quincy, drained of tears, left the room in search of Janelle. She needed that combination of abrasiveness and pity only Janelle could provide. She was like human sandpaper in that regard. Rough and soothing in equal measure.

In the great room, she found Ramdy stuffed into one of the armchairs. Amy sat on Rodney's lap, one lithe arm around his neck as they made out. They reminded Quincy of swimmers, mouths open, gasping.

"Where's Janelle?"

The female half of Ramdy surfaced, catching her breath, annoyed to be so disturbed. "What?"

"Janelle. Have you seen her?"

Amy shook her head before diving back under.

Quincy then headed outside, creaking across the deck. It was a clear night, the full moon coloring the trees pale gray. She paused on the deck steps, listening for signs of Janelle. Footsteps on the grass, for instance. Or the throaty laugh that was so familiar she could pick it out in a crowd. She heard nothing but the last of the season's creepers in the trees and the distant, forlorn hoot of an owl.

Rather than go back inside, Quincy kept walking, drawn into the woods. She found herself following the same path they had trod earlier, the leaves still tamped down. It was only when the forest floor began to rise that Quincy thought about turning back. By then it was too late. She needed to push on, even though she wasn't sure why. Call it a hunch. An instinct. A certainty, even, surging with the blood inside her veins.

The large rock peeked into view as she neared the top of the incline. Its sheer size created a break in the canopy of tree branches overhead. It was like a hole in an umbrella, silver moonlight pouring through it, raining down on two people atop the rock.

One of them was Janelle.

The other was Craig.

He lay on his back, shirt off and balled under his head to form a makeshift pillow. His pants had been shoved to his ankles, circling them like manacles. Janelle sat on top of him, riding him. Each thrust moved the skirt of her dress. An ebb and tide of fabric across Craig's bare thighs. The top of her dress was pulled down, exposing breasts so pale they practically glowed in the moonlight.

"Yes," she moaned, the word a wisp mingling with the night air. "Yes, yes, yes."

Anger and hurt clenched Quincy's stomach, like there was a hand there holding her insides, squishing them as it curled into a fist.

Yet she couldn't look away. Not with Janelle moaning like that, her movements more desperate than passionate. It was all too beautiful and painful and grotesque.

Then the sobs came, burbling out of her. Quincy slapped a hand over her mouth to block the sound. Even though she shouldn't have cared if they heard her. Even though all she wanted to do was scream to the sky, her banshee's wail riding the breeze.

But the angry fist inside her kept squeezing, increasing her anger, her pain. She slipped back through the woods, fresh tears forming where the earlier ones had dried. She could still hear Janelle as she slid down the incline, her repeated moans like a taunting bird in the branches.

Yes, yes, yes.

33.

"Why?" I say, still on the floor.

Sam ignores me, instead crossing the room to silence the CD player. Then it's on to the knapsack, where she pulls out her black jeans and begins to slide them on under the skirt of the red dress.

"Why?"

"Because it needed to be done," Sam says.

"It didn't," I say, rising to my knees. "You just felt like it did."

Because she knew how much it would hurt me once I found out. And I was certain she intended to make sure I found out. This was just another way to mess with me, to wake me up, to make me angry.

I claw at the wall, using it to help me rise to my feet. Still unsteady, I lean against it, leveling my gaze at Sam. She's removed the dress and is now yanking her Sex Pistols shirt over her head. Then she sits on the bed, replacing the fuck-me heels with her combat boots.

"You're sick," I tell her. "You know that, right? You can't stand to think that one of us could have a normal life. That at least one of us could actually be happy."

Sam goes to the window, throws it open, and lights a cigarette. Puffing out smoke, she says, "You have me all figured out, don't you?"

"I do. You came here and saw that I was normal and stable and decided that you had to fuck it all up."

"Stable? You sent a guy to the hospital, babe. He's still in a goddamn coma."

"Because of you! You wanted me to do it!"

"Keep thinking that, Quinn. If you need that lie to be able to live with yourself, then keep on believing it."

I look away, not sure what to believe.

It feels as if gravity has failed and everything once secure and settled in my life is now tumbling in midair, suddenly just beyond my reach.

"Why Coop?" I ask. "It's Manhattan. There are a million guys you could have picked. So why him?"

"Insurance."

"For what?"

"That detective came by again this morning," Sam says. "Hernandez. She said she wanted to talk to you. When I told her you were away, she said she'd be back and that you shouldn't have left town."

Because my running off with my lawyer boyfriend made me look suspicious. Of course it did.

"I didn't know what to do," Sam says. "So I called Coop."

I suck in my breath, suddenly numb. "You didn't tell him about the park, did you?"

Sam rolls her eyes while hissing out smoke. "Hell no. I told him that we should get to know each other better. That he should come to the city if he could. He did."

"And you seduced him."

"I wouldn't say that," Sam says. "He was more than willing."

"Then why did you do it?"

Sam lets out a weary sigh. She looks so tired, so defeated by life.

So utterly damaged.

"Because I thought it would help us," she says. "You, especially. If the police are able to trace that guy's beating back to us, we're going to need someone on our side. Someone other than Jeff."

"A cop," I say, grim understanding settling over me. "One who can defend us to his colleagues. One too blinded by emotions to do the right thing and turn us in if he suspects something."

"Bingo," Sam says. "But you know all about that, don't you?"

"I've never tried to fuck Coop."

A snort from Sam, nostrils streaming smoke. "Like that matters. You're still using him. For years, you've used him. Texting him at all hours. Beckoning him into the city at a moment's notice. Flirting with him every now and then to keep him interested."

"That's not how it is," I say. "I would never do that to him."

"You do it all the time, Quinn. I've seen you do it."

"Not on purpose."

"Really?" Sam says. "You mean to tell me this weird, creepy thing between you two has nothing to do with what happened at Pine Cottage? That you've never noticed, not even the tiniest bit, that you have him wrapped around your finger?"

"I don't," I say.

Sam stubs out her cigarette. Lights another. "Lies, lies, lies."

"Let's talk about lies," I say, pushing away from the wall, strengthened by anger. "You lied when you told me you never met Lisa. You did. You stayed at her house."

Sam stops inhaling on the cigarette, her cheeks slightly sucked in, smoke gathering in her mouth. When she parts her lips, a grayish cloud rolls out like a fog bank.

"You're crazy."

"That's not an answer," I say. "At least admit you were there."

"Fine. I was there."

"When?"

"A few weeks ago," she says. "But you already knew that."

"Why did you go? Did Lisa invite you?"

Sam shakes her head.

"So you just showed up like you did with me?"

"Yup," Sam says. "Unlike you, she actually said hello when she realized who I was."

"How long were you there?"

"About a week," Sam says.

"So she liked having you there?"

It's a wasted question. Of course Lisa liked having Sam there. It's what she lived for—taking troubled young women under her wing and helping them. Sam was likely the most troubled of them all.

"She did," Sam says. "At first. But by the end of the week, Lisa couldn't deal with me anymore."

I infer the rest. Sam showed up out of the blue, knapsack bulging with Wild Turkey and expressions of sisterhood. Lisa gladly let her crash in the guest room. But that wasn't enough. Not for Sam. She needed to pry, to needle. She probably tried to shake Lisa out of her complacency. To make her get angry, to make her a survivor.

Lisa didn't let her. I did. Both of us paid a very different price.

"So why did you lie about it?"

"Because I knew you'd become a drama queen if I told you. That you'd start getting suspicious."

"Why?" I say. "Do you have something to hide? Did you kill Lisa, Sam?"

There it is. The question that's been itching at the back of my brain for days, now spoken, made real. Sam shakes her head as if she pities me.

"Poor, sad Quincy. You're more messed up than I thought."

"Tell me you had nothing to do with her death," I say.

Sam drops the cigarette, making a show of grinding it out on the hardwood floor with the toe of her boot. "No matter what I say, you're not going to believe me."

"You've given me no reason so far," I reply. "Why start now?"

"I didn't kill Lisa," Sam says. "Believe me or not. I don't give a fuck."

A beep rises from deep within my pocket. My phone.

"That's probably your boyfriend," Sam says with pronounced disgust. "One of them, at least."

I check the phone. Sure enough, there's a text from Coop.

we need to talk

At the window, Sam asks, "Which one is it?"

I don't answer, which is an answer in itself. I stare at the screen, my heart seizing up at the prospect of seeing Coop again. Not just tonight. But ever again.

Sam jams another cigarette between her lips and says, "Run to your little cop, Quincy Carpenter. But remember, watch what you say. My secrets are your secrets. And Officer Cooper might not like yours."

"Go to hell," I say.

Sam lights up and smiles. "Already been there, babe."

PINE COTTAGE
11:12 P.M.

Quincy was out of breath by the time she reached the cabin. Her lungs burned, scraped by both exertion and the night air. Despite the chill, a thin coating of sweat covered her skin, cold and sticky.

Inside, it was quietly chaotic, all dirty dishes and liquor bottles with only dregs remaining. The great room was abandoned. Even the fire had gone out, a trace of woodsmoke heat the only reminder it ever existed.

Sleep. That was all Quincy wanted. To fall asleep and wake up having forgotten everything she had seen. It was possible, she knew. Already her brain was telling her that she was mixed up, saw something she didn't really see. Maybe Janelle had been with someone else. Joe, perhaps. Or maybe Quincy only thought she saw Craig lying on his back, face contorted, pushing into her.

But her heart knew otherwise.

Wiping away tears, Quincy crept down the hall, passing Janelle's empty room. Across the hall, Betz had gone to bed, the closed door shutting out the view of those sad bunk beds. The door to Ramdy's room was also closed, not quite blocking out the violent sloshing sound of the waterbed. Occasional grunts from Rodney rose with the tide.

Quincy turned into Craig's room.

Fuck Craig.

It was her room now.

But it wasn't empty. Someone was on the bed, a vague outline in the moonlit gloom. He lay with his hands behind his head. Quincy faintly saw his wide-open eyes behind his dirty glasses.

"I didn't know where to sleep," he said.

Quincy stared at him, jealous of how comfortable he looked, how oblivious he was. She sniffed. She caught a tear before it could streak down her face.

"Are you okay?" he asked.

"You need to go," Quincy said.

He sat up, concern flickering in his half-obscured eyes. "You're not okay."

"No shit," Quincy said, sitting on the bed. Another tear fell. This time she wasn't able to stop it.

"I saw them leave together," he said. "They walked into the woods."

"I know."

"I'm sorry."

He touched her shoulder, the suddenness of the gesture making Quincy recoil.

"Please go," she said.

"He doesn't deserve you."

When he touched her shoulder a second time, Quincy allowed it. Emboldened, his hand slipped down Quincy's arm to her midriff. Again, she let him do it.

"You're better than him," he whispered. "Better than both of them. So pretty."

"Thank you," Quincy said.

"I mean it."

Quincy turned to him, grateful for his presence. He seemed so sincere. So inexperienced. The opposite of Craig.

She leaned in and kissed him. His lips were hot against hers, kissing back. His tongue slid into her mouth. Tentative. Exploring. It made Quincy almost forget what she had seen in the woods. How Janelle was on top of Craig, riding him, her body radiating lust and pain.

But that wasn't enough. Quincy wanted to forget completely.

Without a word, she climbed on top of him, surprised at how solid he felt beneath her. Like a downed tree. Sturdy oak. Quincy pulled off his sweater, which smelled vaguely of industrial-strength cleaner. The odor stung her nose as she tossed it to the floor and tugged his T-shirt over his head.

She began to suck on his narrow chest, running her hands over the milky skin. So pale. So cold. Like a ghost.

Then her panties were off. His corduroys were at his knees.

On the floor beside the bed was Craig's backpack. Inside was a box of condoms. Quincy pulled one out and gave it to Joe, placing it into his trembling palm.

"Are you sure?" he asked.

"Yes."

"Tell me if it hurts," he whispered. "I don't want to hurt you. I just want to make you feel good."

Quincy took a deep breath and eased herself lower, bracing for the pleasure and the pain, knowing it wouldn't be one or the other.

It would be both at once, forever intertwined.

34.

Coop texts me the name of a hotel a few blocks from my apartment and the number of the room he's staying in. I don't know if he booked the room before coming into the city to meet Sam or after. I decide not to ask.

I pause outside his door, uncertain if I'll be able to face him again. I already know I don't want to. I'd rather be anywhere but this dim hotel hallway with its buzzing ice machine and carpet-shampoo stench. But we have a history. No matter what Coop has done, I owe him the chance to explain himself.

I knock, the door quickly squeaking open beneath my fist. My hand remains clenched as Coop steps into view.

"Quincy." The nod he gives me is quick, shameful. "Come in. If you want to."

Only the past keeps me there. My past. Coop's role in it. The undeniable fact that I wouldn't even have a past if it weren't for him. So I enter, stepping into a room shocking in its smallness. It's nothing more than a large closet someone has managed to fit a bed and dresser into. There's roughly two feet of space between bed and wall, making it hard for me to edge around Coop as he closes the door behind me.

The room has no chairs. Rather than sit on the bed, I remain standing.

I know exactly what I need to do, which is to tell Coop everything. About what Sam has done. What *I've* done. Maybe then I can start the process of getting my life back to normal. Not that it's ever been normal after Pine Cottage.

But I can't confess to Coop. I can barely look at him.

"Let's get this over with," I say, arms folded, shifting weight onto my left leg so my hip angrily juts.

"I'll be quick," Coop says.

He's just showered, steam lingering inside the minuscule bathroom. Dampness clings to his close-cropped hair and his body seems to radiate humidity, sultry and soap scented.

"I need to explain myself. To explain my actions."

"What you do in your free time is none of my business," I say. "It's not as if you mean anything to me."

Coop winces, and I feel a satisfying twinge of strength. I'm hurting him too. Drawing blood.

"Quincy, we both know that's not true."

"Isn't it?" I say. "If we meant something to each other you wouldn't have gone to my apartment to try and fuck Sam while I was away."

"That's not why I was there."

"It sure as hell looked that way to me."

"She called me, Quincy," Coop says. "She said she was concerned about you. So I came. Because something wasn't sitting right with me. I don't trust her, Quincy. I haven't since she arrived. She's up to something, and I wanted to find out what it was."

"Seduction is an interesting interrogation technique," I say. "You use it often?"

"What you saw wasn't planned, Quincy. It just happened."

I roll my eyes, going all big and dramatic, just like Janelle used to do.

"That's the oldest excuse in the book."

"It's true," Coop says. "You don't know how lonely I am, Quincy. So completely alone. I live in a house big enough for five people. But there's only me. Some rooms I haven't entered for years. They're empty, the doors closed."

His confession leaves me speechless. This is the first time Coop has ever opened up to me like this. It turns out we have more in common than I ever imagined. Yet I refuse to feel sorry for him. I'm not ready to forgive him.

"Is that why you wanted me to come?" I say. "To make me pity you?"

"No. I asked you here because I need to tell you something. There's a reason—" Coop stops to clear his throat. "A reason I've tried to be there for you. A reason I've made myself available day or night. Quincy—"

Instinctively, I know what's coming next. I shake my head, my thoughts screaming, *Don't. Please, Coop, don't say it.*

He does anyway. "I love you."

"Don't," I say, this time aloud. "Don't say any more."

"But I do," Coop says. "You know it, Quincy. I think you've always known it. Why else do you think I drive out here at a moment's notice? It's to see you. To be with you. I don't care if it's for one minute or one hour. Just seeing you makes that whole lonely drive worthwhile."

He makes a move toward me and I back away, stuck in a corner between the dresser and the wall. Coop keeps coming, not stopping until he's right in front of me.

"I've never met anyone like you, Quincy," he says. "Believe me when I say that. You're so strong. A true survivor."

He looks at me, his blue eyes making my knees quiver. He touches a thumb to my cheek, sliding it down to my mouth.

"Coop," I say as his thumbnail gently scrapes my lips. "Stop."

"You feel the same way," Coop says, voice husky. "I know you do."

I picture him nestled beside Sam, caressing her neck, lips just starting to push against hers. I hate Coop for doing that. He should have been all mine.

"I don't," I say.

"You're lying."

It's hot inside the room. Stifling, actually. The humming AC unit under the window does little to change that. And then there's Coop, so close to me, emanating a different kind of heat.

"I need to go," I say.

"No, you don't."

When he edges closer, I push back, shoving his chest. He's sweating under his shirt. The fabric beneath my hands sticks to his skin.

"What do you want from me, Coop? You said what you have to say. What else do you want?"

"You," he says softly. "I want you, Quincy."

Contrary to what I've told Sam, I have thought about what could make me succumb to my attraction to Coop. Those blue eyes always struck me as the likely culprit. They're bright as lasers, seeing everything. But it's his voice that finally does it. That soft confession pulling me into his arms.

It's our first embrace since Pine Cottage. The first time he's wrapped those strong arms around me. I expect the memory to tarnish this new embrace. It doesn't. It only makes it sweeter.

With him, I feel safe.

I always have.

I kiss him. Even though it's wrong. He kisses back, lips hungry, biting. Years of pent-up lust are finally being released, and the result is more need than desire. More pain than pleasure.

Soon we're on the bed. There's nowhere else to go. My clothes come off. I don't know how. They seem to simply fall away, as do Coop's.

He knows what he wants.

God help me, I let him take it.

He was still asleep when Quincy slipped from the bed and crossed the room on tiptoe, hunting her shoes, her dress, her panties. It hurt to move. Soreness lingered between her legs, flaring whenever she bent over. Still, it wasn't as bad as she thought it would be. There was consolation in that.

She dressed quickly, suddenly aware of the sharp chill hanging in the room. It was as if she had a fever. She shivered from the cold even though her skin was burning hot.

In the hall, Quincy ducked into the bathroom, not bothering to turn on the overhead light. She had no desire to face herself in the mirror under that harsh glare. Instead, she stared at her dark reflection, most of its features erased. She had become a shadow.

A chant popped into her head. Something from grade school. She and her friends in the pitch-black girls' room, repeating a name.

Bloody Mary, Bloody Mary, Bloody Mary.

"Bloody Mary," Quincy said, eyes on her eyeless reflection.

Once out of the bathroom, she paused at the entrance to the great room, fearful that Craig and Janelle might have returned, drunk and giggling and pretending like nothing had happened between them. She only proceeded once she heard nothing. The cabin was silent.

Quincy headed to the kitchen, standing there, pondering her next step. Should she confront them? Demand to go home? Maybe she'd look for Craig's keys and take his SUV, leaving all of them stranded without their cell phones.

The idea made her smile. Already she had entered the second stage of grief, which she learned in psych class only three days earlier. Janelle skipped that lecture and Quincy had yet to give her the notes. She didn't know that second rung in the ladder of grief. But Quincy did.

It was anger.

Full-throated, bitch-on-wheels anger.

Quincy felt it warm in her stomach. Like heartburn, only hotter. It pulsed outward, zipping through her arms and legs.

She went to the sink, ready to put that fiery energy to use. That was her mom's way. Good old passive-aggressive Sheila Carpenter, cleaning instead of screaming, fixing instead of breaking. Never, ever saying what she felt.

Quincy didn't want to be that woman. She didn't want to clean up the mess that everyone else had made. She wanted to get mad, dammit. She *was* mad. So angry that she plucked a dirty plate from the sink and prepared to smash it against the counter.

It was her reflection that stopped her. That pale face staring back at her from the window above the kitchen sink. This time she couldn't avoid it. This time, she saw herself clearly.

Eyes red with tears. Lips curled into a snarl. Skin throbbing pink from anger and heartbreak and shame that she had just given herself to a complete stranger.

That wasn't the Quincy she had thought herself to be. It was someone else entirely. Someone she didn't recognize.

Darkness crept up around her. Quincy sensed it moving in. A black tide washing onto shore. Soon it had surrounded her, shrinking the kitchen, eclipsing it. Quincy could only see her face staring back at her. The stranger's face. Until that too was consumed by darkness.

Quincy put the plate back in the sink, replacing it in her hand with something else.

The knife.

She didn't know why she grabbed it. She certainly had no idea what she was going to do with it. All she knew was that it felt good to hold it.

With the knife firmly in her grip, she passed through Pine Cottage's back door, crossing the deck in three quick strides. Outside, the trees closest to the cabin stood like gray sentinels guarding the rest of the forest.

On her way past, Quincy slapped one with the flat of the blade. The impact shivered into her hand and up her arm as she moved deeper into the woods.

35.

A door slams shut, echoing down the hall and jerking me out of a dead sleep. I open my eyes with a gasp, dry air scraping across my tongue. Morning sun burns through the window in a diagonal streak that lands directly on my pillow. Clear and sharp, it feels like needles poking my retinas. I roll over, cursing the sun as I throw my arm across the other side of the bed.

It's empty.

That's the moment I remember where I am.

Who I was with.

What I've done.

I leap from the bed, head dizzy, room spinning. I make it as far as the minuscule bathroom before collapsing to the floor, its tile cold beneath my bare ass, knees drawn to my chest. My thoughts are clouded, indistinct. I feel of this world but not part of it.

It's a hangover, I realize. A guilt hangover. Haven't had one of those in years.

Memories creep in at a steady pace, like the tick of a clock's second hand. Tick, tick, tick. Within a minute, it's all come back to me. Every slutty, sordid detail.

Coop, obviously, is gone. He could have even been the source of the slamming door, although I suspect he slipped out quietly, preferring not to wake me. I can't say I blame him.

At least he was gentlemanly enough to leave a note, hastily scrawled on hotel stationery. I saw it sitting next to the TV as I wobbled to the bathroom.

I'll read it later. Once I'm able to pick myself up off the floor.

My entire body is sore, but in that satisfied way that comes after getting what it wants. It's the way I sometimes feel after jogging. Exhausted and sated and just a little bit worried that I might have overdone it.

This time, I have no doubt. I've overdone things in the most cataclysmic way.

I look at my hands. Most of the black polish Sam painted on has chipped away, leaving only flecks. There's crud beneath the nails. More polish, most likely. Or maybe flakes of Coop's skin from when I scratched at his back, begging him to fuck me harder. His scent remains on my hands. They smell of sweat, semen, and, faintly, Old Spice.

I climb to my feet and go to the bowl-size sink. I splash cold water on my face, careful not to look at myself in the mirror. I'm afraid of what I'll see. Actually, I'm afraid I'll see nothing at all.

Two steps later I'm at the bed again, sitting down. Coop's note stares at me from its spot beside the TV remote.

I grab it and read it.

Dear Quincy, I'm ashamed of my behavior. As much as I wanted this to happen, I realize now that it never should have. I think it's best if we don't communicate for a long time. I'm sorry.

And that's that. Ten years of protection, friendship, and idol worship lost in a single night. Tossed away as easily as I toss the crumpled note at the plastic trash can against the wall. When it misses and bounces onto the floor, I crawl over, pick it up, drop it in.

Then I pick up the trash can and fling it across the room.

After it slams into the wall and drops straight down, I grab something else. The remote. This, too, goes flying, breaking apart against the bed's headboard.

I lunge for the tangled sheets drooping onto the floor, tearing at them, twisting them around my balled fists, holding them to my mouth to muffle my sobs.

Coop's gone.

I'd always assumed this day would come at some point. Hell, it had almost already happened, right before that threatening letter pulled him back into my orbit. But I'm not prepared for a life in which Coop isn't there when I need him. I'm not sure I can handle things on my own.

But now I have no choice. Now there's no one left in my life but Jeff. Jeff.

Fuck.

Knowing how much I've betrayed him sends a wave of nausea pushing into my gut, jabbing me. This will devastate him.

I decide on the spot to never, ever tell him what I've done. It's my only option. I'll find a way to forget about this musty room, these tangled sheets, the feeling of Coop's chest against my breasts, his breath hot in my ear. Like Pine Cottage, I'll block it all from my memory.

And when I face Jeff again, he won't suspect a thing. He'll see only the Quincy he thinks he knows. The normal Quincy.

Plan in place, I sit up, trying to ignore the guilt squeezing my insides. It's a feeling I'll need to get used to.

I check my phone and see three missed calls and one missed text from Jeff. I can't listen to his messages. The sound of his voice will break me. But I read his text, every word of it weighted with worry.

why aren't you answering your phone? everything ok??

I text him back.

sorry. fell asleep as soon as I got home. will call you later.

I tack on an *I love you* but delete it, worried it might make him suspicious. Already, I'm starting to think like a cheater.

Besides Jeff, I've missed one other call. It's from Jonah Thompson, received shortly after eight. Roughly an hour ago. When I call back, he answers after only one ring.

"Finally," he says.

"Good morning to you too," I say.

Jonah ignores me. "I did a little digging on Samantha Boyd, aka Tina Stone. I think you'll be very interested to see what I came up with."

"What did you find?"

"It's hard to explain over the phone," Jonah says. "You need to see it in person."

I sigh. "Bethesda Fountain. Twenty minutes. Bring coffee."

PINE COTTAGE
11:49 P.M.

The moon had slipped behind some clouds, leaving the woods darker than before. Quincy had trouble staying on the path, the ground beneath her feet a dim muddle of leaves and underbrush. But she had reached the incline. She could feel the weight of extra effort tight in her calves.

She had no plan. Not really. She just wanted to confront them. She wanted to go to that rock, stand before their panting, moon-streaked bodies, and tell them how much she hurt.

The knife would make them believe it. It would make them scared.

Soon Quincy was halfway up the incline. Heart pumping hot blood. Breath escaping in ragged puffs. As she marched upward, she was struck with the sensation that she was being watched. It was nothing more than a tickle on the back of her neck, telling her she wasn't alone. She stopped, looked around. Although she saw nothing, she couldn't shake the feeling of eyes on her body. It made her think of the Indian ghosts rumored to roam the forest. She welcomed them, those vengeful spirits, eager to have them join her cause.

A sound entered the woods. Quick footsteps shush-shushing through the fallen leaves. For a moment, Quincy thought there really were ghosts in the forest, a herd of them coming toward her. She glanced behind her, expecting to see them swooping through the trees. But this ghost was all too human. Quincy heard gasps of exertion, heavier than her own. Soon the sound was right behind her, making her spin.

Joe appeared, awake now and hastily dressed. His sweater was on backward. The tag scraped his Adam's apple as he stared at Quincy.

"I need to be alone," she said.

His breath was still heavy, gasping out words. "Don't do this."

Quincy turned away. Just looking at him made her queasy. She still felt him inside her. The burning between her legs both shamed and excited her.

"You don't know what I'm going to do."

"I do," he said. "And it's not worth it."

"How do you know?"

"Because I've done it. And I felt the same way then that you do now."

"Leave me alone."

"I know you want to hurt them," he said.

The thick darkness that had enveloped Quincy suddenly vanished, leaving her dizzy and disoriented. She saw the knife in her hand and sucked in air. She couldn't remember why she had picked it up. Had she honestly intended to use it on them? On herself?

Shame burned through her. She shook her head back and forth. The dark forest blurred.

"It's not what you think," she said.

"Isn't it?"

"I wasn't—"

She stopped talking, knowing that whatever she said wouldn't make sense. Words had failed her.

"You should go back," he said. "It's not right to be out here like this."

"They hurt me," Quincy said, suddenly crying again.

"I know," he said. "That's why you should go back now."

Quincy wiped her eyes. She hated herself for crying in front of him. Hated how she had enjoyed being with him. Hated the fact that, out of everyone in that cabin, he was the only one who saw the real Quincy.

"I will," she said. "Where are you going?"

He stared forward, as if seeking out a location in the far distance, somewhere beyond the trees.

"Home," he said. "You should go home too."

Quincy nodded.

She dropped the knife.

It landed on its side, cushioned by leaves.

Then she ran back the way she came, passing him, trying to ignore the way the moonlight clouded his glasses, turning the lenses opaque. Like a fog.

36.

Twenty-five minutes after hanging up with Jonah, I'm in Central Park, rushing through the Baroque tunnel that leads to Bethesda Terrace. I spot him through the ornate arches at the tunnel's end, seated at the fountain's edge. Pink shirt, blue pants, gray sport coat. Towering above him is the Angel of the Waters, a flock of pigeons resting on her outstretched wings.

"Sorry I'm late," I say, sitting beside him.

Jonah sniffs. "Whoa," he says.

I too can smell myself. I'd wanted to take a shower in the hotel, but there was no hot water left. I had to make do with a few well-placed splashes from the sink before putting on the clothes I've been wearing since the day before.

While dressing, I thought about how many miles these clothes have traveled in the past twenty-four hours. From Chicago to Muncie and back again. From Chicago to New York to that Spartan closet of shame. Now they've made their way into Central Park, stinking and sweat-stained. After today, I think I'll burn them.

"Walk of shame?" Jonah asks.

"Save it," I say. "Where's my coffee?"

Two cups sit by his feet. Beside them is a messenger bag, filled with what I hope is enough information about Sam to force her out of my life. If not, I'd settle for getting her out of my apartment.

"Pick your poison," Jonah says, raising the cups. "Black or cream and sugar?"

"Cream and sugar. Preferably intravenously."

He hands me a cup marked with an *X*. I gulp down half of its contents before coming up for air.

"Thank you," I say. "No matter how many good deeds you perform today, nothing will top this."

"You'll be rethinking that in a minute," Jonah says as he reaches for the messenger bag.

"What did you find?"

He unzips the bag and pulls out a beige folder. "A bombshell."

Inside the folder are dozens of loose pages. Jonah riffles through them, fingers nimble, allowing me only brief glimpses of photocopied news articles and files printed from the Internet.

"A search of Samantha Boyd turns up all the usual information about the Nightlight Inn," he says. "She's the lone survivor. A Final Girl. Went off the grid eight years ago and was never seen or heard from again until a few days ago."

"I already know that," I say.

"Tina Stone is a different story." Jonah finally stops flipping through the folder, landing on a news clipping. He hands it to me. "This is from the *Hazleton Eagle*. Twelve years ago."

My heart thumps loud in my chest when I look at the clipping. I recognize it. The same one was at Lisa's house.

HAZLETON, Pa.—A man was found stabbed to death yesterday inside the home he shared with his wife and stepdaughter. Responding to emergency calls, Hazleton police found Earl Potash, 46, dead in the kitchen of his Maple Street duplex, the victim of multiple stab wounds to the chest and stomach. Authorities have ruled the incident a homicide. The investigation is continuing.

"How did you find this?"

"Through a LexisNexis search on Tina Stone," Jonah says.

"But what does this have to do with her?"

"According to the newspaper, Earl Potash's stepdaughter confessed to killing him, citing years of sexual abuse. Because sexual assault was a factor, her name was shielded in court records."

Now I know why Lisa had the article.

"It was her," I say. "Tina Stone. She killed her stepfather."

Jonah gives a firm nod. "Afraid so."

I gulp down more coffee, hoping it will chase away the headache that's again blooming in my skull. At that moment, I would likely kill for a Xanax.

"I still don't understand," I say. "Why would Sam change her name to be the same as a woman who murdered her stepdad?"

"That's the strange thing," Jonah says. "I'm not sure she actually did."

Out of the folder come several pages of medical records. At the top is the name Tina Stone.

"Aren't medical records also supposed to be classified?" I ask.

"Clearly you've underestimated my powers," Jonah says. "Bribes are a great motivator."

"You're despicable."

I flip through the records, which begin with last year and go backward. Tina Stone went to the doctor sporadically, always in the case of an emergency, and usually without health insurance. I see a broken wrist four years ago, the result of a motorcycle accident. A mammogram a year earlier after she found a lump that ended up being benign. An overdose of anitrophylin eight years ago. That one gives me pause.

There's a second overdose attempt one page and two years before that. I look at the date. Three weeks after Pine Cottage.

"This can't be Sam," I say. "The dates don't match up. She told me she didn't change her name until a few years after Pine Cottage."

The realization, when it comes, almost sends me reeling backward into the fountain. I drop the folder, its pages scattering, forcing Jonah to scramble for them before they can blow away.

I remain motionless when he returns to my side, folder tucked under his arm. "You get it now, right?"

"Tina Stone and Samantha Boyd," I say. "They're not the same person."

"Which begs the question, which one is in your apartment?"

"I have no idea."

But I need to find out. Immediately. I stand, legs wobbly, prepared to leave.

Jonah stops me, an apologetic look pinching his face as he says, "Unfortunately, there's more."

He opens the folder, flips to a page in the back. "There's an incident where she ODed."

"I know," I say. "It's from before the alleged name change."

"You might want to look at where she overdosed."

Jonah points to the name of the facility where Tina Stone was treated.

Blackthorn Psychiatric Hospital, located just on the other side of the woods from Pine Cottage.

Looking at it makes me instantly woozy. Worse than when I woke up that morning. Almost worse than the moment I realized I had beaten Ricardo Ruiz to within an inch of his life.

Tina Stone was a patient at Blackthorn.

The same time He was.

The exact same time He went to Pine Cottage and gutted my world.

PINE COTTAGE
MIDNIGHT

The first scream arrived when Quincy reached the cabin's back deck. It blasted from the forest, swooping toward her as she climbed the stubby wooden steps. Quincy turned toward the sound, too surprised to feel afraid.

The fear would come later.

She scanned the dark forest behind the cabin, whipping her gaze from tree to tree, as if the scream had come from one of them. But she already knew its source.

Janelle.

Quincy was certain.

A second scream erupted from the woods. Longer than the first, it became a crackle of noise stretching across the sky. It was also louder. Loud enough to spook an owl from the upper branches of a nearby tree. The bird skated past the deck, wings thumping, vanishing over the cabin roof.

The sound of its retreat blended with the approach of something else.

Footsteps. Reckless ones.

A moment later, Craig burst out of the woods. His eyes were blank, but there was a crazed jerkiness to his movements. His shirt was back on. So were his pants, although Quincy noticed how the fly was undone and that his unbuckled belt jangled and flapped.

"Run, Quincy." He stumbled forward, frantic. "We gotta run."

He was on the deck by then, making an attempt to drag her along as he streaked past her. Quincy's arm went limp in his hands. She wasn't going anywhere. Not until Janelle was with them.

"Janelle?" she shouted.

Her voice echoed, bouncing through the woods, creating new calls, each one more faint than the last. They were answered with another scream. Craig yelped when he heard it. He did a little shimmy, as if trying to shake something from his back.

"Come on!" he shouted at Quincy.

But a fourth scream lured her forward, to the deck's top step, the toes of her shoes peeking over the edge. Behind her, Craig tried to get inside, blocked by the others pushing their way out.

"What *was* that?" asked Amy, fear slashing her voice.

"Where's Janelle?" asked Betz.

"Dead!" Craig yelled. "She's dead!"

But she wasn't. Quincy still heard her choked breaths hissing in the night. Footfalls as quiet as cats' paws stumbled through the woods.

Janelle appeared suddenly, materializing like one of her Indian ghosts along the tree line behind the cabin. She didn't stand so much as hover, only the instinct of standing keeping her upright. Dark blooms of red dotted her dress at her shoulder, chest, stomach.

Both hands were at her neck, one clamped tightly over the other. Blood streamed from beneath her palms—a crimson waterfall running down her chest.

That's when the fear struck.

A gut-tightening, body-stilling fear that left the others motionless at the back door.

Only Quincy managed to move, the fear pushing her forward, off the deck, into grass just starting to gather frost. It crunched under her feet as she moved to Janelle. Cold wetness seeped into her shoes.

Then she was at Janelle, reaching out, catching her as she drooped forward. Janelle's hands fell away from her neck, exposing the wide slash across it. Blood poured from the wound, hot and sticky, all over Quincy's white dress.

Quincy covered the gash with her hands. The pumping blood tickled her palms. Then Janelle's body went slack, the weight shifting onto Quincy, making her twist onto her knees. Soon she was seated on the ground, Janelle a rag doll in her lap, staring at her with wide, terror-struck eyes as her breath rattled.

"Help!" Quincy screamed, even though she already knew Janelle was beyond help. "Help! Please!"

The others remained on the deck. Amy curled against Rodney, the hem of her nightgown flapping. Betz began to sob uncontrollably, the sound rising and falling. Only Craig looked at them. Quincy felt like he could see into her very heart. Like he knew every one of her awful, awful secrets.

She stared at him, seeing a new rush of fear in his eyes.

"Quincy! Run!"

But Quincy couldn't. Not with Janelle still dying in her arms. Not even when she felt a new presence in their midst. Something vile, seething hate.

He was upon them before she could turn around to look. Fingers dug into her hair, collecting a handful, yanking hard. Pain shimmered through her as she was whipped around, seeing what the others saw.

A figure looming.

A knife charging.

A silvery flash.

The stabs arrived almost simultaneously, one right after the other. Two sharp strikes of pain in her shoulder. Hot ones. Searing through skin and muscle. Nicking bone.

Quincy didn't scream. It hurt too much. The pain screamed through her instead.

She slumped over, Janelle rolling from her lap. They lay together on the ground, face-to-face, Quincy staring into Janelle's dead eyes. Blood pooled in the grass between them, melting the frost, steaming slightly.

He was still there. Quincy heard the even rhythm of his breathing.

A hand touched her hair again. Not pulling. Caressing.

"There, there," he said.

Quincy saw him on the far edge of her vision, still a shadow. And as she waited for that final bite of the knife, he began to move.

Past her.

Past what had once been Janelle.

On his way back to Pine Cottage.

It was the last thing Quincy saw before pain and grief and fear overwhelmed her. Black clouds rolled across her vision, blurring the world. She closed her eyes, welcoming oblivion, letting the darkness take over.

37.

Jonah begs me to let him come back to the apartment with me, but I won't allow it. He says it's too dangerous, and he's right. Yet his presence would only complicate things. This needs to be between me and Sam.

Or Tina.

Or whoever the fuck she is.

Once again, I practice caution when entering the apartment. And once again, I wish that she isn't there.

But she is. In the foyer, I hear the steady flow of water coming from the hallway bathroom. Sam is in the shower. I go to the bathroom door and hover there until I hear noises from the other side. A cough from Sam. A clearing of her cigarette-agitated throat. The shower continues to flow.

I hurry into Sam's room, where her knapsack still leans in the corner. I can't open it. My hands are shaking too much.

I take some deep breaths, aching for a Xanax despite knowing I need a clear head. Yet addiction wins out, pulling me into the kitchen long enough to pop a single Xanax into my mouth. I then take several gulps of grape soda, continuing to drink long after the pill has slipped down my throat.

Properly fortified, it's back to Sam's room. My hands are steadier now, and the knapsack opens with ease. I root through it, pulling out stolen clothes, black T-shirts, an array of worn bras and panties. A bottle of Wild Turkey emerges—a fresh one, still unopened. It clunks to the floor and rolls against my knees.

Inside the knapsack, I swat against items that have slid to the bottom. A brush, deodorant, an empty pill bottle. I check the label. Ambien. Not anitrophylin.

I find the iPhone Sam took from my secret drawer. The same phone I had stolen from the café. It's turned off, the battery likely dead.

At the very bottom of the knapsack, my fingertips skim across a cool slick of glossy pages. A magazine.

I yank it out, flipping it over to look at the cover. It's a copy of *Time*, dog-eared and threatening to rip from its stapled binding. The photo on the front shows a ramshackle motel surrounded by cop cars and scrub pines dripping with Spanish moss. The headline, in red letters slammed over a slate-gray sky, reads: HOTEL HORROR.

It's the same issue of *Time* I devoured as a child, shuddering beneath my covers, dreading the nightmares to come. I riffle through the pages until I find the article that prompted so much childhood fear. It features another picture of the Nightlight Inn—an exterior shot of one of its rooms. In the open doorway, there's a flash of white. One of the victims covered with a sheet.

The article begins next to it in a narrow column of text.

You think it only happens in the movies. That it couldn't happen in real life. At least, not like that. And certainly not to you. But it happened. First at a sorority house in Indiana. Then at a motel in Florida.

The passage has the ring of something familiar. A kiss of déjà vu. Not from my childhood, although I had certainly read it back then. This memory is more recent.

Sam said it to me during her first night here. The huddled girl talk. The Wild Turkey passed between us. Her sincere soliloquy about the Nightlight Inn.

It was a load of bullshit, lifted word-for-word from this magazine.

I stuff her belongings back into the knapsack. Everything but the magazine, which I can use as ammunition against her, and the stolen iPhone, which can be used against me. The magazine is rolled under my arm. I shove the phone down the front of my shirt, securing it beneath a bra strap.

Satisfied I'm leaving the room in almost the same condition as when I entered, I hurry back to the kitchen and grab the grape soda, carrying it with me to my laptop. I take another sip as I crack open the computer and click my way to YouTube. In the search field, I type "samantha boyd interview." It yields several versions of Sam's sole TV interview, all of them uploaded by the same freaks who run murder-porn websites. I click on the first one and the video begins.

On-screen is the same TV newswoman who had slipped the Chanel-scented interview offer under my door. Her expression is benign—a mask of impartiality. Only her eyes betray her. They're black and ravenous. The eyes of a shark.

A young woman sits with her back facing the camera, barely in the frame. What can be seen of her is in silhouette. She's a half-girl, blurred beyond recognition.

"Do you remember what happened to you that night, Samantha?" the newswoman asks.

"Sure, I remember."

That voice. It doesn't sound like the Sam I know. Interview Sam's voice isn't as clear, the diction less precise.

"Do you think about it often?"

"A lot," Interview Sam replies. "I think about him all the time."

"You're referring to Calvin Whitmer, right? The Sack Man?"

There's a tilt of darkness as Interview Sam nods and says, "I can still see him, you know? When I close my eyes? He had cut eyeholes into the sack. Plus a little slit right over his nose for air. I'll never forget the way it flapped when he breathed. He had tied string around his neck to keep the sack in place."

She stole that line too. Saying it to me as if for the first time.

I go back to the start of the video, slightly dizzy as Miss Chanel No. 5 trains her shark eyes on Interview Sam.

"Do you remember what happened to you that night, Samantha?"

I blink, my eyes suddenly tired.

"Sure, I remember."

The voices on the computer become distant and vague.

"Do you think about it often?"

Numbness creeps into my body. Hands first, then up my arms like a line of fire ants.

"A lot. I think about him all the time."

The laptop screen goes fuzzy, the interviewer's face lurching out of focus. When I look away, I see the entire kitchen has turned into blurred streaks of color. I glance at the grape soda, which has brightened into a Wonka-esque neon purple. My hands are too numb to lift the bottle, so I bump it with an elbow, its dregs fizzing. Swirling along the bottom are powdery bits of Xanax that glow blue.

A voice rises behind me.

"I knew you'd be thirsty."

I spin myself around to see her in the kitchen, dressed and dry. The shower still runs in the distance, as muffled as Interview Sam's voice trickling from the laptop. It was a decoy. A trap.

"Wha—"

I can't speak. My tongue has thickened, feeling like a fish flopping in my mouth.

"Shhhh," she says.

She's turned into a shadowy blur, just like her counterpart still talking on my laptop. Interview Sam come to life. Only she isn't Sam. Even the pills wreaking havoc on my nervous system can't suppress that. It's a moment of clarity. My last one for God knows how long.

Maybe forever.

"Tina," I say, fat tongue still flip-flopping. "Tina Stone."

She makes a move toward me. I react by reaching for the wood-block knife holder on the counter, my arm moving in slow motion. I grab the biggest knife. In my hand, it weighs a hundred pounds.

I stumble forward, legs useless, feet as heavy as rocks. I manage one weak jab before the knife drops from my limp-noodle fingers. The kitchen tilts, only I know it's really me who's doing the tilting, falling sideways, everything a sickening blur as my skull smashes against the floor.

ONE YEAR AFTER PINE COTTAGE

Tina was among the last to go. She sat on her squeaky bed, staring blankly at the one on the other side of the room, most recently occupied by a stringy-haired pyromaniac named Heather. It had been stripped of sheets, leaving only a lumpy mattress with an oblong urine stain. On the wall beside it, not quite hidden under a coat of paint, were the curse words scrawled in lipstick by Heather's predecessor, May. When she got transferred, she bequeathed her stash of lipstick to Tina.

All told, Tina had spent more than three years in that room. The longest time she had spent in any one place. Not that she had a choice. The state decided that for her.

But now it was time to go. Nurse Hattie shouted it from the hallway in that grating hick accent of hers. "Closin' time, folks! Everybody out!"

Tina lifted the knapsack that leaned against her bed. It used to be Joe's. His parents left it behind when they cleaned out his room after he was killed. Now it was hers, and everything she owned was inside, which wasn't much. Its lightness astonished her.

As Tina left the room, she didn't look back. She had moved around enough to know that long last looks didn't make leaving any easier. Even if you had been dying to leave since the moment you arrived.

In the hallway, Tina took her place with the other stragglers, lining up for one last head count. Instead of seeing that everyone was there, the orderlies were making sure no one stayed behind. At noon, Blackthorn's doors were closing for good.

The majority of Blackthorn's patients were still too crazy to be let loose upon the world. They had already been transferred to other state facilities, Heather among them. Tina was one of the few deemed mentally fit to be released. She had served her time. Now she was free to go.

After head count, she and the others were shuffled through the wide and drafty rec room, which was already being cleared of furniture. Tina saw that the TV had been dismantled from the wall and that most of the chairs had been stacked in a corner. But her table was still there. The table beside the grated window where she and Joe would sit and peer out at the woods on the other side of Blackthorn's scrubby patch of lawn, naming all the places they would go once they got out.

Tina did allow one last look at that, instantly regretting it, for it made her think about Joe. She had been ordered not to think about him.

Yet she did. All the time. Leaving wouldn't change that.

She had also been ordered not to think about that night. About the terrible things that happened. All those dead kids. But how could she not? It was the reason the place was closing. The very reason she and the others were being marched out.

Some of the orderlies came by to watch them leave. Matt Cromley was there, that perm-headed prick. He had put his hand down Tina's pants so many times she lost count. She glared at him as she passed. He gave her a wink and licked his lips.

Parked outside was a van that would take them to the bus station. After that, no one gave a damn where they went as long as it wasn't there.

As Tina climbed aboard, Nurse Hattie handed her a large envelope. Inside was the name of a social-services agency that would help her find employment, her medical records, all necessary prescriptions, and cash that Tina knew would last only about a measly two weeks.

Nurse Hattie put a hand on her shoulder and smiled. "Have a great life, Tina. Go make somethin' of yourself."

TWO YEARS AFTER PINE COTTAGE

There was no one home. Tina kept telling herself that as she knocked again on the sun-bleached door. There was no one home, and she should just leave.

But she couldn't leave. She was down to her last dollar.

Tina tried to make a go of it, and for a while she had. Thanks to that nice lady at social services she had a job, even though it was bagging groceries at a gritty-floored supermarket, and a place to live at a boardinghouse built for people like her. But all those health-code violations killed the store, which meant she couldn't pay for the boardinghouse. Those unemployment checks barely covered food and bus fare.

So now she was back in Hazleton, still knocking on the door of a duplex she hadn't seen in four years, praying no one would answer it. When someone did, she almost ran away. She'd rather die of starvation than be there. But she willed her legs to remain on that worn welcome mat.

The woman who opened the door was fatter than when Tina last saw her. An ass as wide as a love seat. She held a baby on her hip—a writhing, crying, red-faced little shit in a drooping diaper. Tina took one look at it and her heart sank. Another kid. That poor, doomed thing.

"Hi, Momma," Tina said. "I'm home."

Her mother looked at her as if she were a stranger. She sucked in her fat cheeks, lips puckering.

"This ain't your home," she said. "You made sure of that."

Tina's heart seized up, even though this was exactly what she had expected. Her mother never believed that Earl did those things to her. The touching and the fondling and the sliding under her covers at three in the morning. *Shh*, he'd say, with beer stench on his breath. *Don't tell your momma*.

"Please, Momma," Tina said. "I need help."

The baby fussed even more. Tina wondered if the kid had been told about his half sister. She wondered if she'd ever been mentioned.

A man's voice cut through the cries, coming from the living room. Tina had no idea who he was. "Who's at the door?"

Tina's mother stared at her. "No one important."

THREE YEARS AFTER PINE COTTAGE

The bar was packed for a Tuesday night. All the stools were filled. Tables too. Nothing like two-dollar beers to bring in the barely functioning alcoholics. The crowd kept Tina hopping her entire shift as heaps of empty mugs and ketchup-smeared plates came her way. She washed them all, her hands submerged in the water so long her fingers had become shriveled and bleached.

When her shift was over, she whipped off her hairnet and shucked her apron, stuffing them into the laundry bin by the kitchen's back door. She then headed into the bar itself, claiming the employee-eligible free drink that was supposed to make up for how the owner skimped on wages.

Lyle was tending bar that night. Tina liked him more than the others. He had a handlebar mustache, a sexy overbite, and thick, hairy forearms. He poured her drink without even asking what she wanted.

"And a Wild Turkey for Miss Tina," he said, also pouring one for himself.

They clinked glasses.

"Cheers," Tina said before downing the whiskey in a single gulp.

She ordered another. Lyle gave it to her for free, even though she told him she had enough cash to pay for it. She sipped this one, sitting at the far end of the bar, people-watching. The crowd was a nondescript blur—an interchangeable display of big hair, beer guts, and gin blossoms. Tina vaguely recognized most of them.

Then she saw someone she truly did recognize. He was slid into a back booth and getting grabby with a redhead who clearly didn't want to be grabbed. It had been a few years, but he looked exactly the same. Not even his laughable man perm had changed.

Matt Cromley.

The orderly who had groped her and Heather and God knows how many other women at Blackthorn. Seeing him after all these years unlocked the box in Tina's mind where the bad memories were stored. It made her think of all the times he had yanked her into that utility closet, plunging his hand down her pants while hissing, *You're not going to tell anyone, you hear? I can make things bad for you, you know. Real bad.*

The only person she told was Joe. It made him so mad he offered to stab the slime ball, which is what had landed him at Blackthorn in the first place. Some community college shithead had kept bullying him. Joe fought back by driving a steak knife into his side.

Tina declined the offer. Only now she wished she had taken him up on it. Pricks like Matt Cromley shouldn't be allowed to go unpunished.

That's why Tina downed her drink. She slipped into the kitchen for a few supplies. Then she sidled up to his booth, gave him a siren's smile, and said, "Hey, stranger."

Ten minutes later, they were standing in a patch of weeds behind the bar, one of Matt's hands already snaked down the front of her jeans, the other furiously stroking that minuscule prick of his.

"You like that, don't you?" he groaned. "Like the way Matty Boy makes you feel?"

Tina nodded, although in truth his touch made her want to puke. But she endured it. She knew it wouldn't last long.

"How many girls did you do this to?" she said. "Back at Blackthorn?"

"I dunno." He was practically panting, his voice rough in her ears. "Ten or eleven or twelve."

Tina's body went rigid. "This is for them."

She shoved an elbow into his stomach, which made him double over and back away, taking his cold, slimy hand with him. She then whirled around and punched him. Repeatedly. Quick, sharp jabs right to his nose. Soon he was on his knees, holding his hands to his nose to try to halt the blood spurting out of it.

Tina kicked him. In the stomach. In his ribs. In his groin.

Once he was flat on his back and rolling in pain, Tina shoved a dishrag from the kitchen into his mouth. She yanked off his jeans and underwear. She tore at his shirt, ripping the seams until it was nothing but shreds stuck to his shoulders. Then she tied rope she had found under the kitchen sink around his wrists and ankles. Once he was good and secure, Tina whipped out the black dry-erase marker swiped from the whiteboard that listed the daily drink specials. Cap between her teeth, she jerked the marker open and scrawled three words across Matt Cromley's naked torso.

MOLESTER. PERVERT. SCUM.

She took his clothes with her when she left.

NINE YEARS AFTER PINE COTTAGE

It was October, which meant she was thinking about Joe. It always happened when fall rolled around. Even nine years later that crisp chill in the air took her mind back to him in his sand-colored sweater, sneaking down the hall. *Wait for me!* she had whispered frantically at the back door, trying to catch up to him.

Each year, she thought it would be different, that the memories would fade. But now, though, she suspected they were a permanent part of her. Just like the tattoo on her wrist.

During her smoke break behind the diner, Tina rubbed her thumb across the tattoo, feeling the dark smoothness of the letters.

SURVIVOR

It had been six years since she got it. Long before she'd found her way north to Bangor. She got it in a fit of inspiration after writing all over Matt Cromley's pink and pudgy body. She didn't regret it one bit. It made her feel strong, even though she later worried that some customers would be put off by it and tip her less. Instead, most folks gave her more. The pity tippers. Thanks to them, she had been able to buy a car. It was nothing but a thirdhand Ford Escort, but she didn't care. Wheels were wheels.

Inside the diner, the lunch crowd was starting to trickle in. Tina recognized the majority of the customers. She'd been around long enough to know who they were and what they wanted. Only one customer was a stranger—a goth kid draped in black. The way he kept staring at her creeped her out. When she went to take his order, she said, "Do I know you?"

The kid looked up at her. "No, but I know you."

"I don't think so."

"You're that girl," he said, eyes locked on her tattoo. "That girl who almost got herself killed at that hotel all those years back."

Tina snapped her gum. "I don't know what you're talking about."

"Your secret's safe with me." The kid lowered his voice to a whisper. "I won't tell anyone you're Samantha Boyd."

When her shift was through, Tina went straight to the library and its bank of outdated computers. Sitting among the elderly and Internet-deprived, she Googled the name Samantha Boyd.

They didn't look so alike that they could be mistaken for twins. She was a bit thinner than Samantha, and their eyes weren't quite the same. But the resemblance was there. It could be even stronger if Tina made her hair as dark as that goth kid's.

She thought of Joe again. It couldn't be helped. A search of his name brought up the same picture that had been printed everywhere after the Pine Cottage murders. And wherever Joe's picture appeared, one of that girl always followed.

Quincy Carpenter. The survivor.

Tina stared at Quincy's picture. Then at Joe's. Then back to Samantha Boyd, her dark-haired doppelgänger.

In the back of her brain, something clicked. A plan.

NINE YEARS AND ELEVEN MONTHS
AFTER PINE COTTAGE

Tina hauled her knapsack from the trunk of her Escort, assuring herself that she could actually pull this off. She'd planned this for almost a year now. She'd done her homework. She'd memorized her lines.

She was ready.

With the knapsack thrown over her shoulder, Tina marched up the flagstone walkway and rang the doorbell. When a kind-eyed blonde opened it, Tina knew exactly who she was looking at.

"Lisa Milner?" she said. "It's me, Samantha."

"Samantha Boyd?" Lisa replied, surprise thickening her voice.

Tina nodded. "I prefer Sam."

38.

I'm awake, only my eyes don't know it yet. The lids refuse to lift no matter how much I contort my face. I try to raise my hands and force the eyelids open with a finger. I can't. My hands are lead, resting in my lap.

"I know you can hear me," Tina says. "Can you talk?"

"Yes." The word can't even qualify as a whisper. "What—"

It's all I can manage. My thoughts are equally as weak. Snails plowing through a field of mud.

"It'll wear off," Tina says.

It already is. A little. Feeling creeps back into my body. Enough for me to know I'm sitting up, something strapped diagonally across my chest. A seat belt. I'm in a car.

Tina sits to my left. I feel her presence. I hear the leathery squeak of the steering wheel in her hands even though the car isn't moving and the engine is silent. We're parked.

I try to move, twisting against the seat belt.

"Why—"

"Relax," Tina says. "Save your strength. You're going to need it soon."

I continue to writhe in the seat. I reach for the door handle. My heavy fingers merely claw at the air.

"You could have made this easy, Quinn," Tina says. "Trust me, I wanted it to be easy. I wanted it to last a day. Two, tops. I show up, make nice, and then have you tell me everything you remember about Pine Cottage. In and out."

My fingers finally connect with the door handle. Somehow I'm able to pull it. The door falls open and a rush of woodsy October air hits my face. I lean toward it, trying to roll myself out the door, but the seat belt stops me. My hazy mind forgot about it. Not that it matters. Even if I was free of both seat belt and car, there's no way I could escape. Not with most of my body feeling like marble.

"Whoa there," Tina says as she pulls me back into the seat. When she reaches across my lap to close the door, I swat at her arm. The blows are so weak I might as well be petting her.

"This doesn't need to be hard, babe," she says. "I just need the truth. What do you remember about Pine Cottage?"

"Nothing," I say, my tongue loosening. I'm even able to speak a full sentence. "I don't remember anything."

"You keep saying that. But I just can't believe you. Lisa remembered everything. It was in her book. Sam did too. She told that interviewer all about it."

My mind continues to pick up speed. My mouth follows suit. "How long have you pretended to be her?"

"Not long. A month or so. Only once I realized I could get away with it."

"Why?"

"Because I needed to know how much *you* knew, Quinn," she says. "After all this time, I had to know. But I needed help. And since I knew you and Lisa wouldn't otherwise give me the fucking time of day, I pretended to be Sam. I knew it was risky and that it might not work. But I also knew it would get your attention. Especially Lisa. She did everything she could to help me find out more about Pine Cottage. I told her it would help you. I said getting you to remember would aid the healing process. She bought it for a few days before she started having second thoughts."

"But you kept at it," I say. "You called my mother."

Tina doesn't sound surprised that I know this. "Yeah, once I realized Lisa wasn't going to do it. Then she kicked me out."

"Because she found out who you really are," I say, all this talking giving me strength. Energy stirs within my body. My hands are lighter. So are my legs. I can speak without thinking about it.

"She found my driver's license. Did some digging."

"Is that why you killed her?"

Tina pounds the steering wheel so hard the whole car shudders. "I didn't kill her, Quincy! I liked her, for God's sake. I felt like shit when she learned the truth."

"But you came to me anyway."

"I almost didn't. It didn't seem like the best idea." A laugh bursts out of her, inappropriate and thick with irony. "Turns out I was right."

"What are you looking for?"

"Information."

"About what?"

"Joe Hannen," Tina says.

The name is a lightning strike, zapping me awake. My eyes flicker open, pink-orange light catching in my lashes. Sunset. A strip of dying light crosses over the dashboard, collecting and reflecting off something Tina has placed there.

A knife. The one from my kitchen.

"Go ahead and try to grab it," Tina warns. "I guarantee I'm faster."

I lift my gaze from the knife to the windshield above it, dirty with wiper streaks and splotches left by wet leaves. Through the grime, I see trees, a gravel drive, a run-down cabin with cracked windows flanking a moss-flecked door.

"No," I say, clenching my eyes shut again. "No, no, no."

I keep saying it, hoping enough repetitions will make it not true. That it's just a nightmare I'll soon wake from.

But it's no nightmare. It's real. I know it as soon as I reopen my eyes.

Tina has brought me back to Pine Cottage.

39.

Time hasn't been kind to the place, which sags under the weight of decay and neglect. It looks less like a building than something foul that's emerged from the forest floor. A fungus. A poison. Leaves blanket the roof and surround the fieldstone chimney, which rises jaggedly like a rotten tooth. The cabin's exterior, weathered to a dull gray, is pockmarked with moss and dying plant sprouts that curl from nooks in the wood. Although the sign still hangs over the door, one of its nails has rusted away, slanting the words.

"I'm not going in there!" Hysteria colors my every word, which pop out in panicked squeaks. "You can't make me go in there!"

"You don't have to," Tina says, much calmer than I. "Just tell me the truth."

"I already told you what I know!"

She turns to me, elbow resting on the steering wheel. "Quinn, no one believes you can't remember anything. I read that transcript. Those cops think you're lying."

"Coop believes me," I say.

"Only because he wanted to fuck you."

"Please believe me when I say I don't remember anything," I beg. "I swear to God, I don't."

Tina shakes her head and sighs. Opening her door, she says, "Then I guess we're going in."

My body starts to buzz. Adrenaline churns my blood. I see the knife on the dashboard and lunge for it. Tina does too, snatching it away from my springing hand.

She's right. She *is* faster.

I go for the keys next, aiming for the plastic key fob. Again, Tina beats me to it. Yanking the keys from the ignition, she carries them and the knife out of the car.

"I'm coming back in a second," she says. "Don't try to run. You won't get far."

She heads off to the cabin, leaving me alone in the car, scrambling to come up with a plan. I jam my thumb into the buckle at my hip and the seat belt recoils with a snap. I then search my pockets for my phone.

It's gone.

Tina took it.

But I have another. The memory of it is a whirling dervish in my drug-addled brain. I shove my hand into my shirt, fingers fumbling for the stolen phone still secured under a bra strap.

Through the windshield, I watch Tina at the cabin's front door. She stands directly beneath the crooked Pine Cottage sign, trying to get inside by jiggling the doorknob. When that doesn't work, she throws her body against the door, leading with her shoulder.

I turn on the phone, holding my breath as I check the battery level. It's in the red. There's also barely any signal. A single bar appears and disappears in quick intervals. I estimate there's enough juice and signal for one call.

I hope.

But calling 911 isn't an option. Tina will hear me talking. She might take the phone away. Or worse. I can't risk that, even if I suspect that worse part is going to arrive eventually anyway.

That leaves texting. Which leaves only Coop. Because I'm not using my phone, I know he won't recognize the number. That might work to my advantage, considering what happened last night.

I look to the cabin again and see Tina still shoving herself against the door. Now's my only chance.

I text Coop quickly, summoning his number from my hazy memory, fingers skating across the quickly dying phone.

its quinn sams holding me hostage at pine cottage help me

The phone beeps when I hit Send, confirming the text is on its way. Then the phone's screen goes black in my hand, the battery giving up the ghost. I shove it into my pocket.

At the cabin, Tina succeeds in breaking through the front door. It yawns open, the threshold a dark and festering mouth, ready to swallow me whole. The car's headlights point directly at it, the beams slicing the quickening dusk all the way into the cabin, where a patch of dusty floor basks in the glow.

That glimpse inside the cabin triples the dread that's formed in my lungs. It feels like glass, puncturing the spongy tissue, cutting off airflow. When Tina marches back to the car, I have no choice but to run.

Only, I can't.

Standing is far different from sitting up. Now that I'm out of the car and on my feet, the drugs take hold again, knocking me off balance. I drift sideways, steeling myself for the inevitable fall. But Tina is there, holding me upright. The knife flies to my neck and hovers there, blade scratching my skin.

"Sorry, babe," she says. "There's no getting out of this."

Tina hauls me toward the cabin as I thrash in her grip. My heels dig into the gravel, doing nothing to slow us, twin trails of resistance all I have to show for the effort. One of my arms is trapped under one of hers. The arm that holds the knife, which I can't see but can certainly feel. My chin bumps the hilt every time I scream. Which is often.

When not screaming, I try to talk Tina out of doing whatever she intends to do.

"You can't do this," I say, huffing the words, spittle flying. "You're like me. A survivor."

Tina doesn't answer. She just keeps dragging me to the cabin door, now only ten yards away.

"Your stepfather was abusing you, right? That's why you killed him?"

"Something like that, yeah," Tina says.

Her grip loosens. Just a hair. Enough to make me know I'm getting to her.

"They sent you to Blackthorn," I say. "Although you weren't crazy. You were protecting yourself. From him. And that's what you've been trying to do ever since. Protect women. Hurt the men who hurt them."

"Stop talking," Tina says.

I don't. I can't.

"And at Blackthorn, you met Him."

I'm no longer talking about Earl Potash. Tina knows this, for she says, "*He* had a name, Quincy."

"Were you close? Was He your boyfriend?"

"He was my friend," Tina says. "My only fucking friend. Ever."

She stops our tumultuous drag to the cabin. She tightens her grip around me, the knife's edge pressing into the flesh right under my chin. I want to swallow but can't, out of fear it will cause the blade to break the skin.

"Say his name," she orders. "You need to say it, Quincy."

"I can't," I say. "Please don't make me."

"You can. And you will."

"Please." The word is choked out, barely audible. "Please, no."

"Say his fucking name."

I swallow against my will. A gulp that forces my neck further onto the knife blade. It stings like a burn. Hot and pulsing. Tears pop from my eyes.

"Joe Hannen."

A rush of vomit follows, riding the words as they spew from my mouth. Tina keeps the knife where it is as I heave up the contents of my stomach. Coffee and grape soda and parts of pills that haven't yet wormed their way into my body.

When it's over, I don't feel any better. Not with the knife still at my neck. Not with five short yards separating me from Pine Cottage. I'm still sick, still dizzy. More than anything, I'm spent, my body weakened to the point of paralysis.

Tina resumes pulling me to the cabin and I comply. There's no more fight left in me. All I can do is cry as strands of puke droop from my chin.

"Why?" I say.

But I already know why. She was here that night. With Him. She helped Him kill Janelle and all the others. Just as she had helped Him kill those campers in the woods. Just as she later killed Lisa, despite her claims to the contrary.

"Because I need to know how much you can remember," Tina says.

"But *why*?"

Because it will help her decide if I need to be killed too. Just like Lisa.

We're at the door now, that insidious mouth. A chill whispers from deep inside, faint and shivery.

I begin to scream. Panicked ones that erupt from my bile-coated throat.

"No! Please, no!"

I grab the doorframe with my free hand, fingernails digging into the wood. Tina gives one sharp tug and the wood snaps in my grip, breaking away. I drop the splintered chunk and keep screaming.

Pine Cottage has welcomed me home.

40.

I fall silent once I'm actually inside.

I don't want Pine Cottage to know I'm here.

Tina lets me go and gives me a shove. I tumble into the middle of the great room, skidding across the floor. Inside, it's blessedly dark. The grimy windows block most of the waning light from outside. The open door lets in the yellow glow of the headlights—a rectangle of brightness stretching along the floor. In its center is Tina's shadow, arms crossed, blocking my escape.

"Remember anything?" she says.

I look around, curiosity mingling with terror. Water stains darken the walls. Or maybe it's blood. I try not to look at them. There are more stains on the ceiling, circular ones. Definitely water damage. Nests and cobwebs crowd the rafters. Sections of floor are splattered with bird shit. A dead mouse lies in a corner, dried to leather.

The whole place has been emptied, all that rustic furniture carted away and hopefully burned. It makes the room seem bigger, save for the fireplace, which is smaller than I remember. Seeing it brings to mind Craig and Rodney kneeling before it, boys trying to act like men, fumbling with kindling and matches.

Other memories fly at me in short, startling bursts. Like I'm flipping channels, stopping for a second on each, catching flashes of movies I know I've seen.

There's Janelle, dancing barefoot in the middle of the room, singing along to that song we both loved until everyone else started to hate it.

There's Betz and Amy, preparing the chicken, bickering until they giggle.

There's Him. Staring at me from across the room. Dirty lenses hiding his eyes. Almost as if he knows what the two of us will be doing later.

"I don't," I say, my voice amplified in the empty room. "There's nothing."

Tina leaves the doorway and jerks me to my feet. "Let's take a look around."

She pulls me toward the open kitchen, now a shell of its former self. The oven's been removed, leaving a vacant square of leaves, dirt, and gauzy strips of dust. Gone too are the cupboard doors. Bare shelves sit exposed, littered with mouse droppings. But the sink is still there, rust holes in four different spots. I latch onto its edge for support. My legs remain unsteady. I barely feel them. It's as if I'm floating.

"Nothing?" Tina says.

"No."

So it's into the hall, Tina leading the way, her merciless grip pinching the flesh of my upper arm. She stomps. I float.

We both stop when we reach the bunk-bed room. Betz's room. Empty except for a single gray rag bunched in the center of the floor. The room holds no memories. Until tonight, I've never set foot inside it.

When I say nothing, Tina pulls me to the room I was supposed to share with Janelle. Just like at school. One of the two beds remains, stripped of its mattress. It's been pushed away from the wall, nothing but a rust-mottled frame.

This room brings back memories. I think of Janelle and me talking about sex while trying on dresses. Things would have turned out differently had I not worn that white dress Janelle let me borrow. If I had insisted on spending the night in here and not in the room just down the hall.

Tina shoots me a look. "Anything?"

"No." I've started to cry. Being here again, reliving things again. It's all too much.

Tina wastes no time in pulling me to the room across the hall.

The waterbed is gone, of course. Everything is. The only notable detail in the empty room is a large swath of floor turned dark with rot. It stretches to the doorway and under our feet before crossing the hall to the last bedroom.

My bedroom.

I hesitate at the doorway, unwilling to enter. I don't want to be reminded of what I did in there. With Him. And what I did after. Marching like a madwoman into the trees. Clutching that knife. Leaving it there once I came to my senses. Practically placing it in His hands.

It's all my fault.

He and Tina might have killed them, but I'm the one to blame.

Yet even though he had the chance, He didn't kill me. He made sure I'd live, giving me those nonlethal wounds that made Cole and Freemont so suspicious. I was spared because of what He'd done to me. What I had let Him do.

Having sex with Him was the only thing that saved my life.

I know that now.

I knew it all along.

Tina notices something in my face. A twitch. A flinch. "You remember something new."

"No."

It's a lie.

There *is* something new. A slice of memory I've never had before. I'm in this room.

On the floor.

Water seeps under the closed door, rolling toward me, then around me. It soaks my hair, my shoulders, my whole body, which convulses with pain and terror. Someone sits next to me. Tears chime inside his ragged breaths.

You'll be okay. We'll both be okay.

From the other side of the door comes a terrible slick-swish. Footsteps in the water. Right outside.

More memories. Brief snippets. Pounding on the door. A rattling of the doorknob. A slam. A crunch as the door breaks open, smashing against the wall. The flash of moonlight on the knife, glinting red.

I scream.

Then.

Now.

The two screams collide until I can't tell which is in the present and which is in the past. When someone grabs me, I start yelling and kicking, fighting them off, not knowing who it is or when it is or what's happening to me.

"Quincy." It's Tina's voice, cutting through the confusion. "Quincy, what's going on?"

I stare up at her, firmly in the present. The knife remains in her hand, a reminder that I can't disappoint her.

"I'm starting to remember," I say.

41.

Details.

Finally.

In my memory, I'm edging in and out of consciousness, my eyes opening and shutting. Like I'm in a closed-off room and someone is flicking the lights. I've rolled onto my back, hoping it will make the stab wounds at my shoulder hurt less. It doesn't.

Blinking at the swirling stars overhead, I hear the others on the deck, screaming and scrambling to get inside.

What about Quinn? It might be Amy, her voice plaintive. *What about her?*

She's dead.

I know that voice. Definitely Craig.

The back door is slammed shut. A lock clicks.

I want to look but can't. Pain tears through my shoulder when I try to turn my head. It hurts so bad. Like I'm on fire. And the blood. So much blood. It pumps out in time to the panicked thrum of my heart.

He's still crossing the frost-crusted grass to the cabin, feet crunching over it. When He reaches the deck, the grass crunch changes to wood creak. Inside Pine Cottage, someone screams at the window, the sound muted as it bounces off the glass.

Then the window shatters.

I hear another click, the creak of the door, screams of multiple people making their way deeper into the cabin. They fade until only one scream remains. Amy again. She's screaming and screaming just inside the now-open door. Then one of her screams is cut short. A sickly gurgle follows.

Amy is silent.

I moan and close my eyes.

The lights are flicked off again.

I'm jostled awake by hands on my arms, pulling me to my feet. The movement reignites the pain blaze at my shoulder. I cry out and am instantly shushed.

Quiet, someone whispers.

I open my eyes, taking in Betz on one side of me and Rodney on the other. Betz's hands are stained with blood. Every place she touches leaves a red print. I'm covered with them. Rodney is also bloody, smears of it on his face and shoulder. A tourniquet has been wrapped around his forearm, damp with gore.

Come on, Quinn, he whispers. *We're getting out of here.*

They throw my arms over their shoulders, not caring how it hurts so much I want to scream. I swallow the sound, choking it down.

As we leave, I get a glimpse of Janelle, lying right where I left her. She's on her side, head lolled, eyes wide open. One of her arms is pitched forward, stretching across the blood-drenched grass, as if she's begging me to stay.

We leave without her, the three of us crossing to the cabin. Betz and Rodney do all the work. I'm just along for the ride, weak from blood loss, delirious from pain. I'm so helpless that Rodney's forced to lift me up the deck steps.

The two of them whisper over me as I'm planted upright again.

Is he there?

I don't see him.

Where'd he go?

I don't know.

They grow quiet, listening. I listen too, hearing only night noises—the last of the season's crickets, bare branches crackling, the ghostly whisper of falling leaves. Everything else is silent.

Then we're moving again, faster this time, crunching over a pile of glass near the door before bustling into the cabin.

Amy is just inside the door, propped against the wall like a discarded doll. She even resembles a doll. Eyes as blank as plastic buttons, arms limp at her sides.

Don't look, Rodney whispers, his voice breaking. *It's not real. None of this is real.*

I want to believe him. In fact, I almost do. But then we step in a slick of blood and I skid forward, releasing a yelp. Rodney slaps a hand over my mouth. He shakes his head.

Then we're on the move again, into the great room, toward the window by the front door.

Where are we going? I whisper.

Rodney whispers back: *As far away from here as possible.*

The three of us stand at the window, watching. For what, I don't know. Until suddenly I do.

Craig is outside. Running in a crouch toward the SUV that brought us here. The SUV where all our cell phones have been stowed. Craig opens the door slowly, hands shaking, recoiling when the interior light pops on. Then he's inside, starting the engine.

Now! Rodney yells.

Betz flings open the front door and we hustle outside, caught in the SUV's headlights, our shadows looming large against the front of the cabin. I turn to look at them—three dark giants, menacing and tall.

A fourth giant joins them. He holds a knife, its shadow on the wall three feet long.

Suddenly I'm being jerked back toward Pine Cottage. There's more screaming. From Betz. Maybe even from me.

Inside the cabin, Rodney slams the door shut and slides the ratty armchair against it. Betz and I return to the window. The SUV's headlights sweep over us as Craig steers it into a U-turn.

He's leaving! Betz yelps. *He's going without us!*

The SUV gets about ten feet before it slams into a large maple next to the driveway, shaking loose leaves that rain onto the windshield. Steam hisses through the dented grille. The engine sputters and dies.

Inside the SUV, Craig slumps over the steering wheel, his chin pressing on the horn. The noise breaks the night silence with a steady blare.

The shadow with the knife is upon the SUV in an instant, flinging open the door and dragging Craig from the front seat.

The blare of the horn stops. Silence reigns again.

Despite his collision with the steering wheel, Craig is still conscious. Yet he doesn't make a sound as he's shoved to his knees beside the SUV. He simply stares forward, his eyes sparking with terror.

I turn away from the window, suddenly dizzy. I collapse against the wall, sliding down it, feeling the floor rise up to meet me. Just before everything again goes dark, Craig finally screams.

Later.

I don't know how long.

I'm on the floor in one of the bedrooms. My room. I recognize the quilts on the wall. Water trickles beneath the door. I don't know where it's coming from. A burst pipe? A flood?

All I know is that I'm wet and bleeding and more scared than I've ever been in my life. When I whimper, Rodney says, *You'll be okay. We'll both be okay.*

He's huddled beside me, one of the quilts from the wall thrown over his shoulders. There's blood in his hair.

Where's Betz? I whisper.

Rodney doesn't answer.

Outside the room, everything is quiet. Even the crickets. Even the trees and the leaves. But then a sound emerges on the other side of the door.

Footsteps.

Slow, cautious ones that slosh through the water in the hall. Each one reminds me of my mother's mop sliding across the kitchen floor.

Slick-swish.

Slick-swish.

They stop just on the other side of the door.

I look to Rodney, my eyes asking the question I dare not speak: *Did you lock the door?*

He nods. The doorknob rattles.

Then something slams against the door, bending it, wood bulging outward. Fear lifts me to my feet as the door is rocked by another slam. It bursts open and I see a knife, glinting darkly.

I scream.

I close my eyes.

The knife pushes into my gut. Filling me. A steel-sharp rape. I take a rattling breath through gritted teeth as the blade is pulled out and I slump to the floor.

Quincy, no!

It's Rodney, pushing past me, throwing his body in front of mine. I don't open my eyes. I can't. The lights have gone out. All I can do is listen to the scuffle moving out of the room and into the hall. I hear Rodney grunting and cursing and shoving.

Then a single, strangled yelp.

Then nothing.

Later still.

I wake again in the wet room. My room.

The cabin is silent. So are the crickets and trees and leaves. Everything's either dead or fled. Everything but me.

I sit up, the pain at my stomach surpassing the pain at my shoulder. Both still bleed. My dress is soaked with blood and water. Mostly blood. It's thicker.

Somehow, I get to my feet, now bare, shoes God knows where. Somehow, these weary legs take me through the open door. And somehow I remain upright in the hall, even after I spy Betz dead in the other room, surrounded by liquid from the knife-pierced waterbed.

Rodney is farther down the hall, also dead. I avoid looking at him when I step over his corpse.

It's not real, I whisper. *None of this is real.*

I don't see Him until I'm all the way into the great room, standing by the fireplace, shivering from cold and blood loss. He's on all fours next to Amy, like a dog sniffing at a carcass, wondering if it's worth consuming.

Strange sounds rise from the back of His throat. Tiny whimpers. The dog's in pain.

Then He notices I'm there, head whipping around to face me. The knife is on the floor beside Him, black with fresh blood. He grabs it, lifts it over His head.

I was leaving, He says, breathing hard. *I heard screams. I came back. And saw—*

I don't hear the rest because I'm too busy running. Terror and hurt and rage burn through me, mixing together, bubbling under my skin like a chemical reaction. I keep on running.

Out of the cabin.

Into the woods.

Screaming all the way.

42.

The memories arrive all at once. A zombie horde back from the dead, grasping at me with peeled-skin hands. I try to fight them off but can't. I'm surrounded, overwhelmed and convulsing as memory after memory returns. All those sounds and images I had kept at bay for so long. They're all back, lodged into my mind, unshakable as they play over and over in an endless loop.

Amy and her dead doll eyes.

Craig being dragged from the SUV.

Betz and Rodney with their palpable horror and desperation. They saw more than I did. They saw it all.

Yet I saw something they couldn't. I saw Him. Crawling around Amy, whimpering, grabbing the knife, raising it.

That image is the one that repeats itself most often. There's something off about it, something I can't quite comprehend.

Breaking free of Tina's grip, I rush down the hall, my numb legs propelled only by the insistent tug of memory. My breathing is shallow. My heart clangs in my chest.

I don't stop until I'm in the great room again. Right back where we started. I stand exactly where I stood a decade ago, staring at the spot where I last saw Him. It's almost as if He's still there, frozen in place for a decade. I see the raised knife in His hands. I see His smudged glasses. Behind the lenses, His wide and uncomprehending eyes are full moons of fear.

Of me.

He was afraid of *me*.

He thought I was going to hurt him. That I'm the one who had killed the others.

I drop to my knees and gasp, inhaling dusty air, coughing.

"It wasn't him," I say between body-rattling coughs. "He didn't do it."

Tina swoops toward me, the knife lowered, now forgotten. She kneels in front of me and grips my arms tight. So tight it hurts.

"Are you sure?" Hope colors her words. A trembling, uncertain, pitiable hope. "Tell me you're sure."

"I'm sure."

I now understand why we're here. Why Tina sought out Lisa and me. She wanted me to remember everything, to prove Joe's innocence, to declare once and for all that he didn't do it.

It was all for him.

For Joe.

"I wanted to come with him," Tina says. "I wanted to run away. Together. But he told me to stay. Even after I followed him down the hall to that broken door. He said he'd come back for me. So I stayed behind. Then they told me he was dead. That he'd killed a bunch of kids. But I knew he didn't do it."

"I didn't know," I say. "I truly thought it was him."

"So who did it? Who killed them?"

Disbelief rises like bile in my throat. I cough again, trying to dislodge it. "Someone else."

"You?" she asks. "Was it you, Quinn?"

God knows she has every right to think that. I'd forgotten so much. And she's seen me angry. That was her goal, after all. To poke me, get me mad, see what I'm capable of. I didn't disappoint.

"No," I say. "I swear, it wasn't me."

"Then who?"

I shake my head. I'm breathless, exhausted.

"I don't know."

But I do. At least, I think I do. Another memory arrives. A straggler.

It's a memory of me running through the woods, seeing something else.

Someone else.

"You're remembering something," Tina says.

I nod. I close my eyes. I think. I think until my head throbs.

And then I see it, as vibrant as the day it happened. I'm running through the woods, screaming, that branch all but punching me in the face. I see headlights. I see a man silhouetted in the brightness.

A cop. I see his uniform.

It's covered with something dark and wet. In the dim moonlight, it almost looks as if he's been smeared with motor oil. Yet I know that's not the case. Even as I run toward him, I know his uniform is covered with blood.

My blood. Janelle's blood. Everyone's blood.

But I'm too scared to think clearly. Especially with Joe somewhere in the woods behind me. Chasing me. The taste of his lips still on mine.

So I make a beeline toward the cop, embracing him, pressing my dress to his uniform.

Blood against blood.

They're dead, I gasp. *They're all dead. And he's still out here.*

And suddenly Joe's there, bursting through the trees. The cop draws his gun and fires off three shots. Two in the chest, one in the head. As loud in memory as they were in real life.

I hear a fourth shot.

Louder than memory.

Definitely real life.

It blasts through the cabin, vibrating off the walls. The energy of the bullet streaks from the open door into Pine Cottage. It has a presence, a force that fills the room.

A splatter of hot liquid hits my face.

I shriek when I feel it, my eyes flying open to see Tina slumping onto her side. One of her hands flings outward past her head, knuckles against the floor, knife skittering from her grip. A thin pool of blood starts to roll out from under her, spreading fast.

She's not moving. I'm not even sure she's still alive.

"Tina?" I say, shaking her. *"Tina?"*

Noise drifts from the doorway. Someone breathing. I look up and see Coop standing there. Even in the darkness, I can make out the glint of his blue eyes as he lowers the gun.

"Quincy," he says with a nod.

There's always a nod.

43.

I notice the ring immediately. The red class ring he wears in place of a wedding band. It's familiar, yet foreign. I've seen it so many times that I've come to not see it. Taken it for granted, like so many other things about Coop.

That's why I didn't recognize it when I saw it in that photograph on Lisa Milner's dresser. Coop's face wasn't in the picture. It was just his hand thrown over Lisa's shoulder, the ring right there, visible yet not.

But now it's all I see, worn on the same hand that holds his Glock. Although the gun is lowered, his index finger continues to twitch against the trigger.

"Are you hurt?" he asks.

"No."

"Good," Coop says. "That's real good, Quincy."

He takes another step closer, his long legs covering twice the distance of a normal stride. One more step and he's right beside us, towering over Tina and me. Or maybe it's just me now. Tina's likely dead already. I can't tell.

Coop gives the knife near Tina's hand a rough kick, sending it sliding into a distant corner, where it's swallowed by the shadows.

There's no point in trying to run. Coop's finger never leaves that trigger. One shot is all it would take to put me down. Just like Tina. I'm not sure I even can run. Grief and pills and the weight of remembering that night have left me paralyzed.

"For a few years there in the beginning, I always wondered how much you knew," Coop says. "When you asked to see me in the hospital that day, I thought you were toying with me. That you wanted me to be there when you told the detectives you remembered everything. I almost didn't come."

"Why did you?"

"Because I think I loved you even then."

I sway slightly, dizzy from disgust. When I drift too far to the left, Coop tightens his finger around the trigger. I force myself to stop moving.

"How many were there?" I ask. "Before that night?"

"Three."

There's no hesitation. He says it with the same ease with which he orders his coffee. I was hoping for at least a pause.

Three. The strangled woman on the side of the road and the two campers stabbed in their tent. All of them were mentioned in the article I found at Lisa's house. I think she knew what happened to them. I think she died because of it.

"It's a sickness," Coop says. "You need to understand that, Quincy. I never wanted to do those things."

I sob. When snot starts leaking from my nose, I don't bother to wipe it away. "Then why did you?"

"I've spent my whole life in these woods. Hiking, hunting, doing things I was too young to be doing. I lost my virginity on that big rock up on the hill." Coop cringes at the memory, hating himself. "She was the school slut. Willing to do it with anyone. Even me. When it was over, I puked in the bushes. Christ, I was ashamed of what I'd done. So ashamed that I thought about snapping her neck right there on that rock, just so she wouldn't tell anyone. It was only fear of getting caught that kept me from doing it."

I shake my head and put a hand to my temple. With every word, a piece of my heart breaks off and falls away.

"Please stop."

Coop keeps talking, his words carrying the relieved rush of confession.

"But I was curious. God help me, I was. I thought the military would shake it out of me. That killing for my country would make me not want to do it. But it didn't work. All the messed-up things I saw over there only made it worse. And not long after I got back home I found myself back in these woods, in a car, getting sucked off by some whore trying to hitchhike her way to New York. That time I wasn't afraid. War had beat all the fear out of me. That time I actually did it."

I keep my expression blank, willing myself not to show the fear and disgust churning inside me. I don't want him to know what I'm thinking. I don't want to make him mad.

"I swore I'd only do it that one time," Coop says. "That I got it out of my system. But I kept coming back to these woods. Usually with a knife. And when I saw those two campers, I knew the sickness hadn't left me."

"What about now?"

"I'm trying, Quincy. I'm trying real hard."

"You weren't trying that night," I say, trembling with desire to glare at him, to show him how much I hate him. There's nothing left of my heart. It's been reduced to knifelike shards.

"I was testing myself," Coop says. "Going to this cabin. That's how I'd do it. I'd park down the road and walk up here, peeking in windows, both hoping and dreading I'd see something that would bring the sickness back. Nothing ever did. Until I saw you."

I think I might pass out. I pray that I do.

"I was supposed to be looking for the kid who escaped from the psych hospital," he says. "Instead, I started circling this place, ready for another test. That's when I found you in the woods. With the knife. You walked right past me. So close I could have reached out and touched you. But you were too angry to see me. You were so angry, Quincy. And so fiercely sad. It was beautiful."

"I wasn't going to do what you think I was," I say, hoping he believes me. Hoping that one day I'll believe it too. "I dropped that knife."

"I know. I watched you do it once he showed up. Then you left. And he left. But the knife stayed. So I picked it up."

Coop takes another step closer. So close I can smell him. A mix of sweat and aftershave. I'm hit with flashes of last night. Him on top of me. Inside me. His scent now is exactly the same as then.

"I never meant for all that to happen, Quincy. You've got to believe me. I just wanted to see where you were headed with that knife. I wanted to know what made someone as perfect as you so angry. So I went to the rock and saw them, and I knew that's what upset you. The two of them screwing like filthy animals. That's what they looked like, you know. Two grunting, dirty animals that needed to be put down."

Coop lightly swings the hand that holds the gun, his elbow bending and unbending, as if he's no longer willing to point it at me.

"But then your friend ran," he says. "Craig. That was his name, right? And I couldn't let him get away, Quincy. I just couldn't. And there you were. And your friends. And I knew I had to get rid of all of you."

I'm crying more now. Tears of shame and sorrow and confusion soak my face. "Why didn't you kill me too? You killed the others. Why not me?"

"Because I could tell you were special," Coop says slowly, as if he's still amazed by me all these years later. "And I was right. You should have seen yourself running through those woods, Quincy. Strong even then. Even more, you were running *toward* me, wanting me to help you."

He gives me a bright-eyed look of admiration. Of awe.

"I had no right to snuff that out."

"Even though there was a chance I could suddenly remember it was you?"

"Yes," Coop says. "Even then. Because I knew what was happening. I had created another Lisa Milner. Another Samantha Boyd."

"You knew who they were," I say.

"I'm a cop. Of course I knew," Coop says. "The Final Girls. Such strong, defiant women. And I had made one. Me. In my mind, it made up for all the other bad things I'd done. And I swore I'd never let anything bad happen to you. I made sure you'd always need me. Even when it looked like you were drifting away from me."

At first, I don't know what he means. But then realization settles onto my shoulders, weighing me down. I slump further against the floor.

"The letter," I say weakly. "You wrote that letter."

"I had to," Coop says. "You were straying too far from me."

It's true. I was. Getting the website off the ground, moving in with Jeff, finally becoming the woman I'd always wanted to be. So Coop drove to Quincy, Illinois, and mailed that typewritten threat, knowing it would make me run back to him in a heartbeat. And I did.

A question unfolds in my mind, curling open like a flower. I'm afraid to ask it, but I must. "What else have you done? After that night? Were there more bad things?"

"I've been good," Coop says. "Mostly."

I shudder at the word. So much horror resides in those two tiny syllables.

"It's been hard, Quincy. There were times I came so close to slipping. But then I'd think of you and manage to stop myself. I couldn't risk losing you. You've made me behave myself."

"And Lisa?" I say. "What about her?"

Coop hangs his head, looking truly regretful. "That was out of necessity."

Because she suspected something. Probably after Tina arrived seeking answers about Pine Cottage. Lisa looked into it because that's the kind of person she was—big on details. And she kept looking after Tina left. She found those articles about the murders in the woods, wrote a few emails, pieced it together that Joe likely wasn't physically capable of killing everyone at Pine Cottage. Not someone as big as Rodney or as athletic as Craig. Coop was the only person there that night strong enough to overtake them.

That's why Lisa emailed me right before she was killed. She wanted to warn me about Coop.

"You knew her, didn't you?" I ask. "That's why she invited you in, gave you wine, trusted you."

"She didn't trust me," Coop says. "Not that night. She was trying to get me to confess."

"But she trusted you once."

Coop offers the slightest of nods. "Years ago."

"Were you lovers?"

Another nod. Almost imperceptible.

I'm not surprised. I think again of the photo in Lisa's room. The way Coop's arm had been so casually thrown over her shoulders suggested ease and intimacy.

"When?" I say.

"Not long after what happened here. I asked Nancy to put us in touch. Once I realized I had created a Final Girl, I wanted to meet the others. I wanted to see if they were as strong as you."

Coop puts a matter-of-fact spin on it, as if the whole twisted idea makes perfect sense. As if I, of all people, should understand the urge to compare and contrast us.

"Lisa was impressive, I'll give her that," he says. "All she wanted was to help you. I can't count the number of times she asked me how you were coping, if you needed help. I feel bad about what happened to her. Her concern for you was admirable, Quincy. Noble. Not like Samantha."

I try not to show my shock. I don't want to give Coop the satisfaction. But he sees it anyway and gives a half smile, proud of himself.

"Yes, I met Samantha Boyd," he says. "The real one. Not this cheap imitator."

He dips his chin in the direction of Tina's body and purses his lips. For a sickening moment, I think he's going to spit on her. I close my eyes to avoid seeing it if he does.

"You knew all along she wasn't Sam?"

"I knew," Coop says. "I knew it the second I saw that picture of you two in the newspaper. There's a bit of a resemblance, sure. But I knew she couldn't be the real Samantha Boyd. What I didn't know was what to do about it."

My mind flashes back to last night, when I came home and found the two of them together. I recall the way Coop's hand was on her neck. It looked like a caress. It could have been a clench. He had planned on killing Tina too. Perhaps right there in the guest room.

"Why didn't you tell me?"

"I couldn't," Coop says. "Not without making it known that Samantha Boyd was dead."

I groan, my pain and sorrow finally too much to keep hidden. I keep on groaning, getting louder, trying to block Coop's confession. But I've heard too much already. I now know that Coop also killed Samantha Boyd. She didn't drop off the grid. He had erased her from it.

"Why?" I moan.

"Because she wasn't like you, Quincy. She didn't deserve to be mentioned in the same breath as you. I flew all the way down to a shit town in Florida just to see her. And what I found was a weak, chubby piece of trash. Nothing like the Samantha Boyd I'd pictured. I couldn't believe this was the girl who'd survived what happened at that motel. She was scared and meek and nothing at all like you. And so eager to please. Christ, she practically threw herself at me. At least Lisa showed some restraint."

Suddenly, it all clicks into place. All those details. Like a necklace of beads. One stacking on top of the other, forming a full circle.

Coop had slept with all three of us.

Sam and Lisa and me.

Now two of them are dead.

I'm the last one left alive.

I continue to cry. Sorrow wraps around me like a fist, squeezing out the tears.

"She didn't even ask about you," Coop says, as if that justified her death. "Samantha Boyd, your fellow Final Girl, was so interested in getting into my pants that she never bothered to ask how you were doing."

"And how was I doing, Coop?" I say, my words as bitter as my tears. "Was I doing okay?"

He puts the gun away, sliding it gently back into its holster. Then he comes closer, sidestepping Tina's body, kneeling to where I've collapsed on the floor until his blue eyes are looking directly into mine.

"You were doing great."

"And now?"

I tremble, afraid he'll touch me. Not wanting to know what kind of touch that will be.

"You can still be great," Coop says. "You can forget everything. About tonight. About ten years ago. You forgot it once. You can forget it again."

On the floor, something pokes into my leg. Something sharp.

"What if I can't?" I ask.

"You will. I'll help you do it."

I risk a glance away from Coop to look down, seeing that it's a knife jabbing me. The same knife that dropped from Rocky Ruiz's pocket. Tina had kept it for safekeeping. Now she pushes it toward me, somehow still alive, staring up at me with one bloody eye.

The tattoo peeks out from the sleeve of her jacket. Although it's upside down, the word remains clear.

SURVIVOR

"We can go somewhere," Coop tells me. "Just the two of us. We'll start new lives. Together."

He sounds so earnest. Like he almost believes it's possible. But it's not. We both know that.

Yet I continue the charade. I nod. Slowly at first but picking up speed as Coop leans in and touches my cheek.

"Yes," I say. "I'd like that."

I keep nodding until Coop kisses me. First on the forehead, then on both cheeks. When his lips touch mine, I will myself not to retch or yelp or squirm. I kiss him back while dropping my right hand to the floor.

"Quincy," Coop whispers. "My sweet, beautiful Quincy."

Then his hands are around my neck, squeezing gently, trying not to hurt me too much. He's crying too. His tears mix with mine as his grip tightens around my throat.

My thumb brushes the knife blade, sliding across its shivery edge.

Coop keeps squeezing my neck. His thumbs slide against my trachea, pushing. Then he kisses me again. Breathing air into my lungs even as he's squeezing it out. He keeps crying. Moaning words into my mouth.

"Quincy. Sweet, sweet Quincy."

My fingers find the knife's handle. They curl around it.

There's no more breath in me. It's all gone, even though Coop continues to kiss me, puffing apologies past my lips.

"I'm sorry," he whispers.

I raise the knife.

Coop's still squeezing, still kissing, still apologizing. "I'm so, so sorry."

I expect Coop's body to put up a fight, as if he's made of more than just skin and tissue. Yet the knife plunges into his side with ease, surprising him into stillness.

"Quincy."

There's shock in that single word. Shock and betrayal and, I suspect, a little admiration.

His hands don't fall from my neck until I remove the knife. Blood spews from the wound, sticky and hot. Coop tries to pull away from me, but I'm too fast. The knife goes in again, this time in the center of his stomach.

I twist it and Coop's body spasms. Flecks of blood and spittle fly from his mouth.

He puts his hands on mine, trying to remove the blade. I grit my teeth, grunt, hold the knife in place. When Coop's grip weakens, I give the blade a final twist.

"Quincy," he says again, blood bubbling at the back of his throat.

I give a single nod, making sure he sees it before his eyes roll back in his head. I want him to know that I'm more than a survivor, more than the fighter he always imagined me to be.

I'm his creation, forged from blood and pain and the cold steel of a blade.

I'm a fucking Final Girl.

FOUR MONTHS AFTER PINE COTTAGE

Beige wasn't Tina's color. It washed her out, fabric and skin almost indistinguishable from each other. Other than her pallor, she looked good. Same taut features. Same prickly body language. Only her hair was different. It was shorter, and deep brown instead of raven black.

"You'll look like a different person when you get out," Quincy told her.

"We'll see," Tina said. "Fifteen months is a long time."

They both knew it could be shorter than that. Or not. It was an unusual situation. Anything was possible. Although Quincy was surprised by the length of the sentence, Tina wasn't. It's amazing the ways police can get you when you're pretending to be someone else. Criminal impersonation. Identity theft. A dozen different types of fraud. The charges against Tina were so varied, stretching across several states, that Jeff warned she could spend up to two years in jail.

Quincy hoped it was less. Tina had been through enough, although she swore it was all worth it.

Some of it might have been. Mostly the part about clearing Joe Hannen's name. His innocence had been proclaimed to the world, which is what she wanted all along.

Yet Tina had almost died, thanks to Him, the new person whose name Quincy could no longer utter. The bullet He fired missed Tina's left lung by a few millimeters. It missed her heart by even less. The blood loss was enough to give doctors some concern, but all in all she recovered nicely. She healed up just in time to be sent to prison.

"You know you don't have to do this," Quincy said, not for the first time. "Just say the word and I'll confess to everything."

She looked around the visiting room, which was packed with other women in beige and their guests. Hushed conversations rose from the neighboring tables, in all manner of languages. Through the grate-covered window, Quincy saw dirty snow drifting against a tall security fence, looped at the top with barbed wire. She honestly didn't know how Tina could stand it there, even though she was assured it wasn't that bad. Tina told her it reminded her of Blackthorn.

"It's not like your confession would get me out of here any faster," she said. "Besides, you were right. I made you do that to Rocky Ruiz."

Rocky emerged from his coma at roughly the same time Quincy was shoving that knife into Him for the final time. Rocky's memory was hazy, though, less from the beating and more from the fact that he was strung out on crack when it happened. But he knew he had been attacked. Against Quincy's wishes, Tina confessed to it. Rocky didn't argue, and Detective Hernandez didn't press the issue. Jeff suggested a plea deal, with Tina to serve time concurrently for both the assault and the fraud.

"You didn't make me do anything," Quincy said. "My choices are mine."

That much was true. It was the repercussions of those choices that she couldn't control.

"Have they found the real Samantha yet?" Tina asked. "I've been asking the guards for news."

"Nope," Quincy said, capping the word with a popping sound. "They're still looking for her body."

Once it became clear that Samantha Boyd had been murdered, police in Florida went all out trying to recover her body. Quincy had spent the past four months monitoring the news as authorities searched swamps, dredged lakes, dug up dirt lots. But Florida was a big state, and the odds were slim that she'd ever be found.

Quincy concluded that maybe it was for the best. Until they found Sam's body, it would feel like there was another Final Girl out in the world. That it wasn't now just her.

"How about Jeff?" Tina asked. "How's he doing?"

"You probably talk to him more than I do," Quincy said.

"Maybe. The next time I do, I'll tell him you said hi."

Quincy knew it would do little to change things. Jeff had made his opinion of her very clear that long, torturous night when she confessed all her misdeeds. It destroyed her to see him veer between love and anger, sympathy and disgust. At one point, he simply latched on to her, begging for a logical reason why she had slept with Him.

She couldn't give one.

That's why she decided it was best for them to go their separate ways, even if Jeff could possibly find some way to forgive her. They weren't right for each other. They both should have seen that from the start.

"That would be nice," Quincy said. "Tell him I wish him well."

Quincy meant it. Jeff needed someone normal. And she needed to focus on other things. Like getting the website back in working condition, for starters. And laying off the wine. And quitting the Xanax.

The day after Jeff moved out, Quincy's mother arrived for an extended visit. They did all the things they should have done years earlier. Talking. Crying. Forgiving. Together, they flushed all those little blue pills down the toilet. Now whenever Quincy got the urge for one, she sipped a bit of grape soda in an attempt to fool her Xanax-deprived brain. Sometimes it worked. Sometimes it didn't.

"I read your big interview," Tina told her.

"I haven't," Quincy said. "How was it?"

"Jonah did a good job."

After Pine Cottage Part II, Quincy gave exactly one interview—an exclusive to Jonah Thompson. It had felt like the right thing to do, considering that he helped her, in his own smarmy way. All the major news outlets from Trenton to Tokyo picked it up. Everyone wanted a piece of her. But since she was no longer talking, they settled for Jonah instead. He was able to parlay all that attention into a bigger, better gig. He started at the *New York Times* on Monday. Quincy hoped they were ready for him.

"I'm glad it turned out well," she said.

The room began to empty around them. Visitation was almost over. Quincy knew she should leave too, but one more question lingered in her head, begging to be asked.

"Did you suspect that He was the one responsible for Pine Cottage?"

"No," Tina said, understanding exactly whom she was referring to. "All I knew was that it couldn't have been Joe."

"I'm sorry that I blamed him all these years," Quincy said. "I'm sorry it caused you such pain."

"Don't be sorry. You saved my life."

"And you saved mine."

They stared at each other, not speaking, until the guard stationed at the door announced it was time to leave. When Quincy stood, Tina said, "Do you think you'll come back sometime? Just to say hi?"

"I don't know. Do you want me to?"

Tina shrugged. "I don't know."

At least they were honest with each other. In a way, they always had been, even when they were lying.

"Then I guess we'll have to wait and see," Quincy said.

Tina's lips curled upward, on the edge of a smile. "I'll be waiting, babe."

Quincy drove her rental car back to the city, squinting against the sunset reflecting off the snow that had been pushed onto the highway's shoulder. The scenery passing the window was underwhelming at best. A dull line of strip malls, churches, and used-car lots full of vehicles stippled white by road salt. Yet one business caught her attention—a sliver of storefront squeezed between a pizza place and a travel agency closed for the weekend. A neon sign glowed pink in the window.

TATTOOS

Without thinking, Quincy veered into the lot, shut off the car, and walked inside. A tinny bell over the door chimed her arrival. The woman behind the register had ruby bow-tie lips and a constellation of pink stars inked onto her neck. Her hair was the same color Tina's used to be.

"Can I help you?" she asked.

"Yes," Quincy said. "I think you can."

An hour later, it was finished. It hurt, but not as much as Quincy expected.

"Do you like it?" the pink-starred girl asked.

Quincy turned her arm to examine her handiwork. The ink there was still wet and stinging, dark against the peach fuzz of her wrist. Pinpricks of blood bordered each letter like lights on a marquee. Still, the word was easy to read.

SURVIVOR

"It's perfect," Quincy said, marveling at the tattoo. It was a part of her now. As permanent as her scars.

She was still staring at it when breaking news flashed on the tattoo parlor's TV. Quincy had snuck a few glances at it while all that black ink was being pushed just beneath her skin, more focused on pain than whatever it had to offer. But now she was riveted, held in place by what she saw.

Several teenagers had been found dead at a home in Modesto, California, the news anchor announced. In total, nine people were killed.

Quincy rushed from the tattoo parlor, driving fast back into the city.

Once home, she spent the rest of the night flipping among the cable news channels for more information about what was being called the Massacre in Modesto. Eight of the victims were high school seniors—attendees at a house party held while one of the kids' parents were away. The other person killed was a maintenance worker at their school who showed up unannounced with a pair of sharpened garden shears. The only survivor was an eighteen-year-old girl named Hayley Pace, who managed to escape after killing the man who slaughtered her friends.

It didn't surprise Quincy when one of the newscasters mentioned her name. It was the first incident of its kind since Pine Cottage, after all. Her phone had buzzed all night with calls and texts from reporters.

At three in the morning, she switched off the TV. By five, she was at the airport. When the clock struck seven, she was in the air, heading to Modesto, pain from the tattoo still pulsing at her wrist.

Quincy waited for the press conference before sneaking into the hospital. The news vultures flapping near the front doors were too distracted by a progress report from Hayley's doctors and parents to notice her rushing inside, hidden behind owl-eyed sunglasses picked up at an airport gift shop.

Inside, she had no trouble sweet-talking the motherly woman at the information desk into giving out Hayley's room number.

"I'm her cousin," Quincy told her. "Fresh off a plane from New York and dying to see her."

Hayley's hospital room was dim, solemn, and choked with flowers. Like a church sanctuary. Like Hayley was already in the process of being enshrined.

She was awake when Quincy entered, propped up on a pile of pillows. She was a plain-looking girl. Pretty, but no knockout. Straight brown hair and a pert little nose. In a crowd, she would have been easy to overlook.

Except for those eyes.

They're what drew Quincy deeper into the room. As green and bright as emeralds, they flashed strength and intelligence, even in the midst of deep pain. Quincy saw a little bit of herself in those eyes. Tina too.

They were radiant.

"How are you feeling?" she asked as she approached the bed.

"I hurt," Hayley said, her voice slurred slightly by that uneasy mix of fatigue, painkillers, and grief. "Everywhere."

"That's to be expected," Quincy said. "But it will go away in time."

Hayley's eyes never left hers. "Who are you?" she asked.

"My name is Quincy Carpenter."

"Why are you here?"

Quincy clasped one of Hayley's hands and gave it a tender squeeze.

"I'm here," she said, "to teach you how to be a Final Girl."

ACKNOWLEDGMENTS

Writing a book is a solitary endeavor. Publishing one, on the other hand, is a team sport, and I feel blessed to be part of a brilliant, dedicated team that spans continents.

Thanks are due to my agent, Michelle Brower, whose enthusiasm for *Final Girls* helped me set a record for speed writing; Chelsey Heller, who got it into the hands of editors around the world; and everyone at Kuhn Projects and Zachary Shuster Harmsworth. Special thanks to Annie Hwang at Folio Literary Management, who took the first stab at my unwieldy first draft.

At Dutton, I must thank my amazing, awesome editor, Maya Ziv, who is never less than a delight to work with; Madeline Newquist, for keeping things running smoothly; Christopher Lin, for his amazing cover design; and Rachelle Mandik, for sparing me from much grammatical embarrassment. A big thank-you also goes out to everyone at my British publisher, Ebury, especially my editor, Emily Yau, whose unabashed excitement for this book was clear from the very start.

I also owe a huge thanks to fellow writers Hester Young, Carla Norton, and Sophie Littlefield for putting their stamp of approval on an earlier version of the book. Your support made all the difference.

Finally, I need to thank all the friends and family who offered me emotional support during the dark period in which *Final Girls* was written, especially Sarah Dutton. May your gingerbread houses always earn blue ribbons. As for you, Mike Livio, no amount of thanks would be enough. None of this would have been possible without your quiet strength and unflagging insistence that, yes, I could actually do this. So I have, and I owe it all to you.

READING GROUP QUESTIONS

1. The title of the book – *Final Girls* – derives from a film motif from 90s cinema. How is this explored in the novel, and what other themes are there?

2. How did the flashbacks to Pine Cottage impact the story?

3. Culpability is an important theme within the book, and the ethics of what you will do to survive – after all, all three Final Girls had to kill in order to escape. To what extent do you think the characters can get away with this and how are they affected by it? As Quincy begins to spiral, how much do you approve of her actions?

4. As a character, Samantha Boyd portrays a very different response to being cast in the role of a Final Girl – do you empathise with her story? And as her relationship with Quincy develops how does your opinion of her change?

5. What do you think of Quincy's relationship with her mother? Do you think her mother suspected her of being a murderer and how does this inform their relationship?

6. How does the author explore the role of journalists and the media?

7. How real did you feel the 'connection' was between the Final Girls or is it merely a device created by the media?

8. How important is trust in the novel? Does your trust in the characters change as the story progresses?

9. Stephen King compares this book to *Gone Girl*, which has the ultimate twist in psychological fiction. What did you think of the twists in this book? Did you see them coming, and did this affect your overall enjoyment of the book?

10. How do you think things will change for Quincy at the end of the novel? Will she be able to finally 'move on' and how does this change the way she views the term 'Final Girl'?